CHASING THE GODDESS

A Novel By

Bill Froehlich

For
Katrina
and the lightning bolt moment

AUTHOR'S NOTE:

After many exciting years of writing, directing and producing motion pictures and television, my desire to continue as a storyteller has deepened with this my first solo novel. The writing takes place in a state of inspired exploration of life's experiences, my imagination, and the unknown for the world is more than we know and something sacred emerges from every story that comes to us so I invite you into this soul journey story.

The Setting:

Life held many surprises before the pandemic compressed experience into endless waiting and the world held its breath. In the fall of 2019, this story was one such surprise.

Bill Froehlich
(November 2025 California)

PROLOGUE

"Be careful when a naked person offers you a shirt."

An African saying

The man was unknowable, this man, Eli Cross. Not because he was secretive. On the contrary, he was open, disturbingly so, and projected an energy of pure potential, a lively inner *presence* that arose by resisting the temptation to fully conceptualize an identity and thereby be limited by that concept. It captivated people. He radiated confidence without attempting to do so and utilized that perception to great effect.

Years of exotic foreign travel provided insight into the pliability of human behavior even across cultural differences. He developed an artist's eye of possibilities for the images and stories needed to sculpt a person's imagination into his masterpiece of desire.

The best art was often deceptively simple.

He could anticipate someone's next thought and set it in motion hurtling down a path conjuring images and assessments to his advantage. He knew the mind told stories, constantly creating the incessant swirl of thoughts, and with the right suggestion, a tale would arise, be woven in someone's mind, a self-perpetuating cavalcade of conclusions that were utterly convincing of who he was, and what he was going to do; people then thought they knew him. But they would be wrong. They had merely boarded a runaway train of thought with his light touch the hand of the engineer.

Much of this guesswork—the insatiable desire to pin him down and categorize him like an insect on an entomologist's mounting board—had been committed to paper. Assiduously archived in painstaking detail, the data of Eli Cross—what was generally agreed upon—was immortalized in the files of Interpol, the Police Nationale of France, the Préfecture de Police de Paris, MI-5, New Scotland Yard and its Art and Antique Squad, The BKA and Bundespolizei of Germany, The Guardia di Finanza of Italy, Policia Nacional of Spain, the Singapore Police Force, the Criminal Intelligence Service Canada

(CISC), the FBI Art Crime Team, the LAPD, the NYPD, as well as most law enforcement establishments throughout the United States, all listing him as a *thief*, and begrudgingly, for Search-Engine-Optimization, as a *Master Thief.*

The files were thick, but filled with conjecture, coincidence and circumstantial evidence only; no connecting criminal facts were provable. He had never been caught with his hand in the cookie jar. *Never caught.* That was all that was knowable.

It irritated the most righteous of law enforcement—maddening like the incessant itch of a tropical rash—that he could not even be properly defined by the categories of the official forms. *Nationality*: American, possibly; Canadian by way of Montréal or Québec perhaps; then again European, possibly, perhaps France or England, but Switzerland could not be ruled out; New Zealand could not be ruled out either, nor Singapore for that matter. He seemed to be an ex-pat from everywhere. He had a continental flair, but not necessarily by lineage.

It galled those assigned—or addicted—to tracking him, which were mostly men, that he was also charming, assured and drop dead gorgeous, standing over six feet tall with a thick head of lustrous, dark hair and luminous blue eyes flecked with splashes of green. His dashing good looks stole one's breath and drove a stake through the heart of their self-esteem.

Beauty, he knew, could be its own decoy.

A stunning achievement to have so many of the world's vast alphabet soup of law agencies clamoring to lock his body in a small space for years; even more so to exasperate them to hell and back by their not being able to do it. What really drove many of them straight up the wall pushed them to the edge of insanity; they liked the guy! A few really liked him and hated him all at once which turned their stomachs into ulcer soup. Others flat out hated him and wanted to shoot him dead for their own health reasons. Those miserable bastards racked up divorces like pinging pinball machines. However one looked at it, Eli Cross had a knack of getting under the skin; parasite or warm fuzzy, one never knew.

Having duped both the authorities and his targets, many of whom never knew they were fooled, he turned his focus to creating one final masterpiece. His simple and delicious recipe: a web of trust woven with the strands of doubt and desire dazzled as a soufflé of hubris and human behavior. What he didn't concern himself with at those moments of past victory—attempting an iron discipline of thought—was what happened when you no longer can trust anything or anyone? This time would be different.

His web of deception now held a secret purpose known only to him.

Only one man, an NYPD Robbery-Homicide cop, got close to knowing that secret; but he was dead.

Unwritten by those living was the feeling of him they all carried in their gut... *dangerously unknowable.*

The horse knew him. The glistening, grey Arabian, *Saudade,* who carried him effortlessly over the French countryside near St. Tropez, knew him intuitively and undeniably. Together, they split the wind as their thunderous momentum propelled them along cliffs extending skyward from the azure waters of the Mediterranean. Thrashing hooves ripped apart the fertile earth as flesh strained against leather and forcefully expelled breath heralded another burst of speed.

Saudade also trusted him, utterly. Perhaps being one of the few who did or could. But then, horses were real to their core, being fully present. A person awakened to who they really were in their presence. This was an offering the horse gave to whoever was aware enough to receive it. It was grace.

This magnificently muscled creature, designed by nature to flee from all it did not know or trust, never fled from Eli Cross. He first spoke to Saudade in a language the horse understood: the language of movement, a non-predatory expression, until Saudade was willing to release his sense of self-preservation to Cross and be in harmony with his leadership; a trusting with his life. No human held such a depth of connection with Cross.

Perhaps this hinted at the horse's name—Saudade—even its sound when spoken—*so-dazh-zhey*—held the feelings—for from the Portuguese, it translated as *"the love that remains" after someone is gone, a yearning, a longing.*

ℬↄ

The soft, tapered bristles of the delicate paint brush barely touched the paper yet the water colors flowed independently of her artistic guidance. Nathalie Seeger knew precision eluded her attempts to control the flow of paint. She knew with increasing frustration that she couldn't control the paint no matter how sharp her focus.

Worse yet, she couldn't remember the face she wanted to capture with any precision. Tom's face. She wanted to capture the sensual memory of that face, a face she had kissed so often, and so recently.

The noise didn't help; the symphonic cacophony of sirens and car horns that made up the night music of New York. Even eight floors up the sounds penetrated. Wide awake, Nathalie Seeger should be sleeping; she had a big day coming up. She longed for stress-free sleep; yearned for the peace from knowing her ducks were all in a row. But she knew she had only one duck—the job she had to nail to prove herself.

Jerry had called from his late-night vantage point at The Waldorf Astoria, the job site. A new wrinkle needed to be dealt with. A last minute unexpected delivery of new state-of-the-art high security jewelry display cases required a shift in plans. It ratcheted up the pressure on them to pull off the job. *No big deal, we'll adjust* she had told him with her best confident tone.

But she couldn't remember Tom's face. Her thoughts fled here—not the pressing job—but the fading image of his face. This was a man she thought she loved—what the hell was she thinking—was she even thinking?! Now there were only feelings left—sharp penetrating shards of feelings she couldn't control. She couldn't control the paint. It all escaped her grasp. She had taken up painting as a refuge for her mind and soul. Water colors, an aggressively independent medium, needed nurturing from one's soul to flow in harmony. She felt all out of nurture, in command of nothing.

The city offered no solace. Its prominent buildings were modern masterpieces carved into the sky shoving aside the clouds, even blocking out the moon, and down below smaller blended structures of aging bricks mortared with sweat, blood and immigrant vision. To her, New York was an elegant, sensual storm; an in your face city not to be ignored. She liked it.

She clearly felt a storm was coming.

❧

In most cities, buildings were erected. In St. Tropez, they were kissed up against each other. Architecture was energy and generated feelings. Even the sun felt romantic in Southern France. Perhaps that was why Eli Cross lived there. Then again, maybe it was what they expected. And maybe he wanted it that way. The yachts anchored in the harbor and the artsy trend-setting streets splashed with pastel colors created an undeniable sense of style known the world over and to be part of that was like wearing the right clothes. It all set up to create a feeling. He liked that.

A sprawling villa commanded a view of the Mediterranean and the seaside landscape. The villa was as old as the land, but lovingly restored to its original grandeur, including the prominent stables. Seemingly impenetrable thickets marked the outer property edges and these rows of heavy brush added protective walls with their craggy and twisted wooden arms reaching for sea and sky, wildly untamed yet seductively aromatic.

The villa also had another distinct quality cherished by its owner. It was isolated.

Elements of behavior that were precise in their design unfolded in a rhythm that was natural; the discipline behind the actions unseen in the casual execution.

So it was that Marcel, the lanky stablehand, ambled toward the stables while a black Mercedes limousine rolled easily out of a multi-car garage as Saudade—in a mane-flying leap—cleared a thicket row and then abruptly a white perimeter fence by the villa's name plaque; its letters creatively gouged out of a wooden plank: *Maquis sur-mer.*

Eli Cross commanded the Arabian across the lush grounds with an effortless touch, a serene confidence.

Those who worked for him were loyal, well-paid and skilled at their jobs. They were aware of his reputation for it was the first thing Eli Cross would tell them when they sought their current position. But none of them had any hard evidence of how he got that reputation which allowed them to respond honestly to the legal authorities who pestered them from time to time.

There was something about his smile—they all felt it—a sly, charismatic force drawing one into an irresistible yet enigmatic lair. Perhaps the unknown kept them on edge. They knew only what he wanted them to know; yet they realized he knew all about them.

Marcel, in his early twenties, applied because he loved horses and the villa's stables were spacious and immaculate with five horses to care for and exercise; he regularly worked one Camargue, the native working horse of France, two Andalusians, a Lusitano and a Selle Francais sport horse. Saudade, the Arabian, was clearly the most loved of all and ridden only by Cross. Marcel wondered what Cross might do if anything ever happened to Saudade under his care.

Marcel's mother knew he liked this man, yet asked her son once if he ever worried for his own safety. After a thoughtful pause…he replied: "Sometimes." Those speculations would not bother Cross; he liked their not knowing.

They all arrived at the stables in a natural flowing rhythm propelled by expected discipline. The limo rolled to a stop as Cross dismounted gracefully and Marcel took the reins.

"It's time," Cross said simply.

"Would you like to shower first?" Marcel asked.

The driver opened the limo door for Cross.

"No, I'll do that on the plane."

The day before had been hot. Oppressive humidity had released relentless rivulets of sweat from the slightest effort. It was the last hurrah of a lingering summer.

This day the air was suddenly crisp. The skin tightened. Autumn insistently arrived. Change asserted itself. To most on the verge of risking everything, the sudden shift might have aroused suspicion, a possible ominous sign.

Not to Eli Cross. Given what he was about to attempt, it all made sense to him.

Expect change. That was solid ground, not shifting sand.

He slipped inside the limo and with the closing click of the door the rhythm was complete. Eli Cross was a man who went after what he wanted. He felt the wind at his back; clearly a time to strike.

∞

Across the pond it was still the middle of the night.

Nathalie thought she knew Tom. She was wrong. He had left. A month ago.

She told herself she didn't really know why. That allowed her to keep piling the blame on him...*the asshole.*

The nightgown she wore told a different story—and she knew it—and it pissed her off. She still wore it though—even now in the middle of the night staring out at the city—this nightgown that was torn the night her boyfriend Tom left.

Tom had not torn it.

She had.

Emotionally gobsmacked—*heartbroken* she had told herself—when she had watched him walk away from her. Not a word from his lips. Before he reached the door, she had yanked on her nightgown tearing open a flap of fabric above her left breast. The grating sound of the ripping lace had not stopped him as she had hoped. He had not even paused or turned around.

When the door had softly clicked shut—a *click* that had echoed around her apartment—and he was gone, she had stared stunned at her reflection in the large plate glass window, the lights of the city shimmering around her.

This was the French lace nightgown she had ordered from Paris to please him. Paris! For him...*the asshole.*

That night—and this night—the torn flap fell open exposing the curves of her left breast and rested precipitously just above her nipple like an open wound to her heart. *An open wound to her heart...yeah, that felt right...like a righteous scar.*

She had trusted him. Actually it was more like she had decided to trust how she knew *he could be.* She felt she really knew *he could be* the man who respected and liked her independence.

He didn't like her independence. He told her he did, but he didn't.

So she had been a chump.

That was why she tore the nightgown. That was why she still wore it...to remember. She still wondered though, just couldn't help it; it was so hard to admit being fooled.

Why all the deception? He could've been straight with me. I should've seen it—felt it—something. I just couldn't sense that he was...an asshole—and assholes shit on you—that's what assholes do. No more assholes! Simple, right? But assholes...disguise themselves. Next time eyes wide open—no bullshitting myself—I'll spot those red flags a mile away! The next romantic bastard better be real or be prepared to be neutered. Why the hell else would I pay all that money for Cutco knives?!

No comfort or answers came from her incomplete water color painting of Tom's face—and barely half a face at that—which lay on her kitchen table. Only pain flowed from the runaway colors that resembled a child's fever dream.

Her focus shifted quickly to her work, to finish her prep. Time to lock up the *props.* She stashed a Zeiss telephoto lens into her hidden safe in a wooden night table by her living room couch. She tossed in a security earpiece with attached miniature hand mic and it landed on a black metal box about the size and thickness of a hardback novel like *Don Quixote.* She slapped the safe door shut and locked it. The faux, wood-covered, outer door of the night table made it seem innocuous except for the 8x10 framed photograph lying face down on its top surface.

She stared at the back of the photo frame.

Her inner debate lasted only seconds. Nathalie grabbed the frame, turned it over and worked the glass cover loose which protected the photograph—the photograph of Tom. Once unprotected, she clawed at the photo; her fingernails shredded it into little strips with a few jagged pieces stuck along the outer edge.

One jagged piece contained a partial slice of Tom's right index finger but a full image of the more prominent middle finger. How apropos, she thought.

She flipped the bird to the shredded image and plopped it face down on the table.

This night in the reflection in the window, more jagged pieces caught her attention; the jagged edges of the ripped lace caressing her exposed breast seemed erotic. Naughty. Sort of like the city that lay before her, the taunting, tempting Big Apple, and she a badass Eve.

She wondered about the trend of those first designer blue jeans, the ones from Paris. Had it been an unspoken partnership between the two cities? The elegant designer-created jeans born in Paris shipped to New York City where they were torn strategically and only then sent out into the world as the uniform of the radical, yet stylish, rebel woman.

God she loved Paris, all its glorious art, continental class, and innate sophistication; then again, she adored New York with its intimidating style, vibrant culture, and irrepressible individuality. Maybe this made her schizophrenic but she didn't care. And maybe she wasn't a chump but an erotic rebel.

Yeah, she could make that play. That would keep the boys on edge; give her the advantage, which was what she needed. Then her intelligence—her wit and wiles—would win the day. She knew that. She also knew there was so much she was hiding.

So…maybe…she shouldn't overlook *erotic rebel.* She could make it her own version of brass balls needed to take on the boys. Her imagination took flight. *Erotic Rebel* would demand some sort of cool costume, a uniform even—alluring, definitely alluring—that would accentuate the curves and compress the cellulite. *The boys* would be toast.

Her father had worn a uniform. Looked great. Kicked ass. That memory froze her thoughts for a jarring moment.

Her imagination fractured into shards of doubt and the dagger-like points perforated her fantasy wings. Her hopes crashed hard into reality. She knew the *erotic rebel* plan had serious potential pitfalls for her. For one, *erotic rebels* needed to keep a straight face while being forcibly erotic. Too many self-conscious smirks might give her away, but the idea of compressed cellulite felt really good.

No, wit and wiles were the solid, safe bet. Wit and wiles would be her badge. She knew they were a potent potion when liberally applied; yet even a subtle drop or two caused great speculation of what the sorceress might do, with her doubt being the only diluting agent. Nathalie wanted her place at the table in business and the boys wanted theirs, usually wanted it all. Feminine sorcery seemed like fair play.

Nathalie knew she could be formidable. She had proven that in her work, at least to herself. But her best friend, Megan, told her she could be a delusional doofus when she tried too hard.

Formidable and delusional doofus. Hard to reconcile. That she knew and it did not fill her with confidence. Neither did hearing the

Joni Mitchell refrain *"I really don't know love at all"* rattle around in her head when she thought of Tom.

Then there was job at the Waldorf Astoria to pull off—a presentation of precious jewels—where she could score some real points and prove her worth. Prepped and ready to go, she knew she was good at what she did. On this chess board, she felt the queen had all the right moves to best the king.

So the would be erotic rebel with the torn nightgown took a moment to reassess.

She knew how to check things out; she was after all an investigator of sorts. She handled insurance cases—more forms than field work—but felt her willingness to go the extra mile, to take risks, gave her an edge over most of the boys in her line of work. She insisted she could handle field work; she owned a pair of sneakers.

She was Nathalie Seeger. She felt that was enough.

Out of spite, she turned the shredded photo of Tom back to the propped upright position on her night table—the jagged pieces still stuck along the edges—but the center of the frame was empty; the image of Tom was gone.

Ready to move on…

However, the twinge in her gut felt like a whispered plea: hoping that *alone* wasn't a synonym for *independent*. She wanted to know that for sure.

CHAPTER ONE

Man is not what he thinks he is; he is what he hides.

André Malraux

The Bombardier Global 6000 swept through the clouds. For its six thousand mile cruising range, this trip barely registered as a blip, but even a blip in a fifty million dollar aircraft was pleasurable.   A significant part of the pleasure for Eli Cross was the jet's ability to relocate quickly to far flung destinations. It fit his sense of humor as a getaway vehicle and there was no reason that a quick, unscheduled departure couldn't be a thing of beauty.

Luxury flowed inside where soft cream-colored leather seating and rich dark wood engaged the senses. A fully stocked galley capable of handling any meal also contained an enviable wine collection. Each reclining leather chair had a computer screen.

The sole item on the mahogany dining table was a jet black knapsack, fully packed.

On this trip…there were no passengers to be seen. At the rear of the cabin was a bedroom. Laid out neatly on the satin spread of the bed were clothes of stealth—all black.

At the back of the bedroom was a door and behind that door the sound of a running shower. Had someone else been present, they would've smelled a light but deeply masculine scent…just a hint of fresh musky cologne, but extremely distinctive that lingered like a memory.

Out the window, the whisper-smooth jet sliced through soft mountains of clouds on descent, breaking through into clear blue sky. Below was a winding river. The Rhine.

Germanic castles rose majestically up from the river banks. These rock-walled fortresses were once the domains of noble knights, lords and ladies, but now the domiciles of the uber-wealthy and ancestors clinging to a pastiche of royalty. Still the architectural majesty was ever-present. Cylindrical turrets linked by parapets topped with crenellated battlements of carved stone projected an expression of fortitude, an engulfing beauty that dwarfed the human form and conjured apparitions of wielded sword, lance, and bloody battle ax.

In a patch of forest, thick brush gave way as Eli Cross pressed through the foliage dressed all in black with the knapsack slung on his back. He hiked with purpose but ease, slipping past the clinging branches as if he was gliding on a dance floor; his casual movements masked the disciplined athleticism that made them.

He kept moving steadily until he attained the high ground of a clearing on the mountainside which overlooked the Rhine and a restored ancient castle that rested atop a small hill guarding the bend in the river. Cross took a moment to appreciate the grandeur before him. It was a blending of olden times in a modern age.

To fully honor this experience, he pulled wine, bread and cheese from his black knapsack and sat back against a tree and waited.

The sun finally dropped below the horizon and pulled down the curtain of night.

The lights of the castle glistened as a Mercedes limousine glided across the narrow, stone bridge over the water-filled moat and then through the open, iron gate to the round keep. Cross watched intently but without concern. He knew what would transpire inside the walls when the Mercedes parked in the guest area. His research was thorough. But there was still time to relish the final slice of cheese and bread. Nothing needed to be rushed, especially a fine glass of Bordeaux.

Savoring this moment always had deeper meaning than mere pleasure. It rose from a feeling cauterized into the marrow of his soul. In these moments he honored why he was here, his real purpose. Each savored sip of wine heightened his resolve and renewed the solemn commitment made in his youth from a day he would never forget. It was the source of his *saudade*, the yearning and longing that drove him.

His eyes never left the target below. An innate sense of timing guided his decision of when to move. The last sip of wine preceded his action. Calculations clicked confidently through his mind like the precise movements of a Swiss timepiece; a world created for him with consummate skill. The alpha predatory spirit fully engaged.

Within seconds, he descended into the mountainside's darkness.

⁎

A butler opened the enormous castle doors to two couples adorned in formal evening attire from famous designer names. Status achieved by association. They were all here to impress the owner of the castle or at least be seen to be on his level. Inside the extensive foyer, two suits of armor flanked a steel shield with the family crest of a rearing lion.

Striding forward with the proper sense of a theatrical entrance befitting his title, the master of the castle, Baron Johann von Hellerstadt greeted them with a glass of champagne in hand.

"Dieter, I welcome your friends," and then the Baron paused with a practiced grin, "to my humble pad."

"Baron, where is Siglinde?" Dieter threw a furtive glance to the sweeping staircase.

"Down in a moment. It's her jewels, Dieter," then continued with impish delight, "there are so many."

"Then take us to your other woman," Dieter exclaimed with a sweep of his hand.

The Library doors swung open and Baron von Hellerstadt swelled with pride as he led his guests over to *the other woman*. Mounted on the wall in the place of honor over the cavernous fireplace was an original Renoir, the voluptuous nudity of *Reclining Nude from the Back, Rest after the Bath*, the oil masterpiece from 1909.

The guests were suitably impressed but Baron von Hellerstadt was most pleased about the glint of envy he spotted in their eyes and the grimace on their lips. He took this opportunity to extend the duration of his delight by pouring champagne for everyone.

"You have given her a special place of honor, Baron," Dieter offered, "but may I say that your Siglinde is far more beautiful and lively."

"You may say. I heartily agree." Baron von Hellerstadt paused to stare at the painting. "But my beautiful wife is not worth sixty-eight million euros."

Dieter and the Baron clinked their champagne glasses in triumphant acknowledgement. Everyone raised their glasses toward the painting.

"Well Baron, for once, a mistress who pays you," Dieter grinned at his well-timed riposte.

With a nod, Baron von Hellerstadt was actually quite pleased with the snarky remark.

Outside there was movement in the night just below the tallest turret. A black rope snaked around a battlement along the connecting parapet at the base of the tower. A silent but swift tug lashed an intertwined knot tight against the stone battlement. The other end of the thick rope slithered then dropped over the side into the blackness. It dangled against the outside wall adjacent to the soft light from an open window.

Encased in his stealth black attire, Eli Cross—a black velvet pouch-type bag dangling from his waist and a black cylindrical tube strapped diagonally on his back like a quiver of arrows—descended the rough-hewn castle wall on the rope and slipped into the open window.

The room was a spacious lady's boudoir. A lady with money and accustomed to adornments. Cross moved past the king-sized bed encased in a pink canopy. An evening gown and lace panties neatly arrayed on the bed. The light that spilled out of the castle window from the boudoir flowed from around a walled corner where the bath was located. Soft sounds of movement emanated from the bath. Someone was there.

Cross hesitated. Slowed his breathing. Listened. And waited.

Outside, the moon waited for no one, and briefly broke out of thick cloud cover and cast its glow at the castle window. Inside the effect was instant. The glint of moonlight caught the faceted edges of jewelry displayed on top of the ornate antique wooden dresser and sprayed glistening reflections of light around the boudoir. With a stride quick and soft like a cat, Cross moved to the jewels.

They were laid out ready to be worn. Ready for Siglinde. Was she the one in the bath? Cross knew she was if his research was correct. If… But reality had a way of sabotaging research in the moment.

Eli bypassed the jewels and edged his way silently toward the bath. Out of the pocket of his black pants, he extracted a hinged black metal rod and unfolded it. Attached on its tip, a small circular mirror, the kind used by a dentist. He extended the mirror around the corner. Though the image was small, it was clear.

Naked before a floor length mirror, luxuriating in her own reflection stood Siglinde, an Austrian blonde whose dynamic curves put the Renoir to shame. Not to be rushed, she indulged her naked ritual of sensuality taking pleasurable delight in allowing droplets of perfume to splash onto her aroused nipples. A natural blonde from head to toe, her thick, lustrous hair cascaded over her shoulders while the golden triangle of hair between her legs had been carefully brushed into a sweeping swirl which darkened as the scented droplets flowed to their final rest.

The temptation to stay and appreciate, even to taste and sample her delights, made the air thick and heavy with desire. This was nature's power. Women had it. Men, both in myth and reality, fell under its spell and succumbed. Like savoring the Bordeaux, Cross drank in her delicious sensuality until discipline turned him back to the hard beauty of the jewels.

Outside, the moon drifted back behind the clouds and the sparkling jewels suddenly fell into milky shadow. Wasting no time, his black gloves lifted a large diamond necklace from the dresser and silently slipped it into the black velvet pouch. Emerald encrusted bracelets, sapphire and diamond earrings, a ruby ring, a Tsavorite garnet ring, several smaller opal necklaces and a mother of pearl brooch still remained. Adorned with jewels was how Siglinde planned on greeting her guests.

Siglinde, utterly comfortable in her perfumed nudity, entered the bedroom and lifted the lace panties from her bed. Her evening gown clearly would not accommodate a bra. Her round natural breasts were still defiant of gravity. An eerie stillness settled in the darkness. She sensed something…something not right…but only silence persisted. A soft rustle of clothing brushed aside the silence as she stepped into her panties. Adoring guests awaited her.

A scraping sound near the window drew her attention—perhaps only a tree branch—then moonlight entered the open window, once again bathing everything in a soft glow.

She gasped! The air in her throat expelled in a burst of terror! Her eyes filled with horror!

Her jewels were gone!

So was Cross. No unseen movement or sound from leaving. He simply wasn't there.

A blood-curdling scream erupted from her lungs!

Even from a woman easily irritated when everything did not go her way, Baron von Hellerstadt had never heard such a scream. That outburst paled to the next wave of screams—not of terror—but eruptions of volcanic outrage!! Hot lava of imperious swearing flowed down from above!!

The Baron and his guests raced from the library fearing that hell had opened its gates! Wanting no part of hell unleashed—not the hell of a woman in mortal danger, but a pampered one denied her pleasure—Dieter and the guests made a hasty retreat out into the night and their Mercedes escape limo.

Baron von Hellerstadt, then all alone, gingerly climbed the staircase as Siglinde's screams sputtered into choking, coughing sobs and wailing! Lacking a husband's protective instinct or any control over his second prized possession, the Baron cringed and slowed his climb.

In the empty library, the Renoir adorned the wall all alone. The naked woman with her back and face turned away from all who would gaze upon her was still most alluring and inviting and not at all bothered by the unfeminine outrage that poured down from upstairs. Resplendent and casually stretched out on her bed, legs slightly bent with the left one resting comfortably on the top side of her right, while a white cloth underneath her languidly cascaded off the edge with a large colorful pillow propped under her right arm and shoulder. The blended background earth-tone colors of cream, moss green, brown and gold greatly added to the enveloping feeling of relaxation. Eli Cross felt relaxation to be most appropriate if one rested in this position since 1909. His black-gloved hand lightly patted her bare bottom.

℃

In the soft, golden light of dawn and through the mist which rose over the Rhine, the castle appeared almost as the apparition of myth. A knight astride a Holsteiner returning from battle once graced these very grounds. But this morning, the sounds clattering across the stone bridge were not from horse hooves but the tires from a Volkswagen van; Eli Cross, attired in a dark blue business suit from the German designer Hugo Boss, the van's driver and sole occupant.

In the castle's cavernous foyer, Cross wasted no time in presenting Baron von Hellerstadt his business card. The Baron had the exhausted look of a man who had been up all night dealing with calamitous events. Gone was the prideful grin, replaced now with a piercing scrutiny of this new visitor.

"Guten tag, Baron von Hellerstadt," said Cross.

The Baron merely studied the business card, glancing up every now and then at Cross's face as if proof of his profession would be written upon it. The embossed card held the imprint of **Veritas**, an international insurance company with headquarters in Zurich. The name on the card was **Helmut Hauer** with the **Fine Art Retrieval Division**.

The Baron addressed this new visitor with a certain entitled annoyance. "You are early."

"Yes, is it a problem?" Cross waited, his patience unflinching.

"No..."

"Good. I need to verify the authenticity before the insurance payment can be made."

"The thief also took two million euros in jewels," a point made by the Baron with the lingering expectancy of compassion and understanding.

"Something we don't cover."

"I'm aware of that, but surely—"

"Our policy prohibits contacting the authorities due to the *unusual way* in which you obtained the Renoir." Again Cross waited. His face registered no opening for argument.

"Let me show you what remains," said the defeated Baron.

What remained was the frame of the Renoir which still hung above the fireplace in the library. But only the frame and an old blank protective backing with some jagged pieces of the painting along the frame line now adorned the wall. The Renoir had been cut out, apparently rather quickly and crudely!

Cross and Baron von Hellerstadt moved toward it with reverence.

"I had no idea," said Cross with astonishment. "To desecrate such a work of art is...vile." A grimace of disgust furrowed his brow. "Tests will need to be run on the pieces remaining. I will require the entire frame."

Cross looked to Baron von Hellerstadt and simply gestured for help to remove the frame. The two men very carefully lifted the remnants of the desecrated Renoir off the wall. The Baron knew that Cross was all business, so he got right to the point of the payment.

"Once you authenticate, then the payment will be in full, the coverage of my policy."

"Baron," said Cross with studied assurance, "Your policy will be to the letter. You have already paid the substantial deductible for your premium policy so you are fully vested. As I understand it, the covered amount for the painting's loss would be seventy-two million euros."

"Seventy-two." The Baron was pleased at that.

"Yes, for you a four million euro profit. Two of which I imagine would cover the unfortunate loss of your wife's jewels. But for the art world, a terrible tragedy."

"Yes, terrible," said the Baron, attempting to hide his relief.

Out in the castle courtyard, the two men loaded the frame into the back of the Volkswagen van carefully securing it for transport. Cross shut the door. The Renoir frame tucked inside. Cross, with practiced indignation, wiped off some castle dust from his Hugo Boss suit.

Baron Johann von Hellerstadt, gripped with a sudden rush of concern, did not want to let Cross leave without some additional level of assurance. "What are the chances for recovery?"

"For the painting—or what is left of it—there is grave doubt. The nature of this theft is already a travesty. You must brace yourself. The Renoir may never be yours again."

"But my insurance payment—"

"Will be placed in my hands, I guarantee it."

The Baron smiled. "Then I will say auf Wiedersehen."

Cross offered a professional smile in return.

ℴ⁍

The Bombardier Global 6000 descended toward the sparkling lights of Paris at night. The Eiffel Tower's bright beacon swept the sky, a welcome to the city of light and love.

The main court of the Musée du Louvre, the Cour Napoléon, stood eerily deserted. No security personnel, none whatsoever. The air deathly still. The grandeur of the massive façade, though subdued in the breathless darkness, dwarfed a single man or woman; its parade of elegant archways mere curved holes in the night with the ornate pillars more like giant soldiers guarding the walls.

Something sinister slipped past those guards this night; it was darkness itself. A pressing canopy of darkness engulfed the extensive grounds like a death shroud. A haunting change for this most magnificent of museums, a treasure of France and the world, to not be accented by artistically arrayed beams of light in the night. The light had vanished. Human hands brought down this darkness. Quickly. Silently. Very skilled hands stealing the light.

Clouds even encased the moon in shadow like an accomplice until a slash of light broke through and struck the glass panels of I.M. Pei's the Louvre Pyramid. A distorted shape slithered along an inner corridor beneath the towering, glass-arched ceiling. Splotches of moonlight fell upon the walls dripping in priceless paintings.

In the hallway which connected Neoclassicism and French Romanticism, the shadow's movement suddenly stopped, then melted into a wall pocket in the darkened corridor.

Within that blackness, the sudden illuminated glow from tritium gas vials in the dial of a Luminox Navy SEAL wristwatch's hands appeared. They indicated 2:55 am. When the second hand swept up to twelve, the illumination slid back into blackness. The shadowy movement reemerged as a figure dressed in stealth black.

It was Eli Cross.

In appreciation, he paused, and took a moment to look up. He was after all in the Musée du Louvre, considered the largest castle in the world. At this moment he knew he was in the space that once was the apartment of the French king. With masterpieces from around the world surrounding the walls—many collected by the monarchs of France—Eli Cross knew not to neglect the ceiling.

Safely distanced from human touch, the ceiling of the Salle des Sept-Cheminées held every reason to look up to the heavens. The ornate skylight was surrounded by the Victories, the life-sized winged figurines by the sculptor Francisque-Joseph Duret whose two bronze figures also graced the entrance to Napoleon's tomb at Les Invalides. Eli Cross had always appreciated the Victories for they seemed eternally ready to take flight, a quality he keenly cultivated.

Art was not come by easily, *so attention must be paid,* and if one was going to *remove art* from its rightful home, it seemed only fair that it was first admired. Removing a masterpiece from this ceiling would make an amusing challenge, he thought. Some might even consider the theft an act of righteous reciprocity. A fair amount of the art within the Louvre arrived under less than auspicious arrangements; many pilfered from original owners, ripped out of tombs meant to be sealed for eternity, and looted in battle as the spoils of war. A cop might call sections of these hallowed halls an evidence locker of stolen property. The ethics of ownership created such a slippery slope that Eli Cross felt almost noble about his musings of personal art *liberation.*

Tonight though there was only a small patch of time allocated for rumination.

On this night, he hoped during this caper in this hallowed space, that he would not see the faces; the dead faces that haunted him in the dark. But this night was no exception. Even in his state of heightened focus for the job at hand, they were with him. They were what drove him. They were part of who he was and would be that way forever. There was certainly no going back and changing it.

He pushed a dolly loaded down with a packing crate, its wheels padded to muffle sound. He knew where he was headed. The route had been well planned. The silence within the massive hall was unsettling; even more so, the complete lack of security. He stopped again.

His black-gloved hand pulled back the black sleeve on his arm to reveal the black Navy SEAL watch. The illuminated second hand swept up to 3:00 am. He tugged the sleeve back down and plunged the space around him into darkness once more.

The padded wheels moved forward.

The plan was simple, but precise. He knew there would be no security personnel in this section at this exact time. Move, wait, move again, and always be where they were not.

Precisely how the Mona Lisa had left the Louvre in 1911. The thieves had hidden in an art-supply closet until everyone had gone. They simply were where the security guards were not. Not an intricate plan, but Einstein once remarked: *"When the solution was simple, God was answering."*

Strangely enough, it took more than Leonardo da Vinci's God-given talent to bring world fame to the Mona Lisa. When recovered—two years later—people the world over wanted to know: *who was this smiling woman who had been taken from France's most illustrious museum?*

Fame delivered by the hand of a thief.

So it could be done. A masterpiece taken from the Louvre. Simplicity had its own reward.

The Mona Lisa had long intrigued him. A smile so mysterious it beguiled those who gazed upon it. Eli Cross felt he knew her secret. Her eyes gave away nothing, an enigma; yet he sensed a deep well of her own saudade behind her smile, an acceptance of life's irony. He liked that she hid her secrets well; he knew his own guarded secret. Everyone hid something; his talent, constantly honed, unlocked the secrets of others exposing their vulnerability to him. A well-planned theft was a work of art when the elements of the vision's possibilities became practical…and then profitable. Nothing human was perfect, even art, and his excitement rose from where the flawed *moment* in the theft would occur, then to elude that *moment.*

He knew he would face her smile again and share that *moment* together.

Cross stopped the dolly when French Romanticism changed to a special one-time exhibit on Impressionism. With three swift, practiced movements, he ripped the packing crate open; the packing material wrapped in such a way to emit no sound when torn.

Inside the crate was a frame—the frame that once held the Renoir.

Cross stood in front of an empty wall space between a Monet and a Cezanne. He lifted the desecrated Renoir frame into the empty space on the wall.

The placement of the frame and its missing painting—with only jagged pieces remaining along the edge—in between the two Impressionist masterpieces on either side seemed an act of revenge, a twisted and cruel display of humor.

Eli Cross took a moment to admire his work. He then moved to complete his task.

His black gloved hand felt around the frame's edge and carefully took hold of a jagged piece of painting that remained stuck in the frame. He then peeled the jagged piece backwards, which pulled the attached blank backing from the frame's edge, revealing the untouched Renoir masterpiece underneath! The false backing with its expertly forged jagged pieces of the Renoir cleverly positioned and glued around its edges imitated a painting that had been crudely cut from its canvas. The original masterpiece had never been removed, never touched, never desecrated!

Suddenly, a piercing beam from a spotlight snapped on trapping Cross in its glare!

Aiming the light was an armed museum security guard.

Cross sighed, accepting the inevitable that this was the end of his perfect plan.

The guard was not alone and Cross nodded to his other *captors*. They were an illustrious ensemble to be sure—The French Minister of Culture, the Curator of the Louvre as well as the Director of the Louvre—and surrounded him by the Renoir. No escape.

In the dignified tone of a diplomat, the French Minister of Culture addressed the man they had caught in the beam of the spotlight. "You should be aware, Monsieur, that the Louvre does not usually house the work of the Impressionists and this special celebratory exhibit of Impressionism is on loan from the Musée d'Orsay, the Musée de L'Orangerie and the Musée Marmottan Monet. The government of France has an invested interest in the presentation of the art masterpieces under its watchful eye."

The Director of the Louvre continued without missing a beat. "And as the eyes of the world are always focused on the activities at the Louvre, should anything go missing it would be an embarrassment that would be difficult to explain."

The Curator of the Louvre picked up the sentiment. "To say nothing of the insult to the art world which Parisians, and may I say, all of France, would take personally."

"Have you anything to say, Monsieur?" asked the Minister of Culture.

"Oui," Cross replied, and then turned to the Renoir. "C'est magnifique, n'est-ce pas?"

Cross did not make a move to flee; unlike the readiness of the winged Victories gazing down from above, he merely continued his admiring gaze of the Renoir. The three men and the guard did not rush to grab him and apply shackles and haul him off with incensed indignation. No, they waited. So Cross turned to face them once again.

"Pierre-Auguste Renoir, an inventive artist who helped birth the impressionist style. Most worthy of this exhibit of Impressionism. *Reclining Nude from the Back, Rest after the Bath.* A work of great passion."

"We honor the passion of the artist," the Curator said, referring to Cross.

The Director said hopefully, "I imagine you were able to obtain something for yourself?"

Cross produced the black velvet bag and gave it a little shake rattling the precious jewels inside. "For travel expenses."

"Indeed," said the Director.

"Poetic," chimed in the Curator.

"The government of France is once again grateful." The Minister of Culture extended his hand. "Merci, Monsieur."

Cross shook his hand. "De Rien."

"Au contraire, Monsieur. To France it is far more than nothing. It is…everything. C'est tout."

"Ah oui," agreed Cross, "Et pour France, toujours l'audace."

"Oui, monsieur, always daring," agreed the Minister of Culture, very pleased. "It is why we turn to you. Et maintenant, a tout a l'heure."

The men left Eli Cross by the Renoir and melted back into the darkness of the Louvre, content once again with being in control of all that they surveyed.

Cross was also very pleased with the casual and informal nature of their adieu. He had wanted it to seem as if they were friends. Friends could be useful. Eli Cross knew that was an edge to his advantage; their devotion to the art and culture of France and to *friendship*. The set up was crucial and the best ones took time. Patience yielded great wine among other things of value. Perhaps, one night this advantage may bring into his arms the Victories from the ceiling.

But not this night, for as grand of a challenge as that would be, it was not at the heart of his deepest desire. It was not his *everything.* The Renoir retrieval had been a side trip leading to his next step; it had been a mere prelude, a chance to warm up and be loose.

To lay it all on the line, that was *everything* to Cross. Was that perfect moment even possible? His next key heist would test *that moment* and set things in motion.

It was more dangerous than anything he had attempted before. There would be no turning back. It was to be the ultimate test, a swan song perhaps. His skills and readiness were at their height. To put his very life on the line would change—or end—that life forever.

He had to know if it was possible to meet *that moment*. The yearning to know had deepened for years. Underneath everything he did, *saudade* drove him.

Beware the wounded animal.

In this moment, he felt a long way from home.

The Bombardier was fueled at Orly. This trip would not be a blip. This was a long flight.

CHAPTER TWO

*A woman is like a tea bag - you can't tell how strong
she is until you put her in hot water.*

Eleanor Roosevelt

The Red Hook Container Terminal in Brooklyn, New York handled any type or size of cargo. On any given day the stevedores manned the gantry cranes and unloaded road salt to de-ice snow-clogged winter streets as well as pallets of tropical bananas for the grocery stores. Other days the big cranes swung loads of steel or lumber from the massive cargo ships to the docks where longshoremen would man the forklifts and reachstackers to move them along to the next transportation method or warehouse storage at the terminal. They handled arriving fleets of autos and even yachts.

The crisp cool air of the last autumn before things changed invigorated the work. No disruption to the flow of goods intruded yet. No collapse of the supply chain. There was plenty of toilet paper. The following year's numbers would be the same as those designated for perfect vision; yet the world would be seen quite differently. Change was in the air. The goods wrestled off the ships this day by hardened people who needed no masks to do their job flowed as they should. That trust would be tested soon in the following spring.

These stevedores and longshoremen were a breed of toughness with their own code hewn from their rock-ribbed determination, trash-talking sass, tradition and pride lathered in blood, beer, sweat and salty language. The pay was good, the camaraderie even better, and the fights were the best. Nobody, but nobody, called them pussies, not even the Teamsters. Some tough son-of-a-bitch women had broken through the barriers and joined this gritty band of brothers. There was a steep price to pay—enough abuse to choke a cow—and when they had won hard-earned respect they were still called *women longshoremen*. No one could pronounce or even utter the term *longshorewomen*. It was not allowed to exist. This was a tough man's world.

The first photo of Neil "Grab Ass" Grabowski on the docks was taken with a telephoto lens and clearly showcased his tattooed forearms and barrel chest as the longshoreman heaved crates onto a truck bed. The shutter clicked off a rapid series of shots which looked almost like a herky-jerky dance of images of "Grab Ass" working up a monster sweat. This was one tough son-of-a-bitch bastard.

"Oh, Mr. Grabowski, you are a fine physical specimen. And very photogenic."

The voice behind the camera belonged to Nathalie Seeger, the same Nathalie Seeger of the torn nightgown and shredded Tom photograph, now working an easy fact-gathering case. This simple job at the wharf merely paid the rent. She planned to knock this off—no problem—then change for the Waldorf-Astoria gala, the career-making opportunity set for the afternoon. It had all the makings of an ordinary day of business for her. She'd not given it a second thought when she rolled out of bed. Even if she had, she wouldn't have had the faintest idea that the next twenty four hours would irrevocably change her life.

She clicked off one final photo of Neil Grabowski flashing a two-fisted bird at his giant hulk of a working partner, appropriately named Bubba. A name Ms. Seeger assumed he used with pride. The final photo finished her portion of the job. Wrapped up. So simple…until Nathalie decided she should go the extra mile just to be better.

"I think we should meet."

Nathalie dismantled the heavy lens from the digital camera and packed it in her equipment bag. Her perch on the roof of a warehouse overlooked the entire terminal. She seemed somewhat out of place, alone on the expansive roof in a sleek, navy blue Ann Taylor business suit with slacks. Much better she thought than a torn nightgown and more professional than *erotic rebel.* The dose of practicality was provided by the sneakers. Skechers were her preference. But even in a business pants suit with sneakers, she was very female.

Her toned, nicely proportioned body—in her own words *nothing got in the* way—along with her tomboy athleticism served her well in her work. She was not obsessive about her looks but she enjoyed looking good when the occasion required it. Her hair had a stylish layered cut above the shoulders that was so practical it looked carefree and sexy just out of bed which worked well on the many days that the alarm didn't go off and on the few days when the hangover still lingered. She actually was quite happy with her hair, it blew dry quickly and the rich browns with natural highlights gave her the impetus to prove that blondes did not have more fun. Mainly it stayed out of her way and she didn't have to bother with it.

This was New York City and she felt in competition with—well with everyone—but especially the guys. She fretted that her femininity was being left behind in the race to keep up, to maintain a business-edge. Tom's leaving did not help. This concern shoved a wedge of doubt into her self-confidence and her self-esteem, but especially into her desire to be an independent woman standing on her own two feet—an appendage to no one. Basically that meant her emotional stability was on roller coaster rails rising and dropping between rock star and total loser; an exaggeration perhaps, but that was how she would describe it when fishing for sympathy.

Nathalie wanted life to have a little kick to it; it's why she followed her own path and did what she did for work, and why she liked being single. She wouldn't have minded being in love, just didn't trust it. She was stubborn that way. She came by her stubbornness honestly. A dyed-in-the-wool, life-long, New Yorker father and a French—one-time art student—mother.

Nathalie was the French spelling of Natalie, the suggestion of which came from her mother. Her father always referred to it as the *suggestion* he graciously accepted, when the reality was that there were certain arguments that French women did not lose. Ever. Nate Seeger was no push-over, but neither was Odile Trenet. Nathalie was clearly her own woman and though comfortably into her thirties, she thought of her parents often, especially her father. But at this moment, she felt she needed a plan to do the right thing in dealing with Mr. Grabowski.

She needed to *take it to him.*

℘

Down on the dock, Grabowski slammed a boat hook into a large wooden crate and ripped the slats apart to expose wine cases packed inside.

"Hey, Bubba, what's that look like to you?"

The lingering hulk, Bubba, was even bigger than Grabowski and just as refined.

"Damaged shipping crate," said Bubba matter-of-factly.

"Yeah," Grabowski replied, "Total loss."

Grabowski sliced open a wine case with the boat hook and extracted a bottle.

"Helluva shame," Bubba said with practiced remorse.

"Terrible tragedy," Grabowski replied in their long-running routine.

Grabowski flipped the bottle to Bubba. A group of longshoremen gathered 'round. Bottles tossed with wild abandon got snatched out of the air by guys until one was caught by—

Nathalie as she stepped into the midst of the rough longshoremen with confidence.

"Mr. Grabowski…" she addressed him with a tilt of the wine bottle, like a nod to his tossing skills.

Grabowski looked up from the wine crate. "Me?"

"Mr. Neil "Grab Ass" Grabowski?"

Grabowski claimed the name with pride. "Yeah."

"She's got you pegged," Bubba said, clearly enjoying this encounter.

"We need to talk," Nathalie said simply.

"The ex-old lady send you?"

"No," said Nathalie firmly. She continued more softly, "I have an offer for you." She turned her back to the others. "A private offer." She gestured away from his buddies who drew closer. "Best if we do this alone," she whispered.

"You're a fine lookin' babe. We just gonna talk…all alone?" Grabowski made sure his buddies had heard that taunt.

The longshoremen were now getting into this and more had gathered around to witness Grabowski toy with this woman. It was a great break from their brutal physical routine. Their mate was going to provide some raucous and raw theater and if they were lucky it might be something that got out of hand.

"Bring her back when you're done," Bubba cried out.

Nathalie handed her bottle to the mountain that was Bubba. "Don't let the wine go to your head." Then she turned to her subject. "Let's step over here, Mr. Grabowski?"

Grabowski looked at Nathalie with a shit-eating grin and said, "You got somethin' to say," and turned to his crowd of co-workers with his arms opened wide, "say it."

This drew a series of whoops from the riveted stevedores and longshoremen. Even the lone woman, stout and tanned, with a short cropped cut of dark blonde hair and an eagle's claw tattooed on her neck grinned at Nathalie as if to say *you asked for it, Honey.*

"I'm Nattie Seeger," she said to Grabowski keeping her voice low, "a free-lance private investigator hired by the insurance company you're ripping off with your disability claim."

"I can't do shit with this back," Grabowski feigned a sudden grip of pain.

"I have photos of you doing all sorts of shit with that back."

She looked Grabowski straight in the eye with an appeal to his humanity and his reason. She thought it was a moment of compassion expressed to someone who worked hard to make ends meet. It seemed the right thing to do, to give him a chance. So very slowly and with a deliberate tone, she told him, "However, I'm giving you the opportunity to return the insurance company's money before I submit the proof. No legal repercussions. A clean slate for you."

"I gotta pay alimony with that money!" These words left a bad taste spurting out of his mouth.

"You haven't paid alimony or child support in six months," Nathalie said simply.

"I ain't payin' that bitch for the kid."

"You are the child's father."

His past relationship clearly held some bitterness for Grabowski. "Look, she had the kid, not me. All I did was screw her," he snapped.

"All it takes to earn the title." Nathalie had no more time or sympathy for his pathetic one-sided view of his marital responsibilities. Doing the right thing didn't include coddling well-practiced assholes. "All right, we're done here."

Grabowski took a quick stride forward as she stepped away and grabbed Nathalie by the ass and pulled her into his groin! "Wanna go a few rounds with the champ?!"

His co-workers erupted in cheers as he pumped himself against her a few times. Up until this pivotal moment, his co-workers had heard nothing of Nathalie's fair offer.

"I'm only going to tell you once to let go of me," Nathalie said this so only Grabowski could hear her.

"Or what?" Grabowski laughed. His look intensified. This was his moment, the time to make his play. "I oughta do you right here," he said loud enough for everyone to hear.

The longshoremen were clearly itchin' for a show. This *woman* set foot in their territory making demands of one of their own, so that gauntlet thrown made this encounter a blood sport the way they looked at it. She was a woman to be taken, if "Grab Ass" was man enough.

"Do her, Grab Ass! Do the bitch!" Bubba played his role whipping up the crowd.

Grabowski's lips moved toward hers, but stopped when he found a Sig-Sauer 9mm "short" pressed against his nuts. He hadn't seen her reach behind her Ann Taylor blazer and slip the semi-automatic from its leather holster clipped to her belt.

"We're not in love and I'm not in the mood." Nathalie knew she had to regain control of the situation and the crowd and this would give her the space she needed to walk away. Any reasonable man would take the hint and back off. Game over. But this was not a reasonable man.

Grabowski wasn't going to let some bitch in a business suit take control of anything involving him. He grabbed her hands and held the gun against his genitalia!

"You wanna screw me with this?!" Grabowski humped her gun over and over.

"This is not smart," she said to him knowing she was losing her edge over the situation. It didn't help her confidence that the stevedores and longshoremen were taking sides.

"Do her!"

"Shoot him!"

"Nail her!"

"Blow his balls off!"

This was not good on so many levels. Nathalie knew she was no physical match for this brute. Her desire to do the right thing had gone terribly wrong. This was not the way to compete with the boys. No, this was how the boys crushed you. They never would've offered him a way out. File the photos and fuck him. What the hell was she thinking?! She was being *a girl,* that's what she thought!

Propelled by the jeers and cheers, Grabowski humped harder! A demented sexual frenzy infected the crowd of dockworkers jacking them up. This type of energy wiped out reason, obliterated humanity, and created a thirst for more action. In this atmosphere, rape would be nothing more than street theater, performance art, and these were rabid art lovers now.

"Back off!" Nathalie insisted.

Her heart beat rapidly, her skin flushed red from rampaging fear! She knew she had fallen into a deep pit of danger, a trap of her own making!

"I'm gonna do you now!" Grabowski knew he had the crowd with him but he also knew his manhood and standing in this tough community required that he delivered the whole nine yards. He let go of the gun and grabbed her suit jacket!

A gunshot ripped the air!

Everyone stopped!

A smoking hole had been blown through Grabowski's pants below the groin! Everyone stared. There was no blood...just smoke curling out of the hole in his pants.

Grabowski stared...mouth agape.

"Sorry. I missed," said Nathalie taking control of her breathing. She backed off a couple steps hoping that she had made her point and that now they could get real in a business-like fashion—like her leaving.

"You bitch!" Stunned at first, Grabowski went from dumbfounded to pissed-off in less than three seconds, his face a crimson red of rage.

The longshoremen whooped it up! This was a twist they hadn't expected from a city chick in a business suit. "Now that's sexual harassment!" someone yelled out. The catcalls erupted like the crescendo of an exploding fireworks display.

"Balls on fire!"

"That pussy's packin'!"

"Yeah, Honey with a heater!"

"Scorched his sack hairs, baby!"

"Better count your balls, Grabowski!"

No way in hell Grabowski wanted to lose face in front of his friends and co-workers. But they were having a great time. It was instantly clear to him that this was emotional life and death if he was ever to hold his head up high on the docks again. He walked toward her with cold, dead eyes.

"This time you better kill me." He kept coming right at her.

Nathalie knew this time she was going to have to shoot him for real unless she found an alternate solution fast! She backed up and suddenly saw a cargo net swinging overhead from a giant hundred foot tall Liebherr gantry. She saw her way out, slipped the Sig in her belt-clip holster and clambered up a pyramid of crates scrambling for her life!

Grabowski went right after her!

When Nathalie reached the top crate, the stack teetered from the imbalance of her weight and Grab Ass Grabowski pawing at her feet as he clawed his way up the stack. She leaped off and grabbed onto the passing cargo net, which swept her off the dock and out over the water, but not until Grabowski had made a flying leap at her legs and latched on!

Both were carried out over the water!

The one hundred and fifty foot reach of the Liebherr gantry's arm swept the cargo net over a docked private yacht. Grabowski clawed at Nathalie legs with such venom he shredded her pantyhose beneath her pant leg and stripped her grip from the net!

They both plummeted down onto the yacht and crashed through the glass skylight over the main cabin and landed on the master bed below in a shower of glass!

Nathalie struggled to get up, but Grabowski yanked her down by her hair! He grasped her neck and pressed her into the mattress, while up above, longshoremen leaped aboard the yacht and peered over the skylight cheering on the show down below!

Grabowski yanked her gun and holster from her backside and tossed it off the bed, then fumbled at the belt and zipper on Nathalie's pants. Nathalie was choking from his grip.

"Kiss me," she gurgled.

"What'd you say, you bitch?!"

"If you're gonna do me, kiss me," she managed to choke out.

That prompted a chorus of "Kiss her!" from up above!

Grabowski fed off their frenzy. He let go of squeezing Nathalie's neck and pressed her down into the mattress from the front to re-grip. He then jammed his hand behind her head and pulled it up toward his lips! As he lowered his lips to meet hers, Nathalie's left hand clamped onto his nuts and her right hand slipped a bottle of champagne out of the bedside ice bucket and christened his face with it, launching Grabowski off the bed!

Whistles and cheers rained down from the longshoreman audience above! This was their kind of kick-ass show!

Nathalie straightened her clothes and rustled her fingers through her hair. One more reason, she thought, to love her easily managed hairstyle. She retrieved her Sig Sauer, stepped over the unconscious lump that was Grabowski, and headed up the stairs to the main deck.

She stepped into the sunlight as longshoremen slapped her on the back.

"Lady, you're pretty good," Bubba offered.

"Good?" Nathalie turned to him. "I'm the best, pal."

Nathalie strode through the parting mass of men and one tattooed woman, accepting the slaps on the back and butt as the adrenalin pump kept her moving quickly through the raucous gauntlet. She figured she had maybe five minutes to clear the dock area before the adrenalin crashed and then just like *the girl* she didn't want to be, she'd probably faint.

On the roller coaster rails of her life, this fleeting moment was a boost to the self-confidence and self-esteem. At this moment, *rock star*. But she knew full well that she had been a single heartbeat away from *total loser*. It pissed her off that she couldn't completely own this *rock star* moment without the doubts lingering around waiting for recognition; unlike the men she felt in competition with—those bastards and their egos kept the doubts at bay.

Somehow…somehow she felt she just had to be better.

She picked up her pace, cleared the crowd, rounded the corner of the warehouse…and once all alone, vomited on her brand new Skechers.

CHAPTER THREE

*The greatest enemy of knowledge is not ignorance; it
is the illusion of knowledge.*

Stephen Hawking

It was only fitting that Madison Avenue was a one-way street heading north. In the advertising world and to a large degree the world of financial investments, true north was getting people to believe that whatever you were selling was right and that it was okay to believe, in fact it was required to believe to be *in the know.* In this way, people were manipulated and controlled. Just like in politics, reality was illusion and illusion was reality.

Nathalie watched the sea of people converge on the buildings. It was a wonder that anything fully real ever got done, she thought. The coming spring would empty these streets from pandemic fears, but now she was swept along with the rising tide of pedestrians who flowed into one of the steel and concrete monoliths.

In the lobby of Delacorte, Redfield & Nanning, there were Hockneys, Lichtensteins and Turners gracing the walls of this brash new advertising firm. The elevator doors opened and Nathalie moved to the reception desk. As she expected, the person greeting the arriving guests or clients was a woman—always stylishly attired with perfectly coiffed hair—and most importantly, pretty and sexy with a voice like smooth Bourbon going down. This one was exceptional.

"Nathalie Seeger to see Megan Hollister. She's expecting me."

The supermodel receptionist checked a list.

"Yes, I have you right here, Ms. Seeger. Do you know the way?"

"Yes, I do."

Nathalie entered the inner corridor and even though she employed her most confident walk, she wondered how she could be feeling so inferior. She knew the answer. The answer was very clear. The receptionist was breathtakingly stunning. Nathalie felt a gasp of breath leave her body when she had first seen the absolutely gorgeous human being who greeted her.

This was by design.

After witnessing such human perfection, anyone's ego would be brought down a notch. The stunned effect would leave them vulnerable to the *suggestions* they would hear of how best to do business with this advertising firm, this firm which had already set the gold standard right outside their door; leaving one to wonder what other *great ideas* would they find inside. If the receptionist was this *perfect,* the anticipation of how exceptional the ad executives were could easily make one feel…inferior.

Of course the tickling feeling made from her shredded pantyhose which suddenly dangled from underneath her pant leg in ragged strips and flapped against her ankles added to the inferiority. It was not her best professional look.

This fresh inferiority complex carried into a large and efficient office bullpen where the graphic artists of DRN worked out of open cubicles subdividing an entire wing like a maze. Nathalie followed the twists and turns of the cubicle maze and finally stepped into a single cubicle where Megan Hollister sat with her feet propped up on her desk.

Megan was hip, playful and filled with an artist's insecurity. She made insecurity a badge of honor and this was one of many reasons that qualified her as Nathalie's best friend. Megan was living proof that intelligence, talent and insecurity could go hand-in-hand.

She was a graduate in Interior Design with an emphasis on Graphic Design from Cornell University in Ithaca, New York. After graduation, Megan had returned home to Queens and looked for a job…and looked…and looked. Her parents were driving her nuts at the time so to escape the haranguing *to find a job with your fancy degree,* she rented a dingy flat on the Upper West Side with a view of a single tree three blocks away in Central Park if she stood on a stepstool and looked out the top of her kitchen area window.

Nathalie did not know Megan then and had graduated herself from Columbia University in the city with a degree in Creative Writing and a plan to follow that up with a masters at Columbia in journalism. That plan fizzled and never panned out. Megan and Nathalie's background would not have normally connected them. It took a boyfriend to do that. At that time it was Nathalie's Italian boyfriend, Vittorio, at Columbia who was an actor in the drama program.

Vittorio didn't go back to his parents in Florence one summer and instead got a part in an off-Broadway play where Megan was designing scenery—a job Megan did not tell her parents about because the pay was pathetic. One night after rehearsal, Vittorio smiled at her, and three drinks later she was flat on her back with Vittorio on top of her and their clothes scattered about her studio apartment. Vittorio was a good actor but he was an even better performer in bed. He was after all, Italian.

On opening night, Nathalie came to see the play. She arrived early to get a good seat. Suddenly, the scenic designer—Megan—began hacking at the scenery with a hammer! Nathalie, the only one in the audience at the time, shouted out at Megan to stop—*her boyfriend was starring in this play*! Megan stopped and stared at her for an unnervingly long time.

Megan told Nathalie—then referred to as a salacious hussy—there was only one male actor in this play. That actor was *her boyfriend*, and that actor, she had just discovered, had been having an affair with the leading lady during the entire rehearsal time. Nathalie stared at Megan for an unnervingly long time. She then asked Megan if there were more than one hammer.

Together, Megan and Nathalie plotted revenge. They had such fun and so many laughs devising horrid plans to eviscerate Vittorio that they never got around to acting on them. They also discovered that their boyfriend, Vittorio—who ultimately turned out to be Vinnie, from the Bronx—was just not worth the time. So the boyfriend was caput, but a lifelong friendship commenced.

Nathalie looked at Megan, so relaxed at her desk, and decided to vent at the gross injustice perpetrated out at the receptionist desk. "Have you seen—"

"Oh yeah, I've seen—the creature out front—we've all seen her." Megan had been holding in her venting until Nathalie arrived. "You know what really sucks, I mean sucks the wazoo. That ugly sow with the golden voice is a Stanford graduate."

Nathalie's mouth dropped open.

"Yeah, truly, totally," moaned Megan. "There are not enough plastic surgeons in the world to save me. With her around, a man would only pay attention to me because of—" She pointed at her perfume ad campaign, "La Jeunesse! A man will tear your clothes to get to... La Jeunesse!" She tossed a sample bottle at Nathalie. "Have a sample."

With one whiff, Nathalie grimaced. "You can fry brain cells with that."

"Exactly," Megan agreed. "When a man is chemically brain-dead you can get him to like you and then I won't have to hate the creature out front. They'll sell a ton of this shit."

"That's great, nice campaign," Nathalie said while looking around for something. "I'm running late, so ahh…"

"There's the dress," Megan pointed to the corner of her cubicle.

In the corner, a life-sized cardboard cutout of Donald Trump wore a cocktail dress; Megan's dress which Nathalie was borrowing. Nathalie peeled off her clothes down to bra and panties—and shredded pantyhose.

"Good look," said Megan referring to the pantyhose.

"Things didn't quite go as planned at the docks."

"So I'm guessing you didn't just take the photos then simply drop them off at the insurance company he was defrauding."

"Not exactly."

"Which means you—channeling Mother Theresa—tried to offer a way for him to redeem himself."

"Yeah," replied Nathalie as she slipped out of her ripped pantyhose.

"He was…displeased," said Megan

"You could say that."

"My Jewish friends would call you a shiksa shit-head," Megan added.

"Hey, I was a badass," Nathalie retorted.

"Un huh. Translation, I almost had to pick you up at the hospital."

Nathalie had no snappy comeback. Her bravado finally cratered and tears welled up in her eyes. She fought hard to keep them from falling. Her arms shook as she gathered her clothes and searched for a place to put them. Reality roared in like a raging tsunami for her morning was not a slick and safe Hollywood movie scene but a terrifying assault. She had been scared shitless and she could still feel the grip of his greasy hands on her legs ripping her pantyhose. A sickening feeling of inadequacy sank into her soul. She had been lucky. Her body started shaking from fear and abject failure when Megan's hand touched her forearm in tender support.

"So ah, just a typical first date then, another *Me Too* story," Megan said as she held her hand on Nathalie's arm, the bonded touch of a real bestie.

Nathalie brushed the tears from her eyes. "Well…there was champagne."

Grady, a young draftsman, stuck his head in the cubicle with a color one-sheet.

"Megan, here's the—" Grady stopped, taking in Nathalie's state of undress. "Sorry," then he suddenly made a connection. "You know your bra's on the *Victoria's Secret* website this month."

Unperturbed, Nathalie continued dressing—new pantyhose—the cocktail dress—heels.

"Forget it, Grady," Megan said as she grabbed the one-sheet. "She's not your type. She's human."

"Yeah, well…" Grady backed out, but flung out one last attempt at making a favorable impression with the near-naked lady. "Maybe later." He was then sucked back into the maze.

"I'll give him points for being hopeful," Nathalie quipped.

"Yes, for guys, an erection is hopeful," added Megan.

"I gotta guard some jewels—big display at the Waldorf. You wanna come see what you can't afford?"

"I can always lower my self-esteem another notch." Megan grabbed her purse.

℘

Outside, along Madison Avenue, Nathalie and Megan tried to hail an *Off Duty* cab. No go. Not a single one responded. They both realized this might take a while.

"How's your mother?"

"Why are we talking about my mother?" Nathalie said, slightly put off.

"She's my idol."

Nathalie avoided responding with an attempt to flag another *Off Duty* cab. No luck.

"C'mon, inspire me.," Megan urged.

"All right..." But Nathalie was not pleased. "Three."

"Three?! She's dating three guys?! Jesus, I'm just seein' Randy, that doesn't even count as one. And you're not seein' anyone!"

"I don't wanna talk about this."

"Why don't you let me set you up with—"

"I'm not ready yet. I still have Tom's tire marks across my heart."

"C'mon, look at your mom."

"I am... and that's what hurts." Nathalie paused and looked Megan in the eye with a vulnerability reserved only for a trusted best friend. "I don't think I'll ever get over my father's death... I guess she has."

Megan knew well enough to not open this Pandora's box further. This was unresolved pain in process and not the moment to step into that process, even as a bestie.

Fighting back the tears, Nathalie stepped out to flag another *Off Duty* cab which again failed to heed her signal. "The *Off Duty* guys used to stop," she spit out in frustration.

"They're just pullin' a macho trip."

"Well I can play that game too!"

Nathalie, not about to let a man best her, walked to the edge of the sidewalk, hiked her dress over her knee, and extended a beckoning leg!

"It worked for Claudette Colbert in *It Happened One Night,*" Nathalie said with assurance.

"Go girl, go," Megan laughed.

Sure enough, the very next cab pulled up alongside them at the curb. Pleased with her triumph, Nathalie then saw the cabbie—it was a woman—who rolled down the passenger window!

"It's women like you who give our sex a bad name! How the hell are we supposed to get any equality when you carry on like a couple of tramps?!!"

Launched with a grunt of disgust, spittle spewed from her lips toward Nathalie as the cabbie floored the cab and squealed away in smoking indignation; leaving them to face the strange, equally indignant stares from those walking by.

"Maybe she doesn't watch old movies," Megan offered.

"I feel like such a criminal," Nathalie said and hung her head.

Reluctantly, they started walking, quietly, with a slow, deflated gate.

"Nice legs though," Megan said. "Just sayin'."

ℰℭ

The Waldorf Astoria was lingering grandeur. Even the soon planned renovation and restoration wouldn't remove the layers of nostalgia. Memories, like settling dust, worked their way into the granite and marble and embedded for eternity undisturbed by any attempt to tear down and apply a *fresh look.* Architecture, though solid, held within it the energy of change.

Nathalie and Megan scrambled out of an arriving cab into the Park Avenue entrance.

In the three-tiered Grand Ballroom, whoever was here was somebody—the moneyed elite—and dazzling, sparkling jewelry abounded. Some descended from necklaces down the alluring cleavage slopes of pampered breasts. Some of the breasts were as expensive as the jewels. Wrists weighted down with adornments so dazzling they blinded the eyes and swelled the egos. The voiceless and silent cry of *look at me* was thunderous.

The same for the black tie tuxedoed men who sported rings and watches whose value could alleviate poverty in third world countries. Some gay and straight chose the same diamond studs for an ear or two. Slender pins with a masculine line adorned with diamonds, rubies, garnets or emeralds set off many a lapel. All of this done with the nonchalant savoir faire of a casual outing as if the glittering adornments were merely a trifle worthy of only castaway comments.

The real players, a select few of the men and the jewelry-adorned women were here on serious business. The jewels, though appreciated, were merely an acknowledged entrance requirement. This was networking, showcasing and power positioning of the highest order.

Looking and acting the part garnered multi-million dollar deal connections for the newer members of the moneyed-elite. Others merely took their place at the top of the money mountain sporting the cool air of attained power. The casual conversations strategically dropped by this crowd, strewn with subtle innuendos of power plays, rattled and confused the competition. It was the sound of savage civility.

At the presentation and display area, the latest and newest design offerings of jewels rested in three large locked glass cases arrayed for maximum viewing. Even a quick glance from discerning professional eyes would have estimated a value of forty million plus.

The jewel cases were watched by Jerry Glendon, an alert, wiry and athletic man in a tuxedo with a small, nearly invisible, security earpiece in his right ear. Like the U. S. Secret Service agents, a small cord extended from the earpiece down underneath his tuxedo collar and emerged from his right sleeve into a slender microphone cupped in his hand. His eyes anxiously scanned the room until he spotted Nathalie and Megan as they entered the ballroom.

Nathalie struggled to insert an earpiece into her ear without drawing attention. The earpiece was almost too big and wouldn't stay inserted in her ear cavity.

"You want help with that?" said Megan noticing the wrestling match.

"So much for one size fits all," replied Nathalie as she jammed it into her ear and held her finger on it. Jerry's annoyed voice vibrated in her ear.

"You're supposed to be fully dressed before you arrive!"

Nathalie's eyes swept the room and met Jerry's gaze, his cupped hand up to his mouth. He was not pleased. "You're late," he said into his hidden microphone.

Nathalie wormed her way quickly through the crowd with Megan tagged along behind her. She spoke into her own cupped hand quietly as she worked her way to Jerry and the display cases.

"Had to walk part way," she explained. "Trouble getting a cab, you know how it is. Hard to believe this is the last event before they close it down for three or four years."

"Just get over here." Jerry dropped his hand back down to his side.

Megan tugged on Nathalie's cocktail dress. "Did you see that obscene broach? I want it."

Nathalie scooted past the last group of invited guests blocking her route to the jewelry display cases and came face to face with Jerry as Megan hustled up behind her.

"Who the hell is this?!"

'I'm nobody, a nothing," Megan offered. "I'm—"

Nathalie cut her off. "She's cool. She's my best friend."

"Everyone else is in place. You're eyes and ears only. Leave any rough stuff to us."

"Being a girl and all…"

Jerry was not at all concerned about hurt feelings. "Just mingle. We don't want people to know you're part of security. And keep that damn thing in your ear. And you," Jerry turned to Megan. "Since you're nothing, act like it."

Jerry moved off as Nathalie pushed her security earpiece back into place.

"What's his problem?"

"Tight underwear," quipped Nathalie. "This is an easy gig. It's not as if the jewels in the display cases are gonna get up and walk away. Not with the security they've got set up." Nathalie swept two champagne glasses off a passing tray. "So let's enjoy this."

The waiter, Ramone, moved off through the crowd and brought an iced tea to Jake Kracauer, whose steely eyes scoped out the room. Kracauer did not acknowledge the waiter. His eyes never left the milling jetsetter crowd. He was not a member of security. No earpiece. No watch or rings or distinguishing adornments of any kind. His Armani tux was classical but not flashy. It was however superbly tailored around a muscled and athletic body. Jake Kracauer was ruggedly handsome with the swarthy skin tone of a Cossack heritage. His brown eyes revealed a calculating coldness. He radiated energy of quiet, coiled command, braced for action.

Unobtrusively, while he sipped his tea, his other hand reached behind him and worked the lock on a closed door with a thin, pronged, edged file. Once he heard and felt the *click* of the tumblers and the lock opening, he pocketed the metal pick and patiently waited. His actions unnoticed as the gala was in full swing.

The members of the chamber orchestra, all dressed in tuxedoes and black gowns, played flawlessly through a blended medley of Claude Debussy's music. The massive ballroom filled with a dreamy and moody emotional landscape. Society photographers seemed to dance around the mingling couples in a choreographed flow of movement. The flashes of light from their cameras leaped off the facets of the jewels and spun out into the air among the glitterati. Caterers and waiters replenished the elegant buffet for patrons on their way to gaze appreciatively at the special jewelry display cases. The tuxedoed security staff did their best to remain respectful yet unobtrusive, but they scrutinized everyone.

A caterer slipped in between patrons and around conversation groups in a fluid rhythm like a well-choreographed dance. Nathalie drained her champagne glass and placed it on his moving tray as he passed by. Her eyes scanned for trouble as Megan emerged from the crowd.

"The cheapest item is some little rock on a necklace for twenty thousand," said Megan.

"Chump change." Nathalie's eyes remained on the job.

Megan fingered her necklace. "I got this out of one of those arcade games, you know the steam shovel with teeth. Least I worked for it."

Nathalie's interest stretched across the ballroom to a young busboy. He surreptitiously looked to see if anyone was watching him. Anyone as in security personnel.

"You think any of these stinking, filthy rich men are single? Megan wondered.

Nathalie, barely listening to her, adjusted her position to get a better view of the busboy.

"Check 'em out... if you're really that shallow."

"I can be very shallow," said Megan as she moved off in a determined search of tall, dark, filthy rich and disgustingly handsome.

The busboy edged closer to a group of women guests engrossed in conversation. While holding his tray of a few dirty dishes, he deftly slid his other hand into two purses and slipped the stolen items under a large embroidered napkin on his tray. When a woman turned to face him, he merely nodded and gave a slight half bow of apology for touching her and then moved on.

Nathalie quickly walked up to Jerry, who scanned a different area.

"Game time," said Nathalie as she pointed. "Busboy. He's got some fast hands," she added and headed straight for him.

"Nathalie," said Jerry as he tried to grab her and stop her to no avail. "Seeger, leave this to—" But Nathalie cut a beeline for the busboy. "Goddamnit!" Jerry immediately circled around three women admiring their necklaces while speaking into his hand mic. "Greg, close in on position seven."

The busboy lifted a jeweled pill dispenser from another woman's purse bagging another score. Before he could slip his prize under the napkin, Nathalie's hand peeled back the embroidered napkin for him and exposed his loot. It was all small stuff; a gold lipstick tube, silk handkerchief, two jeweled compacts, and a pocket watch.

"Not a very good take, said Nathalie casually.

"What's it to you?" replied the busboy. Clearly startled, his attempt to be cool rapidly collapsed.

"My job and I like to do it well." Nathalie briefly opened her purse so he could see her Sig Sauer 9mm short. "This is noisy, it'll ruin the party."

The busboy saw Jerry and Greg close in from either side.

"If we leave quietly, maybe we can forget all about this," said Nathalie.

"I can walk?" The busboy was skeptical.

Nathalie looked at Jerry for confirmation, but he was hesitant.

"It's not procedure."

"But it is discreet," said Nathalie. The guests around them were oblivious. "For the moment," Nathalie added.

Reluctantly, Jerry nodded. Nathalie bundled the busboy's loot in the napkin. Jerry grabbed his arm. They quietly escorted him toward the main entrance where they opened the doors for him.

"Time for a career change." Nathalie looked the busboy directly in the eye.

The busboy quipped, "I made more money parkin' cars."

Jerry watched him walk away. "Little prick."

"Yeah," said Nathalie, "probably just trying to feed his family." She then quickly added, "Letting him go was a good idea…for a guy."

"Seeger, ya got a few good moves in ya, I'll give ya that, but basically you're a pain in the ass." Jerry looked out over the crowd. "I've never felt comfortable around people with this kind of money. They expect too much."

A woman screamed!

Nathalie and Jerry then saw her clutching the bare area where her necklace used to be! Others near her searched the floor.

"No," she called out horrified, "someone touched me! Someone stole my necklace!"

Jake Kracauer stopped abruptly short as he neared the jewelry display cases. His eyes flicked toward the security guards by the cases but no one reacted to him as all eyes were drawn to the hysterical woman. His eyes registered a quick change of plans then he slipped out through the door whose lock he had picked earlier.

Just then, another woman screamed, and no one saw Kracauer leave.

The second woman desperately searched for her missing bracelets.

Yet another frantic cry from a third victim, "My rubies! They're gone!!

Waves of panic rolled through the crowd as Nathalie and Jerry guarded the main entrance.

Jerry's eyes darted around the ballroom. "What the hell's goin' on?!"

"Nobody got by us," said Nathalie assuredly as she scanned the crowd. "They're still here! Gotta be!"

Jerry barked into his security mic! "Seal off the exits—lock it down!"

Security personnel sprang into action taking one, two steps…then the ballroom lights went out! Waves of fear flooded through the crowd at the sudden crash of darkness.

"Jesus Christ!" Jerry, flustered, yelled into his mic, "Block the displays—now!"

Security ringed the jewelry display cases, each officer facing away from the case itself, eyes on the crowd, forming an impenetrable barrier. No one could get past them. Inside the display cases, the jewels rested safely on their velvet pads in the darkness.

Nathalie and Jerry raced through the anxious crowd deftly moving people aside to get to the display cases. The emergency lights clicked on. Nervous energy burst through the throng of the glitterati and they shoved each other aside like scared peasants to get to the exits.

"Keep those exits sealed! Don't let anyone push past!" Jerry shouted into his hand mic, knowing it might be futile to stem the rush, but at least he'd have someone else to blame. He had to get to the jewels!

The security guards formed an impenetrable barrier around the display cases. The security team's main objective was safe from prying hands, so they thought.

All the guards continued to face away from the cases, their focus on the bustling crowd of people. The noise of panic in the ballroom dominated the senses. Eyes sharply focused on the swirling chaos of the frightened crowd. Some of the glitterati collided with the display guards as they rushed to flee the ballroom! The guards did their best to deflect the crushing throng of the privileged patrons.

Inside the display cases, a safe environment prevailed; no broken glass or intrusion to worry about from the scuffling crowd. The locks on the glass tops remained untouched. However, change had asserted itself inside the seemingly sealed cases. The velvet pads that held the jewels were now empty. Millions of dollars of jewels—all the jewels—were gone.

Nathalie and Jerry squeezed through the panicked people to their ring of security personnel around the display cases just as the wail of sirens from the street penetrated the crowd noise. A quick glance indicated that the display cases were undisturbed, the glass unbroken.

"Maybe that busboy was working in tandem with someone we didn't see," said Jerry, now noticeably calmer.

"No way," said Nathalie quickly to slip any blame coming her way *as a girl*. "You know we had it covered."

Uniformed cops burst into the ballroom from the main entrance.

"Good," snapped Jerry. "Tell that to the boys in blue."

Nathalie braced for the tsunami of cop questions and demands. "Look, we just stick with procedure." She glanced around for an exit path that would force Jerry to have to deal with the NYPD. "You know tell 'em nobody leaves until…"

It was then that she glanced once again at the display cases, a glance that lingered.

"…until they're fully searched," her words slowed and her voice softened, "and then they can…go." There were times when the mind refused to take in the full reality of the moment. This was one of those times for Nathalie. The best she could manage was a catatonic stare at the *empty velvet pads*, and from her lips a slow exhale of pained breath and two slurred words. "Oh no…"

Jerry wasn't listening to her—typical guy—so she placed her hand on his shoulder and turned him around to see the empty display cases.

"Jesus Christ!" Reality rushed from Jerry's mouth with no problem. "It can't be... How the hell... The company's gonna crucify us!" In a flash, Jerry was emotionally twelve and about to get grounded permanently if he didn't come up with a superhero-size excuse. "I gotta…I gotta…fuck!"

The incoming cops barreled right toward him. He needed to stave off the criminal reveal until he had his story straight in his head so he might keep his job. He left Nathalie by the display cases and moved to head off the cops.

"Guys, it's cool, we got this," he called out hoping it would stop the tsunami. It didn't. Jerry got surrounded and peppered with questions.

Nathalie stared at the floor. Piece by piece she felt her clothes—her neatly put together confidence costume—peeled off her in ragged strips by a man's hand and layered in a crisscrossing pattern on the floor by her feet. Total raw nakedness. Crushed confidence. Proof of her incompetence with no idea how it happened. Her wild imagination of being stripped naked made as much sense as what had happened. This distortion of reality meant one thing, her career salvage, if possible, commenced with her next breath.

"Excuse me, I'm with her," insisted Megan as she struggled in the grasp of a security guard near the display cases.

Nathalie tapped the guard's arm. "It's okay, she's good."

Megan squeezed through the ring of security up to the cases.

"What's goin' on? I didn't see anything. Is it really that bad?"

Utterly dismayed, Nathalie pointed to the empty display cases.

Megan placed her hand on Nathalie's arm. "Hope your boss has a sense of humor."

CHAPTER FOUR

When Stardust gets in your eyes…it's still just dust.

A Scorned Woman

At night, during countless celebrations, the grand ballroom had been a dreamscape of beauty bathed in splashes of colored light, the emotions deepened by the music of an orchestra. The senses and the imagination soared.

This night, with roped-off sections of yellow tape, the dream plummeted from once lofty visions down into the crass scribbles of human cataloguing, just another statistic, a crime scene. Forensic personnel poured over the area, isolating elements, dusting, and cataloguing, then handing the filled and *clear* evidence bags to uniformed cops who carried these *clear* evidence bags outside in a steady stream right before everyone's eyes. The parade of perceived progress.

Detective Ramsey had his subject cornered away from the display cases. A rather attractive one at that, and given the crime level, he felt she was significantly incompetent. "According to your statement," Ramsey paused and gave Nathalie his best demeaning and lingering gaze, "security guards were positioned by the display cases all evening, and not one saw anything unusual or suspect."

Like a piece of meat, Nathalie had been slapped on the chauvinistic grill before. She knew to not even acknowledge the slight. Instead she caught a whiff of distinctive cologne which drew her eye to a uniformed cop weaving through the flowing line of cops who carried the clear evidence bags. She leaned and tilted her head to get a better look because his face became obscured by other cops as he worked his way over to the display case on the far end.

"But…the display cases are totally empty." Ramsey looked up from his notepad. His face flushed with irritation seeing that this *woman* wasn't even listening to him but checking out some other cop. "Maybe you have some brilliant explanation for this, otherwise…"

The uniformed cop at the display case, face still obscured, deployed an *opaque* evidence bag. The bag was all she could see at that moment.

"Hey!" Ramsey snapped at Nathalie.

Nathalie jerked her head back from watching the uniformed cop.

"Is this how you pay attention? I think I understand how these jewels got up and walked out of here."

Nathalie didn't take the bait and merely pointed at a detective who stared up at the ceiling. "Maybe he knows where they are. Then again," Nathalie called out to the detective, "You won't find much up there."

Lieutenant Victor J. Donelli didn't acknowledge her, just stared up at the high ceiling. Nathalie wasn't even in his world until he wanted her to be. He was pushing past sixty, retirement coming up fast, but could still knock a face in if so inclined, and he was often inclined. "They used to hang the star ball," Donelli pointed, "right there. Guy Lombardo. Yeah…for my parents he was the man. Those were some good times. They're all shadows now. And what you don't know could fill this room." Donelli moved off, no need to even look at her.

"You're not real smart," Ramsey said to Nathalie. "He's the last person you wanna piss off."

A great shattering clatter of falling and breaking dishes turned everyone's head!

Two young busboys, one black, the other Puerto Rican, had collided with their large stainless steel trays loaded down with dishes from last night that were finally being allowed to be removed from the crime scene. The two lads, now pissed off, shoved each other both slipping and falling over the pile of broken dishware, then scrambled up again only to slip and fall onto the pile once more. Hurled racial invectives filled the ballroom as they scuffled.

Nathalie had always hated the "n" word even when spoken in jest or as righteous endearment by someone who was black and she had always wondered what the hell *spic* meant. Who thinks up this crap, she thought, it's so pointless, except to aggravate and demean. But she still couldn't help laughing at the clumsy and noisy spectacle of the two young guys wrestling on top of a mountain of broken dishes. It required four uniformed cops to break up the melee and then force the lads to clean up the mess.

Smelling the distinctive cologne again, Nathalie turned back from the farcical dish spectacle and scanned the crowd and saw the same uniformed cop now carrying a full *opaque* bag marked: "NYPD EVIDENCE." His face still obscured by the crisscrossing bodies of other cops, he headed for the exit.

Nathalie struggled to get a good look, stepped to the side allowing her a clean angle to him right at the exit. Just as the uniformed cop strode into her clear line of sight, Ramsey stepped in front of her blocking her view.

"I'm not through with you yet, Honey."

"Honey?! We must be married then," said Nathalie. "That would make you, Dickhead."

&

Midtown North Precinct was a cold, stone slab. Four stories of harsh edges. At night, an artless, foreboding fortress. Upon entering, one's sphincter immediately puckered.

In the dark recesses of a bullpen area the sputtering green glow from the exit sign sent eerie waves of light rolling across the space. The work day long done, desks day-driven by crime statistics and data crunching sat empty. The hustle silenced. The lights off. Only the soft white light from a lone computer screen rose above a cubicle in the far corner. And voices. Quiet voices edged with wariness.

"I'm only doin' this out of respect for your father. I could get my ass canned," whispered Sally. Her head peeked around the cubicle wall to see if they were still alone. They were. She ducked back out of sight.

Sally Maguire was damn nervous. She was also damn sexy. A short layered cut of golden hair offset by smooth tan skin. Jade green eyes that many a man swore beckoned when she grinned, which was often. The curves didn't hurt except if you were a man and prone to staring. She had the kind of sexiness that oozed fun because she didn't care what others thought about her; except her bosses, because she liked her job. She kept it cool around the bosses.

"These guys would never let an ass like yours walk out of here." The reassuring whispered voice belonged to Nathalie. She knew cops, male cops. Testosterone was plentiful. Even female cops had to be able to surf those waves of testosterone and not be drowned by them. Testosterone valued an extremely well-formed ass. Did she know for sure that Sally wouldn't get fired? Well…she needed Sally to help her now and she bet—or hoped—that a great ass would give Sally a few screw-ups before being shit-canned. But hope only goes so far.

Sally chuckled. She knew her ass attracted a lot of eyeballs. Drool was at times common also. "Men are easy to read, aren't they?"

"I want to get the goods on this one." Nathalie impatiently pointed at the computer screen.

Sally worked the keyboard. Her fingers flew over the keys. "How do you know it's a man?"

"It smells like him."

"I'm accessing the data base now."

Nathalie waited for the data to emerge. Her assessment was already forming. "How many uniformed cops do you know that wear cologne?"

"They reek of Right Guard, not cologne, maybe Old Spice if they're desperate," said Sally as she punched a key. "We're in. Searching…and locked. Here's your first one."

The computer screen revealed a photo and data block on a white male: JAKE KRACAUER. Thick dark hair swept back. Piercing brown eyes given a savage edge by the three deep-set crow's feet lines that extended from only his right eye. Strong prominent cheek bones of Cossack heritage. Manly. A striking, confident face.

"What do you think he smells like?" Sally was intrigued.

Nathalie stared at the screen noticing that three suspects hit the search criteria. "Can you print these for me?"

"Sure."

"Let's run 'em all. Maybe I'll get lucky. I'm gonna need it to face the boss tomorrow."

Sally fingered a few more keys. "How deep in the shit are you?"

Nathalie sighed. "So deep they can't even see my ass."

A new photo and data block printed out—a different white male—MARTY LEFKOWITZ. Tight wiry hair. Angry eyes. A smug, crooked smile. Defiant. Dangerous.

છ

Vorhees International Insurance commanded the top floor of a steel and glass structure that shot straight up imposing its presence on the sky. The elegant office of Edward Vorhees overlooked the bustling South Street Seaport.

Edward Vorhees exuded the confidence of an overachiever and the barely contained disdain for *lesser folk*; someone who had gained his influence by being relentless and anally careful. He liked his view of the East River. He liked overlooking this historic area that was thought of as the place where the story of the city first began. He liked that it was adjacent to the Financial District. He really liked money. He did not like parting with it unintentionally.

So it was that he stood behind his desk, facing the window which overlooked the historic area, and listened with clenched jaw to his employee, Simmons, as Simmons finished reading out loud the "damage list."

"Next, one Ginsee ruby necklace valued at fifteen, and also a Pirot diamond bracelet last appraised at eighty-seven five. With the jewelry from the display cases, our total liability comes to just over fifty two million dollars."

"Thank you, Simmons," Vorhees said, never taking his gaze from out the window. "The day, however, was not a total loss. We have Ms. Seeger to thank for that."

Nathalie sat deep in a huge, leather chair in front of Vorhees' desk that dropped her below desk level. The Vorhees desk was mahogany and massive, an impenetrable barrier between Vorhees and whoever was on the other side. Nathalie attempted to sit up straight and as high as possible, but the leather was designed to be slippery. She slid down into the recesses of the chair like a captive child.

"Ms. Seeger," Vorhees continued calmly, "stopped the theft of one tube of lipstick, a compact—gold-plated—and a handkerchief...which I believe was monogrammed." Vorhees paused...an unnatural and deeply disconcerting pause. "Its value has yet to be determined."

Simmons, the clean-cut company man, took his position standing at the corner of the enormous mahogany desk. Nathalie wondered if he was now the official executioner for Vorhees and she waited for the swift descent of the ax.

Designed to increase her discomfort, which had not escaped her attention, Lieutenant Victor J. Donelli of NYPD Robbery-Homicide leaned against a book shelf of somewhat priceless first editions on full display, his arms folded in the pose of official and professional disdain. This was the same Lieutenant Victor J. Donelli that Dickhead Ramsay had said *He's the last person you wanna piss off.* She knew every execution needed a cheering crowd.

Vorhees milked the silence then turned and faced Nathalie.

"And the busboy thief, who we now know was probably a decoy, you allowed to walk away."

Nathalie hiked herself up against the back of the chair...then slid right back down into it.

"Yes, well, Mr. Vorhees, this is an unusual situation."

"Yes, this does not happen to me every day."

"I can well imagine, your reputation is beyond reproach."

"Apparently not. I hired you because we felt you were the best, but—"

"I am..."

"It seems there's somebody better."

Nathalie locked eyes with Vorhees. "At this point, we don't know how the jewels were taken." She looked directly at Donelli. "But no one walked in off the street and sauntered out with them."

Lieutenant Donelli looked at her as if she was navel lint but said nothing. Maybe she could ignore him. She turned back to Edward Vorhees. Him, she had to impress.

"They were prepared—and well-practiced—a professional," she stated.

Vorhees merely listened, his clenched jaw tightened. Nathalie took that as a clear sign to rocket ahead before the ax fell. She referred to her print-outs as if they were scripture.

"My research has yielded several possibilities. The most prominent is a man whose M.O. fits this heist."

Now Donelli was listening.

"He's a master thief," she quickly punched the next phrase, "with an international reputation. Scotland Yard refers to him as the Prince of Darkness. They say he's—"

"Like a shadow," Donelli cut her off. "With you all the time, but you never know it."

"Yes..." Nathalie wondered for a nanosecond if Donelli might actually turn out to be an ally. "His name is—"

"Eli Cross." Her supposed ally cut her off as if she was indeed lint to be brushed aside.

"This is Lieutenant Victor Donelli of Robbery-Homicide," said Vorhees. Clearly this was his go-to-guy and she was superfluous, if not lint.

Nathalie played what she hoped would be her ace of spades. "Did you know my father?"

"Yeah, I knew him," said Donelli.

Nathalie eased up.

"So did Cross," Donelli said.

Nathalie's sphincter tightened.

"Your father tried to nail Cross a couple times. No luck. No one's ever caught Cross with the goods."

"Victor," said Vorhees dismissing the lint, "is this our man?"

"Every crime has a personality. And this is Eli Cross."

Nathalie confidently rejoined the conversation. "At least two other jewel thieves..." She held up her print-outs for emphasis. "Marty Lefkowitz and Jake Kracauer should also be investigated. Eli Cross is not the only—"

"I've tracked Cross for fifteen years," said Donelli. "You're not even in the game. Edward, this is Eli Cross and no one else. He likes to live on the edge. I'm gonna push him over and recover the jewels."

That was all Vorhees needed to hear. With a nod to Simmons, his ax-man turned to Nathalie.

"Ms. Seeger, you may pick your check up from personnel on the way out."

Nathalie knew that lint didn't get up and walk out. Lint was brushed aside like it was nothing. These chauvinistic, testosterone sacks were going to respect her, goddamnit.

"Mr. Vorhees, you don't owe me anything unless I recover the jewels." She turned defiantly to Donelli. "And this Seeger is definitely in the game—for the whole ride."

Feeling her dignity sufficiently recovered, Nathalie pushed herself up from the slippery leather chair only to slide forward onto her knees on the floor. "So..." She stood up with as much confidence as could be mustered from the tattered remnants of her self-esteem. "Let's get started." She made a move toward the door before any other disaster befell her. She stopped at the door and pointedly turned around.

"Why would NYPD use opaque evidence bags?"

"We don't," Donelli responded. "Evidence bags are clear." Not just lint, but ignorant lint, he thought. Sad and pathetic. Her father would be spinning in his grave.

"Thank you," Nathalie said. *Clear* was her point.

"Glad to add to your vast knowledge."

Nathalie rifled an up-yours-grin to Donelli and slipped out the door. Vorhees was back to gazing out the window at the South Street Seaport. She knew he had long ago moved on to other matters. She had work to do…her reputation, her career, her livelihood were all on the line.

Ⅎℂ

The Waldorf Astoria's Grand Ballroom was still roped off as a crime scene. Nathalie meandered among the tables, now cleared of food and drink, and purposely ended up over by the end display case that once held the jewels insured by Vorhees International Insurance. The protective, security-enhanced cases were untouched from the day before.

Nathalie stared at the empty velvet pads... thinking.

In frustration, she kicked the side of the display case! She squelched a cry of pain in her foot and bent down to rub it. Her fingers then felt a split in the side of the shoe from the force of her kick. *What an idiot! These were good shoes!* Then, adding to her dismay, she saw the side of the supposedly secure display case where she had kicked it. Her kick had shoved it open.

It had actually been left slightly ajar—on purpose she thought—a subtle invitation to look inside. So her kick had easily opened it further until her shoe scrunched up against the metal hinge which kept it from opening fully. The hinge had caused the pain and the split in her shoe. There was now a gap, an opening—large enough for a man's arm to fit through—which further revealed the hinged edge separating the bottom half of the side panel. This was clearly by design.

Nathalie applied pressure widening the gap exposing an inner cavity. The lead lining inside the cavity added weight and made it seem solid and not a hollow base. Soundproofing material encased the inner walls. From the outside and from above looking down through the protective glass, the display case offered no indication that there was a hollow inner core underneath where the jewels had been displayed.

Telescoping columns rose up from this inner floor and connected to the underside of the display flooring above. Lifting her head to look down inside the display area down through the glass, she saw that these telescoping columns connected to the exact spots where inside the glass-protected display area the velvet pads rested and had cradled the jewels during the event.

Nathalie reached in underneath past the hinged opening and manipulated a telescoping column manually. It collapsed within itself which lowered the velvet pad. At the bottom of its travel, the velvet pad tilted, allowing any contents to slide off into a padded storage tray…quietly…undetected. When she released the telescoping column, it extended, raising the pad back to its original position in the display case and sealing off any indication that there was an inner cavern underneath. The action could have been initiated by remote control.

It would have appeared that the jewels were stolen, somehow lifted from under the glass—the locks swiftly opened during the jostling crowds—while in fact they remained hidden beneath in a hollowed-out core that by the known design didn't exist. Retrieving the jewels could have occurred at any time. Even during a distraction of busboys shoving and shouting and wrestling in a pile of broken dishes.

Right under our noses. In an opaque evidence bag, Lieutenant Douche Bag! Men could be such… She then realized that someone had in fact *walked in off the street and sauntered out with them* contrary to what she had confidently proclaimed, which made her cringe at being a first-rate douche bag…and now with bad shoes.

CHAPTER FIVE

*I may neither choose who I would, nor refuse who I
dislike; so is the will of a living daughter curbed by
the will of a dead father.*

**William Shakespeare
Portia, Merchant of Venice Act I Scene II**

There was no accounting for *strange* in the decisions of Nate Seeger's life. This hardened, no-nonsense cop's fascination with police work germinated in the good-natured antics of a sixties TV comedy *Car 54 Where Are You* when he was a boy. Goofy but sweet TV cops Toody and Muldoon were not Riggs and Murtaugh or Crockett and Tubbs or even Starsky and Hutch and definitely not a darker Benson and Stabler. Tough and kick-ass and cool were not in their nature. Yet a young Nate Seeger wanted to be a cop because of these loveable dimwits. To the dismay of Dispatch, he called his first patrol car, Car 54.

When Nate landed in Robbery-Homicide, he was the polar opposite of bumbling; he built the best clearance record in the precinct. He and his partner were called the Wrecking Crew. When a perp was processed by Nate Seeger, it became known as *being Muldooned*, and it was a charge that usually stuck, all the way to the Big House. The word on the street was clear, whatever you do; don't get your ass *Muldooned.*

A line from the theme song of that same TV comedy—*There's a traffic jam in Harlem that's backed up to Jackson Heights*—led to the cobbled-together purchase of a small Tudor-style house several blocks off Roosevelt Avenue in Jackson Heights, Queens that had a small garden in what could actually be called a backyard, which Nate had referred to as *grass in the rear,* and was subsequently interpreted and dubbed *ass grass* by his then four-year-old son, Ian.

A saunter of several blocks through Jackson Heights was a cultural tour round the world with enough temptation for any foodie seeking an array of international cuisine choices. This eclectic and lively atmosphere captured the heart of the former Odile Trenet when Nate was courting the French beauty who was born and raised in the 6th arrondissement of Paris—St-Germain-des-Prés, Les Deux Magots, Café Flore, Luxembourg Gardens and the Latin Quarter—and whose family summered in Arles in Provence. If Jackson Heights intrigued her enough to leave all that stunning architecture and history and Southern France sunshine to stay and marry him, it was worth the almost hour commute to his Manhattan precinct.

She would forever be a mystery to him. He had treasured her.

The life of Nathaniel ("Nate") Seeger was now relegated to cherished and haunted memories for his family and friends and perps. His work—his passion—was in boxes of files, police case files, piled in a study closet. Nathalie stared into the open door of the deep closet recounting her travails to someone inside.

"The jewels were there all the time. Took them out right in front of us. Dressed as a cop."

Standing in the study closet, hauling down a file box was Ian Seeger, Nathalie's younger brother by three years. A sharp mind but with a body that has betrayed him, saddling him with a disabled leg, requiring a cane to get around. No way could he have followed in his father's footsteps. The desire was there, the idolizing of a dad, but also the relentless feeling of not measuring up. As close as he could get was chasing criminals with words. At first journalism and a crime beat, then later adding making it all up as a novelist, and not yet a successful one. Not at all the man he wanted to be.

"My first byline for the Times had something like that" Ian reminded her. "Remember that Bayside animal lab raid?"

Ian almost stumbled with the box and Nathalie took it from him as he leaned against her. She knew better than to say anything and quickly placed the file box marked: NATE SEEGER ROBBERY/HOMICIDE CASES atop the coffee table next to another file box.

"Would've been easier if Pop put all this shit on computer," Ian sighed.

"Once he got sick, he lost interest. I thought he had tossed everything."

"No way, you know that, Nattie. This is gospel, holy writ, life's blood. He only lost interest 'cause he couldn't do shit anymore, didn't have the energy, which had to just fucking…"

"I know." Nathalie struggled not to bring those images up again.

Ian hauled a third box from the closet. "Jesus, this must have bricks in it." He heaved the heavy box onto the end of the coffee table next to the previous two. All marked *ELI CROSS*.

"He probably told mom to bury it all with him so he could work on it in the afterlife, like all the shit the Egyptians loaded into the tombs with the mummies so they had tools and stuff. Perps couldn't walk scot-free just 'cause they croaked. I think I was ten when he told me that."

On the walls of the study, they were surrounded by citations, NYPD medals, press clippings and photos of Nathaniel ("Nate") Seeger, a man whose rugged life-force bled through his photos as if he was still present.

Nathalie traced the edge of a photo of her father with her hand…

"It all looks just like it did when we'd sneak up on him in here."

The echo of a memory broke through her thought carrying with it her father's voice. *Nathalie, you stand tall, back straight, chin out. You're my tough little copper.*

"But it feels so… far away."

"I feel like he's gonna walk in and kick my ass for goin' through his stuff," Ian said.

"Well before he does, let's get at it."

It was as good an excuse as any to cap the emotional memories. They quickly settled in and became engrossed in reading the files.

"I can't believe this is all Eli Cross," said Nathalie grabbing a file.

Ian glanced at a report page. "One take was four point three million. Not bad for a night's work." He read further down the page. "Couldn't tie it to him though."

"Competed in downhill ski events; Chamonix, Kitzbühel, Val d'Isére," Nathalie said. Intrigued, she ran her finger down the page, searching, and was quickly disappointed. "Never won." She checked the file date. "At least then." Only a moment later to be suddenly surprised. "Top ten at Whistler once."

As files were grabbed and perused, they spoke out loud to themselves as much as each other. They both felt like they were working a case, taking on their father's mantle, a drive to get the job done. For Ian, this was the gist of a novel possibly. For Nathalie, it was a way out of career jail.

She was an independent female who had chosen to prove she was as good as any man at this job and was none too pleased she had fallen hard on her ass. Now the best man she had ever known had boxes of files on this guy Cross and she felt in her bones that her father had the goods on this thief and she could ferret it out from his case work. She was hopeful.

"He has a villa in the south of France with horses, including an Arabian." Ian stared at a photo...imagining the lifestyle.

"Seems he started in his twenties, maybe even earlier. Crewed on a Windjammer. In the Caribbean. One morning, in port at St Bart's, the tourists' jewels and Cross were gone." Nathalie stopped reading...her imagination transported to the exotic locale. "The jewels were never found. The connection to Cross purely coincidental. He totally skated. Seems this guy never trips up. That's catnip to a cop."

Ian suddenly laughed. "Holy shit, he tried out for the Yankees. Just showed up at spring training. The balls on this guy..." He read more. "He didn't make it—of course—it's the fuckin' Yankees. So there's something he's not good at." He read a little further. "Whoa, hit a home run though in Yankee stadium...to right center. Jesus Christ, this scouting report had him tagged as *active consideration*. You gotta wonder, did he like baseball, or was he just...I don't know..."

Nathalie merely shook her head. Her focus was a surveillance photo of Cross in midtown Manhattan. His back was turned, only a glimpse of the side of his face. In the background, Nathalie recognized the bleak façade of the Midtown North Precinct, her dad's precinct. What was Cross doing there? Mere coincidence?

In her growing desire to know all about this mystery man, she felt a twinge of obsession. She sensed intuitively that this was not a good thing. Her gut warned her not to get carried away, to keep it professional; be sure to leave personal matters out of it.

Ian picked up another file, read, then stopped. "Summer of '99, he was in Paris."

Nathalie snapped out of her reverie.

"So were Mom and Dad. Could they possibly have..."

"I don't know," Ian wondered. "They never talked about that trip."

"They weren't talking much at all when they got back."

"And then they separated for a year. You don't think that..."

Nathalie finished his thought "...he had something to do with it?"

Both siblings got very quiet...wondering about their parents.

Nathalie walked out of the study with part of a file and sought quiet refuge in the Seeger living room. The décor had a distinctive European style. Framed poster art of a Renoir exhibition in Boston showcased the image of the impressionist painter's work *Dance at Bougival*, sometimes referred to as *The Dancing Man*. Its placement on the wall behind the black baby grand piano was intentional.

As a child, and even as a young woman, Nathalie always felt that it represented her parents. The man's handsome bearded face was masked by his yellow straw hat but his strong body language held the woman with clear romantic intent. The woman's burnished orange flowered hat captured the gaiety of the moment in color, but it was her soft and sweet abandonment in his arms that made one feel his breath upon her cheek and her delight in being adored.

Nathalie fingered the piano keys... and stared at the many framed photos atop the piano. One photo stood out to her. It was Nate Seeger kissing a beautiful woman with the Eiffel Tower behind them. There was a handwritten inscription: *Je t'aime, mon amour.*

Nathalie turned her attention back to her father's file. Once again, her father's voice flooded in on her as she read. *Cross plays the game like an artist. If you want to defeat your enemy, first make him your friend.* Nathalie read on until Ian hobbled in with his cane, flipping through pages.

"Pop couldn't nail this guy."

"Or didn't want to."

"Really?" said Ian intrigued.

"Cross wrote Dad a letter." She held up the letter as she read out loud to her brother.

"Nate, our swords have crossed, I hope with honor, but perhaps you do not see it that way. For me, facing you added a luster to the game. You were fair, but you never relented. And I thank you."

For a moment, Ian just stared at his sister as they both let those words sink in, then he showed her a page from the file he was holding.

"Look at this margin note Pop wrote. Still tough to read his scribbles."

Ian handed Nathalie the file and she read her father's words out loud.

"I knew him too well. Maybe he wanted me to. No regrets."

"I knew him too well," Ian repeated. "Jesus."

"Maybe he wanted me to. No regrets," Nathalie repeated softly. It was hard to believe her father had written those words. "Did dad get used? 'No regrets.' What the hell, Ian?!"

"I know…makes you wanna *Muldoon* Cross's ass, doesn't it? And yet…"

They barely had a chance to register the impact of this confession when the front door swept open and in strode Odile Trenet Seeger—their mother—a classy French beauty, who embodied *joie de vivre* and *savoir faire*. At sixty four, she could've easily graced the pages of Vogue, passing for a woman fifteen years her junior. Odile was a woman strangely out of place in Queens, except she was the one being kissed in the photo on the piano.

"Nathalie, Ian, bonjour. Ca va bien?"

"Oui, ca va. Et tu?" responded Nathalie.

"Ah, oui," said Odile, a clear glow about her. "Y a-t-il des colis pour moi?"

"No mail yet," replied her son.

Nathalie and Ian were edgy, guilt rising, as they glanced at the files.

Odile had clearly seen the boxes. "Qu'est-ce qu'il y a?"

"Nothing's wrong," said Nathalie, lying through her teeth.

Odile switched to English with ease. With a wry grin she directed her attention to her son. "You aren't moving in again, are you?"

"No, no Mom. Just researching a new book."

Odile saw a file labeled: *"Eli Cross."* A flash of fear lit up her eyes. Caught off guard, she glanced away, quickly switching subjects.

"Combien de temps restez-vous?"

"Might stay for lunch," Ian covered.

"Where were you?" pressed Nathalie.

Odile knew her daughter was probing. "Montreal."

"Montreal?!"

"Oui, Montreal. Jack took me to dinner last night at a marvelous French restaurant."

"Just a little hop to Canada," mused Ian.

"Who's Jack?" Nathalie had to know. This did not feel good to her.

Odile looked once again at the files spread everywhere.

"This is for a book?"

Covering quickly, Ian spilled out, "Yeah...a cop thriller, like before."

His mother held his gaze, testing his veracity. Ian exhaled slowly but did not falter in his commitment to his lie.

"I'm expecting company later," Odile said.

"I'll clean it up," said Ian.

Nathalie watched her mother slip into the master bedroom. It did not escape her attention that her mother would not look at her directly. Nathalie waited for the bedroom door to close then turned to her brother and whispered.

"Did you see her eyes when she saw the file?"

Ian nodded, completely transfixed with the intrigue.

"Holy shit..." Nathalie knew without a doubt her world had just irrevocably changed.

CHAPTER SIX

Stolen kisses are always sweetest.

Leigh Hunt, British poet

Rockefeller Center rose dramatically into the night sky. Nathalie in a stylish evening suit which clearly stated *classy, professional woman* stepped out of a cab into the fresh breeze of the cool, night air. She entered the lobby, crossed to the elevator, and then got swept inside by a romantic couple gliding in a dancing embrace when the doors opened. As the elevator lifted up, the young man and woman were oblivious to Nathalie as they twirled into a kissing embrace.

The floors floated by. Nathalie stared at the couple but heard her father's voice from something she had read in the files. *Eli Cross's style is that life is to be felt, explored, experienced, and not left wanting at the end.* This couple was wasting no time, embracing life with both arms, hearts on fire, and joy running over. What was Nathalie doing? Digging out of a shithole of her own making, she thought. Sweet.

The Rainbow Room was stylish elegance and charm sixty five floors above Manhattan. Dining and dancing encased in the sparkling lights of the city. The elevator doors opened and the young couple broke their embrace and glided out leaving Nathalie with a wistful smile, transfixed until the doors began to close, then she slipped out.

Nathalie took a moment to take in the splendor. She had last been here in 2008 tracking down an embezzler for a client during the financial crisis, testing the waters of her independent investigator profession; one of her first opportunities to do more than get coffee and pastries. Little did she know at the time that the Rainbow Room itself would fall victim to the global financial squeeze and close its doors in 2009. She had not been back since it reopened in 2014, so even if an asshole, holier-than-though, chauvinistic prick of a cop had invited her, she was planning on savoring at least the view…for a moment.

The lit up skyscraper jewels of this great city lay before her through the almost floor-to-ceiling windows. The light leapt off the giant chandelier in the center of the main lounge and dance floor and splashed over the elegant tables and chairs. It was easy to feel special here. But she had work to do.

The Maitre'D looked up from his reservation book.

"Good evening."

"The reservation is under Donelli," Nathalie said.

"He has not yet arrived, but I'll be glad to show you to your table."

"Fine, thank you." Nathalie followed him to the table. He seated her and presented her with a menu. "Are you sure that Victor Donelli made this reservation?"

"Yes, Lieutenant Victor J. Donelli. He was very clear about the Lieutenant part. Enjoy your evening."

Nathalie suddenly flinched as she noticed being watched by a face she had recently carefully studied. It was Marty Lefkowitz—last seen on the police print out—now somewhat hidden at a corner table. His haunting, disturbing eyes were drilled right at Nathalie. She averted her gaze and lifted up her menu hoping he hadn't seen her recognition.

Nathalie studied the menu while wracking her brain as to how in the hell he knew who she was and why he was here. It was no coincidence, she knew that. This did not bode well. To make matters worse, she had left her Sig Sauer at home. Her mental wrangling ended with a jolt as a shadow fell across her menu. She looked up to see a tall, dashing man in a tuxedo smiling down at her with eyes that looked into her and through.

"Hello, I'm Eli Cross."

For a moment—just a moment—Nathalie was off balance. Cross held out his hand. His eyes never left hers. Nathalie took his hand and felt his gentle strength.

"Nathalie Seeger."

"Yes, I know."

It was strangely all so simple, so normal, so very natural, and that chilled her to the bone. Cross sat himself at the table. Two out of her three suspects were now here. She wondered if Jake Kracauer would arrive before she ordered. She also knew she was on her own.

"I didn't think this place was quite Lieutenant Donelli's style," Nathalie said as nonchalantly as possible, "but then, people can surprise you."

Cross stared at her with piercing, but appreciative eyes. It wasn't unsettling, but what the hell was he doing here tonight and why the set up? Cross kept staring and smiling an unnervingly warm smile.

"Something wrong?" Nathalie had to figure him out fast.

"On the contrary. You have your father's eyes."

Okay, now it was unsettling. She would remember this moment later as pleasantly uncomfortable. His gaze was uninhibited, the kind that makes a woman breathe...slowly.

"And his smile," Cross added, not for effect, but because it was true.

The moment was damn near perfect...not forced or false. The bit about her smile definitely got to her because her mother always remarked that she had her father's smile. Here he was—Eli Cross—in the flesh, staring at her. She had read file boxes on him, and yet looking into his eyes, she knew full well she didn't know him at all. That disturbed her. So did his looks.

Blue eyes flecked with green offset by thick, dark hair, lips that seemed invitingly soft and a face that sent—*goddamnit why'd he have to be so breathtakingly handsome*—an uncomfortable warmth spreading across her skin. She hoped to hell she wasn't blushing, that would send a very poor signal. This was her prey she reminded herself—her prey—and you do not blush in front of your prey. *And his fucking nose was perfect. Shit.*

It took Nathalie a breath to get back in stride.

"I'm sorry I don't have any jewelry you might like," Nathalie said, very pleased with her riposte. She hoped that should square things up.

Cross was not at all put off. In fact he seemed very pleased with himself, entirely at ease. He stared at her. Nathalie held his stare...unflinching. An engaging smile slid across his face.

"So, it begins."

His eyes found the menu and dropped away from hers. Nathalie continued staring, not sure of anything just then. She took a slow breath...he was fascinating. She had to force herself to remember that he was also considered a criminal with an international reputation.

The next action that roused Nathalie's suspicion was ordering. He did not order for her right away. That was surprising. She had expected this smooth alpha male to order for her. Too many dates had done just that, establishing their dominance by choosing her food as if she were a child incapable of knowing what she might like; and even worse was the self-assured acceptance that she would like whatever they had ordered for her without ever inquiring about her tastes. She hated that, even from guys who were good in bed.

She waited for him to take the helm and order for them. This she knew would tell her something. But he gestured for her to order first. She dipped her head in acknowledgement but gestured back for him to go ahead. She wanted to see how far he took the green light. He ordered medallions of beef for himself and then shocked her by waiting for her to tell the waiter her choice.

She was going to have the salmon, but now certain that he was up to something, she switched to filet mignon to throw him off. She had no sooner ordered than she felt like an idiot. She was reading too much into everything. What the hell difference did it make what she ordered! She decided then and there that she would simply let things be normal. But then the wine arrived.

Nathalie watched the deep red liquid curl and billow in her glass, refracting the light in splashes of rich, ruby color. It was from a bottle that the waiter had brought over without Cross ever mentioning a word. How did Cross know what she would order and that she would want wine and that the perfect selection would be red?

A chilling feeling rose up her spine…how much did Cross know about her? Did he have file boxes? She had not forgotten about Marty Lefkowitz at a dark corner table. Did Cross know him? Did Cross know he was there?

She felt like she was the only one who might not know what the hell was happening. This was not a good feeling. The evening was clearly in motion as she watched Cross as he slid the bottle over the top of his glass and poured.

"I had this sent here from Provence."

"Should I be impressed?" Nathalie said casually.

Both were trying to key in on the other.

"Only by the wine. It's from a very small vineyard outside of Arles. Each year, the owner Jean-Pierre creates a special blend for his friends. He has the touch of a master and I'm always honored that he feels me worthy of his artistry."

In this moment Nathalie saw a sincerity that couldn't be denied. But what of the other moments? What was being set up here? How was she being played? Her mother summered in Arles in Provence before her father swept her away. Was there any connection with this Jean-Pierre and his Provencal vineyard?

Too many questions. No answers.

She cautioned herself to have patience. She was patient with longshoreman Grabowski and she nailed his ass.

"Then I'm honored that you're sharing it with me," said Nathalie, playing it cool.

She raised her glass and he lifted his to meet her gesture. She sniffed the wine's bouquet.

"Cabernet?"

"Ah oui," he smiled. He continued in natural conversational French to regale her with how the sauvignon perfumes are difficult to obtain and maintain in the wines and just how his friend Jean-Pierre meticulously developed his own consistent method to capture the flavor.

"Oui, ca c'est vrais. Maintaining the bouquet and sauvignon flavors is difficult," responded Nathalie.

He obviously knew that she knew French by speaking in French as much as he did. She had responded in French then slipped into English as if to say *I get it, but let's keep it simple and get on with whatever this is.* It annoyed her however that his flawless accent sounded like a native Frenchman, but only when he spoke French, leaving no clue as to his native land. The romance language of love, so smooth and naturally seductive, made her want to listen to it all night long. She imagined many a woman's panties had slipped to the floor from the silky sound of the words flowing from his lips. It also made her feel that her French accent had drowned somewhere in the Atlantic between Queens and Paris.

Nathalie sipped the wine and Cross watched her eyes sparkle from the taste. She could not hide her pleasure.

"Your friend Jean-Pierre is an artist."

"Yes, someone who makes the world a better place."

"And you?"

"I learned that the world is what you make it. I decided to make it profitable."

Cross savored a swallow of the cabernet.

"You see yourself as an entrepreneur?"

On this night, a special musical ensemble, a small chamber group provided lilting music. Not the usual entertainment for the Rainbow Room and Nathalie wondered if Cross had them brought over from France as well.

"I've always had a fascination with art," said Cross.

The music changed to Gershwin's "*Embraceable You.*"

"My parents instilled in me an appreciation of all things beautiful." He paused and stared at her, long enough for appreciation but not discomfort. "And this song should not be denied."

He extended his hand.

"Would you care to dance?"

Nathalie was game. Wasn't this what it was all about anyway, she thought, a dance? Wasn't a dance meant to lead to something? The truth perhaps? No one able to come straight out with it; only dance around it, until the truth was felt. She was confident she could handle this.

Cross led her from the table to the intimate dance floor overlooking the city lights.

Nathalie's fingers nestled into his left hand as he slipped his right arm around her waist. For a moment, Cross merely gazed into her eyes...holding her still. Entwined couples flowed around them. Nathalie could hear her own breathing as she looked into his eyes. His arm gently tightened around her waist and Nathalie murmured an involuntary moan, then his left hand pressed lightly against hers, turning her gently and they moved with the flow of the music as he guided her gracefully among the dancing couples.

He moved her not so much from pressure, but more from a feeling, as if they weren't even touching; but they were, and his eyes never left hers.

She couldn't help thinking about the Renoir image of the dancing couple behind her parents' piano. The truth was this was heavenly. She knew she had to snap out of it or end up in a hell not of her choosing. She had to take the lead back.

"I like your cologne."

"A gift from another friend."

"I've come across it once before."

"A lucky moment...it's very rare."

He twirled her away, only to meet her closer...more intimate. Or was it challenging? The feeling of enticing danger lingered. She caught herself holding her breath. She had to press on.

"Why baseball?"

"I wanted to know what it was like to hit a home run in Yankee stadium."

Nathalie searched his eyes for the little boy inside the man. She knew she should be aware of *the man* who was probably manipulating her, but she couldn't help herself.

"And…?"

Cross gave an honest answer. No need to hesitate. "Addicting."

Nathalie was looking for more.

"Same as skiing?"

"It's the speed," he said looking into her eyes. "You can never go fast enough."

"Have you ever found yourself not wanting to stop?"

For a fleeting moment, she saw a glimmer of light—a spark—race across his eyes. It was what she was looking for, the passion that drove him. It was dangerous...and intoxicating.

When the music stopped, he led her back to their table as effortlessly as they had graced the dance floor. Nathalie caught sight of Marty Lefkowitz hastily leaving his table for the exit; his body language an expression of annoyance and impatience. He'd had enough or seen enough, she didn't know which, nor of the point as to why he was there at all. She clearly noted that Cross paid no attention to Lefkowitz. Working together or mere coincidence?

Too unknowable this night. She needed to stay alert. Every action had some meaning to it. She knew this was a fluid game.

The exploring with Cross continued through the savoring of after-dinner drinks. He suggested Chartreuse for her. This immediately put her on high alert. Did he know that this French-style digestif was first introduced to her by her mother because it was her mother's favorite? Had he once ordered one for her mother? That thought did nothing positive for her digestion. Nor did the realization that the drink's strong content could easily leave her very relaxed, which could very well be his intent.

She threw him a curve and ordered a Kahlua neat.

He asked for a Chairman's Reserve Forgotten Cask Rum. She recognized it as a limited edition bottle and knew it would not have been the first time he indulged that drink. The aroma and overall sensuousness of its dark aged look and flavors blended well with his cologne, conjuring up images of South Sea island adventures. The combination had a definite allure.

Whatever it was he was doing, he was good at it. The preparation—or set up—was nuanced and natural. If she didn't remain sharp, she knew she could slip under its spell unawares. She felt there had been moments where he could have stolen a kiss and she wouldn't have even known it. My god, it was all so…infuriating…because it felt so, so very delicious.

"So why am I sitting here?"

Cross took a slow sip of his rum and stared at her across the top edge of his glass.

"Perhaps part of it is memories."

He then tilted his glass toward her.

"To your father."

Nathalie was taken by surprise with the sadness that crept into his eyes...it was genuine.

"I miss him," he said.

"He tried to put you in prison."

"Yes," he said with clear affection.

His vulnerability was like a magnet...drawing her closer. So subtle and so effective and so…*goddamnit*…she had to keep her focus.

"Were you in Paris the summer of 99?"

"Yes. As was your father and your beautiful mother. How is Odile?"

"Busy," she finally replied. The thought of all of it—her mother and men, and even this man—made her very uncomfortable.

"She's a remarkable woman."

Nathalie desperately wanted to know more about his connection to her mother but knew that desire expressed too quickly was a weakness he could use against her. Let him keep guessing where her feelings on that sensitive subject resided.

"And the other part of why I'm here?"

"I was hoping we could help each other. You're working for Vorhees International Insurance and they suspect me."

"Lieutenant Donelli suspects you."

"I'm sort of a career obsession for him. Your reputation is on the line with the theft of those jewels."

"No thanks to you."

"Exactly—but thanks to someone imitating my style. Right down to my cologne. The first time was two months ago in Vienna."

"Too competitive for you?" Nathalie quickly assessed the veracity of his words.

"Inconvenient. You see, I've gone straight with the job I have, though understandably, some people doubt this."

"Since wherever you go, expensive things disappear."

Cross gave her a slight nod, a touché gesture. Then his eyes darkened.

"What I do now is very...secretive. My employers trust me with certain art masterpieces."

"Sounds like you set them up to steal them."

"If too many people come to believe that, then I become ineffective. So you see, my reputation also hangs in the balance."

Nathalie showed him no reaction.

"I do not steal them."

She still gave him no reaction.

"You'll just have to trust me on that."

Nathalie looked for a falter in his gaze...there was none. After all the nuance and atmosphere and testing and exploring, it came down to something so simple.

"That's what this is all about," she said matching his stare. "Trust."

An enigmatic smile slid across his face. "I must stop this impostor. It'd be nice to have a Seeger on my side for a change."

For a change? She thought about those words. At this moment she couldn't even be sure if her father had been in cahoots with him some time in the past. Her father's words *no regrets* haunted her. Was she being lured *to be the Seeger on his side* for the second time?

She fingered her Kahlua glass, revealing nothing except her own enigmatic smile. She didn't know what his enigmatic smile hid, but she knew hers hid shameful, sexy excitement with equal parts terror of being a gullible screw-up. Talk about boys against the girls, she thought. This had all the markings and banners of being the Super Bowl. She wanted to suit up—for combat—not as a cheerleader—but a player!

Cross knew that for all his skills at gauging what moves human behavior, there was always a dark, recessed corner of a woman's nature that remained dangerously unknowable. Hence the risk, as well as the heady anticipation of those unknown moments that gave life its…razor-sharp edge. Was it ever possible, he thought, to stay one step ahead of a woman's nature and the moment of its expression?

"Don't give me an answer now," he said. "Tuesday, meet me at The Baronfeld Museum. Three o'clock. It will help your decision."

CHAPTER SEVEN

*Being a woman is a terribly difficult task, since it
consists principally in dealing with men.*

Joseph Conrad

The jogging path in Central Park was a great way to meet men. This day it had another purpose. An attempt to understand them. Neither Nathalie nor Megan had the faintest idea what jogging had to do with figuring out the male sex but it made them feel like they were accomplishing something. At the very least, they felt they looked good in their latest Fila jogging outfits. Twenty bucks a pair at Costco with designer-looking cred. Keep 'em guessing was the plan. Probably the best advice in dealing with men…so they hoped.

"Only boring stuff happens to me. You're lucky," said Megan.

"Yeah, lucky. If I blow this job, my free-lance days are over. No one's gonna hire me."

They passed a bicyclist kneeling down adjusting the chain assembly on his bike. He was turned away from them and wore a helmet and sunglasses; three reasons why Nathalie did not recognize Marty Lefkowitz. When they had sufficiently moved on at a distance that wouldn't arouse suspicion, he mounted his bike and followed them, keeping pace, but not closing the gap.

"Maybe Eli Cross can help. You gotta get the jewels back, right?"

"Cross is too casual about going straight after all these years."

Megan glanced back as they rounded a curve and noticed Lefkowitz on the bike.

"They're only supposed to be going in one direction on a bike—the other direction! Pisses me off! They can run ya down and not give a shit." She then yelled back at him. "You're goin' the wrong way!"

Lefkowitz did not slow down or even acknowledge her, just kept pace with them.

"He's not changin' direction!" Megan yelled at him again while pointing in the other direction. "Hey, asshole, the other way! Go the other way!"

Lefkowitz paid her no mind.

Megan couldn't believe it. She had been summarily dismissed by this bicyclist.

"He's either deaf—or a prick—or he's following us," said Megan.

"Maybe a deaf prick who just likes the way we look in our spiffy new Costco jogging suits."

"Well my ass is bouncing all over the place, that can't be too appealing," whined Megan.

For the first time, Nathalie glanced back at the bicyclist. It couldn't be, she thought. She had to look again to confirm it.

"Shit. He's definitely following us. And he's more than a prick," said Nathalie, worried.

"What? How do you—do you know him?"

"Sorta," said Nathalie. "His name's Marty Lefkowitz. He's a jewel thief and a suspect from the heist. He had his eye on me at the Rainbow Room too."

"Jesus Christ, why didn't you say something?! Now I've pissed him off. Is he dangerous?!"

"I don't know, let's find out."

Nathalie turned around to face the oncoming Lefkowitz whose focus was riveted on them.

"Fuck, seriously?!" Megan jerked Nathalie back into jogging mode, shoving her forward.

"We're out in the open with people running around," Nathalie said assuredly.

Megan pushed Nathalie faster. "People get killed out in the open all the time!"

Lefkowitz increased his pace, gaining on them.

Megan panicked. "He's getting closer!"

"Good for him," said Nathalie calming herself.

Lefkowitz pumped the pedals harder, fully intent on overtaking them. Megan glanced back freaking out at the obviously guilty thief barreling to kill them!

"Do you have your gun in that fanny-pack?!"

"No," Nathalie stated.

"Jesus Christ!"

Lefkowitz was almost beside them. Megan gasped and grabbed Nathalie's arm in a vise-like fear grip! Lefkowitz angled the bike right at Nathalie. She turned her gaze directly on him.

"Hello, Marty."

Lefkowitz registered momentary surprise at being called out by name. He swerved aside and quickly veered left at the fork in the path. His facial expression unmistakable—pissed—for she knew him and was unfazed.

"Hello Marty?!!" Megan hauled Nathalie to a breathless stop. "Are you nuts?!"

Nathalie watched Lefkowitz disappear along the left fork.

"You gotta know how to deal with these guys."

"I know that look," gasped Megan. "You didn't have clue, did you, not a clue?!"

"Well, he's a man, so—"

"That is not reassuring!"

"Now he knows I'm on to him."

"Yeah, and me too—and I called him an asshole!"

"I gotta figure out whether he's working with Cross or not."

"For a woman who's not dating, you got a lot of guys interested in you."

"Lt. Donelli thinks Cross is the only one to worry about."

"After what you told me about last night, I'd be worried about what to wear when I see him again."

They exited the park onto Central Park West.

"This wouldn't have happened if we belonged to a gym," bemoaned Megan.

&

Nathalie's apartment was in a condo-converted, pre-war building on the Upper West Side at 79th midway between Central Park and Riverside Park. Nineteen floors of dark, red brick and about a hundred units, not that Nathalie ever bothered to count. Basically a tall rectangle with some slight architectural "indented" deviations for a touch of style.

A realtor would regale one with the facts that dogs and cats were allowed, so were protruding air conditioners. There was a full-time doorman, a laundry in the building even though most units had their own washer & dryer installed, and there was a live-in super—also a bike room. The last point was useful knowledge when it was revealed that there was no gym and no garage. There was also no concierge and no sundeck.

The location however was rather fabulous. It said something about her character. At a certain point, some years back, she had sworn she would live in an area worthy of her dreams, a locale that raised her sense of self-worth. She knew she might have to finagle her way there, but get there she would. It was time, she had thought, her home mirrored the confidence she felt in her ability to do her job, to hold her own in a man's world as a woman. Her father's guidance and encouragement along with her mother's insistence on living with style had grown roots in her soul.

However, Nathalie's strongest memories and reveries about this location were mostly…sexual.

Next door was the historic 1895 Blessed Sacrament Convent Academy building. Nathalie's sexual reveries had nothing to do with the religious aspect, although it has been reported that repressed Catholic sex—when released—generated an almost indecent level of orgasm. Nathalie, being amorphously Protestant, could only wonder.

Catholic ownership continued for a little over a hundred years and then the building was sold. At this time, with all the changes in building ownership, Nathalie lived next door to a Jewish day school which conjured up thoughts of discipline and guilt but rarely sex.

The reveries came from the geographic positioning of her apartment unit and the romance of architecture. The historic building was a tall four-story brownstone with sweeping curved lines. It had the flair of Renaissance Revival and greeted the pedestrian with open arms created by an exterior stone staircase split by a center cylindrical column and embraced by two other columns on the outer edges of the steps. The columns extended to the base of the second floor. The outside sections of the buildings swept inward in graceful curves and greeted a recessed portico which was protected by a second floor balcony.

There were six windows on each floor; two on each of the outside curved sections that swept inward and two in the center flat rectangular panel of the building which met the inward sweeping curves. All the windows had deep brownstone-style edged frames to them.

To the uninitiated, a carved panel above the portico running the length of the building contained a flourish of what seemed like regal symbols which added to the European flavor. It clearly stood out from its neighboring structures with a special allure. An author might exclaim *it was the stuff dreams were made of.* Perhaps a princess might be lodged there on a visit—or horny Catholic school girls as it were.

That's where the positioning of Nathalie's apartment launched her reverie. She was on the eighth floor and her windows overlooked the roof of the convent building which was only a short drop below. In her daydreams, she imagined an adventurous and amorous lad leaping from the apartment window onto the roof, scaling the outer walls to an open window and deflowering a sexually-repressed school girl—*sweet surrender at sweet sixteen*—then barely escaping when the nuns were aroused by her screams of ecstasy. Nuns intuitively knew that certain rapidly repeated breathless cries of *"Oh God,"* were not expressions of devout religion.

When Nathalie, bored conjuring up that dreamscape, her other go-to dream was of a handsome prince—or randy rogue—leaping from the brownstone roof into her open apartment window, without tearing the fluttering lace curtains, and then ravaging her before leaving with a gentle kiss upon her lips. What he was doing in a Jewish day school was never considered in her dream.

The other sexual memory was real. But that lingered from across the street at the treasured landmark of the Lucerne Hotel. Its European-style architecture and old-world prestige beckoned the cognoscenti of travel and class. The magnificently carved entrance columns announced that all who entered must surely be of world-renown.

After Vittorio—Vinnie, from the Bronx—and one or two others, and before the most recent tire-marks-across-the-heart Tom, there was Graydon Hutchings. There was much to remember about Graydon.

She met him on what was a good day, a very good day. She had just landed the apartment owned by an older couple—her parents' friends—on the eighth floor of the building across the street from The Lucerne.

This condo was a sublet for Nathalie and only affordable because the older couple knew her parents from long ago and had always thought of Nathalie as *that lovely, sweet, young woman*. Obviously, Nathalie felt, they didn't really know her—especially the *sweet* part—but she was not about to correct them and possibly lose out on their fiscally irrational decision to rent to her. Some creative finagling was added to her *sweetness* in negotiation as she pressed the family-friend connection to full advantage to engender trust. They could trust her to take care of their place.

They could've easily charged Nathalie $5,500 a month or more for the two-bed, two-bath rental. Instead she ended up paying a scandalous $2,000. From that moment on, she knew *sweetness* could never be underestimated, even if it wasn't rock solid real. Nathalie also knew that when they passed, their adult kids were going to launch Nathalie's cheap ass right out—by the window if necessary—just as sweet as can be.

Having closed the deal, that day—that very good day—was to be her first night in the new pad. To celebrate this amazing and fortuitous turn of events, which got her out of a dump near 50th and 11th in Hell's Kitchen, she stepped into Nice Matin NYC, the French-Mediterranean restaurant par excellence at The Lucerne.

Her mother loved the food there which reminded her of the cuisine in Nice. Whenever her mother felt like injecting her tough, city-cop-detective husband with some Provencal culture she would drain his wallet at Nice Matin NYC. Nathalie planned on taking advantage of the Lucerne's Wine Hour to kick off her first night in new digs.

Graydon Hutchings entered her life by backing into her and spilling her wine glass onto the sleeveless, V-neck, navy Donna Karan dress she had borrowed from her costume designer friend at the Met. He insisted on making amends over dinner at Nice Matin NYC.

He was cultured, confident and scull-rowing fit with an accent honed at Oxford. It was endearing in a sly rugged way when he insisted that his character-imbued broken nose was not from rugby, but from smacking himself with a scull oar. Whatever caused it, the nose was slightly cocked at a sexy, jaunty angle to Nathalie. She wanted to straighten it with kisses before the salads arrived. His enchanting accent made certain expressions like *spot on* seem remarkably classy when used to simply describe precision. On any day after, her taste buds needed no assistance to summon the memory of the potato gnocchi with lobster, cream & peas.

It was his sense of humor though that tipped the scale. Subtle and sly and deliciously wicked without a hint of crassness. That had to be his British upbringing, to have at least the mirage of decorum, she thought. *My father's only a viscount but I have a deluxe king suite tonight. While we savor a digestif, they have bathrobes, so I can have the hotel dry clean your lovely dress.* Years later she still remembered those exact words that caused her to skip dessert in hopes of other delights. Who knew that *they have bathrobes* could be so disarmingly enticing.

In the well-adorned deluxe king suite, the wine-impacted dress slipped off but the bathrobe never slipped on. The after dinner drinks had been ordered and with a gallant toast Graydon slipped off his shirt with practiced ease. When the bellboy arrived to pick up the special expedited dry clean run, a well-muscled, scull-toned, naked arm extended the dress out the partially opened suite door.

With her first sip of the digestif, he undid her strapless bra and let it slide to the floor. With his first sip, she unzipped and dropped his pants. A second sip from Nathalie brought the descent of her panties by his fingertips. His drawers fell, twirled off her fingers, as he took a final sip. He tossed their glasses onto the center of the bed, briskly whipped off his socks in a flourish, and proceeded to back her up. Not to the bed, but to the far wall. He gently pressed her against the wall and consumed her lips with a soft, wet kiss.

Tingling anticipation of something delightfully naughty spread across her skin like warm goosebumps. Nathalie thought this very good day was turning into a very good night. She also thought that sculling was amazingly beneficial to men because he was incredibly fit in all possible ways. After this evening, she declared to herself that he was *fucking fit*.

He was also knowledgeable and knew where all her sensual buttons were and how to press them. So practiced was he that she felt willing to let his touch take the lead in this scintillating dance. And a dance it was, not only against the wall, but all around the suite, on or against every piece of furniture, in positions before now only imagined. Through all this, his lips remained connected to hers with soft caresses. It was a performance like no other she had ever experienced.

Rivers of sensation flowed together to generate rushing rapids of feelings both exciting and eerie. The physical sensations were delightful but the disorienting effect of engaging with all the furniture gave her…pause…for where was this going? She knew she was not a gymnast. Strange was overtaking delight but his *button pushing* so encapsulated precision that the words *spot on* rushed into her mind, but the words *Oh God* escaped her lips.

Gripped in the clutches of a sensual out-of-body experience, the phrase *roller coaster romance* raced through her swirling thoughts; each thought spinning before her mind's eye like Dorothy watching the tornado whip images past the open window of her Kansas farm house. A sudden surging wave of electrical tingling rushed like a tsunami along her legs and she wondered if *Elmira Gulch* would be peddling by her next to do God knows what! Her body's sensory overload made her quiver all over allowing only one clear thought: *this probably never happened to Auntie Em.*

The sensual performance dance from this uber-fit Brit ended on the last piece of furniture touched—the bed—and her insides exploded with feelings at a level she'd never experienced before. He collapsed next to her and whispered: *your dress will be ready in the morning.* In five minutes, he was asleep.

So it was that Nathalie's first night in her new apartment was spent at the hotel across the street; she dreamed that night of moving to London at the soonest possible date.

In the morning, draped in her perfectly cleaned and still-borrowed Donna Karan V-necked sleeveless dress, Graydon escorted her to breakfast. This was after having bent her over one of the deluxe king suite stuffed chairs and entering her from behind until her knees buckled from rapturous shaking, and she collapsed like a rag doll over the back of the chair, head down into the cushion, not wanting to move until…well until he might want to do that again.

Just before they walked into the hotel's restaurant to be seated for breakfast, an exquisitely beautiful Indian woman who had just checked-in strode up to Graydon and threw her arms around him and pulled his face toward hers and gave him a deep, sensuous kiss. Her name was Eshana, and Nathalie later learned that in Hindi, that meant *desire.*

This woman was breathtaking. Her olive skin looked like living silk and her dark brown eyes were deep pools of liquid light. Her jet black hair was impossibly radiant, throwing off splashes of light that seemed to leap out of its dark lustrous layers as she swept it from side to side. Not only that, but her body was female perfect, with curves so balanced that her breasts were harmoniously round and her hips projected sensuous pleasure and infinite fertility. Her voice was an enticing blend of a soft British accent with a slight Indian intonation rolled into the rhythm of her sentences and phrases. Clearly the sound of an international Aphrodite.

Nathalie thought as she looked back upon this moment, that what she had felt, and her remembered description of that feeling, might be carrying it a bit too far—*but damn it*—Eshana was the prototype for God's perfect female—irresistible to the male—and Nathalie felt if she was ever going to test her attraction to women, and what it would be like to make love with a woman, it would be with Eshana.

Graydon was rather comfortable and nonplussed when he introduced her to Nathalie.

"Eshana, this is my new friend, Nathalie, and Nathalie, this is my wife, Eshana."

Nathalie had never forgotten the impact of those words either…*my wife, Eshana.*

At breakfast, Nathalie didn't know whether to be furious and expose Graydon as an unrepentant cad as he gracefully placed his napkin in his lap or to be civil and *sweet* and not ruin Eshana's marriage. The answer became clear—if not wild and crazy—during her yogurt parfait.

With nothing having been said between husband and wife, Eshana turned to Nathalie with engaging eyes. "I'm glad you and Graydon so thoroughly enjoyed each other. He never invites anyone to breakfast who isn't suitable."

"Excuse me," Nathalie said attempting to feign ignorance.

"You are lovely, Nathalie, sweet and rather alluring," said Eshana with affection.

"I knew she would like you," Graydon said to Nathalie.

After breakfast, we should…" Eshana gestured toward the lobby.

"We should what?" Nathalie felt that was an invitation to The Twilight Zone.

"We should all go back upstairs and thoroughly enjoy each other," stated Graydon happily.

"At least until lunch time," chimed in Eshana.

Graydon signaled the waiter for the check.

"How lovely and…unexpected," said Nathalie totally at a loss for her next move.

Her thoughts tumbled around in her head as she sought an escape. When it came to sex she thought she was open but not loose. She was willing to experiment to a point and realized she had just encountered her point while eating a yogurt parfait. From that moment on, a yogurt parfait eaten by anyone in her presence brought on a cascading flow of images of intertwined limbs and lips. She would only ever order one herself when her mood was stable and her head clear.

A threesome had always seemed enticing in her imagination. Staring it right in the face, even with the world's sexiest woman and a performance-king of a man, it somehow just didn't seem like…her. Strange, when she thought back upon this moment, how one got to know things about who they really were deep down when it was all on the line. Besides, she didn't think she'd survive the orgasm assault from both of them. One can only quiver and quake so much. These two clearly didn't fit the joke of *no sex please, we're British.*

She politely excused herself, claiming a pressing business meeting to which she was now late, and left the hotel never to see either of them again. She thought of it as an escape. She had never told anyone about this—even Megan—and it was so far her one and only one-night stand.

What turned out to be most disturbing about it all was how angry and thoroughly confused it had made her for months afterward. She didn't want to have sex with anyone then. There was nothing wrong with the sex with Graydon. It wasn't a moral thing or a religious hang-up. No, she had entered into the escapades of that night freely and with abandon. It was the best physical sex of her life. It was sensual art. It was performance art. But the performance was so emotionally impactful, her heart wanted more. It made her angry to know that it was only *performance.*

It also confused the hell out of her. Why couldn't she just enjoy it as a memory of a mind-blowing, body-shivering, soul-shaking night of sex? Many people never have an encounter like that in an entire lifetime.

It took her a while to realize what had destabilized her world was that *she had felt used, set up,* because there was no real attempt to *connect* with her. He had been setting her up for the anticipated threesome with his wife. He'd been hunting for a vulnerable or at least willing participant...or victim. He had no regrets about using her. It confused her that she wasn't totally on board with *"if it feels this good getting used, oh you just keep on using me till you use me up."* That lyric was from a Bill Withers song she had always loved. But for months, she hated it and couldn't listen to it even for a second. That made her really angry because she loved Bill Withers' music. Why hadn't she simply been able to go with the flow, to experience this...unknown?

Graydon's sexual skills had set off physical and emotional fireworks inside her sending a flood of oxytocin throughout her body. She hungered to bond with him. She learned in those months which followed that her heart wanted *real* and that night wasn't real. It was decidedly unreal, on many levels. She had been fooled. Fooled by someone who really knew what they were doing. Knew what it would do to her and knew how she would react. With that realization, she couldn't get the Who's song lyric out of her mind for months: *"we don't get fooled again."* It became like a mantra loop running in her head until it became a pledge for all her future relationships.

She was disappointed in herself. She had let herself down and not protected herself. She had let her heart trust the feelings that were aroused that night. She trusted that those feelings meant this was something real and deep. But her trust was violated. Never again. If she was to trust, it would only be on her terms.

She learned a lot about herself from that night and the next morning. But that was all years ago.

ᴇᴏ

The present moment held the dilemma of Eli Cross and Marty Lefkowitz and not…well, not getting killed in attempting to recover the jewels.

Nathalie and Megan, no longer jogging, approached Nathalie's building.

Megan looked across the street at the Lucerne Hotel.

"I love that hotel, it feels so romantic." sighed Megan.

Nathalie felt a sudden rush of heat between her legs. "Have you ever stayed there?"

"At those prices, are you kidding? I looked in the lobby once. It's just got that European je ne sais quoi, ya know. Like your master thief."

"Yeah," said Nathalie. "Je ne sais quoi with him is the problem."

"You wanna get to know him?"

Megan's tone hooked her attention as if she had a simple answer.

"He likes women. There's your game plan. You are investigating him."

"Why does this not sound smart?"

"You wanna reel him in, right?" Megan paused. "You gotta lure him with something."

"We're not dealing with Vinnie here. This guy's a cut above. Way above," Nathalie added almost wistfully.

Megan clearly heard the tone in her voice. Nathalie may have thought she covered her feelings well, but the yearning was all too apparent.

"He got to you. Are we smitten here?"

Nathalie continued inside her building's lobby crossing to the elevator without comment. She pushed the elevator button.

"I was very professional," Nathalie said somewhat defensively. "Even on the dance floor."

"Which you forced yourself not to enjoy."

"That's right. Even though he did move well."

The elevator doors opened and once they were both inside, Nathalie pushed the button for the eighth floor.

"I didn't have to think of where to put my feet. He just led, and…" Nathalie stared at the advancing floor numbers.

Megan sighed at her wistful friend. "Yeah…we're in deep trouble here."

Inside Nathalie's apartment, sunlight filled the space and offered a view of The Lucerne.

The furnishings were minimal, space being filled when budget, quality and sales meshed. She did have good taste, interspersed with funky quirks, which accounted for the bronze sculpture of a hole in the ground with a rabbit's ass protruding up out of the hole and the hand of an Alice in Wonderland girl grabbing the rabbit's tail. The girl wore a Mad Hatter hat and had a rhinestone-etched tattoo on her arm that spelled out *Hare Raising;* purchased at an embarrassing price one afternoon after she and Megan had consumed an experimental plate of hash brownies. The non-refundable sale meant it would forever be displayed…without explanation. It was art and she was sticking to it.

"I never tire of these beamed ceilings," said Nathalie as she stepped inside into the foyer.

"I wouldn't know what those are," sighed Megan.

"Oh here we go."

"Yeah," injected Megan. "I think you're gonna get along just great with this thief since you are stealing this two bed, two bath for two thousand a month from that sweet old couple and I'm getting squeezed for twenty-one hundred for a hole-in-the-wall studio that has a view of Central Park three blocks away but only if you haul a kitchen stool over to the window and stand up on it on your tip-toes, then you can see the top of a tree."

"You did that all in one breath this time."

"I've been practicing." Megan plopped herself in a chair. "You still have no remorse."

"None whatsoever. Beer, wine or tea?"

"Beer, I love my fat ass."

"You've never apologized for getting me to buy Alice," Nathalie said pointing at the sculpture and handing Megan a Blue Moon.

"And why should I when it fills out that space so well."

Nathalie plunked herself down on her couch and opened her own Blue Moon.

"I really gotta figure out this guy."

Both women quietly sipped their beer. They've been trying to figure out men for years.

"So he steals a little. You can change him," offered Megan. "Where does he live?

"He has a villa in the South of France."

"Really?" That sounded awfully nice to Megan. "If you marry this man, you could be set for life. I could come visit."

Nathalie sipped her beer. She wrestled with saying what she was thinking. Then what the hell, she knew it would spurt out of her sometime, at least now they were not in public.

"I think my mother had an affair with Eli Cross in Paris, when she was there with my father in '99.

"Holy shit..." Megan stared at Nathalie to see if she was serious. Nathalie's lost look told Megan she was very serious. Megan waited for Nathalie to gather her thoughts.

"When my parents came back from that trip, they separated for a year. Maybe because of Cross...and yet my father liked this guy."

"That takes a lot of charm."

Nathalie drilled Megan with a pissed-off glare.

"I'm just sayin'," Megan shrugged, totally at a loss.

Nathalie moved to her window...maybe there was an answer out there somewhere.

"I need to know more about Eli Cross before I know what to do."

"Well, then…wear that blue dress with the slit up the side."

Megan's one-track solution didn't sound overly professional to Nathalie. She sipped her beer and stared out the window hoping some fully formed plan might appear in the cloud patterns. Instead her eyes were drawn down to the street eight floors below. A chill ran up her spine. Marty Lefkowitz sat on his Blackhawk motorcycle at the curb smoking a cigarette. He brazenly looked up directly at Nathalie's window and blew out a trail of smoke.

This case had now gotten too close to home.

CHAPTER EIGHT

Mysteries abound where most we seek for answers.

Ray Bradbury

Nathalie's parents' house in Jackson Heights was mostly dark when Nathalie turned the front door lock with her own key and entered the foyer where the lights were off.

The living room was lit with candles and sound emanated from the stereo system in the sexy and smooth stylings of Gilbert Becaud singing "Et Maintenant." Nathalie listened. There were no other sounds.

"Mom... It's me."

No answer. She cautiously peered down the hall and saw a dim light coming from the master bedroom. She worked her way along the wall toward the bedroom, her breathing edgy, frightened about what she might find; she drew her Sig Sauer out of her purse. Suppose Eli Cross had snuck in to see her mom…and pick up the affair! Following her training, she pointed the gun into the room first, aimed directly at…a sexy dress!

A quick glance showed her no one was in the room. The dress was laid out on the bed next to a pair of black silk stockings. On the nightstand, a package of condoms. Nathalie moved toward the condoms, transfixed on them, until Odile suddenly came out of the bathroom in black lace panties with garter belt and a black lace bra!

"Mon Dieu," her mother cried out!

Nathalie gasped and spun toward her mother, lowering her gun.

"Sorry, Mom. I called out and didn't hear anything so, I…"

"It's okay, Nathalie, I just didn't hear you." Odile smiled about the music wafting in from the living room. "Gilbert Becaud can fill a room, can't he?" She noticed the gun as she sat on the edge of her bed. "Did you think I was in danger?"

Odile pulled the stockings up her legs and clasped them with the garters. Definitely old school, but with legs like hers, any man would enroll.

"That's quite an outfit." Nathalie did not mean it as a complement.

"So I've been told. But then you are not here to advise me on my wardrobe, are you?"

"No... I have to ask you something."

She watched her mother dressing and was seeing her for the first time as a sexual being.

"This is not easy for you, is it?"

"You're my mother."

"And I am a woman. Your father was comfortable with that. If he was still here, I would be with him."

"I used to believe that, but I see you doing things I didn't expect and..."

"And you wonder how well you know your mother."

Odile snapped the last garter and looked at her daughter. She was completely at ease until…

"Did you have an affair with Eli Cross in Paris the summer of 99?" Nathalie surprised herself with her demanding tone.

Odile slipped into her dress, without responding, then...

"You feel this from reading your father's files?"

"I don't know what to feel."

Odile finished her make-up in the mirror, judging how much to reveal to her daughter.

"Even parents need some privacy."

"I need to know about him."

"Eli Cross…he may not be knowable."

"But you were with him," Nathalie pressed on not relenting.

Odile looked at her daughter, choosing her words carefully.

"Nathalie, there are things that you may not be able to understand."

"You're not going to tell me." Nathalie knew her mother and her evasive French ways.

Odile remained silent.

Nathalie's feelings swirled. She grew unsteady. She looked at a framed photo of her parents displayed on the vanity. She couldn't take her eyes off it, and then in frustration she glanced over at the condom package on the nightstand by the bed. Nathalie set her jaw and strode defiantly to the bedroom door.

"I'll leave you to your... evening."

She stopped at the door.

"I had dinner with him last night," Nathalie said not facing her mother, but then turned and registered the look of shock on Odile's face. She then administered the coup de grace.

"I'm meeting him again."

And with that she was gone.

"Nathalie..." Odile fought a sudden rush of tears that filled her eyes.

ℂ

A hallway vending machine got whacked with a cane and a Snickers candy bar dropped down into the receiving ledge. Ian Seeger bent over and grabbed it, but before he could stand up, he got a photo shoved in front of his face. The photo was a police surveillance shot of Nathalie dancing with Eli Cross in the Rainbow Room. Ian stood up to face Lieutenant Donelli.

"He's settin' her up. I don't know what, but he'll ask her to do something with him—to trust him."

"She can handle herself," said Ian as he broke open his candy bar. He pushed past Donelli brushing aside the photo, none too pleased that it had been jammed in his face.

"Really? I must've missed her last MMA match," said Donelli.

Ian hobbled briskly with his cane through the City Desk Bullpen of The New York Times as Donelli followed him back to his desk. Ian sat down ignoring the detective, but Donelli wasn't going anywhere.

"What do you expect me to do?" said Ian as he gathered a pile of notes and tried to turn his attention back to the article-in-progress on his computer. He knew full well that Donelli wanted him to get his sister to back off. She had stepped on his dick in the Eli Cross case.

Because Ian worked the crime beat for The Times, and was his father's son, too many shields on the force thought they could count on him to do them favors.

"You know I read your last novel," said Donelli.

"You were the one. Never would've guessed."

"Yeah bright boy, it didn't catch on, but you know your shit," said Donelli with respect. "You know damn well how this goes down. This guy works all the angles. Whatever it takes not to get caught."

Donelli then laid out several surveillance photos of Eli Cross at an outdoor shooting range. His targets were not bullseyes. They were all silhouettes of people. Based on the bullet pattern hits—head and heart—Cross was an excellent shot.

"He cut a deal with the French government," said Donelli. "As long as he's not stealing the masterpieces of France, they look the other way."

"Does he have some arrangement here?

"Someone's greased the wheels for him. You don't get away with shit for this long without bein' connected."

"He told Nathalie he's gone straight."

"Yeah…" Donelli waited for Ian add it up.

"But why would you do that if you're protected?" Ian didn't like where this might be headed.

"That's a faint up the middle to set up an end run," Donelli said.

"For what purpose?" Ian did know his shit and Donelli had his attention.

"Cartier's jewelry bash of the decade is goin' down next weekend in the Hamptons. The international jet set will be there in full glitter."

"Cross knows you're watching him," said Ian.

"Damn right he does. That's what he wants. He'll hit that party just to take the jewels out right under my nose. He might take your sister out with 'em, if she's in the way."

Ian knew that Nathalie plowed ahead hell bent on recovering the jewels that had been taken out right under her nose at the Waldorf. She was self-confident enough—or arrogant and pig-headed enough—to think she could stop Cross the next time. Nathalie always told him that she knew what she was doing. This time he wondered how much was bravado.

He felt that true knowledge came from experience, and after having read his father's files, he knew that Nathalie had never experienced someone like Eli Cross. The underlying problem he faced was that Nathalie didn't like taking his lead when he told her something; he was the kid brother. So, he knew he would now have to add *checking out Cross* to his list. Maybe his dad couldn't nail him or didn't want to, maybe this fell to the son.

"I gotta get this in," said Ian as he pounded away at the computer keys again.

"Yeah, you don't have to listen to me," replied Donelli. "I'll still buy your next book. The one about a murdered sister. Maybe that'll sell well. A real heart-tugger."

Ian didn't react. He was not going to give the prick the satisfaction. He knew all too well that Donelli took great pride in his ability to irritate people and used it to maintain his edge. He knew his father thought Donelli was a first-rate cop but only a second-rate prick because he lacked wit. Ian simply focused on his computer and started typing, and sure enough, Donelli turned and left.

The only problem now, he thought, was how to keep his sister from getting killed.

CHAPTER NINE

If you obey all the rules, you miss all the fun.

Katharine Hepburn

In the desired Beekman area of Manhattan, where Irving Berlin once resided, The Baronfeld Museum was an elegant mansion that handled the elite in art. Private collections lent their priceless treasures to The Baronfeld for the acknowledged prestige. Only a limited number of patrons were admitted at any one time and reservations were difficult to acquire as the demand was quite high and the qualifying entrance requirements were stringent. To be seen at The Baronfeld was paramount for an art world traveler. Yet the public at large scarcely knew of its existence. There was no advertising, no promotion; it was a destination which was simply known if art was of serious interest. Perhaps its most unique trait was that through the years, The Baronfeld Museum resided in different countries on different continents; changing locations whenever the owners became restless.

The Baronfeld family was notoriously private; their whereabouts on any given day were closely guarded secrets. Even the death of a family member might not be announced for years. The living members utilized an assortment of legal aliases that were changed to maintain privacy. The term *more money than God* clearly applied. The family name did not appear on any of the vast business holdings in their international financial web save one…the museum.

The mansion was a new construction that took the place of three multi-million dollar townhouses which had simply been removed to create the space desired for the exhibits. A casual passerby saw no sign and would merely assume it was a wealthy residence.

But the Baronfelds were eccentric and clever and built a stunning work of art on the inside. The design and construction were modeled after the famed Isabella Stewart Gardner Museum in Boston which was fairly plain on the outside but grandeur in the style of a Renaissance Venetian palace on the inside, multi-leveled with an open-air garden courtyard in the center. It didn't bother the multibillionaire Baronfeld family that the Boston museum had been the sight of the biggest art heist in history in March of 1990 with 13 pieces stolen at a value of $500 million and empty frames left on the walls.

Eli Cross had not been in Boston that March night. It was one theft not attributed to him.

This late August afternoon, Eli Cross and Nathalie Seeger both came from different directions; Nathalie from the west and Cross from the East River, two opponents closing in on each other.

As he walked toward her, Nathalie recalled many a scene from classic westerns as the lawman and the outlaw strode down the dusty street of Dodge City or Tombstone toward each other with a six-iron strung on their hips for the final showdown.

She couldn't help smiling though she knew this was deadly serious. This was her father's nemesis, or his friend, or maybe both. And what was he to her mother? And more so, what had he done to their marriage? Yeah, this was deadly serious.

It was exactly three o'clock.

"Glad you decided to meet me."

"And right on time," said Nathalie.

"Well done."

"You knew of course that I would probably have to look up the museum, since I had never heard of it—most people haven't—and that there was no listing because that's the way they want it; to say nothing of the fact that it moves around the world from year to year because the Baronfeld family is…quirky…and has way too much money."

Nathalie recognized that Cross had been keenly observing her while she rambled on. Was he assessing her as an opponent or even worse…as a woman? At least she sensed the hint of a smile. Why did this feel so personal to her? Was he that good? She told herself that she had not been smitten at the Rainbow Room. No, she clearly told herself that she had been put on guard, that's what she had felt. Then why was she was pissed that she had to remind herself that this was not a date. This was business.

Clear your head she could hear her father say.

She knew the real reason the *thought of a date* pissed her off. She felt her mother was seduced by him and that affair almost wrecked her parents' marriage. That disgusted her. The fact that she had to remind herself that this was not a date—even for a fleeting nanosecond—really disgusted her.

This man standing before her had a way about him that was almost impenetrable. Yet, he was so natural and relaxed. Well, she was a Seeger, and she knew how to relax if that was what it took to nail this bastard. She would *not be fooled again.*

"I trusted you would find it." Cross nodded his approval of her detective prowess. There was something else that he sensed in her; it was the same feeling he had when they were in the Rainbow Room. If it was true, if he could trust that feeling, he didn't know how to handle it yet. It was the illusive *something* that he never thought he would ever encounter. He knew there was more work to be done.

Nathalie felt back in stride. "I have a friend at MoMA and she…"

"Yes, friends are very useful. Was she impressed that you would have a reservation?"

"Yes, very, and a little jealous."

"Good, then she knows her art."

Cross gestured for them to head inside. On their way to the front entrance, Cross noticed two security guards sneaking a smoke outside a side door. Nathalie caught his observation but purposely made no mention of it.

He pressed the entrance buzzer and waited. Nathalie was alert but professionally relaxed.

The door opened.

He presented his reservation which was on his cell phone screen.

They were ushered inside. It was surprisingly simple to her.

As they strolled down a corridor between exhibits, Nathalie knew the trust game was in motion. Cross had been speaking about an artist since they entered the first hall. Nathalie only half-heard him as she contemplated why she was really here. She promised herself she would be alert to any slips in his demeanor which might give her a clue as to his true nature. There was no denying—if she were completely honest—that beneath the surface there was a sexual tension.

Listen, she told herself, listen to what he was saying. Stop drifting with mental conjectures and disturbing physical sensations.

Cross paused in what he was saying. He could tell her thoughts were elsewhere. "Did you have a thought on that?"

"On what?"

"What I was saying."

"No…no, I was just listening. Go on," Nathalie said, recovering quickly. She didn't want to get tripped up like that again.

He looked at her for a brief moment which he sensed made her uncomfortable. However brief, it was a calculating moment. The sum of it was that she could be formidable.

"So…for reasons which remain unknown, he didn't paint again until 1915. It wasn't the same. But his early works were… well, you saw them. The Baronfeld usually contains art that has never graced the inside of any other museum. These are private collections. Very private."

"Did you ever want to be an artist?"

"I've had my artistic moments. The French Ministry of Culture awarded me a "Chevalier dans l'order des Arts et des Lettres" for contributions to the arts of France."

She wanted to climb into the world she saw in his eyes…but she was not so swept away by that feeling that she missed him *eyeing* the security cameras. He calculated as he spoke.

"I remember the first moment looking at a masterpiece; how it felt. I imagined the artist standing before his work. The passion that flowed through him."

"Or her," Nathalie interjected.

"Yes…or her. I wanted every waking day to feel like that."

Nathalie sensed in that an element of truth for him. But what was art for him? Was theft something he had raised to an elegant art? Was that how he created his masterpieces?

An exhibit room focused on a presentation of ancient art; a protective glass case commanded the center of the room. Underneath the protective glass a rare manuscript of verse lay open with brittle leather bindings. The pages were a slightly wrinkled and yellowed parchment, once fine vellum. The glass casing suddenly reflected the images of Nathalie and Cross looking down at the open parchment page.

"A four hundred and eighty year old manuscript written in Old French," said Cross, "the author was a French monk escaping persecution."

As Nathalie gazed at the calligraphy of the ancient script in Old French, Cross glanced again at the security cameras. Nathalie noticed but didn't let on as she read the manuscript.

"Old French is…different," Nathalie realized. "What does it mean?"

"It is personal. Close your eyes. I'll translate."

Of course, she thought, he would be well-versed in understanding a language not spoken since the sixteenth century. Who wouldn't be? He lived in France, but was he French? Probably not, but maybe so, yet there were no clues that resonated. His talents and accomplishments and most especially his unknowability were irksome. Staring at him gave no further hints.

"You really must close your eyes to fully appreciate it," insisted Cross.

"Is this where I discover how good a pickpocket you are?"

"Close your eyes," he said, ignoring her jab.

He waited until she complied. In the brief silence, she opened her eyes to peek. He caught her looking and she slammed her lids shut again in guilt. Cross watched her face scrunch up from the forced effort and for a moment he studied his guest, his adversary or perhaps his partner or simply an asset. A sliver of a smile slid across his lips. He began translating.

"My love bringeth a naked heart that crieth twice, upon first sight, and from whispers of death's delight."

He waited for her to feel the words. Nathalie opened her eyes.

"What did you see?"

"A beach," said Nathalie. "Cape Cod. It was windy. Getting dark. Cold. He was leaving."

"That's what it means then—this moment—the feeling it forms. Read it again, it will be different."

Nathalie pointed to a section further down the page. "And what is this? Something about the goddess. Read that to me."

"The goddess," repeated Cross. He stared at her as if divining her soul, to know her true thoughts.

She could swim in his eyes; they radiated blue and green, a deep ocean, with his gaze a riptide dragging her focus to him. To keep her edge, she pointed once again to the manuscript.

"Yeah, the goddess—in the manuscript," she said to take his eyes off of her.

Cross turned his gaze back to the ancient page.

After a moment of reading over the words, he said "I'll phrase it in a manner more of our time," He gathered his thoughts. "The goddess is but for a moment, and yet, for all eternity. Chasing her is elusive for she is ever-present, though seems unattainable. Acquiring her is sweet surrender."

"And who or what is the goddess?" Nathalie asked. "Or do I have to close my eyes for that too?"

"Don't be so quick to discount the power of myth."

For a moment, ever so brief but ever so real, she felt he gave away a part of himself, a part that was true; he believed in *something*. It was meaningful to him and it was not something physical. Was there a soul in this tightly-wound man that responded to a whisper from the heart? If so, was it what secretly drove him perhaps in ways he himself didn't even recognize? If she could *know* or *feel* what this *something* was then that could reveal what his intentions really were and she would gain the advantage.

Cross moved on to a corridor of Renaissance painters. Nathalie needed to turn up the heat, to dig deeper.

"How do you catch a thief?"

"You must have patience," Cross said simply.

"Meaning no one is perfect, and sooner or later..."

"For every crime there is a moment," he said, "one moment that does not fit."

His words simple and precise, yet his tone and the lilt of his voice commanded her attention; it struck her as declarative yet also beckoning.

He stared at her with such clarity of intent. Had the gauntlet been thrown? Was that *moment* his myth, his grail, his goddess, she wondered?

"The perfect crime is to elude that moment," Nathalie said testing him.

"Yes, but we are only human."

"And all the more interesting."

There was a gleam in Eli's eye. This woman matched him step for step. He liked that.

Pressing him more, Nathalie said "There is a certain...passion to it." She hoped to provoke him, to get an involuntary reaction. Then she saw it; that little spark that raced across his eyes again. "How do you so easily give that up?"

His hesitation showed that he still wrestled with that. An Achilles heel perhaps.

But Nathalie clearly felt that he was not a man bent by fear, no if anything, he was a master of it; not willfully, but intelligently, a projection of confident knowing.

"Sugar Ray Robinson, the great welterweight and middleweight champion, decided to quit boxing when he realized he could see the openings." Cross stated this almost as if he was talking to himself, reminding himself.

"But that's when you want to strike," said Nathalie, "when you see the openings."

"Not for a champion," countered Cross. "For the great ones, your fist is there moving toward the opening before it appears; instinct knowing it will appear. If you're waiting to strike only when you see it, it's not reflex anymore, you're too late. Robinson knew he was thinking about it...and that was too slow. No longer instinctual movement. His moment had passed."

"So he retired, leaving that moment untested," Nathalie said. She saw the resolve in Eli's eye. "Think he ever regretted that?"

Cross paused, not responding, and then offered a challenge.

"You want a quick lesson in the thinking of a master thief?"

Nathalie nodded eager to cross swords with him.

"Hands on, no lecture. We'll steal a sculpture...then put it back."

How far to trust him? Nathalie nodded her acceptance. The game accelerated.

Marble masterpieces, sculptures from the Renaissance adorned another exhibit room. Renaissance paintings were displayed on the walls. Most of these pieces from wealthy private collections had yet to grace the halls of major public museums. In the center, one sculpture commanded attention. It was small in comparison to most sculptures of human figures.

As Nathalie and Cross approached the diminutive statue, several guests who had been admiring it moved on leaving them alone to gaze upon its form.

It was a man and woman entwined. It stood only a foot and a half tall and rested on a display pedestal which was an Ionic-style Roman column that was surrounded by only a waist-high Plexiglas barrier to keep the visitors back.

One could still get close enough to admire its artistry which made the stone appear to be life-like flesh because of its accuracy of muscle and veins on the man pressed against the softness of the woman. The blanched gray and translucent white color of the stone created shadow and light layering a sense of depth to the eye where their bodies flowed into each other and back again; their limbs both theirs yet shared, thus simultaneously distinct individuals and one, wrapped in each other's arms forever locked together in eternity.

An involuntary hushed intake of breath overcame Nathalie from the beauty and precision of the sculpture. Stunned into silence she was unable to look away. Cross was no less impressed even though he had seen it before.

"A recent acquisition," said Cross. "The Cellini Lovers. A newly discovered work of Benvenuto Cellini. Dated to 1570, the year before his death. Its marble taken from the same quarry used by Michelangelo. Ancient and timeless."

Nathalie was indeed quite taken by the exquisite form, surprising herself at how quickly her emotions responded. It was not an intellectual response from understanding sculpture, but the sudden stirring of the heart from the emotional power of image.

"Each flows into the other and back again...endless. La vérité éternelle," Nathalie added.

Cross clearly enjoyed her appreciation of the artist's vision.

"Beauty from the vision of a renowned rogue," said Cross taking pleasure from the use of the word *rogue*. "Benvenuto Cellini was no simple artist," he continued having captured her attention once again. "A goldsmith as well as a passionate sculptor. A most intriguing man, an adroit adventurer in the tempestuous intrigue of the world of the Medicis. A man impossible to simply label by category. Look at the faces of the man and the woman. Does it not capture the feeling of being…human?"

"Their lips so close, the kiss so imminent, and yet forever kept apart."

"Only in stone. In feeling, the kiss has already happened. That's its emotional impact. That's the power of art. The feeling is more accurate than the eye. The yearning for something true to last."

Nathalie knew he meant every word. It was in his eyes. This was a little piece of him to hang onto and see where it might lead. Perhaps possessing the greatness of art made him feel part of it, gave him the justification for stealing it along with a few sparkling baubles here and there.

Cross sat down on a bench against the wall and admired the sculpture from this short distance.

"The impact of its precision is still powerful even as you move away from it."

Nathalie joined him on the bench. "You're right," she said as she gazed back upon it. "So where did it come from, who owns it?"

"The Baronfeld family. They've stated it's their most prized possession."

"Wow, that's saying something. Most prized."

"Yes, quite something."

"So…" Nathalie let her inquiry linger uncompleted. "Is this the something we're going to steal in your lesson—temporarily that is?"

"Yes, it is."

He then pulled a thumb-sized cylinder from his pocket and also a small bottle of Chanel spray perfume. There was no attempt to hide them; in fact he wanted Nathalie to see them.

"Every well-dressed man should have one," he said as if this was explanation enough.

Nathalie referred to the thumb-sized cylinder. "I hope that's not lipstick."

Cross got down to the business at hand.

"Every masterpiece in every room—the sculptures, the paintings on the wall—are protected by state of the art security."

"They actually look quite vulnerable except for the little Plexiglas barriers so people can't easily reach in and touch them." Nathalie was not very impressed at this stage. "At the front entrance there were no metal detectors to pass through."

"That's right. The museum did not want to hassle wealthy patrons with the indignity of being inspected. Everyone is vetted before receiving their invitation. You are licensed to carry your firearm. They would know all this."

"In here, I don't see anything, except the cameras up there." She pointed toward the ceiling and the security camera that commanded a bird's-eye view of the exhibit room.

"Exactly how they want it. What you don't see are the tiny sensor beams one hundred times finer than a human hair protecting every work of art."

Nathalie looked carefully...and couldn't see anything.

"How do you know?"

"Research by Chanel."

Cross stood up, stepped forward and sprayed the perfume bottle. The mist dissipated into a wide spray as it floated toward the sculpture and briefly exposed a few beams.

"Break the flow of the beams even for a millisecond, the alarm goes off." Cross sat back down next to her. "So... how would you do this?"

"I don't know," she said, "but I like the smelling good part." Momentarily stumped, she turned her attention to the lipstick-sized cylinder. "Maybe redirect the beams."

"With mirrors?"

"Yeah, maybe mirrors." She quickly realized that he was setting her up to jump to foolish conclusions. "And, then...maybe…not."

"Keep it simple. That's key. Always. Simple. Less chance of getting caught."

"Okay, well…" Nathalie shrugged, then tossed off, "We could shut the alarm off, then reach in and take it."

"Yes, we could."

Nathalie realized that he was serious; she stared at the statue trying to figure it out.

"We can???"

Cross nodded.

"Okay, glad I figured it out."

She was of course totally lost and stared once more at the sculpture. Cross took this moment to drop his museum guide brochure on the floor. He casually leaned down to pick it up and unobtrusively rolled the small cylinder under the bench. He stood up and offered his now empty hand to Nathalie to stand up.

Cross led her out.

So deft was he that Nathalie was unaware of the cylinder no longer in his possession.

"What now?"

"We wait," said Cross, "for the descent of darkness."

ဆ

The fading sunlight stretched across the Renaissance sculpture exhibit room as the last few visitors exited. A guard soon followed and made a final check in the now empty room. The lights dimmed, the sun retreated further and soon the art was alone, a chalk-white ghost in the darkness and the silence.

Outside, twilight's golden hues, the sun's last gasp before darkness, had long faded into memory. There was only a sliver of moon on this night, so the black of night assumed full command of the area. Two figures sauntered through the growing pools of shadow and dark abyss along the sidewalk. Nathalie and Cross strolled along with no degree of urgency though the attempt of a major theft awaited them.

"You wanted to start at ten o'clock. How did you know that walking every neighborhood street would bring us back by ten—on the dot?"

"Research. Every detail matters."

"Did you actually walk this before bringing me here to the museum?"

"You wanted a lesson. There are many parts."

Cross had simply stated a basic element of *his art,* Nathalie thought.

It dawned on her that she was not this prepared about him—about knowing him—for there was so little that was committed to truth. There were boxes of files, circumstantial evidence, conjecture, but few hard and fast clues as to what to expect. She would have to trust her instincts, like Sugar Ray Robinson. She hoped her *moment* hadn't already passed.

During the walk, he had said very little, mostly about restaurants that he enjoyed. They were some of New York's finest so she knew he had good taste. That didn't seem to be very relevant to stealing priceless art from a museum unless he could always be counted on to celebrate right after with fine dining. It had occurred to her however that knowing your escape route options was a good excuse for casually and innocently strolling around the neighborhood.

The Baronfeld Museum at night was as inconspicuous as a famed museum as it was during the day. The only light was an elegant front entrance sconce in keeping with the neighborhood. A few select solar pathway lights were present for safety. Nothing ostentatious considering the enormous expense for its construction.

As Cross and Nathalie passed by the entrance, Cross glanced over to the side of the mansion and saw the same two guards outside the side door sneaking another smoke. The glow of their cigarettes and the curling smoke created a haunting specter of the danger that awaited them.

"Do you smoke?"

"No…" Nathalie was almost offended that he thought she would indulge in that. She didn't feel the occasional joint or two or three from her past was something to count.

"Good. Bad habit."

He guided her over to a sidewalk bench bathed in the low-level glow from solar pathway lamps. They were a hundred feet from the front walkway entrance of the museum. He sat down and she then joined him after looking carefully at her surroundings.

He checked his watch.

"Is this where we synchronize watches?" she said attempting to be casual. Inside she was twisting knots of tension and alertness because she had no idea what was next. The fact that she could be in danger had occurred to her…more than once.

Another realization shot another chill up her spine. Maybe he had no interest in catching *the imposter* he had told her about in the Rainbow Room. Maybe this *lesson* he was teaching her was the setup for his next theft—*The Cellini Lovers*. Maybe there was no imposter, but perhaps there was a *patsy*—her!

"A good theft requires preparation."

"Good, I'd like to be prepared. What're you considering?"

"Right now, New York traffic."

"So like for the getaway, right? Remember, we are putting this sculpture back, once we steal it, since this is just a lesson."

"No, we don't have to worry about traffic for our getaway."

Nathalie was well aware that he didn't acknowledge her statement about *putting it back*. But to really know him, she had to go along for the ride, and learn. She could just hear her father say: *That's a deadly lesson, kid.* She was definitely her father's daughter though. Her Sig was in her holster, clipped to her pants behind her jacket.

"I noticed there don't appear to be any security cameras covering the outside areas."

"That's right," said Cross. "Good eyes."

"Why is that?"

"It would seem that's how the Baronfeld family wanted it. That way they could state there would be no incursion into the neighbors' privacy from prying cameras. This is a neighborhood with extremely high expectations as to their serenity and identity security. Especially with the prices paid to live here."

"They're not concerned with break-ins then?"

"NYPD's on rapid response to this neighborhood. The outer doors are quite formidable as are the windows. Once inside, any tripping of the alarms would engage the lock-down."

"Lock-down—there was no indication on the doors, how do you—"

"The doors are all electronically wired to dead-lock, shutting everyone inside with no exit. And the guards are well-armed."

"Yeah, but the doors had none of the usual markings for a lock-down," Nathalie protested.

He noticed her consternation at not knowing this piece of information. It was something that someone in her end of insurance investigation would know.

"Don't worry, you would've figured that out with careful research. This new state of the art dead-lock system is virtually invisible. It's completely different from the universally employed system which is easier to spot and the one you're probably familiar with, the one that requires a government warning label. This was designed from a tech start-up in New Zealand. Easy to overlook."

"And you just happened to have been in New Zealand and learned about it."

"Something like that."

"So the Baronfeld got around the government label requirement."

"By the same way wealthy people and companies—

"Have their own rules," finished Nathalie, annoyed as always with this *bend* in the law.

Cross checked his watch again. He looked up and was pleased to see a black van rolling down the street toward them.

"Do we have accomplices?" Nathalie said seeing the van. Her body stiffened, ready for anything.

"Oh, yes, the best."

The driver pulled up right next to them. He got out and handed Cross a black cloth bag with a logo on it that Nathalie could not see. Cross handed the driver two Franklins. The driver nodded then left.

Cross said nothing. He simply held the black bag, with the logo facing away from Nathalie, and he smiled. A very becoming smile.

"Are deliveries part of every theft?" said Nathalie, remaining calm.

"The world is a global enterprise. Some just do things better."

Cross slowly reached into the black bag. Nathalie unobtrusively moved her right hand behind her back until she felt her Sig Sauer in its belt-clip holster. She was ready.

Cross then carefully withdrew two trays of sushi rolls and chopsticks.

"You're enjoying this, aren't you?" said Nathalie, releasing her grasp on the Sig. "Toying with the neophyte."

"There's no reason this lesson can't be enjoyable. There are many things I might call you. A neophyte would be inaccurate and a clear mistake on my part."

At the very least, she realized that everything he did seemed to be some level of a test; research on her was another way to think about it.

"And does this driver work with you?"

"Oh no, a simple text to Nobu Fifty Seven." Cross showed her the restaurant's logo on the bag. "I've been a very good customer. Remember, keep it simple."

Nathalie grabbed a piece of cut roll with her chopsticks. "And enjoy your work."

"That's not a crime. Wasabi?"

Nathalie waved off the wasabi. "So, a good thief prepares." She wanted to keep things on track professionally.

"Yes, and always has a distraction."

Cross took out his cell phone and opened an app. The glow from the screen lit their faces. Nathalie watched in between bites of the sushi roll as he pressed a button labeled: *ENGAGE*. He lifted a piece of the cut roll to his mouth and watched the screen as he ate.

In the sculpture exhibit room that housed *The Cellini Lovers* all was quiet until a soft metal scratching sound came from under the bench they had sat on earlier in the late afternoon. The thumb-sized cylinder that Cross had rolled under the bench cracked open, separated down the center line, and unfolded into a mini-helicopter drone with a fiber-optic nose-lens. It was not much bigger than a common moth.

The tiny blades rotated, built up speed to a whispered whirr, then rose off the floor and floated out from under the bench.

Outside on the sidewalk bench, Nathalie watched his cell phone screen as Cross pressed directional arrow keys with his thumb. The image from the nose-lens rose in the darkened room turning 360 degrees until *The Cellini Lovers* were in view.

The room was empty of security personnel.

"This next step might not be the most peaceful moment while we're eating."

He plucked another piece of cut-roll out of the tray with his chopsticks, doffed it toward her as a salute, dipped it into the soy sauce and wasabi mixture then placed it in his mouth. Savoring the flavors, he slid the directional arrows on the app screen.

Inside the sculpture room, the mini-helicopter drone flew closely past the sculptured lovers and in front of two paintings cutting through invisible beams! The alarm wailed!! Security lights flashed only onto the two paintings and Cellini statue whose beams had been broken!

Outside, Nathalie half-jumped off the bench in an aborted attempt not to flinch as the alarm blasted over the neighborhood, exceedingly loud.

Cross watched the two smoking guards as they tossed their cigarettes on the ground, whipped open the side door and raced inside. Cross watched carefully as the door closed.

"This really is best with wasabi," said Cross referring to the cut-roll.

The alarm noise was deafening. Cross paid no attention to it nor showed any interest in moving away from the bench. With cool but singular focus, he simply manipulated the app and the hovering image from the nose-lens rose higher up toward the ceiling.

Inside the sculpture room, the mini-helicopter rose to just below the ceiling's edge, flew over to the corner, descended and landed on top of a security camera in the upper right corner.

The two guards who had been smoking—security badges labeled Benny Nestor and Gilbert McHugh— rushed into the room with guns drawn!

The statue was fine, undisturbed. The paintings were fine, untouched. Nothing was out of place…except for the tiny object sitting atop the security camera near the ceiling. Gilbert checked the perimeter to see no one and nothing amiss.

Benny pointed a flat screen sensor tablet at the paintings and the Cellini sculpture. The beams appeared on the tablet screen as oscillating lines of blue energy fully operational. Neither one looked up at the security camera where the mini-helicopter drone now seemed part of the camera's structure.

Outside on the bench, Cross gathered their sushi trays and chopsticks and deposited them in the trash can. He folded up the cloth restaurant logo bag and slipped it in his jacket pocket. All this time the alarm was still wailing!

"What now?" Fascinated, Nathalie studied his calm demeanor and precise actions while the deafening noise had lights coming on in neighboring buildings. Her instinct would've been to quickly move to a more secure location.

"We have approximately three minutes to get to our next position before the police arrive."

He gestured for her to follow him. Deliberately, but without panic, he ushered her toward the closed side door where the guards had been smoking.

"They had to keep it unlocked—disengage the dead-lock connection—to sneak a smoke. They will not have thought to reconnect it when dashing in."

He grabbed the door handle to check. The door opened but instead of leading her inside, he closed it again, but not before adding a simple piece of duct tape over the strike plate.

He pointed to a dark outside alcove. He leaned close to her ear because the noise of the alarm filled the darkness around them.

"Will you join me? It's a small space, but..."

Nathalie turned her mouth to his ear. "This is simple?!"

"If you trust human behavior."

What the hell, she thought, and slipped in next to him in the darkness of the tiny alcove.

Off the main lobby inside The Baronfeld was the museum security station. A very nervous guard—badge name Ted Orndorf—stood glued to the security camera monitor of only the sculpture room! The alarm still wailed, the noise inside brutal!

In the sculpture room the alarm wailed and lights flashed!

"Anything?!" Benny yelled to Gilbert.

"Nothing!" shouted Gilbert.

Benny spoke into a small walkie talkie. "Shut it down. Re-arm it. Call it in as a false alarm."

Benny and Gilbert left the exhibit room and in a moment, the alarm shut off.

Merciful silence.

Ted worked the electronic security console and rearmed the system with one hand, punched the hotline button of the landline phone with the other and waited impatiently. Finally..."Yeah, yeah, hello, this is Orndorf at the Baronfeld—Ted, yeah, Ted—it's a false alarm. Send them back. We're okay here. I don't know, some system hiccup, but we're five-by-five. Yeah, roger that. Thanks."

Outside in the alcove, Cross and Nathalie stood face-to-face in the small, dark space.

An NYPD cruiser with lights flashing whipped into a turn at the end of the street and raced toward the museum, then suddenly slowed, the flashers shut off, and the cruiser rolled quietly around the far corner.

Nathalie let out a slow exhale uncomfortably aware that their lips were mere inches apart.

"Now what?"

"We wait."

"Just like this?"

His eyes never left hers as he nodded *yes,* his lips almost brushing hers.

"So, ahh," Nathalie struggled to gather her thoughts. "That little drone device, something you made?"

"No, bought it online. Simple, remember?"

Nathalie licked her lips nervously as they were almost touching his open mouth in the close quarters. "What's your most effective device?"

"Usually a smile," said Cross.

Nathalie noticed his eyes gave no hint of sarcasm and his tone was not flippant, but rather resonated with simple truth. Then he unleashed an enticing wave of energy in a smile that washed over her whole being and lit up their dark alcove. It was beautiful. It was 99% foolproof. Her intuition grimaced from the smile used as a silent stiletto, but her lips involuntarily smiled.

Benny and Gilbert briskly crossed the main lobby, passed through the inner courtyard and right past the outside side door, then eventually stepped into the museum security station where a still nervous Ted Orndorf looked up from the monitors.

"What the hell was that?!" demanded Ted.

"Nothin'. It's cool." Gilbert didn't feel he did anything wrong so things were cool to him.

"Half the neighborhood's awake now and not happy about it! That's not cool! Pissed-off rich people get you fired!"

"The paintings are fine, the stature's there, we're good," said Benny. "No one's getting fired."

"I almost crapped my pants," sighed Ted.

"Well that might get you fired," Benny quipped.

Gilbert hung a high-five to Benny and Ted flipped them both the bird.

In the very quiet, deep, but very narrow alcove, Cross and Nathalie remained pressed against each other in the tight space. The lack of space required a singular focus on composure.

"Warm enough?" Cross never took his eyes off of hers.

"You're like a large hot water bottle," then not able to help herself she added, "with a spout."

Eli's expression did not change. Nathalie felt positive that he secretly enjoyed this moment.

"We could get a room," he finally suggested.

She held his suggestive stare. Cross pulled out his cell phone.

"A room...might be nice," said Nathalie. "But we don't have the statue."

"Right you are. The lesson continues." Cross reengaged the mini-helicopter app.

In the now quiet and dark sculpture room, the mini-helicopter lifted off the top of the security camera and swiftly flew right past a *different statue* and a *different painting*!

The alarm wailed shattering the peace! Lights flashed again and this time only on that statue and that painting!

Benny and Gilbert raced back in with guns drawn again only to find the statue and painting untouched! They hustled to look down the corridors for any activity—nothing—no one!

"Something's wrong!" Gilbert yelled over the alarm.

"No shit, Sherlock!" Benny pointed to the beams. "The beams aren't workin' right!" He yanked his small walkie talkie off his weapons belt and yelled into it. "Shut the alarm off and disarm the beams. Something's screwed up."

The blasting alarm shut off bringing much needed quiet when its last echo faded out. A brief flash of streaked vertical lines of blue light burst next to each work of art around the room as all the beams turned off.

"This time they're stayin' off till you check it out," came Ted's voice over Benny's walkie talkie, "'cause if it goes off again, someone's gonna call up the mayor!"

Rushing through the main lobby and across the inner courtyard, Benny and Gilbert passed by the outside side door again.

"Gotta be a short in the system," Gilbert said, "let's check the main power panels."

The darkness of the outside alcove suddenly illumined with a green glow thrust into it as Cross looked at the luminescent dial of his black Navy SEAL watch.

"Now it gets interesting. They should be checking on the problem, so they probably won't be watching the monitors."

"Probably???" Nathalie sure as hell didn't like the sound of that.

"Yes—and that's the risk."

"And if they're watching?"

"It's good you didn't wear heels."

Not a comforting response either, Nathalie thought, but at least he opened the outside side door for her like a gentleman. Then again, she thought that could make her the first one to get shot. Her senses perched on high alert for this next stage of the lesson.

Nathalie and Cross hustled quietly through the main lobby, across the inner courtyard and slipped down the corridor. Cross paused, halting their progress. He motioned *to listen.*

They heard distant voices from the Museum Security Station... but no one rushed out, so Cross prodded Nathalie onward to *The Cellini Lovers* sculpture exhibit room and the now vulnerable works of art.

Cross sprayed a shot of Chanel perfume mist... no beams.

"I love that fragrance," he said. "You see, we can shut off the alarm..."

He simply stepped up to the Plexiglas barrier leaned over the top of it and removed the Cellini statue from its pedestal.

"And reach in and take it," said Nathalie clearly impressed. She couldn't help a little chuckle out loud. It really was that simple. "Now what?"

"Now we walk out the way we came in."

He proceeded to leave...with the statue cradled in his arm.

"Ah, Eli, not with the statue. Lesson's over. Now we just leave. Quickly, I'd suggest."

"Oh, yes, right. Well..."

He pulled a small, but deadly .25 caliber Baby Browning automatic from his jacket pocket. He turned the tables, altered the game. Nathalie reached for her Sig but stopped in mid-move as his eyes nailed her cold.

"You can leave your Sig-Sauer nine millimeter "short" in your belt clip." His gun leveled right at her heart. "The Browning is small but amazingly effective. And now we leave, quietly, with the statue."

Nathalie couldn't believe that he did this and that she fell for it so easily.

Cross forced Nathalie at gunpoint across the main lobby toward the exit.

"I thought we were trusting each other?" Was this really happening, she thought?

"We were. You did as I expected."

"Somehow I don't think you'll kill me if I call out."

Cross pressed the Baby Browning against the back of her head till it hurt!

"Tough bet to lose."

This guy played a mean game and Nathalie felt trapped and stupid. She needed more time to devise a way out of this. She knew she had to go along with his action right now until she regained her confidence and saw an opening or even better sensed an opening. She could call out, but he could easily shoot her and be gone before any guards would appear. The system remained shut down so there would be no dead-lock, no trapping him inside. He'd be a ghost in the night and she would be dead.

With the exit in sight, Cross suddenly veered them right into the Museum Security Station. Nathalie froze confused as hell as they faced the guards, who turned surprised as hell to see Cross holding a gun and the statue!

For a moment, no one moved. Nathalie prayed to God the guards didn't do anything stupid. This could turn into a blood bath in seconds. Then Nathalie saw it. The guards were not scared. They were not frightened at all. But they were seriously guilt-ridden; the pain of shame etched in their faces.

"Gentlemen," said Cross addressing the guards, "there are a few flaws in the security for the exhibit."

"The alarm wasn't working right," Benny quickly offered.

"Oh, it works fine." Cross then yanked the cigarette pack out of Benny's coat pocket. "They'll be a staff meeting first thing tomorrow—to make changes."

"Yes, sir, Mr. Cross," Benny acquiesced, totally embarrassed.

Cross handed the statue over to Gilbert who cradled it awkwardly like it was a baby.

"Should we call the police on her?" Gilbert wondered hesitantly.

"No...She's with me."

And she was...but she was pissed!

Outside the museum, the sliver of moon still offered little light. A cab waited by the curb with its lights on. Nathalie strode in a determined huff away from the front entrance.

"I suppose that cab is right on time too," she spit out.

"No, he's a little early," said Cross with a slight irritation, though not at Nathalie's tone but at the imprecision of the cab driver's timing.

Nathalie stopped at the curb by the cab and spun around to face Cross. "You used me!"

"You wanted the lesson. Never trust a true thief."

"They trust you to handle security—really—at The Baronfeld?!"

"Several wealthy art collectors who lend their masterpieces to museums do because I know how to think like a thief. The Baronfeld family also asked me to keep an eye on *The Cellini Lovers.*"

"I hope you enjoyed yourself."

Cross opened the door of the cab for her but she did not get in.

"The guy who's imitating my style is very good," stated Cross simply. "If we're going to catch this thief, you've got to learn how to play the game. His game."

The two combatants held unflinching stares. Gamesmanship.

Was she willing to play? Hell yes, she realized. She'd play this to the end. It was as if she suddenly embodied—heart and soul—her father's obsession with Cross. She needed to know who the hell he really was and how the hell to bring him down, even if it killed her!

"What if I had called out or tried to run?"

"I could see it in your eyes. You were running the odds. That gave me time to keep everything moving my way. Sorry about shoving the Browning against your head. That was assurance for me. You okay?"

"As if you really care."

Cross took a breath weighing whether to tell her. "You're a little too cool. You hold your cards tight. It's really a loose game."

"This the lecture part of the lesson?"

"Anger causes mistakes."

Cross gestured for her to get in the cab. Nathalie, still pissed, slipped into the back seat of the cab. To her surprise, Cross got in beside her and shut the door.

"What are you doing?!" Nathalie thought she was done with him for the night. "Cabbie, you don't move." She indignantly turned to Cross. "I don't need a lesson in getting home, besides you don't—"

"172 West 79th street," Cross said to the cabbie. "Go ahead."

The cabbie hit the accelerator.

To her dismay, Nathalie surrendered for the moment. What the hell was she supposed to do? Cross had just called out her address. He knew where she lived. What else about her did he know?

The cab ride back was spent in complete silence. No one spoke. Not even the cabbie. He thought it best not to intervene in what seemed to him to be a lover's quarrel. He had experienced plenty of them. The cab pulled up finally to the front entrance of Nathalie's building. She jerked open the door and got out only to be surprised that Cross got out with her.

"Oh no, you're not coming up," Nathalie snapped.

Cross held his hand up in a peace gesture. "No, no, that's not part of the lesson."

"Then get back in and leave," Nathalie insisted.

Cross reached back into the cab and handed the cabbie a fifty. But he shut the door and the cab pulled away leaving Cross facing a very determined Nathalie.

"I'm serious, you need to leave."

"You're here, safe and sound, apologies if needed. A gentleman always sees a lady home."

"And you're just gonna walk wherever now." Nathalie wasn't buying his gentlemanly routine.

"Yes, it's not far. Just across the street."

A chilled river of goosebumps raced along Nathalie's skin. It couldn't be, no not that. "What?" Nathalie hoped she hadn't heard him right.

"Yes, I'm staying at The Lucerne."

Her face looked as if she'd been pole-axed.

"The Lucerne," she barely managed to whisper.

"Yes, you can see my room from the street here. Tenth floor. Lovely view."

So he was staying at *her special hotel* and probably knew which condo she was renting on the eighth floor, could probably even see inside it if she had her curtains open. She knew in her gut that there was no way on God's green earth that this was a coincidence.

"How long," she pulled herself together. "How long have you been there?"

"Since I came into the city."

"The rooms there…"

"I have a deluxe King Suite."

"…are very nice."

Nathalie simply turned and walked toward the doorman who held the door open waiting for her. She stopped, her head spinning, too much to swallow too fast. She felt she was choking.

Well screw that she thought.

She spun around and strode right up to Cross who still stood there. She grabbed him by his coat jacket and pulled him into a heat seeking wet kiss that left him stunned. He had not seen that coming.

Without a word, she turned away dismissively and left him to wonder what burned beneath the surface.

As she passed her night doorman, Terrence, he gave her a wink, and she reacted with a triumphant little smirk across her lips. *Loose, I'll show you loose!* She had suited up. She could play this game. *He's all mine now, Dad. I'll get him for you.*

Those thoughts carried her to the elevator.

CHAPTER TEN

Ever notice how 'what the hell' is always the right answer.

Marilyn Monroe

Nathalie sat parked just down the street by the big oak tree she climbed when ten. She knew from this vantage point she could see when her mother would leave the house. Hopefully Odile would leave the other way which would be toward the more interesting shopping. She trusted that she knew her mother's habits well enough to not be seen by being tucked safely behind her childhood tree.

But trust was a tough gig and she wondered how much she could trust her own mother given what she had learned. It broke her heart that her mother could've deceived her father that way and with such a younger man. She also felt guilty about needing to sneak into her mother's house.

The proverbial yogurt then hit the fan because Odile came out from the driveway behind the house on a bicycle and rode right toward Nathalie and the childhood oak tree. Nathalie plastered herself down against the seat of the rental car and prayed her mother didn't look inside. There was no garage in her Upper West Side apartment which was one reason why she didn't own a car, so having a rental her mother wouldn't recognize might actually save her ass, hopefully, at this moment.

Nathalie had left the car window open for air and could hear her mother peddling and whistling, getting closer and closer. She always thought it very un-French that her mother whistled. Her father had taught her mother how to whistle explaining that the French female pout that her mother had perfected with her lips would lend itself well to good whistle form. Her mother was quite good at both. Nathalie winced as she recognized the tune she whistled. It was an enthusiastic version of "L'Orange" by Gilbert Becaud. Nathalie loved the song. The wincing came from the subject matter. It was about a thief. Was her mother excited that Cross might be back in her life? God, she really wanted to nail that bastard.

Her mother peddled right by her open car window. Nathalie escaped detection. She slowly raised her head and caught her mother in the side mirror turning the corner. Where was she going in that direction?! And why on a bicycle?! Nathalie had thought for sure she would've taken *Toody*, the 71 Volkswagen Beetle that her father had named after the other *Car 54* TV cop. He loved that bug; though a large man he found the bug easy to maneuver and fun to drive. Why hadn't she taken Toody?! Her mother loved that car as much as her father did.

This simple moment left Nathalie reeling. Did she know her mother at all anymore? It was a haunting feeling.

Now that her mother was gone and not suddenly cycling back, Nathalie gathered her thoughts and focused on why she was there acting like a spy—or thief—in her old neighborhood.

She started the rental car and rolled quietly down the street to her mother's house. It dawned on her that her stealth-like approach was unnaturally clandestine. She knew she was professional and smooth when on a case. Why did this feel so sloppy? She hoped none of the neighbors saw her and asked what she was up to and wanted to chat and catch up. *Oh Nathalie, how are you, what are you up to? Nothing much Mrs. Rinaldi, just gathering some file boxes on the international thief who fucked my mother and almost ruined my parents' marriage, and probably stole the jewels that have my career on the chopping block. How's Mr. Rinaldi, still dead?*

Sarcasm was not going to solve the mystery of Eli Cross. She knew that. No neighbors were present. She quickly went up the front walk, opened the front door, and went inside.

The file closet held all three *ELI CROSS* boxes which Ian had replaced when cleaning up after his *novel research* to quell their mother's suspicions. Nathalie planned on thoroughly dissecting the contents—memorizing if necessary—to learn all she needed to know to nail Cross and complete her father's *Muldooning* of him. Ready and eager, tackle the hard stuff first. Get at it. She hauled out the heaviest box, the one Ian said had bricks in it, and marched with it to the front door.

She looked out the small side panel of window panes that ran vertically next to the front door to see if the coast was clear. She gasped. Couldn't believe it! Ian had just parked his car out front and awkwardly stepped out on his bad leg with his cane. She didn't want to deal with her brother's inquisition and shuffled with the heavy box to the back door and exited.

Ian went to the front door and knocked. No answer. He took out his key and entered.

When Nathalie heard the front door shut, she scuttled out from the side of the house and moved as quickly as she could with the heavy box to her rental car. She wrestled with the key fob button and opened the door, then jammed the box into the front seat and climbed in behind it. She turned the engine over and pulled out quickly without squealing the tires.

Ian stood at the open closet door. One of the *ELI CROSS* boxes was missing. He called out because the closet door had been left open. "Mom? Nathalie?" No answer. He wagered it wasn't his mother who took it. If she had wanted to dispose of these files she would have done so soon after his father died. Still, he wasn't exactly sure why she had decided to keep them. She knew they were there. What purpose did they serve for her? Memories, perhaps? It was unsettling to think of his mother's entanglement with all of this.

So, if not his mother, then clearly Nathalie was digging into the man she felt was the best suspect for the jewel heist at the Waldorf. He knew his sister. She was going to push hard to prove herself to all the men she felt in competition with and to her father. They both were curious as hell as to how and why Cross held such a fascination for their father that appeared to be a strange combination of career obsession and friendship. The *friendship* part was the most baffling. How are you friends with the man you are seeking to arrest unless—it was hard to think it—unless you slipped over to his side?

Ian decided to take both boxes into his possession. They might provide some answers to the nagging questions and doubts, but more importantly it would force Nathalie to come to him. When she did, he would be able to confront her about her plans and see if her head was screwed on straight or if she was taking dangerous risks. Cross was a serious unknown. He had never been caught. How many people paid the ultimate price to keep it that way? His sister's life was on the line and he knew the clock was ticking. Cross had something planned soon.

ℰↄ

Several large blueprint plans were laid out on the King-sized bed in the Lucerne deluxe King Suite. One was for the grounds of an estate labeled: *Borelli*. Another set was for the Borelli mansion, guest houses, art studio and pool house. The plans for several floors of The Baronfeld Museum were also stacked on the bed. Cross looked them over slowly, carefully, with a running stop watch in his hand. He glanced from the Borelli plans and back to the Baronfeld. He clicked the stopwatch and marked the time on a small note pad. The timing he contemplated needed to mesh precisely. Everything depended on that.

The variable and the risk was Nathalie. He still wasn't sure. He knew more about her than she realized. It had all started with Nate and Odile. The two of them surprised him. The adversary cop and the wife. He had played them well, he thought. And then things had changed. The playing field shifted. Something he'd never forgotten; it had brought him inexorably to this moment.

The next level of his plan was clear now. He could lock it in. He reached for his cellphone, brought up a number and called it. "Tommy, file the flight plan for Zurich. Be prepared to re-route mid-air."

The voice on the other end responded. "Roger that. Good luck."

Cross clicked off and tossed the phone onto the bed. He poured himself a glass of chilled chardonnay and relaxed into a deep stuffed chair.

The memory of his father's voice was crystal clear. *Ellie, do you want to file the flight plan?* Ellie was his nickname at fourteen. His father pronounced it by stretching out the ending with a dramatic emphasis as if it were *Elleee* with heavier weight to the *eee* ending. His father said it with a definite French flair to the pronunciation. That made it cool to his teenage self. Made him feel special. Cross smiled at the memory.

The flight was from Rome to Paris. A family business trip that was to involve taking in the sites of Paris—especially the Louvre—for his mother and he and his younger brother, Charles. Young Ellie had a fascination with art and art history. A promised trip to the Louvre two years earlier had been scrapped due to revised business plans. This trip was to make good on that promise. It was also his first introduction to the Bombardier business jet. It was a Challenger 600 owned by his father's corporation and his dad knew how to fly it. For this trip his father would actually be the pilot along with the corporation's long-time co-pilot, Salvatore, who used to fly for Alitalia which really impressed Ellie.

He took another sip of wine and struggled to hang onto fleeting images of the luxurious inside cabin but they were thrust away by the images of rushing water, especially the sharp sound slapping the window. He didn't want his thought to go there. The torn and twisted metal, his mother's arms reaching out. A forced sip of wine brought his focus back. He slammed shut the memories. That long ago trip was why he was here.

His phone rang. He picked it up.

"Yeah? Okay."

He moved quickly to the large window overlooking 79th street. He looked down at Nathalie's building across the street. Nathalie hauled the heavy file box out of her rental car. Freddie, the day doorman, took it from her and placed it inside. She waved and nodded at Freddie and got back in the rental and pulled away.

"One of the file boxes? All right. Thanks, Mosey."

He hung up and stared at her building. He wondered how much Nate revealed in those files. He knew it would make for interesting reading.

ಬಲ

Odile set the groceries down on her kitchen counter. They had fit neatly into her canvas bags which by design fit neatly into the baskets that attached to the sides of the back tire of her bicycle. Riding the bike reminded her so much of her years in Paris. How many times had she left it parked outside of Les Deux Magots café. It was her *thing to do* as a young woman.

She would've preferred this day to have a Vespa. How long that would've lasted on New York's streets was anyone's guess. She had told Nate she would just chain it to something. His reply had been that it had better be a building because he knew of motorcycles stolen that had been chained to a big city mailbox. Both were gone when the rider returned.

Though she still chose to live in New York, mostly because of proximity to her children, the feel of France was always close at heart. Little things made the emotional connection for her. That was why the last grocery item she placed in the refrigerator was Bonne Maman Raspberry preserves made in France. She liked her jams cold. She liked supporting the family-owned French company. She liked being a French woman. It kept her open to adventures.

Marrying Nate Seeger was one. They had met in Paris and fell in love. Hard not to fall in love in Paris even if you lived there. Years later, they had almost come apart in Paris in '99. Every light casts a shadow so it would seem. *Je ne regrette rien.* Those words sung by Edith Piaf the French chanteuse were her mantra for quite some time. *I regret nothing.* It was how she coped. But deep down she knew that famous song was really a celebration for a new love, one that makes the past fade and fall away.

William Faulkner's words from *Requiem for a Nun* haunted her today: *The past is never dead. It's not even past.*

In '99 she was forty-two, and as Nate told her many times then, *a wow of a woman.* She had felt the power, the influence that gave her. She reveled in it. It was her right as a French woman.

Eli Cross was twenty-eight then, if he had told her the truth. His youth and vigor, sensual virility, and self-assured maturity were powerful elixirs. There was no doubt about that. His coup de grace was his style. He had a natural sophisticated class coupled with a razor sharp wit and a mind of the world. He was a magnificent male specimen.

Odile thought she knew herself then so well. But it was Cross who showed her otherwise.

He would be fifty now or at least soon to be. That could be a defining age for a man. A time when he felt an inescapable desire to test himself, to prove that he was the master of time and its inevitable erosion of skills. What form of that would he embrace and how would that involve Nathalie?

She found it ironic that she had been fourteen years older than Cross during that two week encounter in the city of light and lovers, and now Nathalie, at thirty six, would be fourteen years younger. She wondered how he might have changed, if at all. More distinguished most assuredly. Men like Cross aged that way, their allure deepening because of it.

What to tell Nathalie about a man she still did not truly know? What indeed to tell a daughter about something that would carry its own level of pain?

Her memories carried her into Nate's study and the closet holding his police case files. Much of what he knew of his old adversary was in those boxes. Odile had never looked in them, even after Nate's death. Afraid of what she might find? Perhaps. Mostly she didn't want to disturb her own memories of the man she thought she knew—of both men really.

She opened the door. The files were gone.

She knew Ian had been lying about researching a new novel. But now she was more worried about what their contents would reveal to Nathalie. She had no idea what Nate had collected or stated in those files. She had to take a slow deep breath. She felt she had been stripped naked, a haunting vulnerability. The past was not past. It was closing in.

CHAPTER ELEVEN

*As we acquire more knowledge, things do not become
more comprehensible, but more mysterious.*

Albert Schweitzer

The file box sat on the floor of Nathalie's apartment. Most of its contents lay out in separated piles. Nathalie ensconced in reading, but not the file content, sat cross-legged on the floor, a classical art history book opened across her lap. She sensed a pressing need—an intuition—to bone up on Benvenuto Cellini, the Italian sculptor. His newly discovered piece dubbed *The Cellini Lovers* was the one they had *stolen* as part of her embarrassing lesson into the mind of a master thief.

Cross, she noted, had been unusually taken with Cellini. Not just his talent, but his lifestyle. Would that open up any insight into this thief, her main antagonist? At this point, any rabbit trail might reveal…something.

Cellini was clearly a celebrated Renaissance sculptor famous in his own time. He enjoyed the privilege that brought to him. Cross was a clear lover of art as well as a connoisseur. All of which was advantageous knowledge in the pursuit of stealing art. So that connection was clear.

But Benvenuto, clever lad that he was, was also a goldsmith. Another level of craftsmanship applied to an element of wealth. Cross clearly was an accumulator of wealth. They were simpatico in that regard.

Cellini had a serious passion for his work and a talent that lifted him above many practitioners. This brought resentment from those in positions of influence in the world of politics and art. Even though this was the sixteenth century and his work and travels took him from Florence to Rome and to Paris, it was clear that human behavior had not changed that much in almost six hundred years. Cross, she knew, had an international reputation that annoyed the hell out of many authorities. His confidence and allure not only impressed wealthy patrons of art and movers among society's elite but surely elicited deep-seated pangs of envy and jealousy, possibly even revenge.

Cellini was a shameless adventurer with experiences in royal courts, prisons, houses of prostitution and many other levels of Italian society. He was part of the playground of Michelangelo and the Medicis and he seemed to revel in his dalliances in that dramatic arena. One had to be clever as well as talented to survive. Cross dallied in many playgrounds, like Yankee Stadium, and wealthy locales from Monaco to Bel Air to Singapore, as well as tap dancing around the outstretched arms of New Scotland Yard, Interpol and the NYPD.

It was said of Cellini that he possessed an irrepressible sense of humor. Even in her father's notes, Nathalie saw an expression of the absurd in life and a healthy application of irony in how Cross conducted himself. Many times, she felt that Cross was chuckling inside with great delight with what he had just *pulled off.* Clearly their *escapade* and her *lesson* at The Baronfeld were laced with humor if not a barrel of laughs for him.

Benvenuto was a known braggart. That quality Cross did not express. His confidence was so secure in its expression it might be interpreted as bragging, but Eli was too classy in how he presented himself to be branded with that slur.

One thing about Cellini's past did give Nathalie pause. Benvenuto Cellini was also a murderer. It would be helpful to know if that was part of Eli Cross's repertoire and something that drew him to Cellini.

The high-powered binocular brought the image of the cover of Benvenuto Cellini's autobiography into clear view when Nathalie turned the page of her art book to reveal a rendering of that tome.

A knowing smile parted the lips of Eli Cross. He stood a few feet back from his suite window at The Lucerne so that he could not be seen but he could see her with the binoculars. She was doing as he expected. She was working to obtain some information to get the drop on him, to be one step ahead. Like father, like daughter. He greatly appreciated that. He took pleasure in knowing that he would have to be in finest form to meet the challenge of *the moment* that lay ahead for him. A swan song assuredly required elegance.

He placed the binoculars down and returned to the suite's desk where the few disassembled parts of his Walther PPK were awaiting his thorough cleaning routine. Here he enjoyed the pleasure of precision, the embrace of necessary details. The small .25 caliber Browning he had used to keep Nathalie in line at The Baronfeld was not a weapon that he actually used in the field of operation. That Browning was in fact simply a prop, a fake; it would not shoot. He felt it would've been unnecessarily crass to have pointed that out to her that night.

The Walther PPK however was the real deal. Tried and true and trusted. Through the years it had contributed to many successes when in a tight squeeze. The irony of the PPK designation was not lost on him. The German words *Polizei Pistole Kriminal* translated to Police Pistol Criminal. The *Kriminal* was actually in reference to the Crime Investigation Office; it was designated a detective's pistol. He was relying on the same weapon as those hunting him. An even playing field suited his sense of fair play in the battle of wits.

The Walther PPK had been a longtime trusted member of his stable of tools. The fact that this elegant gun became the preferred weapon of Ian Fleming's fictional secret agent, James Bond, amused him no end. But literary and cinematic fame were not the reason he carried the Walther PPK. Like the foundation for his philosophy of the heist, it was a brilliantly simple weapon of precisely the right size and weight, accurate and easy to use and maintain.

The use of a weapon was a last resort decision, but an option he wanted in his arsenal of choices. Its size and weight made it ideal for concealed carry in a pocket if necessary. The safety features were first-rate, easily preventing accidental discharge, but allowing a round to rest safely in the chamber for immediate access.

He appreciated that the first pull of the trigger was smooth but hard. It required a clear commitment. A light touch, accidental or hesitant, would not release the hammer. He knew when it came to firing with intent he would be fully committed; there would be no hesitation.

This particular Walther PPK has a deeply personal connection to him. As he finished the cleaning process and reassembled the weapon, memory transported him back to the first time as it always did. Reliving this moment was a cherished ritual. The gun was an unexpected gift. As a fifteen year old, it wasn't even on his radar. Prior to that moment, he had had no interest in guns. He was told for his new life it would be a faithful companion: *For when you must insist on surviving.* Those were the words he took to heart.

Vano Lakatos, the rugged itinerant Romani gypsy who placed it in his hands taught him many new lessons. Some to give young Eli the will to go on, a reason to live again. Some given in haste, learned while on the run. It was Vano's family who pulled his half-dead body from the water of a sandy cove outside of St. Tropez where he had washed up during the night. Vano's wife, Lavinia, applied poultices of herbs and clay to bacteria infested wounds and gave him eyedroppers of herbal tinctures under his tongue. Vadoma, their twelve year old daughter, fed him by dribbling spoonfuls of broth into his mouth when he could swallow. He slipped in and out of a coma state during much of that time. They did not abandon him. They became a sacred part of his new life.

He pulled the trigger guard open and rested its notched end against the flat underside of the frame then slid the slide on and into position. He slipped in a fully loaded mag, clicked it into place and ratcheted the slide back chambering a round. The safety was locked into position preventing firing. He never tired of admiring the craftsmanship and beauty of its construction—the elegance—and the wording on the side: *Made in France* with a *Manurhin logo* above them made it special.

This model was definitely the German Walther PPK with a slide made in Germany, but the rest of the gun was made in France. It came from the French firm *Manufacture de Machines du Haut-Rhin* located in the Alsace region of France near the German border and the Rhine river. The firm was known in the trade as *Manurhin* for short. They had been licensed by Walther to manufacture the PPK during the years after World War II when Germany was prohibited from manufacturing firearms.

Eli's PPK was from 1984, while they still manufactured the PPK officially for Walther and the year Eli turned fifteen. It was assembled in St. Etienne arsenal and stamped *Made in France.* To have this particular gun made sense to him for *Eli Cross* was made in France.

Nathalie kept her drapes open on purpose. She knew Cross could see her if he was looking. A good pair of binoculars would work nicely she thought. She gave fleeting consideration to undoing an extra button or two on her blouse to fluster his thinking. Sometimes men's brains could be fogged up fairly easily. She wondered if he was susceptible to that or buttoned up too tight.

He had to be aware that her father would have kept files on him. She had propped up the lid against one of her chairs so the large black handwritten letters *ELI CROSS* could be seen with binoculars or a scope. If a scope, was it part of an assassin's rifle? No, she thought that wouldn't be his style—too Hollywood—which was why she thought he'd never carry a Walther PPK; he wasn't playing James Bond.

She shuffled through surveillance photos. *Damn, he sure had the look to play Bond if ever did want to go Hollywood.* She chuckled to herself because she realized that certain things—akin to an undone button or two—could make a woman weak in the knees. *Stay sharp.* She could hear her father's voice bringing her back in line. If her father got taken in by Cross, she owed her dad to not let herself get trapped or tripped up in any way. His stunt at The Baronfeld and how easily she fell for it was proof enough to her to sharpen her claws.

Cross was very smooth in a manner so natural and enticing that one could easily forget the wolf lurking inside. She was sure that many a woman lay on their back in his arms without any recollection how they got there. No Rohypnol, just pure, intoxicating male charm.

Sadly she wondered how her mother could've been one of them.

Bulletin boards on easels stood angled in her apartment living room as a visual web of intrigue if Cross peered in from across the street. She had purposely set them up so that only a few tempting pages from the files could be seen; enough to ignite the curiosity and also generate frustration at not being able to see more. She tacked a large photo of Cross up in a space designed to be viewable from the window. Areas that could not be seen from outside were already filled with computer printouts, notes, more photos, and pages from Nate Seeger's files. They were all about Cross.

Nathalie stuck a photo of her father next to a blow-up of her father's edge notes: *I KNEW HIM TOO WELL. MAYBE HE WANTED ME TO. NO REGRETS.* Nathalie stood back and stared at the crowded board. She spoke out loud to help her zero in and focus and to not feel so alone.

"Okay, Dad, let's work the case. What are you telling me?"

She wanted to will the puzzle pieces of all the notes together.

"*I knew him too well*. Yeah…I think I got a taste of that one at The Baronfeld. I'm gonna get him, Daddy. I'm gonna learn everything I need to know. He's gonna get Muldooned."

She shifted her gaze to two other bulletin boards hoping some trail of evidence bread crumbs would guide her. But too many large gaps left open-ended questions. One section had the police computer printout and photo of JAKE KRACAUER, while another section had the printout photo of MARTY LEFKOWITZ.

"I don't know you guys at all. Not real smart, Seeger."

She knew at this level her suspects played for keeps and what she didn't know could prove lethal. Her father had clearly taught her to *know the enemy*. The level of *unknowability* about Cross seemed to have tripped up her father or possibly corrupted his motives which was a rock she did not want to overturn if she didn't have to. She wanted to cherish the memories and the feeling of being his daughter and not let uncovered truth darken that view or sully those emotions.

If Kracauer or Lefkowitz or both were responsible for the Waldorf jewelry heist, then maybe Cross could remain a fascinating enigma and Nate Seeger remain her idolized father. But the truth has a nasty habit of being relentless. Tough to outrun it or evade it forever. At least she should eliminate the dead ends or the inconsequential. Somehow, in some way, there was a connection to Cross. So…who were these other guys? How did they think? What was their angle and most importantly what was their most exploitable weakness?

She stared at the photo of Marty Lefkowitz. His annoying features hadn't improved.

"What are you all about, Buddy, and what were you doing at the Rainbow Room? Are you working with Cross? And why are you such a nasty-faced son of a bitch? I sure as hell don't like you and I want to know why."

𝔰𝔬

The pitons and carabiners—specific mountain climbing equipment— got shoved aside in frustration. His rough, scarred hands rummaged through one bin after another in an Army/Navy surplus store in Midtown Manhattan. He had already gathered a chosen few. Whatever he was looking for had to be just right. Not the case for his attire; old jeans and a ratty sweatshirt hung just shy of a fashion felony. Underneath the clothes, a taut body capable of receiving and delivering punishment waited. The cold soulless set to his eyes implied he would enjoy both.

Not someone to meet on a first date thought Nathalie. She positioned herself behind a rack of old Army field jackets so she could monitor his activities but still appear as if shopping. To her chagrin, but not surprise, the aggressive squint to his eyes suggested barely restrained violence which had not changed at all from the police photo or the night at The Rainbow Room or the jogging path in Central Park; clearly why she didn't like Marty Lefkowitz.

Encountering violence in the practice of her profession always hovered as a possibility. Her father had told her that many a police officer spent an entire career without ever pulling their weapon in the line of duty. So as an independent investigator seeking resolution for cases—mostly insurance—she took things right to the edge to get closure but without being a thrill seeker. With her skill set, she excelled in tracking down hard-to-find people. Finding Lefkowitz had been child's play. Some of that she knew was her talent; what stuck in her gut was the feeling that he wanted it to be easy.

Nathalie chose this Army/Navy surplus store as the connecting point. In a store with ex-military as fellow shoppers, she reasoned she might be physically safe. She stepped from behind the jacket rack to confront him.

"Not many mountains in Manhattan," Nathalie said.

Lefkowitz snapped his head up from his search. He registered no surprise seeing her. His expression lashed at her like: *I've already had breakfast otherwise I'd eat your face.*

Nathalie simply stared at him across a table piled with coiled nylon cords.

"This stuff's good for a thief," she remarked. "Repel down from the roof...or whatever."

Her eyes riveted to him, challenging but assured. His eyes flickered like a ticking bomb, debating whether to blow-up now, obliterate her on the spot or savor the experience later.

"You're very pretty. Helluva shame."

He swept a coil of black nylon cord right up to her face.

"You like this? Nice color. Think it would hold you?"

"I like the green." Nathalie felt a sudden chill. This might be the first truly warped psychopath she had ever encountered; someone permanently unhinged. She kept her composure…barely.

Lefkowitz dropped the black cord and swept up the green.

"I'm glad," he said with a withering smile, "I'll take it," then whispered, "Don't get too close."

He pursed his lips in a horrific impression of Mick Jagger and spun away. He took the green cord and his small collection of pitons and carabiners and left Nathalie unsure of his sanity. She felt certain he had been one of those little boys who delighted in frying ants with a magnifying glass. A wave of sympathy washed through her for a moment contemplating whether his anger and darkness were retaliation for all the abuse he may have suffered as a child. She would never know. She had to now deal with the adult. Whatever the life ingredients had been in the cauldron of his experience, they had forged a monster.

All she could think about right now was that she hoped to God he was operating independently in whatever he had planned and was not partnered with Cross. If Lefkowitz was behind the Waldorf jewelry heist, she would definitely need to keep her Sig Sauer with her at all times. The most dangerous people were those that were unstable. Like nitroglycerin, they could go off at any time. Keeping an eye on him would be a full-time job unto itself and she had two other key suspects to deal with. A woman's work was never done.

She also knew she was short on intelligence—the kind that's gathered. But she knew who had it. She started preparing for hearing the lecture.

℘

There was actually no place to sit.

Yes, there were chairs—two small ones at the little round dining table and two larger ripped and stuffed ones in the open living space—and there was a worn leather couch. But they were all covered with file papers, research for stories, interview transcripts, newspapers, magazines folded back to particular articles, even the odd East Village receipt for Chinese food delivery scattered here and there. A couple cartons of cashew chicken appeared to be decorative props, the chopsticks protruding from them like flags planted in conquest.

The papers spread around the wooden floors were arrayed in a hodgepodge of expression, more schizophrenic than a masterful Jackson Pollack, and less colorful. On closer inspection, the impenetrable barrier to crossing the room contained a twisting labyrinth with one exit point to the hall corridor.

In the back bedroom, the hope of respite was shallow as half of the bed had surrendered to the incursion of these piles; the other half's rumpled sheets were a half-assed attempt at being Switzerland and temporary neutrality. Despite the visual noise bordering on hoarder madness, the owner knew where everything was—an almost autistic grasp of memory—and he claimed borderline genius because of it.

The sight of his apartment always convinced Nathalie that she and Ian could not possibly share the same DNA. His living habits must remain a closely guarded secret at all costs.

"Where am I supposed to sit?" Nathalie's annoyance had a clear edge to it since she knew full well that he was expecting her and could've cleared out a safe and sane section.

"Well move something," said Ian. He wasn't going to take her condescending or scolding bait. She knew how he worked.

She chose instead to stand and lean against the refrigerator. There was a clear path to the food vault. At least survival had been given some priority.

"This is safer," she said. Out of curiosity, she cracked open the refrigerator door. "Jesus Christ," she grimaced. "Maybe not." She swiftly closed the door.

"So what's up?" Ian smiled toying with her. "I guess you're looking for something."

"You know damn well, why I'm—you'll never get a girl this way, you know that," decried Nathalie changing the subject and gesturing with indignant annoyance at the piles.

"I could meet a fantastic babe who likes it even messier than I do, besides this isn't mess, it's creativity."

"That right there is proof that the novelist in you has warped the real crime reporter. You're living your own *Invasion of the Body Snatchers*."

"You can take that pile off that chair," he said pointing to one of the dining table chairs. "Just don't kick the one under the table."

Nathalie lifted the pile off the designated chair and gingerly placed it on the table in between two other piles. "Katharine Hepburn was right. Men and women should only live across the street from each other and occasionally visit. No woman, who would be classified as a woman, would live like this."

"I've seen your place and you're not exactly channeling Martha Stewart."

"Because I don't look good in orange. And you…oh Ian…"

Nathalie sighed, a breath that left her body trailing heartbreak. He annoyed the piss out of her at times, but he was her baby brother, and she loved him and how he hasn't let his disability stop him…most of the time. The bantering quips faded from her spirit as she surveyed the chaos.

"I've always felt, that all this," she said gesturing at the piles, "was some desperate attempt by my brother to find out who the hell he is. You've been trying to carve out some image between Dad and your journalist hero Scotty Reston since you started at the Times. You wanted to chase the bad guys, but that was a bust," she said pointing at his cane, "so you chase 'em with words. But you act like that's not enough. Dad was proud of you, ya know."

"Yeah, I know, I guess, but that doesn't…" Ian didn't finish his thought because he had no answer for what was missing. What was missing was evidence and validation for his gravitas. His father had accumulated awards and adulation from his peers. The late Scotty Reston at The Times had garnered two Pulitzer Prizes, a Presidential Medal of Freedom, a chevalier of the Légion d'honneur from France and managed to get on former president Nixon's infamous *enemy's list*—all in one lifetime! Ian knew full well—even though he didn't want to admit it—that the piles represented the hope of righting the wrongs. And yet, most of the time he felt he was tilting at windmills.

"Doesn't what? Make everything better?" Nathalie knew just what he was thinking. "Dad kept goin' after the bad guys even though they just kept showin' up like an endless stream. He never quit. You remember, he called it *clearing out*—"

"*The asshole convention,* yeah," Ian chimed in.

"And for the umpteenth time, what's your favorite Scotty Reston quote?"

Ian smiled in spite of his annoyance at having his vulnerability poked. "*All politics are based on the indifference of the majority.*"

"Right. You're trying to get people to give a shit. That's who you are—that's pretty damn good, I think. What's eating at you is you think they don't care. Most do, they just don't know what to do about it. They're scared and they feel powerless. Maybe your words, just maybe, can carve out a way forward."

He stared at his sister surprised. There was no sarcasm in her tone; she was heartfelt and direct. "Wow…did you listen to some insightful Brené Brown podcast or what?"

"I don't know, no, this whole Eli Cross thing has got me—and Dad's files on him better not be scattered all over this floor or I'll kick your ass." Nathalie gazed at the piles and blew out an exhaled breath of frustration. "No, it's, just kinda, ya know, it's got me thinking. I thought I knew Dad, I thought I knew Mom—and now I—maybe I don't even know myself. I sure as hell don't know who the hell this guy is and whatever he's up to. I came here expecting a lecture from you about watching my ass, but all I want is answers. Do you have any fucking answers?! You've read the boxes you took from the closet. I know you're trying to pick up from where Dad left off."

Ian raised a hand in protest but Nathalie waved him off.

"I know you are—you are!"

"What was in the box you took?"

"A lot of questions."

"Sort of what I've found," admitted Ian. "Dad was trying to connect the dots. Questions to answers. Answers to more questions. For someone Dad was trying to nail, he respected the hell out of this guy. Whatever it is Eli Cross is doing, you can bet he's damn good at it. And yeah, I am telling you to watch your ass. He's got plans for you. Intelligence operatives call an easily duped asset a useful idiot."

"If that's what he thinks, maybe I can use that as an advantage," said Nathalie pushing back.

"I'm not sayin' you're an idiot, but Dad…" Ian paused to set up the point he wanted to make. "Dad always felt he could outwit the perps he was after. Sooner or later, they'd screw up and he'd be right there. He knew a lot of them were smart, just not smart enough. It's pretty clear from his notes that he thought Eli Cross was smarter than him—a lot smarter."

"Did he give any specifics?"

"There's a lot that he must've kept in his head. It's not in the notes, but you can kinda read between the lines. It's like something's missing. I've been trying to connect the dots by the questions he asked himself, ya know in the margin notes. One weird thing though. Most of the notes are the type of comments or questions you ask when you're working the case. It's when the notes start getting more personal that it gets a little weird."

"Personal, you mean like feelings? Give me something."

"Okay." Ian got up from his stuffed chair, placing the pile in his lap back on the floor. He picked his way through the labyrinth as easily as following a well-known path home from the grocery store. In the hallway to the bedroom, he liberated a file from one of the Cross boxes and opened the manila folder.

"Okay, here you go," he said. "Dad's got a note here. *Friday 5-7. We TD Bonnaire. Jean-Pierre & Vadoma. EC invested. Cask room-framed old photo-girl & boy-les petites voleurs de vin. Meant to see it??? O liked V. Ex-lover??? Sister???*

Ian trekked back through the labyrinth and showed her Nate's handwriting.

"What's TD?" Nathalie pointed at the note.

"I think an abbreviation for "track down.""

"Jean-Pierre…" Nathalie said thinking back. "Cross said he had a friend Jean-Pierre, a winemaker in Provence. Quite a good one by the way."

"One and the same. There's a Bonnaire vineyard—very small, private—about half-way between Arles and Aix-en-Provence. The winemaker is Jean-Pierre. The wife is Vadoma."

"What's this *We TD*? Who's we?"

"Yeah, I wondered that too. Check the date."

Nathalie looked at the note. "Friday 5-7. So maybe five to seven o'clock."

"Maybe. But maybe Friday May seventh."

"Okay, so?" Nathalie knew he had connected a dot.

"So the seventh of May fell on a Friday in 1999."

"Shit, their trip to Paris. So *We* could be Dad—"

"And Mom," Ian added for emphasis.

"Les petites voleurs de vin," Nathalie repeated the margin note. She and Ian both knew their French. "Those kids. Little wine thieves. And Vadoma, an ex-lover or possibly family, a sister maybe." Nathalie fell in line with her father's reasoning. "He made a point that Mom liked her. *EC invested.* Cross may have put money into setting up the wine business. Was Cross trying to humanize himself knowing Dad would find them? Did he want Dad to know who he was, that an ex would like him or that he has family?"

"I don't know," said Ian. "Other notes seem to indicate that Cross was letting some things leak out on purpose. But Mom could spot a phony real easily and she liked Vadoma. Dad made a point about that. He always trusted her judgement."

"Nothing else about Vadoma?" Nathalie asked.

"Not from Dad. But I checked out the name. Vadoma is a Romani gypsy name."

"Cross isn't a Romani name, if she's family and not an ex-lover that is."

"If that's really his name. Vadoma's maiden name is Lakatos which is also Romani."

"Eli Lakatos?"

"Maybe not even Eli. I mean what do we really know about him?"

"So what're you inferring—if she's not an ex-lover—that he learned to steal from growing up in an itinerant Gypsy family, a nomad around Europe? C'mon that's a little much. Besides, he doesn't have that look; his features have a different ancestry."

"DNA is known for outliers. Don't rule out what you really don't know."

"Yeah, well don't force dots to connect that have nowhere to go."

"Ever think that the Waldorf heist was just a set up?"

"What're you getting at?" Nathalie asked.

"If Cross was the guy, he sure got your attention with it, and knew you'd need to recover the jewels to restore your reputation. Then he comes along and asks for your help."

"He hasn't laid out those plans yet," Nathalie snapped at him.

"It's right in front of your face but he has you so taken with him and his past connection with Dad and Mom that you haven't seen it."

"What?! Just spit it out!" Nathalie knew you don't beat the boys at their own game by not knowing what's right down at the end or your own nose.

"Cartier's bash of the decade—worth a helluva lot more than the Waldorf affair—is taking place this weekend in the Hamptons at the Borelli estate."

Shit, Nathalie thought. She'd pushed that fact away because she wasn't working it; it wasn't on her radar. But it should have been. This was not how you stayed on top—or even alive—when dealing with the criminal element.

"There's gonna be a lot of security," Ian continued to press his point. "It would be another score going down—probably *the* score—because he's got to do it right under everyone's nose. The ultimate test."

"The *one moment,*" Nathalie said out loud involuntarily.

"What?"

"Nothing."

"Donelli thinks he's gonna pull you into this, use you somehow."

"I'm not gonna fall for that," insisted Nathalie.

"You don't even know what he wants yet."

"I can smell a rat good as you."

"There was something else in Dad's notes. He got a feeling about Cross. I'm guessing from some conversations and observation, but anyway, he noted that there was something else to his stealing besides the loot."

"Something else?"

"Something righteous about what he was doing."

"Something righteous? He used those words?"

"Those exact words."

"He didn't indicate how or why?"

"No, it was just a margin note. But based on some of the other notes in other files, other questions he was asking himself, it got me wondering. I know this may be crap—or I want it to be crap—but sometimes you gotta ask the tough questions and be willing to accept where they may lead."

"What are you getting at?"

"That maybe Dad crossed over—maybe just once—to the dark side. That Cross, his lifestyle, the benefits, made it so alluring that Dad hooked up with him for I don't know, a score maybe."

"That's crazy!"

"I don't want to believe that. I really don't. But there were some notes—*retribution, revenge*—hinting that some of Cross's targets may have deserved it. One of Dad's notes was *Justice with style.* As a cop always having to follow the law and being hamstrung by that and watching too many perps walk, that kind of thing could be enticing."

"*Justice with style,*" Nathalie repeated. Her imagination was unleashed and it terrified her and she had to yank it back. "Maybe that's just a wish. I can't see him hooking up with Cross. Not after an affair with Mom. Dad would've been all over him, hell bent on beating the crap out of him, and wanting to nail him even more!"

"If a score is big enough, partners can let a lot of shit slide."

"Partners! Jesus Christ, Ian!"

"Just read it, Nattie—and keep your mind open." Ian handed her the file. "We're in uncharted territory here. Everyone has secrets. The hidden-self inside the self that everyone sees. How well do we know our parents? I know what I feel, what I love, but what do I really know? You really want answers? See how the dots connect, not just how you want them to connect. If it's true, you really gotta watch your ass."

"What else?" Nathalie wasn't ready to swallow all this. She thought she'd choke on it.

"That's as far as I've got. Took me a while to find Bonnaire since I didn't know to look in France until the May seventh connection." Ian pointed at the file. "Have at it and the boxes in the bedroom."

"You got a start on Bonnaire, why don't you apply some of that journalistic acumen and dig up whatever there is on Jean-Pierre and especially *your gypsy* Vadoma."

"We've got less than a week until Cartier's bash," said Ian "So you get some answers too—if there are any. Dad didn't connect the dots, or maybe didn't want to. We don't have that luxury."

Ian stepped around piles and went to his laptop on the table.

"Dad would tell us to *get real.* So here it is: you're in over your head and you know it."

He opened his laptop and got to work.

Nathalie gingerly picked her way through the labyrinth of piles to the hallway and walked into the bedroom. The two remaining boxes of *Cross Files* lay at her feet. If all the answers weren't in here, she'd have to find them elsewhere. She wouldn't admit it out loud, but Nathalie knew Ian was right. The river of doubt reached flood level and she treaded water in the deep end over her head.

CHAPTER TWELVE

"Women who seek to be equal with men lack
ambition."

Timothy Leary

The grass was greener. And there was more of it. The Hamptons had more of almost everything that people wanted. The Borelli estate was a prime example. This sprawling Mediterranean-style villa overlooked the dunes and marsh reeds that led to the beach and the Atlantic. The 25,000 square foot main house had two kitchens, one of which served a banquet room with a proscenium stage. Spread throughout the first two floors were seven bedrooms and twelve bathrooms. The master suite was 2500 square feet all to itself on the third floor and connected to each floor below it by a sweeping private staircase and an elevator. Beyond the main villa there were two guest houses, an art studio by a water lily grotto pond which sat a stone's throw from a pool house that overlooked an Olympic-size pool with a swim-up bar adjacent to the two tennis courts and a basketball court. One could smell the money. The people who graced its grounds through the years were as beautiful as the surroundings.

Cross knew the rich were no different than anyone else; they just killed each other in better environments. He came by his cynicism naturally through experience. He yearned to let it go. Sometimes, but not often, he had some glimpses that all hope was not lost. Perhaps he would find *that moment* which would prove it to him.

His fiftieth birthday was coming up fast. It would be a most appropriate present. If not, pushing himself to the limit and risking it all would be its own reward.

The air was crisp this morning. Late autumn along the Atlantic seaboard contained its treasure of youthful memories for Cross. Summer's fading idyllic magic brought a new and different aura. The heat and the sweat the humidity generated had evaporated clearing the air and giving rise to fresh aromas—a full-throated musky fragrance—

throughout the reeds and grasses of the dunes. It always felt like a cleansing, a clean slate to Eli, bringing in endless possibilities.

The crowds were gone and in that solitude, nature's voice fired up his imagination. That lonely atmosphere which enveloped many a lost adult displeased with their lives instead populated the playground of his mind with vivid heroes and villains in rambunctious scenarios. This spared him the cacophony spilled from the voices of the adult crowd desperately trying to put on airs of superiority to protect fragile egos filled with doubt or the boisterous claims of others who were assured of their entitlement. His little brother, Charles, gleefully played the part of the faithful companion in the scenarios that leapt from Eli's imagination. "CC" was more than a willing playmate; he was a trusted best friend.

Eli quickly brushed the memories from his consciousness like annoying flies. This morning was all about business. Irrelevant warm reminisces had no place in this cold game.

He held in his hand a scope which would usually sit atop a sniper's rifle. Cross lifted it to his eye as the morning sun crested the horizon and he brought the crosshairs of the magnified image up to the top of the multi-level roof of the main house. He panned across studying it as if committing to memory every roof tile.

Cross lowered the scope and made a notation in a little black notebook while comfortably ensconced in the leather seat of a $175,000 Aston Martin DB9 with its top down. Parked unobtrusively at the property's edge, nobody would be suspicious of such a luxury sports car in this environment.

Besides, he was very familiar with the neighborhood and could speak about it as if he belonged. Once he did. Even though many things had changed—renovations from the chronically restless rich— the area still felt the same to him. His childhood summers had been spent three doors down along the coast in his family's escape house on special weekends and for most of the summer.

It was so fitting that Cartier was using the Borelli estate though Cross did not really know the Borellis. Lorenzo Borelli was an Italian shipping magnate and his business was of little interest to Cross. He had met Lorenzo and his wife Lucia once at the baccarat table in the Casino de Monte-Carlo for fast rounds of Chemin de Fer as he set up another wealthy patron.

It had impressed him that husband and wife both played separate but equal hands at the same time and at the same table. But Lorenzo placed no controlling pressure on Lucia. She was quite good and he was surprisingly amateurish. In fact, he took great pleasure in his wife's skills. Eli always wondered if her challenge centered on taking all his money thus keeping it in the family before the other players or the bank cleaned him out. Either way, he remembered a playfulness to both of them quite unusual among the uber-rich.

The Borellis were in residence this week in the Hamptons and presumably would still be present for the gala event. The fact that they might remember him should they spot him did not concern him. On the contrary, he felt it would add to his allure, to the legend he created, and annoy the hell out of Donelli and those tracking him. If he saw them, he might even say hello and remind them of their past encounter at the baccarat table. Having the rich and influential endeared to you was a useful tool, a convenient *get out of jail free card* in the game he played.

For the Cartier event this weekend, he had studied the blueprints of the Borelli grounds and complex to know any changes that had been made over the years. But this compound held a permanent place in his memory because this used to be the Renzinger property. Even now the Renzinger name twisted in his gut, a darkness edged in his soul.

His father's company named CRM—*the C for his father, the R for Renzinger, and the M for Miniatures*—made ultra-tiny computer chips which integrated with larger system chips and provided a faster exchange of information more efficiently. The company was worth a small fortune when his father Roland was the Chairman & CEO and Edmund Renzinger was the President & COO.

At that time, CRM had an offer of sale for 750 million dollars at a time when that was not chump change, but his father had not wanted to sell. Roland had wanted to pour more time and money into R&D as he felt they were on the threshold of a breakthrough with AI, artificial intelligence. It was something he felt could improve their business, but more importantly the world and people's lives.

Progress for humanity was more important to him than profit. He was ahead of his time.

But this was risky then, jeopardizing the company's value and stock.

Edmund Renzinger always had his mind on the money—it was his holy grail—and he wanted the guarantee of luxury and early retirement. He did not want to risk it all on a hope for humanity and have to start all over if Roland's grand ideas proved to be a bust and sank their stock value. Renzinger wanted a long life of skiing in Gstaad, Val d'Isère, Chamonix—wherever the rich and famous played—and months on private islands in the Maldives and the Turks and Caicos Islands along with homes in multiple countries allowing for a constant supply of mistresses.

Renzinger and his wife maintained separate lives and lovers and kept their marriage as a face they displayed for society. They both liked playing the game of deception. Games were designed by nature to have a winner and a loser. That denouement did not engender trust in the players. Isabelle Renzinger shot and killed her husband Edmund only to be shot through the heart by him with his dying breath; a *love story* which spun society gossip for years.

Only Eli knew the reasons which precipitated the deadly end of their marriage by design. His carefully placed bread crumbs of doubt triggered greed and mistrust into an avalanche of murderous emotions. When the salacious and devious elements dripped out from police files, a gossip columnist coined the phrase *a murder so fine and fair* and sold his book to Hollywood. Vano Lakatos would've called it Gypsy magic; *you feel its effect but never the touch.*

The press and the police never knew the whole story; that remained with Eli Cross. Though satisfying, it did not quell the *saudade* within. To end that longing, he knowingly placed his bet on the roulette wheel of fate at the Cartier event. So it was fitting that his ultimate gamble take place at what once was the Renzinger property. The fact that Lorenzo and Lucia Borelli now owned it had a lot to do with Cross. One giant spin of the wheel for either triumphant life or the finality of death to end his *saudade* fed his adrenalin addiction.

The crosshairs of another scope centered on his head this day. The angle of view placed the voyeur on the roof of the same main house. This scope was attached to a Smith & Wesson 586 revolver with an 8 inch hunter barrel—a mean mother that would eat anything. The man behind the scope was Marty Lefkowitz, cleverly hidden behind a roof air-conditioning unit.

Into Lefkowitz's frame of Cross in the Aston Martin came Lieutenant Victor Donelli. With his other hand, Lefkowitz lifted up a military-grade flat-panel sound emitter grid, a portable version for activation in the field during tactical operations. It was capable of delivering and receiving sound waves over a distance. The delivery at full power could knock an enemy combatant on their ass. Another setting could plant a whisper behind someone's ear at a distance. Receiving their conversation, even at this distance, was crystal clear.

Cross didn't bother to acknowledge Donelli who approached from behind him. He expected it.

"Time's running out, Cross. I'll be waiting." said Donelli.

"Someone's got to do it."

Two men from different worlds who didn't like each other.

"Eventually you miss a step. It happens. And at that moment..." Donelli could barely wait for that moment. If desire were drool, he'd be soaking wet.

Eli's eyes narrowed in disgust. "You have no real understanding of that *moment*. You've never had any appreciation of the touch."

"All I see is a lowlife in fancy clothes."

"Crossing swords with you has always left a bad taste in my mouth."

"Maybe this time you'll choke on it."

Donelli turned and walked back down the road toward his car. Some emotions never mature. This could've easily been a pissing contest from high school propelled by acne-ridden angst except these stakes were actual life and death not teenage posturing.

Eli looked up from his little black book and out past the grounds to the ocean. Lost at sea, the longing for better times tenaciously gripped his memory. Crossing swords with Nate Seeger had been part of the elegance of it all. Eli imbued what he did with a sense of art; it was an intentional effort. Even in the simplicity that he insisted upon for any heist, there was a creative flair. Nate, that tough New York *grab-'em-by-the-balls* cop, also played the game with a sense of humor—hence a perp getting *Muldooned*—and more importantly he had an appreciation for the elegance of it all.

Cross knew full well that Nate Seeger wanted to toss his elegant ass in jail and left no stone unturned to do just that. That desire—applied with respect—was what he wanted in an adversary. He also knew that Nate did not know all the reasons for the thefts—what drove them—and why they had started. Some of the bread crumbs were there; he had even planted a few, hoping they would be followed. Crumbs like the vintner Jean-Pierre Bonnaire and Vadoma.

Part of those actions were to keep Nate guessing, but if pressed, Eli would have to admit it was to finally be understood…and perhaps freed from the yearning, from *saudade*. Yet, this day and the days to follow before the Cartier bash, he was compelled to go forward—to clear up loose ends—and he knew Donelli would be waiting.

A telephoto lens image from a new angle near the art studio centered on Cross's head as Donelli left. In Eli's expression, there was a hint of true apprehension. Eventually, you do slow down—you react only when you *see* the openings—and that missed *moment* could be fatal. This pensive image flickered with the click of a camera shutter.

༄

A sheet of white photo paper slid out of a printer with the image of Cross sitting in the Aston Martin talking to Donelli. Annoyed, Nathalie stared at the image in the printer tray.

"What is it with you two guys? What aren't you telling me?"

The bulletin boards dominated the space in her living room as Nathalie tacked up the surveillance photos of Cross, Donelli and Lefkowitz next to Nate Seeger's file note: *CROSS IS A LONE WOLF. TRACKING. CIRCLING. YET PULLS OTHERS INTO THE HUNT.*

Just how many *others* was Cross planning on pulling into his next caper? He had already asked for her involvement. Did the *lone wolf* eventually eat his partners in crime? Nathalie felt no humor in the sudden flash of that thought.

She still did not know Lefkowitz's part in all this which bugged the hell out of her for she felt that this classless, monumental prick shouldn't even be in the picture. In comparison with the likes of Lefkowitz, she understood why her father would've appreciated the elegance and the challenge of Cross. Why Nate Seeger liked Cross was another matter.

Ian's suspicions could not be dismissed. Her brother was too smart, his instincts too well-honed, to not consider the possibility that her father had been tempted by Eli's lifestyle. Who wouldn't be? It was alluring. Was Paris the location of this score? Many of the art world's masterpieces were on display, a tasty challenge to a master thief; capped off by the lucrative backend and the intrigue in cashing in on an once-in-a-lifetime score.

Was that what happened with her mother? Was Eli Cross a tempting walk on the wild side that was just too delectable for her to resist?

Blocking out that image of her mother, her thoughts rushed back to what formed a creature like Lefkowitz. Quickly she brought herself back on track. Whatever happened in Lefkowitz's childhood past was irrelevant at this point for he was too far gone to change. It was enough to know that he was deadly dangerous now.

The one relevant question was his connection to Cross. Was Lefkowitz his hatchet man? Did Cross keep his hands clean of the more distasteful actions, like eliminating people when necessary? Her father had dealt with other elegant criminals who had what he called their *assholes* who dispensed the ugly shit. Was Lefkowitz Cross's *asshole?*

She would put a pin in that for now; it remained an open question.

But Eli Cross was still an unfinished story. She thought back to the photo mentioned in her father's notes. The photo of the boy and girl that hung framed at the entrance to the cask room filled with French oak barrels at the Bonnaire Vineyard in Provence. Clearly a nostalgic and emotional gesture. Someone knew him as a young boy. What was he like? How did he change? And why?! Did that even matter?! *Work the case!!*

Her impatience to *solve the case* plunged her back into more relevant margin notes from her father's files. But then she knew her father wouldn't have mentioned it if it didn't carry some weight. So what did it matter? Maybe everything. Maybe the key. She wanted to know that boy.

She paced back and forth along her own labyrinth of bulletin boards and a few white boards, still angled to entice and frustrate Cross if he peered in from The Lucerne across the street. She had pasted blow-ups of her father's margin notes next to file pages she'd tacked up from the boxes she had brought back from Ian's apartment.

Nathalie desperately wanted to follow the path of her father's thinking, to connect the dots and make the case. She knew there was a pattern here—her father had been looking for it—she just couldn't see it yet. It seemed very strange to her that her father's notes seemed all over the place as if he jumped from thought to thought. Clearly, attempting to understand Cross frustrated him as much as it did her.

There were margin notes about *INTERVIEWS.*

Nate Seeger had made inquiries into what witnesses had seen at the heist locations in question and conducted interviews with those who had an actual relationship or contact with Cross during the time of many of the *incident thefts*. They were all charmed by Cross and didn't even realize how deep the impression was that he had made. Even some of the victims of the crime doubted that Cross could've done it. The common refrain: *it wasn't like him.*

Some margin notes were conclusive. *SET UP.*

Cross created an atmosphere of trust and interest in him which generated an easy acceptance of him in their lives. This started long before the date of any *disappearance of valuables* whether jewels or classic works of art.

CIRCUMSTANTIAL.

There were always carefully constructed reasons for why Cross was *in town* at the time of the heists. All were legitimate. Alibis and timing were tight. Nothing could connect him except *the coincidence of being there.*

WORKED THE PARTIES.

He made their lives seem more vital, more exciting when he was around. He fostered a *presence* that was thoroughly appealing. This modus operandi was present at every crime scene. It was a consistent *M.O.* along with the others. It was a clear pattern of bold and subtle moves on the game board.

LEGERDEMAIN.

This margin note was made with an appreciation of *his style*. Some physical diversion always occurred to turn people's attention elsewhere. The shift of focus was however also psychological, a subtle almost magical touch of suggestion that kept thought centered on other matters. Many times the absence of the items that were stolen was not even noticed for a while.

FENCING.

Inspections of his property, jet, cars, known bank accounts— anything in his possession—never revealed a trace of missing jewelry or art. How the stolen goods were quickly transformed into bankable assets was never traced. He was paid handsome retainers as a *Security Consultant* by governments and corporations with no seeming connection to any of the missing items from the heists under investigation. These were merely some of the many reasons why he had never been caught.

Her father had made one margin note that was a general summation of his own as to how Cross operated and had, so far, gotten away with everything: *Densely complex or utterly simple.*

Nathalie tracked the progression of the file notes down another column of bulletin boards.

SOURCE?

No one seemed to know where his money came from, only that he lived a wealthy lifestyle. It was part of his allure. He wore it well. Even the many international legal authorities who had him under surveillance did not know the source of his wealth. Did he have a deal with Swiss banks? A secret agreement with the French government? He seemed protected or was he just that damn smart.

With each note, Nathalie feared her father became more and more intrigued with the world of Cross. It was quite a skill to keep so much of one's life and exploits a secret from those who were watching. She could tell by the nature and placement of the margin notes that her father developed an admiration for this man. He was no longer just a perp to her father. Was Ian right? Had Cross become a man to emulate?

All of this was destabilizing her sense of both her parents.

The next bulletin board contained three of the more devilish sections, the ones which cried out for concrete answers.

The *SOMETHING RIGHTEOUS?* margin note which Ian had mentioned was accompanied by two others: *RETRIBUTION?* and *REVENGE?*

Many of the thefts happened to wealthy people who were concurrently under investigation or suspicion of fraudulent, criminal or tawdry behavior. For some other victims there was simply common knowledge of less-than-good behavior in business without concern for the consequences to others that hung over their reputations. Was this mention merely coincidence, a warning of human behavior and what greed can do? Or was this the primary reason for the heist? Was it possibly a Cross crusade or simply an unrelated casual connection? The answer to this might shed light on his manner and method and allow her to get ahead of him with whatever he was planning.

Clearly the money mattered to Cross since he put it to good use in accumulating his French villa and the Bombardier Global 6000 in addition to first class taste in horses, cars and clothing. This could of course be simply the cost of doing business, the necessary accoutrements to create and perpetuate the right image. But what if profit wasn't the goal? What if it was merely a by-product of the initial intent? Nate hadn't come to any firm conclusions.

Then there was the note that reached back into the personal past. *WHERE IS FAMILY? ORPHAN?—NO.*

There were holes in Nate's line of thinking on this subject as if some notes had been removed. In a small handwritten scribble were the words *Gypsy training*, but no further explanation for it. Nathalie thought of what Ian had discovered about Vadoma Bonnaire and her Romani maiden name of Lakatos. It all seemed pure conjecture springing from a need to grasp at straws for answers that would stick. It was not every day that itinerate gypsies and the art of petty thievery led to owning a Bombardier Global 6000.

Her father's files had a photo of the Bombardier tucked inside some pages in a different file folder. Nathalie had followed her instinct that this photo was not simply generic and had tracked down the jet's aircraft registration tail number of F-EVLC. The jet was registered in France out of La Môle Airport in St. Tropez. Eli Cross was the owner. That same private jet was currently parked at Teterboro Airport in New Jersey. Eli Cross, the gypsy, owned a fifty million dollar aircraft? No way in hell! She felt the whole gypsy line of thinking was a dead end or a red herring. Probably—maybe—possibly. The man's unknowability was infuriating.

The last two margin notes in this aisle of bulletin boards were the most disturbing. They were margin notes without any further delineation or back-up information. Something was clearly missing. But the notes themselves raised all sorts of alarms in Nathalie's gut.

THE LOUVRE. SIMPLE & ELEGANT. IN & OUT. INGRID KEY TO ML.

These notes were from the Paris '99 trip. They catapulted questions up from the base of Nathalie's worst fears. Had Cross planned on hitting The Louvre? Was this the score that Ian thought their father might've joined, the lure of lifting priceless art from the world's most famous museum? She could not find any evidence of a theft from The Louvre in 1999 but then that's something the museum would want to keep under wraps as long as possible, like perhaps forever. Then again, Cross might've been clever enough to steal some art treasure from the Louvre—possibly with her father's help—and then get a grateful French government to pay for its return and consider him a hero.

And who was Ingrid? An accomplice or merely a useful idiot? Nathalie wondered if Cross had plans for her to be the *new Ingrid.* What was *ML?* Ingrid was the key to whatever *ML* represented. Did *ML* represent the whole enchilada? The Louvre was referred to sometimes as **Museé du Louvre.** Was that the *ML?* Or was it possibly a *who?* Could *ML* be a notation for **Marty Lefkowitz?** She still didn't know how that slimy bastard fit into all this.

As if all that wasn't disturbing enough, the last note grabbed her heart when she tacked it up, and every time since when she looked at it.

O w/C @ G-5 LATE!

This meant only one thing to Nathalie. Her womanly instinct zeroed quickly in on what the letters meant. Her mother, **O**dile, was **with C**ross **at** the **George V** LATE at night! The use of all caps and the "!" was clear emotion on her father's part.

The George V was one of the most luxurious hotels not only in all of Paris but in Europe. Just off the Champs-Elysées in the 8th arrondissement, this palace hotel offered iconic views of the Eiffel Tower from its suites and offered three Michelin-starred restaurants— five stars in total. It oozed romance, Parisian charm, sophisticated style and elegance. Easy to be swept away.

The thought of her mother opening herself to him—skin-to-skin— sent paroxysms of despair and sadness coursing through her body and soul. Did she keep her wedding ring on in between those satin sheets?! Repulsion rushed up like vomit. Her mother had been her trusted confidant, her fount of class, her inspiration. Nathalie felt those disrupting images invalidated her entire childhood. That was a theft she couldn't forgive. The stolen jewels and works of art were things— but this...this went right to her heart. Cross had to answer for the desecration of the memory of her childhood and the respect she held for her parents!

Her emotions plummeted back to earth and focused on her prey with a predator's cold stare. To take down a prey, know all its talents and how they were displayed.

She recalled her own time with him at The Rainbow Room and The Baronfeld Museum. What disturbed her then—and even at this moment—a look in his eyes not forced, nor faked. A *look* between a man and a woman she wanted to trust but couldn't dare, couldn't let herself be lured in…unless…unless it was the real thing. Then what the hell would that mean?! It was a clear conflict between heart and head, intuition and training.

This man had driven such a wedge into her family. She hated him, yet didn't want to. It was nuts! She fought the tears that welled up in her eyes. She wanted to talk to her mom.

Why didn't her father leave her with more information as she wiped her eyes? It was not like her father to leave so many holes in his notes, in his thoughts. Nate Seeger worked a case with precision. But this was different. Why? Why?! What was he leaving out?! It haunted her.

She realized you could ask questions in every direction till you were spinning in circles. *Stick with the clear facts. Connect the dots that make sense. Even more important, trust what you feel.* Those were her father's words. He taught her that. He was still her champion. She owed him to follow through with this case, to listen to that still small voice. Intuition. Don't rationalize it away. Listen to its whisper. Trust it.

She knew she could be as good as Cross. Maybe better. She could crack this case.

Nathalie felt her emotions settle back on track. She rounded the bulletin board aisle and faced the next set of tacked-up notes. She sucked in her breath as a rush of fear gripped her. Right in front of her face stood a note she hadn't seen. It was a plain piece of white paper pinned next to photos of Kracauer and Lefkowitz! The words were made up of cut-out letters pasted onto the white paper. It read: DON'T GET TOO CLOSE.

She ripped the note off the board!

Her eyes darted anxiously around. She had not put it there!

Someone had been in her apartment!!

How did she miss this?! What else did they do while they were here?! Her anger rose up in her throat and then just as quickly she forced herself to control her breathing.

Don't get sloppy!

Suddenly she heard a *click* and turned to see the deadbolt lock on her front door turn.

Training and instinct drove her forward. She knew she had only split seconds to respond. She swept her Sig-Sauer 9mm off her desk, racked the slide to chamber a round, then slipped behind the entry wall of the foyer as she heard the door *creak* open and then *click* closed.

Her heart pounded in her chest!

Footsteps on the hardwood floor came closer. Her hand tightened on the gun grip!

Nathalie sprung out and leveled the gun right at—Megan—who totally freaked and spilled her caramel macchiato all over her blouse and jeans!

"Jesus Christ," screamed Megan!

Nathalie lowered the Sig and decocked the hammer.

"What the hell're you doin' here?!"

"Bloomie's had a sale, remember?!"

Megan brushed at the spilled coffee on her clothes and realized it made no difference so she turned her attention to the Bloomingdale's shopping bag and pulled out a wrapped item.

"You wanted me to pick these up!" Megan peeled the paper back and handed over a trio of lavender lace panties with the sale tag still attached. She wrestled her breathing back to some semblance of normal. "I can't believe I almost got killed over lavender lace panties!"

"Thanks," Nathalie said grabbing the panties, "I forgot about these."

Megan noticed—with a fair degree of annoyance—that Nathalie seemed unscathed about having almost blown a bloody hole through her chest. In fact, Nathalie's focus had already shifted back to her work. Megan scanned the bulletin board labyrinth.

"Wow, this is a real—what do you call this?"

"Workin' the case," said Nathalie as she tossed the lavender panties onto the dining room table.

"I'm impressed." Megan took a quick glance at some of the blown-up margin notes. "So you're gettin' a handle on this guy."

"More like piling up a shit-load of questions."

Megan spotted the binoculars.

"Oh, what're these for?" She picked them up. "Oh wait a minute; he's just across the street, right? Are you…?"

Nathalie looked away. That was all Megan needed to see to get the skinny.

"Oh, you little bitch," Megan chuckled with delight. She picked up the binoculars and pointed them at The Lucerne. "What floor?"

"Stop that!"

Nathalie reached for the binoculars but Megan pulled away.

"C'mon, let me enjoy some of this."

"This is not fun!"

"C'mon, it'll be like dealing with Vinnie together."

"Vinnie cheated on both of us. Neither one of us has slept with Cross!"

Megan pointed at Nathalie. "I know you've thought about it."

"Not with my mom having—"

"Especially with your mom having—you know—I mean, c'mon, I know you, I know how you think."

Nathalie was caught. Megan knew her too well. There was no escaping this accusation. As bad as that thought was, she had wondered what it would be like, if only to understand her mother better—like discovering an excuse for her behavior. There was only one way to stop Megan from digging deeper.

"All right, all right, all right," said Nathalie giving in. "Tenth floor. Far left corner window."

Megan pointed the binoculars at the street level and slowly panned up counting the floors out loud. "First, second, third, fourth, fifth, sixth, seventh, eighth, ninth and there we go. Okay… let's see what we got." Megan worked the focus staring intently. "This isn't great, you can only see a little ways into the suite. Someone would have to step right up to—oh my God!"

"What? What is it?!"

"Holy shit!!"

"Megan, what the hell's goin' on?!"

"He's right at the window! Jesus H. Christ!"

Nathalie grabbed at the binoculars but Megan sidestepped her and kept watching, emitting a low guttural moan. "OHhhhh…"

"What?!!" pressed Nathalie, desperate to know what happened across the street!

"He's fucking gorgeous!" Megan groaned from her groin.

Nathalie grabbed the binoculars away from her.

"You didn't really level with me!" Megan nailed her friend with an accusing finger jabbed at Nathalie's face. "He's—oh my God—he's scorching hot!"

"I know…" Nathalie raised the binoculars to her eye. "Yeah, he's…" Then she lowered the binoculars in defeat and walked away from the window. "But he could also be guilty as sin. What am I supposed to do about that?!"

"Yeah, I know, it's complicated," Megan said sympathetically. "I was just…bein' stupid that's all. You can't really blame me, I mean he's…ya know…whew."

"Yeah, it kind of pisses you off."

"Not really."

"You don't think he uses those looks," Nathalie countered. "They're a tool, a weapon. He used it on my mom."

"Can you really blame her?"

Nathalie hissed to bite back but Megan raised her hands to squash the anger.

"Hey, I'm just tryin' to help you get real here. Your mom's pretty hot too, like sizzling in some of those younger photos. Things happen ya know when two hot people…I mean this was what over twenty years ago? It's not like it's going on now, right?"

Nathalie didn't say anything.

"Right???"

Nathalie was uncomfortably silent.

"Shit…you don't know, do you?"

Megan placed a comforting arm around Nathalie's shoulders. "I'm really sorry,"

"I just gotta work the case. That's what my dad would do."

Megan pointed at the bulletin board labyrinth. "So how's it goin'?"

"Someone got into the apartment. That's why I almost shot you." Nathalie handed her the note with the cut-out block letters. "Left me this."

"Is this some kind of warning?"

"You could say that."

"Jesus, really?"

"You don't break into someone's apartment just for laughs."

"Do you know who it is?"

Megan's fear rose as she watched Nathalie point to photos of Kracauer, Lefkowitz, Cross and Donelli.

"One of these guys," said Nathalie. "And one of them's a cop who knows too much."

"He's a jewel thief too?!"

"I think he'd like to be. He's a pushy prick, so who knows?"

"Then who do you trust?"

The problem simply stated. Nathalie knew it. Now Megan did too and she looked to her friend for an answer. Nathalie usually felt sure of herself in business. She kind of sucked at assurance in relationships, Megan thought, but with the kind of investigations she did, Nattie usually nailed it. Megan knew the girl was good which was why the look of despair on her friend's face scared the hell out of her for the first time.

It didn't seem funny or playful at this moment.

"Maybe they all stole the jewels," said Nathalie.

Then the muscles of her face tightened and she spit the words out through clenched teeth. "I don't know. And that's what pisses me off— I don't know!!"

CHAPTER THIRTEEN

If you're sad, add more lipstick and attack.

Coco Chanel

Nathalie strode down the tenth floor Lucerne corridor like a cruise missile honing in on its target. Ground zero—the hotel suite door at the end of the hallway. Hell bent on running her prey to ground, her mood bold and sassy, no pussy-footing around!

Her fist pounded on the suite door. She braced herself. She knew he was there. She had pinpointed him with the binoculars before leaving her building and dashing across 79th.

Eli Cross swung open the door and with a sweep of his arm and ushered her inside.

He was not at all surprised to see her. That pissed her off. She hoped to spring at him from the jump while he recovered from being confronted by her. But he stood completely relaxed dressed in a long sleeve British racing green polo shirt that comfortably outlined his athletic form. The wrangler blue jeans fit enticingly snug and the tanned bare feet made the killer final touch. *God-damn-it he just reeked of sex appeal.*

She stifled her involuntary gasp of stolen breath and strode inside summoning her resolve, then spun around and spit out her first words.

"Just what the hell is it that you want me to do?!"

"And hello to you," he calmly responded. "Coffee?"

"No, no coffee—yes—coffee would be okay!" She could just kick herself for getting shoved off track. She relaunched her assault. "You wanted me to help you! So—"

"Danish? There's peach and perhaps marionberry."

He pointed to a plate on a room service tray.

"Ah, I don't know—peach—no, marionberry." They both looked delicious to her and she cursed herself for not having eaten before she launched her attack.

Eli placed both a marionberry and peach Danish on a plate and handed it to her.

"Just in case you want to compare them."

He then poured them both a cup of coffee.

"Seriously," she said, "I need to—"

"Black or with a little milk?"

"Ahh, a little milk."

His insistent courtesy dissipated her head of steam; that and his smooth tanned feet with neatly clipped clean toenails sticking out of the royal blue wranglers. She had envisioned her attack upon him as the unleashed fiery *Charge of the Light Brigade* against the Balaclava Heights in the Crimea. Coffee and Danish with a barefoot enemy formed a milquetoast mission at best. He handed her the coffee cup with a gentle smile which almost completed her surrender.

Almost. She simply stared at him. Her enemy. She had to regroup. Surely a soft spot existed, a weak point in his defensive walls, handsome as those walls may be. Perhaps the key strategy proceeded with silent confidence engaged.

She sat quietly sipping her coffee and nibbling on the Danish, first the marionberry, then the peach. To her increasing annoyance, Eli merely watched her back, sipping his coffee and taking small bites from his peach Danish. She realized this could go on until they were both fat or had to pee.

"You want my help," she said finally relenting.

"Yes." He didn't offer anything more, taking a long, slow sip of coffee.

"For all time, or a specific moment?"

He tilted his coffee cup toward her as a touché toast.

"Initially this Saturday night specifically," he replied.

"Dinner and dancing not the goal this time. Since we've been there done that."

He smiled a becoming smile as if from a pleasurable memory that night.

"Cartier's bash in the Hampton's," he said, his tone suddenly serious. "The glitterati will be glittering and the imposter I need to stop will be at play."

"You might not have to worry about that. The incoming weather's looking ominous. Might be stormy that night."

"*A torrent of darkness*," he replied with a more playful tone.

"Usually happens after the sun goes down."

"They won't cancel because of a little rain," he stated confidently.

"The ocean's puckering up. Heavy dark clouds are rolling in."

"Then perhaps *the moon will be a ghostly galleon tossed upon cloudy seas.*"

"Really?"

"*And the road a ribbon of moonlight.*"

"Oh…" Nathalie got it now. "*And the highwayman came riding—riding—riding*"

"Yes," he replied, pleased that she knew the reference; and he continued, "*The highwayman came riding, up to the old inn door.*"

"And this is when you need my help."

Cross nodded for effect, inwardly delighted that she played along.

"*He whistled a tune to the window, and who should be waiting there but the landlord's black-eyed daughter, Bess the landlord's daughter.*"

"Well the eye color's not quite right. And my father never called me Bess."

"But she tried to help him. And he to help her."

"Yes, the Alfred Noyes poem, *The Highwayman,* very romantic."

"Yes, it is." He gazed at her appreciatively.

"Too bad they both got killed in the end."

"Perhaps not the best example when asking for your help, but I do like the poem."

Nathalie enjoyed the repartee but she remained wary of being lured into his web by his charm. She thought of the subtle psychological *Legerdemain* margin note her father had written. "So what can I do that all the cops and security personnel can't do?"

"You've been doing your homework—on me, specifically—learning how I approach my work. The imposter has done the same. He's very good. You may be able to be one step ahead and be there to stop him."

"And where will you be?"

"For obvious reasons, I can't be there," he simply said. By the jaded look in her eyes, Eli realized she didn't buy this line of thinking. "All right. Let's reason this out, shall we?"

"Yes, let's," said Nathalie not wanting to give him any free pass.

"More coffee?" he asked.

"Sure."

He got up and retrieved the pristine stainless steel coffee carafe from the room service tray, then poured both of them another cup all while launching into his reasoning.

"If I am there and visibly present, then Lieutenant Donelli will place all the attention on me and the imposter would be free to pilfer at will and escape to strike again. If I am known to be there but am not seen, then anything missing will be attributed to me."

"But you could be there intent on catching the imposter; if he thinks like you, then you would know how to stop him," countered Nathalie.

"Don't underestimate this thief. If I were there and was spotted, then this man—or woman for that matter—would cancel their activity because the chances of getting caught just got too high. Besides, they want the cops to think it's me. If I'm there it takes away part of their plan, their pleasure. No, this is the night to stop them—if—I'm not there. The lure of achieving success right under the noses of the authorities is too tempting."

"The same could be said of you."

"Yes, I suppose, except that I'm telling you I will not be there. Another Danish?"

"No." Nathalie's diet and her need to focus and not get distracted both contributed to the quick *No*. "Continue the lesson, I'm enjoying this."

"Glad to be of service."

"Wasn't that the highwayman's desire?" said Nathalie with a twinkle in her eye.

Behind her playful twinkle, Eli knew that nothing but the straight truth would satisfy her doubts.

"So," he continued. "If I was there but not spotted by the thief and if I did not find them, then if they were successful it would once again be pinned on me as if I worked with them."

"But you wouldn't be caught with the goods, so it would be purely circumstantial."

"Circumstantial is not a foolproof defense. It has its risks. Jaded juries and pit bull prosecutors have convicted on just such evidence. Then there are the questions. Was the thief working with Cross? Was Cross the diversion? Those questions would be endless and the police would be right in asking them. They could detain me for quite a while. No thank you."

"If you're so sure of your reasons to not be there, then why me?"

"You're very good—and don't be coy and try to deny it."

Nathalie flinched then quickly suppressed her appreciation for the complement. Was it possible he considered her an equal in this game?

"I also told you that I had gone straight. This imposter does think like me and you've been studying."

"Which has left a lot of questions—and don't deny that pleases you."

"We all like to retain a little mystery. Isn't that the desire of all women?"

Eli's smile enticed Nathalie who actually enjoyed the verbal and mental sparring. The battle of wits and reason with a worthy and engaging opponent created a most pleasant way to pass the time. She understood how her father could've enjoyed crossing swords with him.

"Your father came very close and with what you've learned from his files and what you bring to the table with your own talents, your own instincts, you're ready."

Nathalie held his gaze not blinking. She got very still, listened to her intuition and wanted to trust her instincts and feeling.

Eli did not turn away. He seemed to be letting her in, opening himself to scrutiny.

"You think that I know you," Nathalie said. "Yet you pride yourself on being unknowable."

"You have an array of facts, like they all do," Cross said. "Facts matter—cops and law enforcement are led by them—but they don't tell the whole story. Feeling, intuition, instincts connect the dots. Your father knew that. He was a different kind of…adversary. It's difficult to trust intuition. You either do or you don't. I'm betting you do. That's why you can be one step ahead. That's why you might really know me. I'm counting on that."

It unsettled her that he impressed upon her the importance of intuition while she attempted to connect with that very feeling.

"I thought you wanted me to know the imposter," Nathalie said pressing her point.

"Perhaps both of us."

Nathalie saw a glimmer of something different in his eyes, an earnest yearning to his expression, like a plea, perhaps for recognition. Had he really changed? Is this what he attempted to have her see? He told her he had gone straight. But she knew that he wanted her to feel the truth of that if it was true. And if it wasn't true…well, that's how a useful idiot was used.

"Why don't you just tell me straight what I need to know?" Nathalie wanted him to see that she was with him stride for stride and alert to being played, so she laid it on the line: "Unless you like playing this game."

"Once I did, for quite a while actually. I got rather good at it. It's not enough now. Too many things are too real. They must be faced…if there's to be any future in all of this."

"Future in what?"

"The world you so cleverly create and build, that lets you do what you do, can become the very thing that traps you and won't let you go. For what you need to know about me, let's just say that to truly believe, you can't simply be told. You won't trust it. You have to discover the feeling for yourself. I can't help you with that."

For the first time, Nathalie saw the possible chink in his armor, the weakness she hoped to find—the look in his eye—real doubt—a yearning for some kind of answer to quell the feeling he wrestled with. His body language read *cornered* and he quickly got up from his chair and went to the window which looked over to her apartment.

"Your bulletin board walls which you so cleverly angled in your apartment will tell you a lot. Your father dug deep. I know that."

"There are some things missing," she clearly stated, not hesitating to expose his position on the matter. "The dots want to connect, but they don't. I was wondering if maybe you lifted some pages from the files. Like you said, you prefer the term *master thief.*"

"Missing? Your father was too thorough to let something go missing." Cross registered definite concern. He didn't expect to hear this.

"I agree," Nathalie said, "which is why I thought you might've taken some key pages when seeing my mother again."

Cross gaged his words carefully yet sincerely.

"I didn't remove any pages…but maybe your mother…" He didn't pursue that thought.

"What? Took them to cover up what happened?" Nathalie made no attempt to disguise the clear edge in her voice.

"I haven't seen your mother since…Paris…and I respect your mother too much to tell you what happened."

"Do you regret it?"

"Yes, but maybe it needed to happen."

"How the hell did that need to—"

"Some things needed to be shaken loose."

"That tore up their marriage!"

"More than that, but then you weren't there."

"Well I can do something about it now!" Nathalie's anger got the better part of her judgement. She stopped and shut her mouth choking off a potential torrent of invectives. She came here to *work the case* and run this prey to ground, not simply be pissed and argue with him.

"There's no going back," he stated simply but firmly. "Trust me, it doesn't change things."

"Is that how you treat all your lovers?" Nathalie moved in for the psychological kill. "You just move on and leave the past in the past because it can't be changed?! Is that how you left Vadoma?! Another of your precious conquests!"

The ringtone sound of whistling, the music of "Colonel Bogie's March" from "*The Bridge on the River Kwai*," cut off the flow of her words. She quickly reached for her cell phone to see who was calling. It was Ian. She wanted to dispense with him quickly and get back to confronting Cross.

"Yeah, what do you want?! Kind of busy!" she said curtly into the phone.

"I got the 4-1-1 on Vadoma—even saw a photo—and she is one sexy, voluptuous yum muffin! And pure Romani gypsy from an itinerant gypsy family!"

"Vadoma and I," said Cross unable to hear Ian's voice, "are not what you think."

"Hold on," Nathalie said into the phone to Ian. Then she snapped back at Cross. "You expect me to believe you didn't go after a sensuous gypsy woman like Vadoma the way you seduced my mother, I don't think so—"

"No, whoa, no, no he didn't," inserted Ian quickly over the phone! "She's his sister—kind of sister—adopted kind—him not her—sort of. Her family found him in St. Tropez when he lost his family."

Nathalie turned from Cross and walked away over to the window and dropped her voice level. "Lost?"

"Yeah, like in killed, I think."

"What? How?"

"I don't know. Anyway Vadoma adores him. They grew up together—in a gypsy family. Jean-Pierre had no hesitancy in talking with me. I just got off the phone with him so he wouldn't have had time to call Cross and let him know about this. I think he was telling me straight."

"You trust that?"

"Yeah, I do. Jean-Pierre said Cross had changed—or was trying to change—maybe had one last thing to do to put the past to rest."

"Like what?"

"Didn't say."

She looked over at Cross who simply stared at her. "I gotta go," she said to Ian. She quickly clicked off the call.

Cross pointed at her cell phone. "Your father whistled that tune a lot. Your ringtone."

"It was from one of his favorite movies, *The Bridge on the River Kwai*."

"Yes, that's a great one. A David Lean classic. But it was not his very favorite. That would be Frank Capra's *It's a Wonderful Life*."

Nathalie stood shocked at this very personal knowledge he had about her father.

"How did you know that?"

"He told me."

"Why would he…"

"We were talking favorite movies."

"You and my father, just chatting about movies."

"Yeah, his list was quite good."

It flustered Nathalie they would've had such a human moment together.

"Where was this…chat fest?

"Les Deux Magots in Paris. Just the two of us.

In Paris—when her father may have joined him on a score at The Louvre! Mind blowing! Her father and the master thief he'd been chasing for years, chatting as if they were friends while sitting at a café—presumably before Eli had an affair with her mother! "Two guys just hangin' out," she blurted out incredulously.

"I told you I liked your father. And I miss him."

This was almost too much. She had to change the subject before she totally lost it. "So, ahhh, what are your favorite movies?"

Eli lit up, anxious to share. "I really liked your father's choices, but my two favorites are "*Local Hero*, the Scottish writer-director Bill Forsyth's film with Burt Lancaster and Peter Riegert. It's so deliciously droll. And the French filmmaker Claude Lelouch—whose work I love—but it's his romantic classic *And Now My Love* that's one of my favorites. That was the American release title, in France it was *Toute Une Vie*."

Nathalie stared at him open-mouthed. This sudden flow of humanness staggered her.

"Have you ever seen it?" he pressed her for an acknowledgement but didn't wait for even a nod from her. "With Marthe Keller, André Dussollier and the great, singer-songwriter Gilbert Bécaud. Such fun! Bécaud you know was the Frank Sinatra of Europe. The movie's an examination of love at first sight. You really have to see it. But see it in French with subtitles. It's more…natural that way."

Eli perked up again. "Oh—and *Butch Cassidy and the Sundance Kid*—an all-time favorite!" He shrugged as if apologizing. "Cool outlaws."

"You know they get shot at the end."

"Well, that's the myth," he said with a sly smile.

His enthusiasm was infectious. Was this a glimpse of the little boy inside the man? Could a cold and calculating master thief enjoy something as simple as a good movie so much that he would be thrilled in sharing his feelings about it?

Nathalie felt as if another personality had suddenly jumped into his body. It was both endearing and deeply disconcerting.

"What about you," Eli continued, "what are your favorite movies?"

"Umm, I ahh…" This conversation felt more surreal to her.

"Surely there are some you really like more than others."

"Well, yeah..." Nathalie suddenly felt that going with the flow might illuminate something about him that would be to her advantage. "Yeah, I do," she said thinking it through. "*To Kill a Mockingbird.*"

"Excellent, absolute classic," he enthused. "And how can you not like Gregory Peck."

"And "*Field of Dreams,*" she continued, "I really like Kevin Costner and James Earl Jones in *Field of Dreams.*"

"Spectacular choice," Eli said. "Had the last words said to Burt Lancaster in a movie. Remember? Ray Liotta—Shoeless Joe Jackson—said '*Hey Rookie, you were good.*' "

His smile urged her on.

"*Shawshank Redemption,*" said Nathalie. "Definitely one of my favorites."

"And anyone in their right mind," agreed Eli. "Seems we have similar tastes. Perhaps we should catch a movie together sometime."

"Yeah, sure—what?—no! I'm not gonna—with you?!

The conversation had now veered into complete insanity to her. Eli remained very calm, even when she clasped her hands to her head shaking it in sheer disbelief.

"Your father, I believe, had come to understand me. I hope you might be open to that."

What surprised her when she looked up was the sincerity in his eyes. She knew his charm was on full display and she prided herself that she stayed alert to not get carried away with his magnetism. There was however something else in this moment. Something she had never sensed before…a certain innocence that her intuition hinted was too hard to fake, and yet still, she couldn't completely trust that feeling.

Eli decided to bring things back to the business at hand. "I know you've been boning up on the Borelli estate," he said.

"And how do you know—"

"I caught the sun's reflection off your telephoto lens when you were by the grotto pond."

Nathalie thought she had been so careful to stay hidden so this was disappointing to learn. Score another point for Cross. It bugged her that she had no idea who was ahead in clever moves.

"I trust you're not just obsessed with me," Cross continued. "But I do want to warn you about Jake Kracauer and Marty Lefkowitz. I know they're on your list for the Waldorf job if you've done your homework. Don't get too close. Don't press them too hard. Wait for Saturday, you can stop them and recover the Waldorf jewels. I believe it's one of them, maybe both."

This all sounded too convenient to Nathalie. "Don't get too close," she said.

"That's right. They're not good guys."

"Don't get too close…those words…were on a note someone left in my apartment."

"That was me. But it just as easily could've been one of them."

Nathalie swallowed hard to repress her emotions. "You just invited yourself into my apartment."

"You really need better locks. I don't want to see any harm come to you. I know you're not going to back down—not Nate's daughter, not a Seeger—so I wanted to give you a jolt to stay alert. To show you how easy it was to get to you."

Was this a warning to help her, she thought, or an intended threat? The implied danger could just as easily be coming from him.

"You're also in Donelli's way in dealing with me," he added. "He won't take kindly to that. He's a cop who has lost his decency. Your father never lost it. But the bitterness that comes from dealing with *the street* has shredded Donelli's humanity."

"My dad shared some thoughts with me about Donelli."

"Maybe not enough. Donelli was not fond of your father, jealous of his clearance record and his reputation, something Donelli couldn't get for himself. Now at the end of a long run, nearing mandatory retirement and not a lot to show for it has him looking for a little something extra—or a lot—a big bite of the good life. And what wouldn't he do and who wouldn't he shove aside—permanently if necessary—to grab it for himself."

"Why are you telling me all this? Just to throw me off?"

"Let's just say that I owe your father and mother something."

"Maybe what you owe them is letting me bring you to justice."

He knew full well what she was getting at and it was not about any heist since her tone had all the subtlety of a stiletto.

"Maybe I deserve that."

Nathalie felt a real sense of remorse in his response. There was also sadness to it.

"In any event, you need to stay very alert. That at least is a good Seeger trait. So is knowing when to trust. But now you've got work to do."

The level of sincerity and honesty that she felt from him thrust confusion on her desire to hate him. Going with the flow of their very surreal conversation revealed something to her. Not sure whether it provided her with an advantage or a setback.

She discovered that she didn't really hate him; in fact she now struggled with the feeling that she genuinely liked him. Where were those missing pages?! What else had her father revealed about him?! Oh God…she really needed to speak with her mother.

CHAPTER FOURTEEN

Men are afraid that women will laugh at them.
Women are afraid that men will kill them.

Margaret Atwood

The stylish Regency Hotel on Park Avenue on the Upper East Side was a luxurious environment in which to go to work. But that luxury could not prevent you from being killed. Nathalie knew that. Keeping one's distance from the possibility of death therefore had its advantages. She aimed her telephoto lens at the hotel's entrance as Jake Kracauer exited and slipped into a waiting cab. When the cab pulled away and disappeared down Park Avenue, only then did she step out from the shadows across the street.

She was now clear to cross the wide street and *get to work* as Eli Cross had suggested; only he had said she should not get too close to the likes of Jake Kracauer. Well, she thought, at least she had waited until he left the hotel. She needed to know more about Kracauer especially when her main heist subject had told her to stay away.

As she stepped toward the crosswalk, a cane prodded her sharply in the back.

Nathalie whirled to see her brother facing her with a challenging glare in his eyes.

"You're not watchin' your back if a guy with a cane can come up on you," he said.

"I know what I'm doing."

Nathalie's insistent tone meant to Ian she didn't fully know what she was doing; only winging it in a rush to find answers. Traffic whizzed by them and the throng of fast-moving pedestrians flowed around them at the curb like they were an island in the sea.

"You could let the cops do their job and nail whoever it is," suggested Ian.

"I'll clean up my own mess, thank you."

"I think tryin' to figure this guy out has you—"

"What?! Pushing too hard?!"

"Well…" said Ian hoping to calm her down.

"Did you ever stop pushing on a story until you had the goods?!"

"That's not what I mean."

"No, Ian, what you mean is you wouldn't have said any of this if I was a man."

"Now wait," Ian protested, "you're my sister and I'm just lookin' out for you."

"And you're my brother, so I should take your arm and help you hobble along?!"

Her point hit home and Ian relented in his insistence. His sister tried to be as tough and relentless as their father; maybe even more so because she had something to prove to the whole male sex. To Ian, she risked lashing herself to the same rocket sled to hell of getting used by Cross that had snared their father—and their mother.

"I'd hoped you of all people would see me as more than *just a woman.*"

"I do—I do, goddamnit! It's just this guy…he's got me all twisted up. I read the same files you did; you read how confused Dad was about him!"

"Which is why I can't just let this slide."

"What if…look I'll just say it…what if Dad finally thought Cross had changed and wanted to cut him a break?"

"You mean because Jean-Pierre told you he changed or was trying to change, but maybe there was one last little thing he had to do? Well I'd like to nail his ass for Dad when he's doing that one last little thing."

"Jean-Pierre told me that Vadoma had told him they were petty thieves growing up together, but that was for survival, traveling around France. She said he made something of himself and she adores him like a brother."

"We don't know how he ended up in that family or what it means and I'm sure Vadoma does adore him. Wouldn't you adore someone who set you and your husband up in business and keeps you financially stable?"

Ian was out of angles to get her to change her mind. Maybe one last Hail Mary toss. "How do you know that you're not fallin' for this guy like Pop did—or even Mom?!"

"It's not like that!" Nathalie's eyes blazed with indignation.

Ian instantly knew *it was like that!* "Someone's gonna get burned in this game, Nattie!"

"Where's Mom, do you know?" said Nathalie evading him.

"What?"

"Mom! I called her she didn't answer."

"I don't know," said Ian, thrown by her sudden inquiry.

"She's not in Montreal with…Jack?! Is she?!"

"I have no idea," said Ian. "What's that all about?"

"It's about Cross, what do you think?! But right now I've got a brief window of opportunity with another suspect and I'm not gonna blow that goin' round in circles with you!"

She dashed across Park Avenue dodging traffic precipitating a flurry of blared horns then drivers' arms thrust out of windows flipping her off! She rushed into The Regency to get on with it and *work the case!*

At the front desk, Nathalie asked for a clean Regency Hotel bathrobe. She knew the handsome young man at the hotel's check-in would bring her one quickly without involving housekeeping when she smiled at him and told him how soft it felt against her naked skin right after a shower.

On the eighteenth floor hallway, the elevator doors opened to an empty hallway. Nathalie dressed only in the Regency bathrobe clutched her clothes wrapped in the bathrobe's bag. She stepped out into the hallway and quickly hid her clothes behind the large hallway planter next to the elevator.

Jake Kracauer's hotel room door clicked open by a housecleaning maid while right behind her Nathalie wore only the bathrobe and a sheepish grin.

"I feel so stupid about this," Nathalie said, "I'll take my key next time. Thank you."

The maid smiled and then closed the door, leaving Nathalie to her privacy inside.

Immediately, she explored the closet and saw a tuxedo, black leather jacket, several black pants and black running shoes. Appropriate colors for the work of a thief at night, she thought.

In the dresser drawers were several polo shirts. When she moved them she heard the scraping sound of metal against wood. Lifting the pile of shirts revealed a Walther P5 9mm with ankle strap. A good carry gun. Accurate and reliable. Easy to use. She made a mental note that the P5 ejected shells to the left making it easier for lefthanders. She didn't know if Kracauer was a southpaw or not, but every detail might have value later on.

Nathalie replaced the shirts and turned her attention to a briefcase she noticed under the corner table. Lifting it up on top of the table, she discovered it was locked. She pulled a bobby pin from her hair—placed there as a tool not fashion—and inserted it into the latch lock. She twisted the bobby pin and then heard the room door lock click open. That was *not* the lock she wanted to hear open!

Nathalie leaped out of the line of sight as Jake Kracauer shoved open the door and strode inside. Frustrated and in a hurry, he jerked open the closet door and reached for something inside his leather jacket, grabbed it, and turned to leave, but spotted the briefcase on top of the table. That's not where he had left it.

Nathalie hugged the wall in the corner. She saw the briefcase and winced at her mistake. Barely breathing, she listened—ready to be found and confronted—and finally, with relief, heard the door close and click shut. She took a step to move, then trusted her instinct, and waited. Didn't move. Kept listening. All was silent.

Kracauer had not left. He silently positioned himself against the inside wall of the entrance hall near the corner that led into the room.

Nathalie trusted the silence, but only to a point. She slowly inched along the wall toward the corner that brought her closer to Kracauer. Each footstep silently placed. Her intuition halted her.

Kracauer pulled out a switchblade and pressed the release but didn't blunt the blade's whipped opening.

Nathalie stopped her next step on hearing the swift *snap-click* of the opening blade.

Kracauer heard the sound of Nathalie's movement from around the corner and waited with the deadly blade, ready to strike. No one appeared. Instead he heard her voice.

"Hi, housekeeping? Could you send someone up to room 1810. They let me in the wrong room. I'm supposed to be in 1812. I locked myself out. Yes, thank you, right away please."

Nathalie hung up the phone and turned around—gasping for effect—and faced Kracauer holding his switchblade!

"What the hell you doin' in my room?!"

Maximizing her shocked charade, she spewed out a torrent of words.

"Oh my God...please put the knife away. This is all just a silly mistake. I came out of the shower and realized my boyfriend had just left—we're right next door—and he hadn't told me where to meet him. We're from Iowa and this is my first time in New York, and I knew we were gonna have dinner at the South Street Seaport, but I didn't know which restaurant, so I ran down the hall to catch him at the elevator, but he'd already gone. My room door had locked shut when I got back and I was so upset when I finally found the maid that I didn't realize that she let me in the wrong room until she'd already left. I was just calling them to send someone back up to let me in my room."

To punctuate her frazzled performance, she pulled her robe together even tighter, hugging her chest with her fists guarding her breasts.

Kracauer studied her...then closed the switchblade.

Nathalie saw her opportunity. "I should probably wait for them out in the hall, that way you can have your room back." Then with a sigh, she added breathlessly, "I'm really sorry."

She slinked by Kracauer and reached for the door, opened it, and moved to step out when his hand slammed the door shut in front of her and locked it! He grabbed her by the hair and yanked her back into the room and flung her on the bed!

Nathalie twisted onto her back to get up but Kracauer jammed her down with his hand in her face then straddled her and pinned both her arms under his knees! His switchblade flashed open again and he laid it across her throat!

Kracauer leaned close to her face. "Next time you make up some bullshit story about gettin' out of the shower make sure your hair's not perfect."

"My hair's perfect? Thank you," said Nathalie straight-faced knowing she'd blown her ruse.

"There's no way you're from Iowa. You're a New York bitch."

Kracauer slid open her bathrobe with his switchblade. She lay naked except for a lace bra and the lavender panties from Bloomingdale's. His eyes crawled all over her.

She glared at him, defiant even in her helplessness.

"I've seen you around," he said.

"People are watchin' you too."

"They think I pulled the Waldorf?"

"Maybe. But they're giving credit—"

"To Eli Cross," Kracauer said with biting disdain.

"It fits his style. He's the best, right?"

"Used to be. Cross can't cut it anymore. Lost his nerve. Ask him about Monte Carlo."

"What makes you think I'll be talkin' to him?"

"You're a woman. He'll come to you."

The matter-of-fact manner in which Kracauer tossed off that comment touched on the red flag that Nathalie herself had raised. Kracauer recognized that *am I being used* look.

"Ah, I see…already has," Kracauer said, pleased with his assessment. Then he added with a pleasurable smirk, "Did he take you dancing, some place classy?"

Nathalie's eyes flashed with anger at his insight…then drifted into disappointment at the realization of Cross's pattern.

"And you thought you were special," said Kracauer, thoroughly enjoying twisting the psychological knife, at this moment sharper than a real one.

Nathalie did her best to return a defiant glare, but the distinct possibility that she was just one of many *assets* used by Cross was a blow to her confidence.

Kracauer tapped the switchblade against her windpipe. "You sure aren't to me."

A knock on the door was followed by the sound of a key card clicking the lock open.

"Housekeeping," called out the maid as she opened the door.

Nathalie quickly replied, "Be right with you."

Kracauer leaned down close to her face. "If we meet again, we're gonna dance." He snapped the switchblade closed right by her throat and moved his other arm behind him and slid his hand down between her legs. "My way." His fingers rubbed her lavender panties seductively.

The maid waited for Nathalie when she stepped out of Kracauer's room and into the hallway. She closed her bathrobe; doing her best to not seem disgusted.

"Thank you for coming." With a frustrated tug, she finally secured the cloth belt around the robe. Shoving down her revulsion of Kracauer, Nathalie took the maid's hand to keep her close by her and led her toward the elevator. "Slight change of plans. I'm late for an appointment."

Nathalie retrieved her wrapped bundle of clothes from behind the large planter and punched the elevator button.

"Could you leave some extra mints on my pillow? That'd be great. 1812."

The elevator doors opened and Nathalie stepped into the middle of a group of Japanese businessmen, who stared at her bathrobe and apparent nakedness underneath. To their shock, Nathalie dropped her robe and began dressing as the doors closed.

∞

Three suspect photos slid onto Lieutenant Donelli's desk as if dealt from a card deck for a round of perp poker. They were Eli Cross—the King of Crime card, Jake Kracauer—the Jack of Ripper card, and Marty Lefkowitz—the Joker card the way Nathalie thought of them.

"Take your time," Nathalie said. "Did you see any of these men at the Waldorf that day?"

A hand pointed to Jake Kracauer's photo.

"Just this one," said Ramone, one of the catering waiters from the Waldorf event.

"Are you sure?"

Ramone nodded affirmatively to Nathalie as Lt. Donelli propped his feet up on the desk obscuring the photos. Donelli smirked at Nathalie's investigative efforts.

"Yeah, I brought the guy three drinks, all iced tea."

"What was he doing?" Donelli tossed in his two-cent effort as it was after all his office.

"Just watchin'."

"What was he watching?" Nathalie jumped back in wresting control of the questioning.

"Everything. I thought he was one of the security guys."

"Did you see him after everything got crazy?"

"No, just when I brought him drinks."

Donelli's patience for humoring Nathalie evaporated. "Okay, Ramone, thanks for comin' down. We may need you back sometime."

"That's cool. I'm around."

Ramone headed out through the crowded squad room of Midtown North Precinct loaded with perps, witnesses and assorted oddballs.

Nathalie picked up the photo of Jake Kracauer.

"Our new hot suspect."

"That's your rocket scientist deduction," said Donelli with a healthy dose of disdain.

"Ramone's the third waiter that ID'd him! Nobody saw Cross or Lefkowitz!"

"Cross was there," Donelli said matter-of-factly. "He's the only one," he added definitely.

"You just stick with what you want to believe, don't you?" Nathalie really wanted to respond: *Fuck you, you dishrag douche bag,* but she held back...barely

Donelli busied himself with a pile of police forms. "I don't waste time with irrelevant information."

"Jake Kracauer dared me to nail him. This guy's ego's on overdrive."

"That's nice."

"Aren't you going to act on this?!" Nathalie thought of stabbing him in the forehead with the naked pole dancer letter opener on his desk.

"Kracauer doesn't have the touch for a job like that."

"Maybe he's been practicing." Nathalie knew that if—*if*—Cross was right about the imposter, then Kracauer could be the one, and could've been boning up to take the title.

A grisly perp broke free of his arresting officers as if jacked up on PCP and leaped up onto a desk top then jumped from desk to desk kicking cops in the face as they grabbed for him, until he landed on Donelli's desk. He kicked away Donelli's outstretched arms, but Nathalie whirled around, whipped her purse into the perp's face with a heavy thud and knocked him off his feet into the large trash can!

The perp was out cold!

"Not bad," said Donelli. He was actually impressed though he suppressed the feeling.

Nathalie removed a five pound chrome dumbbell from her purse.

"Works every time. Plus adds a little pump to any walk."

The perp's arresting officers high-fived Nathalie then dragged the perp off as Donelli picked up his scattered paper work.

"You like Cross, don't you?"

"Everybody's not dirty, Donelli."

"What is it with you Seegers? Are you all a sucker for this guy?!"

Nathalie studied him... reading his irritation. She wondered what Donelli knew about Cross and her mother. That thought made the bile surge in her stomach.

Donelli shook his head wondering what the hell was wrong with her whole family.

Nathalie thought of what Cross had told her about Donelli. "You're jealous of the way he lives, his style."

For a fleeting moment Donelli flinched.

Nathalie saw the opening and pressed her case. "You want it, but you know you'll never have it. You can't stand that he got away with it—or accept that he's really gone straight."

"You a shrink now?!"

"He found a way to put it behind him, but you haven't."

Donelli just stared back at her—silent—measuring the edge of truth. He knew he deserved a lot more than he had and he planned on grabbing whatever he could from putting an end to Cross. The way he saw it, she was either going to be with him in nailing this son of a bitch or she was going to be in the way. He wouldn't allow anything or anyone to fuck up his plans this time. This was the championship round and he was going to be the only one standing at the bell...whatever it took.

"You know that Cartier's international bash is gonna be in the Hamptons this weekend. And you know the Waldorf event was chump change compared to this. And you know Cross'll be there."

"He wants the imposter caught, but he won't be there," insisted Nathalie.

"Are you sure? Really sure?"

"He doesn't want to risk things being pinned on him." Nathalie felt defensive which seemed suddenly strange to her. Why was she defending Cross, this man who was her prey, and possibly so many other things she hadn't figured out yet?

"That's what he told you."

"Yeah…" She felt a chilled rush in the pit of her stomach wondering if she was so intent on being right in front of Donelli that she wasn't adding up simple math. She hoped Donelli would just shut up and she could take her weighted purse and go home.

"So…Eli Cross isn't interested in risk."

Donelli let his statement hang in the air unaccompanied by any other thought until he saw the hesitation in Nathalie's eyes. She was smart. He knew she'd already connected his dots but he took considerable delight in drawing the thick, unmistakable lines himself.

"Think about this," said Donelli in the tone of a trial lawyer calmly making his slam-dunk closing argument to the jury. "Cross is safe now, with what he says is a good, straight job, and presumably a nice, good, regular salary. But that's the problem. It's safe. And that's not how Eli Cross likes to live."

Nathalie was pissed. At herself. This assholic, bitter prick of a cop had gotten her to face her own charade and its illusion. She had become Don Quixote staring into the mirror and seeing his dream reality shattered. She knew to close this case—and not be snookered by it—she needed to find if Eli Cross had a vulnerable spot. All men had one. Even the unknowable Eli Cross.

It seemed her father hadn't found it in all his years of tracking him. Maybe it took a woman to find it, by being a woman. Did she dare take that step with all the emotional and physical vulnerability it presented? How far was she willing to go?

CHAPTER FIFTEEN

*Only those who risk going too far can find out how far
one can go.*

T.S. Eliot

"Are you makin' it with that art lover hottie?!"

"What?" said Nathalie? She had quickly answered her cell phone at home in her kitchen and did not recognize the voice. She had been expecting Megan. This was not Megan.

"Don't hold out on me girl, I need the down and dirty," said Lisette.

"Is this…Lisette?" asked Nathalie tentatively.

"Oh yeah it's me. Your ears plugged up?"

"No, I thought you were—you don't sound like yourself."

"'Cause I'm at home relaxin'. Bra's off and those bad girls are swingin'. I'm all smooth and sophisticated at the office. I can only be that cool for so long, then I gotta get real." Lisette was in a good mood.

"Well I've only known you from the museum and museum parties and business lunches." Nathalie's guard shot up from this sudden and *different* angle launched at her from her sophisticated professional friend since this was the woman who provided her the information on The Baronfeld Museum so that she could meet Eli Cross.

"Yeah, that's probably gotta change. I've been thinkin' we need to be better friends."

Lisette Granger held an executive level position at the Museum of Modern Art with involvement in art acquisitions. She came by it impressively from a full-ride scholarship to Howard University in Washington, D.C and advanced studies at the University of Florence in art and art history. Fluent in Italian and French, her English was as erudite as needed…at the office.

Among real friends, her Baton Rouge youth rose in full bloom, plenty of soul sister sass. Her first class office sophistication was topped by her striking looks. Luminescent black skin, sparkling eyes, angled facial features like a model but with luscious curves and close-cropped tight hair black as night with a subtle blonde-colored streak on the right side, slightly jagged like a lightning bolt.

"Why now?" wondered Nathalie.

"Takin' a chance, I guess. I've always known you to be direct, a real professional woman who had her shit together," said Lisette pointedly.

"Thank you, I've wanted to be taken seriously." Nathalie had no idea where this conversation was going. The fact that Lisette started it off with a randy reference to Eli Cross—presumably the *art lover hottie*—had her on alert.

"Me too," Lisette chimed in. "Sort of a requirement at MoMA. The straight skinny is that I got a friend who knows your friend Megan and she told me that you two really know how to let your hair down. You get me?"

"Yeah, but I'm not exactly sure…"

"Yeah, I know. Here's what brought this up. I've been invited to one of the city's top art circle social parties at an outrageously expensive penthouse on Beekman Place. It's going to be stuffy as hell. I gotta go and I don't feel like being perfect and professional by myself anymore. I can't bring my boyfriend because he plays baseball for the Red Sox and is a pariah in New York. It's very last minute—like tonight. I can invite a guest. I thought you know how to play nice with the other kids and maybe your Baronfeld mystery guy, who your friend Megan says is smokin' hot, may be there too. If he's anyone in the art world he will be, especially if he has mucho moola. I just wanted to go with someone who'd be in on the joke and we could dish the good shit later. Besides, all you white chicks need more soul sister connection. But if this is too much, then we never had this conversation."

Lisette Granger was one of the sharpest, most stylishly sophisticated and cultured women Nathalie thought she knew. Human beings were mysteriously multi-layered and this casual side of Lisette had been professionally camouflaged. Did she know Eli Cross? Their worlds surely crisscrossed. Had Megan spilled the goods during friendly gossip about what Nathalie felt was privileged information and insight just between the two of them concerning her case and Cross? Was Lisette an ally of Cross, part of his overall plan of distraction and deception? Or was Nathalie just reading too much into everything on this case that still wasn't clear? *What the hell, she thought, let's find out.*

"Okay, I got two questions. One. Are you gonna stuff those bad girls back inside a dress when we go or is this the new Lisette?"

A hearty guffaw burst from the other end of the phone. "That's what I'm talkin'. They'll be cradled in upper class chic couture but exposing enough skin to invite indecent speculation. Now what's number two?"

"Do you know my art guy?"

"Not a clue. He got a name?"

"Yeah, but let's see if you can pick him out just by lookin'."

"Ohhh, I like that. If I spot him, is he fair game or have you claimed him?"

"Fair game."

Another hearty laugh exploded over the phone. "That may call for more cleavage!"

Nathalie thought this was too strange to ignore. To watch Cross *work the room* of potential victims—some of whom were bound to be at the Cartier bash in the Hamptons—made it worth chancing that he might attend this party. The *fair game* idea was a realization that she had been *playing the game* too close to the vest. Eli had even told her that it was *a loose game.*

Maybe it was time to remember that he was a man and she was a woman which tilted the field of play in her favor. If Eli wasn't there, then she'd split early and Lisette would just have to tough it out on her own; she and the bad girls.

℘

The private elevator to the penthouse on Beekman Place happened to be surprisingly empty, though lingering layers of perfume indicated that legions had preceded them, bathed and scented to impress. Lisette's dress, elegantly stated, displayed a delicate balance between classically discreet and an invitation to the devil's playground. The interpretation of which way the balance would tip resided in her smile, something akin to the Cheshire cat.

Nathalie remembered Lisette's hearty laugh about her cleavage when she had stood before her closet wondering what to wear. She had chosen the blue dress with the long slit up the leg that Megan had referenced days ago for her second meeting with Cross. Her gentle curves remained in the shadow of Lisette's, but no one was going to out game her gams in this dress.

"How did you and Megan become friends? My friend Denise Yamura—she works at Lincoln Center—thinks Megan's an original." The sophisticated Lisette emerged once more at the helm with this genuine inquiry.

"She lent me a hammer," Nathalie smiled in remembrance.

"You were fixing something?"

"Oh yeah, the boyfriend we discovered that we unknowingly shared who was two-timing both of us with a third woman."

"You went after him with hammers?!"

"No, the scenery on opening night of the off-Broadway play he was starring in."

Casual Lisette came roaring back with a hearty guffaw. "I may borrow a hammer from you if I my ballplayer guy even thinks of bangin' those dugout groupie skanks."

The elevator door opened into the foyer of the penthouse with the party in full swing. Sophisticated Lisette sparked once again firmly in place, her posture straighter, shoulders back, head elevated. This party existed now as pure business except for guessing Nathalie's art lover hottie.

The art work on the walls alone dwarfed the GDP of some third world countries. Nathalie knew most of these people would also be at the Cartier bash in the Hamptons at the Borelli estate on Saturday. The dazzling jewelry adorning flesh this night would be back in the safe by then. Even more astonishing trinkets would be displayed on body parts for all to see. The only one to wear the same jewels on Saturday, and thus twice in the same week, would be someone who died tonight and their body not discovered until Monday. Even in death they'd be mortified.

Nathalie did not begrudge them their jewels or their wealth. She sensed the pressure to maintain their status among the herd and wanted no part of that parade. The pressure she felt *to keep up and surpass the boys* remained professional and not societal. Her own jewelry which she wore that night—simple yet elegant—resembled mere pauper's pebbles in comparison. She felt neither suffocating impoverishment because of it nor paralyzing mortification for wearing the tiny diamond earrings twice this week. She thought she stood comfortable in her own skin, but seeing herself in a mirror brought a sudden rush of realization that nearly undid her.

Each piece of jewelry had been given to her as a romantic gift from a man—several different men—none of whom were still in her life! Even, Tom, the latest to tread upon her heart now only already a faded memory; the bitterness of the breakup no longer had a bite. The taste was just…gone.

It hit her hard that she had spent a good deal of time with people who no longer mattered, who probably didn't matter when she was with them. Why had she not realized that? It was not that she felt she had needed a man; she did not. Why had she wasted so much time seeking…seeking what?

The jewelry adorning her body, though lovely, suddenly felt cold as if its reflected light came from ice. She desperately searched her memory for a feeling from being with one of them—any of them— that…that mattered. Instead she struggled to even recall their faces. She stared into the mirror so intently, willing the past to be visible, that she did not see the tuxedoed man lean in behind her.

"Not a hair out of place," said Eli.

Nathalie's eyes flash-focused to the image behind her in the mirror. Eli Cross had silently slipped into her life once again unnoticed. He was as gorgeous as the masterpieces on the walls. Adorned in a Giorgio Armani tux, he embodied the epitome of the resplendent male.

"You are quite naturally lovely, and without airs. So why is it that you look…lost?"

The tone of his voice resonated with simple sincerity. She felt no reason to doubt there existed any intent other than appreciation.

"Well I don't know why I was…"

Nathalie fell quiet and simply looked at him; gazed into his eyes and for the first time felt no duplicity. His smile remained genuine, soft, an invitation…but to what, she thought. Her professional wits returned. "These are more your people than mine."

"My people?" Eli questioned his inclusion.

"Yes, well, more like your targets, right?"

"Oh, so I'm scoping them out."

"Saturday is the big night. Most will be there."

"Indeed. And you as well, I hope."

"If I can find something appropriate to wear," Nathalie said.

Cross liked this woman who stood toe-to-toe with him comfortable in her own skin. Nathalie enjoyed returning his gaze without feeling like a gauntlet had been thrown. A strange feeling for her. Simply two people at a party and with a loss for words. A strange, tingling feeling, indeed.

"Would you care for a drink?" Eli finally asked.

"Sure. Some wine maybe."

"Red or white?"

"Surprise me," Nathalie said with an enticing smile.

"I will."

He turned and moved to the nearest bar station with the subtle elegance of a dancer. A true challenge, Nathalie thought, when the enemy was the most pleasing among them all.

"I'm guessing he's not here," said Lisette gliding up next to her.

"What? Who?" Nathalie felt a wave of guilt slam into her.

"Your art lover hottie. I'm not seeing anyone who might fit the description, unless you're dabbling in married men."

"No, no, don't want that complication," said Nathalie quickly. "And you're right, he's not here. I've been to every room. The art is amazing, but he's a no show. Have you paid your respects, kissed the rings?"

"Enough so I can leave whenever you want."

"Maybe a little longer," Nathalie responded.

She saw a woman, around fifty, approach Eli at the bar as if hypnotically drawn to him. Perhaps the forthcoming interplay would give her a first row seat on how Eli set up his victims.

The woman dripped with jewels. Nathalie thought the sheer weight of them had to be damaging to her spine. Stealing a few would be the humanitarian thing for Eli to do. Nathalie figured she represented the quintessential Eli Cross target.

Lisette followed Nathalie's captivated gaze over to the bar.

"Now there's one for you. The man at the bar."

Lisette pointed at Eli.

Nathalie felt caught, handcuffs slapped on her! She didn't want anyone to know her connection to Cross. It would clutter the playing field.

Nathalie decided to deflect Lisette's suggestion and turn the tables.

"What about you? And don't give me any bullshit about the baseball player boyfriend."

"No, can't touch that," said Lisette with a hint of disappointment about Cross.

"Wow…I thought you'd be all over that. What's the catch?"

"I have to do business with him from time to time," Lisette said.

Those words sent a chill up Nathalie's spine.

"With Eli Cross, anything else would be too confusing," Lisette admitted begrudgingly."

"Eli Cross…don't know him, but I get it," said Nathalie. "Outrageously hot hunks can be confusing."

"It's not that, and it's not that I have a boyfriend, who I actually like. No, I don't fully trust Eli Cross, and I don't want to get used."

"He's a player, a womanizer," said Nathalie, pressing her for more precision.

"No, I don't know anything about that, but I doubt he's lacking in dates."

Lisette let rip a bad girl chuckle, but then her demeanor turned serious again.

"No, it's that he provides art masterpiece security for wealthy patrons from time to time…but the rumors are too heavy to ignore that he dances on the other side as well. That's a web I can't get caught in."

"The other side? As in stealing?"

"That's a very crude word for a man of his sophistication," Lisette said. "But if that doesn't bother you, let me know how he is in bed."

"Why would I…"

"Look at him, why wouldn't you? Seriously girl, even for one night, that's a once in a millennium memory." Lisette gave Nathalie a gentle shove toward the bar. "Get on up there. Show a little leg."

Nathalie noticed that the woman who approached Cross simply stared at him, almost stunned. She couldn't take her eyes off of him. How would Eli react?

The bartender poured two glasses of red wine for Cross.

The woman remained laser focused in an eerie and disturbing way. Was she a rich nut job, Nathalie wondered? Some women totally lost their shit with a man that handsome.

Nathalie knew that Eli noticed this woman. Nothing new for a woman to stare at him and Nathalie felt he used it many times to his advantage. She watched him calculate his next move with this woman, clearly a wealthy art patron, and with her cascading jewels she provided a doubly suitable target. But he didn't have to do anything.

The woman made the first move and stepped closer, almost mystified, and placed her hand on his arm before he could take the wine glasses. Nathalie moved close enough to hear her, but not easily seen in the crowd that pressed back from the bar.

"Oh you look just like him or how I thought he would look," said Katharine Otley, the bejeweled woman.

"I'm sorry, what?"

Nathalie caught a flinch in his body language. He leaned back, for once not at ease.

"Oh no, I'm sorry, it's just eerie that's all," said Katharine. "A boy I knew from school. We were just kids, but I had a crush on him."

She stared at him, studying him.

"And you think…" Cross sounded uneasy, a crack in the usual steadfast confidence..

"Well I thought, yes, but obviously no, you couldn't be."

"I see…sorry…did he know you had a crush on him?" Eli looked at her hand that still held onto his arm.

"Oh no, no, I was much too shy then." Katharine suddenly realized she still clutched his arm and quickly removed her hand, embarrassed. "I'm sorry, it's just that…" She couldn't say any more, but kept staring deeply into his eyes as if searching for a memory.

Nathalie watched Cross recover his composure and his charm.

"Perhaps if he met you today," Eli smiled, "he would be the shy one, for you are quite lovely."

"You're too kind." She blushed, embarrassed once again. "I think maybe champagne and memories are a blurry combination. Enjoy your evening."

Flustered, she turned quickly, her necklaces rattled from the sudden movement, and she pushed her way back through the bar crowd.

Cross watched her disappear. Nathalie didn't take her eyes off of him. He had not seen her watching him. That was good, for her front row seat showed her a man off balance for once. A sudden wave of vulnerability washed over him. He reached for their wine glasses, took hold, then thought better of it and simply left them as he moved away from the bar.

Nathalie watched as Eli did not come back in her direction. Stunned, she saw him move decisively to the exit from the penthouse and leave the party.

Nathalie wondered what the hell just happened?! Like a hound on the hunt from a fresh scent, Nathalie cut through the crowd to find the mysterious woman who so destabilized Eli Cross. Nathalie approached Katharine Otley from behind and tapped her on the shoulder.

"Excuse me."

Katharine turned around. "Yes, what is it?"

Nathalie smiled pleasantly and pressed her point. "That handsome man at the bar you were talking to a few moments ago, you thought you knew him?"

"Yes, but it was just silly, obviously. Do you know him? I'm sorry if I…"

"Oh no," said Nathalie smiling to stay in Katharine's good graces. "He's not a boyfriend or husband or anything. I was wondering who he was. He's quite striking. You thought you knew him, why is that silly?"

"It was a very long time ago. I was just a kid, barely fifteen."

The full impact of time suddenly hit her.

"Wow…that's thirty five years ago," said Katharine shaking her head in disbelief. "I'm almost fifty now. I just had a flash when I saw him—totally unexpected—didn't even know the memory was there. It's strange how you retain some feelings and then all of a sudden…but oh no, it's not him, it couldn't be."

"Why not, people can be unrecognizable from when they were kids." Nathalie kept pressing, sensing there some deeper truth to unearth. "Do you look the same?"

"No, not even close," muttered Katharine self-consciously.

"Me neither," Nathalie quickly added to seem simpatico.

"It was his eyes, that's all. He had the same…" Katharine stopped suddenly embarrassed. "What you suddenly remember is so strange—

and all of a sudden." She leaned closer to Nathalie and whispered: "Menopause is a bitch. Probably explains everything."

Nathalie smiled knowingly and touched Katharine's arm in sisterhood support, but her bloodhound instincts wouldn't let go of the scent. "Even so, why couldn't it be him?"

"He was killed in a plane crash with his family."

"Oh, I'm sorry…" Nathalie's intuition was on fire. "Was it with his wife and kids?"

"No, no, long time ago. We had both just started ninth grade. We were the same age. It's so strange, I hadn't thought about him for years until I saw that man's face. Elliot was the first person my age I knew who died. He was only fourteen or fifteen. Maybe that had something to do with it. Sure felt like an emotionally brutal way to lose a school girl crush."

"His name was Elliot?" Nathalie could barely believe what she was hearing.

"Yes, funny, isn't it? I still remember his name even though I never got to know him." Katharine reached back into her memory and responded softly with the fondness of a schoolgirl's first crush. "Elliot Crositer."

CHAPTER SIXTEEN

*"A woman's guess is much more accurate than a
man's certainty."*

Rudyard Kipling

The cleaning crew at DRN had wrapped up. It was late. Only Megan plodded on in her cubicle back in the depths of the graphic artist labyrinth. The fluorescent lights spread a ghastly pall and isolated the walled space like a prison from the glistening darkness of the city with its sparkling and beckoning lights.

The squeaky wheels of the janitorial cart cast an eerie sound that penetrated deep into the workplace as Jordy Barrett reached the exit. The forty year old janitor aged beyond his years wiped his forehead with the gnarled fingers of his right hand. He gazed at the lone light floating up from Megan's distant cubicle and shook his head, a wry smile creasing his lips.

"Megan, you be good," said Jordy, his voice carried across the vast space.

"Aren't I always?" Megan called out. "You can hit the lights, Jordy. I'm out of here soon."

"You best be, you got a life, ya know."

"So they tell me."

Jordy hit the main panel light switch on his way out. The ubiquitous buzz of the fluorescents ceased. Darkness swept the labyrinth except for the small pool of light that rose from Megan's desk lamp.

Her computer rested mercifully dark. Her focus centered on a yellow legal pad with rows of scratched out lines of ad copy. Frustration hugged her. The silence so thick it penetrated the soul. The deep loneliness of this moment echoed like a death rattle in her heart. One day she knew it would all end for her and she wondered where this ad campaign would rank in the cherished moments of her life. She pushed a grim smile out in her pity party parade and envisioned receiving an award for the campaign that launched this new diarrhea medicine. It would be the *Shit Stopper Award.* She'd place the statue next to her cardboard cutout of Donald Trump which she kept adorned with women's clothing.

But if she happened to be rich—that thought an adrenalin rush—she could yell out *fuck this shit* and not suffer any consequences.

She looked down at the drivel she had written: *When the runs have you runnin', the answer is Verawall. It's a pill that works like a cork, only easier. Goes in one end not the other.* She held her pen suspended in mid-air poised for additions, then slashed at the words on her yellow legal pad. Her courage overflowed—being alone—and she bellowed out, "Fuck this shit!"

Her victorious, triumphant rebel yell over the drudgery of her job was short-lived. Welling up from the recesses of truth she couldn't avoid, the haunting lyrics of her favorite songwriter Leonard Cohen *"The rich have got their channels in the bedrooms of the poor..."* whispered out from memory and brought her crashing back into reality.

"Okay, fucked is fucked," she said out loud to herself, "Let's go home."

Her cell phone's ringtone shattered the deathly silence! She jumped like a scared rabbit!

"Fuck!"

It was Nathalie.

Megan stabbed the phone and spit out "You scared the shit out of me!"

"You're alone at the office, aren't you?"

"Yeah, so?"

"You gotta get over here."

"What's wrong?!"

"It's Cross! He's not who he says he is—maybe."

"Maybe as in dangerous?"

"Yeah, maybe. If he lied about that, then—just get over here."

"Are you alone?"

"Yes," said Nathalie.

"Did you change your locks yet?!"

"Yeah, they told me they're pickproof. Better be, they cost a small fortune. I don't think he can get past these. I got a new key for you. Just haul your butt over here. We got work to do"

"Better than diarrhea."

"What?!"

"Nothing," replied Megan quickly. "I'm leaving now."

She slapped off her cell phone and slashed a thick pen strike through her last pathetic ad copy line. She flicked off her desk lamp and swung around in her chair to grab her purse—then stopped cold. A shadowy figure moved into the labyrinth by her exit.

Who the hell was this?! And why didn't they turn the lights on?!

Fear rose up her spine. Her breath froze. The dark figure was a man. A tall man. He wound his way through the labyrinth of cubicles as if he knew his way.

She stayed rock still. Any moment she prayed that he would turn down another twist in the labyrinth away from her. But no…he worked his way toward her cubicle. It was too late. She could not stand up to flee without being seen. She quietly slid down below the top of her cubicle walls and crawled behind the cardboard cutout of Donald Trump. She only hoped the sound of her thumping heart didn't give her away!

The footsteps drew closer and closer. Then they stopped—right in front of her cubicle entrance. She held her breath. She could only see his shoes. They were dark. Black. They were…patent leather oxfords…the kind worn with a tuxedo. She knew it wasn't one of her bosses. They would've flipped on the lights and called out. He remained still and silent.

She dared not move. Surely, he heard her heart because its beats exploded rapidly in her head!

He cleared his throat.

She didn't budge or breathe.

"Megan…"

The voice sounded unfamiliar to her. Maybe he hadn't seen her and probed because he couldn't see in the darkness. She remained as silent as a corpse.

"Megan, why are you hiding behind such a total loser?"

Now exposed—caught—pinned in the corner behind a cardboard Trump. "I knocked my purse to the floor…and was…just picking it up," she mumbled. On shaking legs, she stood up and backed away from the Trump cutout knocking it slightly askew.

His arm reached out—Megan jumped back—to steady the cardboard cutout which teetered off balance. He nodded his approval that the Trump cutout wore a bra and mini skirt.

"Do you know who I am?"

She'd only seen him once—through binoculars.

"Yes…you're…him."

"Him?"

"You're…Eli Cross."

My God he was even gorgeous when it was pitch black. Well almost pitch black. There remained enough light to catch the blue and green in his eyes. She thought she could swim in those eyes. But then… she remembered Nathalie had just told her that he wasn't who he said he was and that he was dangerous…maybe. Maybe, hell, how about definitely?! Who comes to see someone in the dark they've never met unless he came with deadly intent?!

The flash of knowledge that her body would at least be found with some really sexy underwear—the black and gold, lace, leopard-print panties from the Bloomie's half-price sale—kept her from passing out. Her body would look good…if he didn't carve it up too badly. That hope and her wickedly warped sense of humor worked overtime to blow off the tornado of fear that swirled in her gut and whipped her emotions into a raw frenzy.

"You seem nervous," said Cross. He offered no assurances to calm her down.

"I do?" Megan inhaled sharply staving off lightheadedness.

"A little bit, yeah."

"Will it be quick, please?" Megan's whispered plea came with a broken sigh. Her humor ran out of steam. Her sudden emotional exhaustion brought on a resigned acceptance of death that washed over her. Now she felt—and felt deeply—what Nathalie meant by *this isn't a game*. This man, an international thief , obviously had a deadly purpose and somehow for some reason she didn't even know, she was an annoying pawn that needed to be sacrificed.

She hoped her friend would learn of her death in time to save herself. Then again, she hoped in the next life she chose better friends. Her humor made its last stab at keeping her hopeful, but it was no longer funny, and the resignation pushed a tear into her eye and down her face. She knew it was her soul letting go, accepting her fate. Her last vestige of comfort came from the breathy deep voice of her poet champion, Leonard Cohen, rising from memory and coming to her as her personal farewell song: *Everybody knows the war is over. Everybody knows the good guys lost.* Leonard was dead now and soon she would be too. To her grave, she envisioned being carried on her poet's words: *Everybody knows that the fight was fixed.*

"A quick what?" Cross asked.

Megan clutched her purse tightly to her chest. "I know Ted Bundy may have taken his time before he, you know—although you're much better looking than Ted Bundy—so could you just be…quick…" The last words dribbled out of her mouth with a half-hearted plea that she knew wouldn't be heeded.

Cross looked at her with a crooked smile. He reached out and snapped the bra on the Donald Trump cardboard cutout. Megan winced as the snapping sound echoed off the walls.

"I may be many things," said Cross, "but a serial killer is not one of them."

"That's…good," said Megan in a choked whisper. Not entirely convinced, she timidly took a deep breath to speak. "But…have you ever killed…anyone…or two…maybe?"

"You want me to divulge all my secrets?"

The smile on his face seemed genuine, she thought. Megan also knew that *seemed* didn't hold a lot of comfort. At least it gave her some hope that she might be able to talk her way out of whatever it was that might get her silenced and stuffed under some staffer's desk—or worse, stuffed under the receptionist's desk to be found by the Stanford Supermodel in the morning.

"I've never done anything to you, really," Megan stated. Then she struggled to offer something substantial. "I even told Nathalie that you were…"

"What?"

"Attractive?" That sucked as *substantial,* but pitifully that was all she had.

"Thank you" said Cross somewhat amused. "Let me tell you why I'm here."

"Okay…"

"She confides in you."

Those were the first words that held promise for Megan. It meant that she had a use, a purpose, and thus might be allowed to live. Hope rose. "We're besties," she added quickly.

"That's what I figured. That's why I'm here."

Megan unclenched her jaw and inhaled more easily, but then her breath caught in her throat. *What if killing Nathalie's best friend was the message he wanted to send?! Back off or die!* Megan needed to confide something—anything—to him that showed her value if kept alive.

"I can tell you that…" Megan faltered in carrying on. She didn't really know what she could—or should—tell him that would make a difference. But she pressed on anyway. "She feels that…you're…very attractive too."

"Good to know, but…let me come directly to the point."

Megan sensed sincerity in his tone not present before. The difference may be slight, but meaningful. He wasn't toying with her anymore…maybe.

"I need her to be who she really is—to bring it all—hold nothing back."

"Okay…what does that mean?"

"She'll know. Tell her just what I said. Exactly what I said."

"Why don't you tell her this yourself?" Megan stared genuinely confused. It seemed so simple.

"She doesn't trust me yet."

"Well, you know, she thinks you stole the—"

"I know. Just tell her."

"Okay, but why will she believe me and do what you want when I tell her that this is what you told me to tell her?"

Megan stared at him with innocent and logical simplicity.

"That's actually a valid point," he said. Cross debated within himself his next response.

Megan caught a sudden look of commitment in his eyes. An honesty she trusted intuitively.

"Tell her that everything depends on it. Every…*moment*."

Megan clearly felt the extra emphasis he had put on the word *moment*. Cross locked eyes with her. Worried that he might mysteriously and swiftly disappear back into the darkness, she blurted out: "Do you really live in a villa in Saint-Tropez? That's not bullshit, is it?"

"Do you like Arabians?" was his only response.

"Men or horses? I've read you have a few of those around. Horses that is."

"You read that?"

"Yes, I…" she stopped, sensing her stupid mistake.

"Like in a file? A police file?" His direct tone zapped her like an electric jolt.

Oh shit, she realized she stepped right into the trap.

"Well…I was…helping her. She let me…read it."

Megan understood she now plunked herself *in it* up to her neck. He knew she knew probably a lot more of a lot of things that maybe he didn't want anyone to know. He might have to shut her up. Now no hiding that she acted as some sort of accomplice to whatever Nathalie did—like catching him red-handed as a thief—and she stood cornered in her small, tiny, prison-like cubicle which offered no escape. How quickly she went from imagining riding Arabian horses with him in St. Tropez and sunbathing topless at his own private beach to being a cold, dead corpse in leopard-print panties behind a cardboard Trump.

"I won't tell anyone," she whimpered.

"Yes, you will."

"No, I promise I won't." She pleaded for her life with as much emphasis as she could muster.

He uttered his next words with as much clarity and gravitas as the moment demanded. "If you ever want to visit Saint-Tropez and ride Arabian horses, you will tell her exactly what I asked you to tell her."

"Oh…that…yes, I can do that."

Her grin from understanding that he wasn't going to kill her and that he had floated a future invitation to the South of France grew exponentially as he smiled and quietly withdrew back into the darkness of the labyrinth.

Her relief settled into her groin in a most unexpected and surprising feeling. Arousal.

જી

Nathalie opened her door quickly at Megan's knock and pulled her inside handing her a new key as she closed the door swiftly behind her.

"We got a lot of work to do. He may be Elliot Crositer."

"Who's Elliot Crositer?"

"I don't know."

"Then why do you think he's Elliot—who?"

"Crositer."

Megan's disappointment etched in her face like a carving. "Elliot…Crositer? That's not a cool name, that's just like some guy's name. I like Eli Cross. It's just…better."

"He made up Eli Cross—maybe."

"What's with all this maybe shit? I almost maybe got killed!"

"What?!"

"He came to see me—at work!

"Who?!"

"Eli fucking Cross Crositer Elliot that's who!"

"He came to see *you*?!"

"Yes—in the dark—at my cubicle! I was all alone!"

"Did he threaten you?! How did he make you feel?!"

"Not good when I thought he was going to kill me and stuff my body in some dark corner."

"Oh my God, Megan." Nathalie grabbed her in a protective motherly hug.

"I know," Megan said soaking up the sympathy.

"But…well…when I thought I might live and be able to visit Saint-Tropez I wanted him to kiss me."

"What?!" Nathalie shoved her out of the motherly embrace.

"He kind of threw out an invitation to come…to France."

"What?!" Nathalie stared open-mouthed—appalled!

"I know, it was pathetic—putrid actually—I was disgusted with myself to be so…"

"Horny."

"Oh God, my panties were like Niagara Falls, and he didn't even touch me! But not till he left, at least I think it happened after he left, I don't even know anymore!"

Nathalie knew Megan's rambling run-on witticisms masked having been scared to death by her encounter with Cross.

"Randy won't like hearing that," said Nathalie injecting her own humor to alleviate Megan's fear.

"Randy and I broke up."

"What? Oh Megan, I'm sorry. When?"

"Today, this morning actually, so when I was thinking about being ravaged by Eli Cross I wouldn't have been cheating on Randy, just cheating on you...I guess. I don't know what I'm saying anymore, my entire brain is fogged up."

"You're upset about Randy," offered Nathalie attempting to soothe Megan's emotions.

"Yes, I'm upset about Randy...but I'm upset that I'm not upset enough."

Nathalie didn't quite follow that reasoning. "How's Randy taking it?"

"Oh he's fine. We're friends, always have been, still are. We knew we sucked as a couple; it was almost like, ya know, pretend."

This is the first time Nathalie had such a real and penetrating window into Megan's love life. "That's..."

"Pathetic, yeah," sighed Megan. "So you see how I could instantly want to be really unpathetic with your thief—we're not friends."

"Okay, wait a minute," said Nathalie.

She felt Megan's desire to be ravaged by Cross was merely stalling for time.

"Before we plan your wedding, back way the fuck up."

Nathalie wanted to haul Megan back into the real world.

"Why did he track you down? How did he know that you and I—"

"I think he knows everything about everything which is rather freaky. He knew exactly who I was to you and where my cubicle was. It took you a week to remember and find your way through the labyrinth. He just sort of strolled on over...in an Armani tux."

"He probably looked—"

"Yeah he did."

For a moment, both women were lost in their vision of that moment.

Nathalie broke the spell first. "What did he want with you?"

"For me to give you a message."

"He couldn't tell me himself?"

"He said you didn't trust him yet."

"He's got that right."

"He meant what he said, I can tell you that. It was in his eyes—those eyes—he wasn't playin' around. You know how you know."

"Yeah…I know."

"Doesn't happen a lot with guys but when it does…"

"Yeah…"

Another moment of lost reverie…

"So…what did he say?"

Megan paused. She wanted to remember it exactly.

"He said: 'I need her to be who she really is—to bring it all—hold nothing back. Tell her that everything depends on it. Every…*moment*.'"

"That's it?"

"His exact words."

"He actually said 'every…*moment*'?"

"Yeah, he kind of emphasized *moment*."

"*Moment*…okay." It all clicked for Nathalie.

"Okay what?"

"He's going for it." Her thoughts burst into fire—calculating!

"You know what that means?"

"Yeah!"

"He said you'd know that—whatever that is—are you gonna tell me?"

"Yeah, maybe, later."

The use of *maybe* too many times this night did not assure Megan.

"So what do we *maybe* do now?!"

"Okay, we gotta track down Elliot Crositer. Who is he—or was he?!"

Nathalie fired up her computer. She video-called her brother. It was late. She didn't care. He had to be in on this—and she needed him to use his password access to the special New York Times archives. Eli Cross, the unknowable man, with a little digging, might possibly be a little bit more knowable.

ℬↄ

Ian carried his computer connected on Zoom around piles of project file papers stacked in his apartment until he settled in an open space. Megan sprawled on Nathalie's living room floor with her phone. Nathalie poised her fingers on her computer keyboard ready to let them fly over the keys as she surveyed her crime crew. No yellow tape stretched across the scene but it sure felt professional. Nathalie knew her Dad would approve of the family affair effort *to get Cross.* She knew her father had thought of Megan as family: charmingly quirky, half-crazy, preternaturally scared of success, and a lot smarter than she admitted or even knew. He had quite liked her.

They worked quickly. Pieces of information gathered and vetted and then sorted to see if a pattern would fit together and make sense. The international bash at the Borelli estate was a mere two days away. Whatever they discovered had to be relevant and significant enough to provide Nathalie the additional knowledge and insight to gain the advantage over Cross.

They knew there was a plane crash. Katharine Otley had told Nathalie she and Elliot Crositer were fourteen almost fifteen at the time and that was around thirty-five or thirty-sex years ago for her. That would be 1984 or 1985 depending on their specific birthdays. Speculation sped around the room and with Ian on Zoom. There were more plane crashes in the world in those two years than they realized especially if business jets and smaller private personal aircraft were counted in addition to commercial airliners.

"Cross is definitely putting it all on the line on Saturday. That's clear to me," said Nathalie. "He's betting that he can do this right under our noses."

"He might be that good," said Ian. "If he could pull a number on Dad, then…"

"I know, I know," said Nathalie cutting him off. "Let's work this."

"This reminds me of that great movie, *"The Day of the Jackal*, the first one." chimed in Megan.

"From a great book—Frederick Forsyth," Ian piped in giving proper provenance.

"Thank you, Mister Novelist," agreed Megan. "I'm talkin' about how the French and Brits were all after the Jackal and even when his cover was blown he didn't quit. He knew he could pull off the hit with everyone knowing he was going to do it and trying to stop him."

"Cross is not an international assassin, Megan," Nathalie said confidently to shut down Megan's wandering imagination.

"How do you know that? I mean really, how do you know that?" Megan confidently stared right back at Nathalie. She knew she had a good point.

Nathalie knew it too.

"He's an international master thief, that's enough," said Nathalie trying to convince herself.

"But he could also—"

"Megan!" Nathalie sharply cut her off.

"Sis, Megan's right," said Ian. "You wanna do this right, be thorough; we can't rule anything out until we know for sure."

"This is exciting trying to figure it all out," said Megan. "I know he doesn't look like a killer, but then neither did Edward Fox."

"Who?"

"Edward Fox, the British actor who played the Jackal." Megan plowed ahead on the verge of some important insight. "The Jackal was in bed with that countess. Remember that scene?"

"I didn't see this movie," said Nathalie wanting Megan to shift to a more relevant subject.

"That was a good scene," added Ian. "Chilling."

"He just leaned over and softly kissed her on the mouth with his hand gently on her throat. So quiet, no struggle, just a kiss and she was dead." Megan's hand caressed her throat.

"Well you can relax," said Nathalie. "Eli Cross is not going to kiss you."

"He could've kissed me and killed me in my office," retorted Megan.

"He wouldn't have to kiss you. You'd die from the thought of him kissing you."

"Okay, yeah, probably."

"Girls, let's get serious," urged Ian. "A simple Google search isn't bringing up anything on Elliot Crositer."

"So we go deeper," Nathalie pressed him.

"I know you want this to connect," said Ian. "But Elliot Crositer may not be Eli Cross. The names are similar, maybe only coincidental;

it happens, ya know. He may just be a kid who died in a plane crash a long time ago."

"Okay, so if he's not Elliot, then—oh wait," Megan said latching onto an idea. "Maybe Cross took his name to get a passport—like the Jackal did—from someone who was dead!" Megan beamed feeling she'd solved a key element. "Then he could travel under a different name when he had to escape!"

"Cross doesn't use any other fake identities," said Nathalie. "He's just Eli Cross."

"So he doesn't have to hide or escape after stealing stuff?" Megan was disappointed.

"That's how good he is," replied Ian.

Megan turned to Nathalie. "So why Elliot Crositer then? Why do you think this matters?"

"Maybe that's who he really is, or was." Nathalie hoped this would mean something if they found a connection. "Maybe it will tell us something."

"I've heard *maybe* too damn much tonight," said Megan most annoyed.

"Ian, you told me that Jean-Pierre Bonnaire told you that Vadoma said her family found him in Saint-Tropez when he lost his family."

"Yeah," said Ian. "I assumed *lost* meant *killed* somehow but we don't know for sure."

"Okay," agreed Nathalie, "but let's follow that thought. Vadoma told Jean-Pierre that they had grown up together, presumably as kids then. Katharine Otley who knew Elliot Crositer said she was almost fifty and that crash was thirty-five maybe thirty-six years ago, so Elliot would've been fourteen or fifteen. Starting ninth grade was what she said."

"You don't think he killed his family do you?" wondered Megan, then realized how overreaching that sounded. "No, of course he didn't do that, I mean why would he…this isn't like a 48 Hours episode." The blank stares she received told her she should quit while ahead.

"Are you still on the Jackal?"

"No," said Megan. "The Jackal didn't—they didn't know…even who he was."

"Then if we're done with that…" Nathalie paused.

"Yes, yes we are," stated Megan sheepishly.

"Then let's move on to—"

"It was a good movie, that's all," Megan whispered.

"Airplane crashes," stated Nathalie finishing her point. "Let's start with Europe."

℥

Eli Cross sat in the dark in his suite at The Lucerne. He loosened the tie that went with his tux. He hadn't removed his jacket.

The curtains stood open across the street in Nathalie's apartment. He could see Nathalie and Megan together. It pleased him his plan worked out so far. He didn't know what Nathalie thought of his sudden exit from the party. He couldn't concern himself with that. Something to keep her off balance wasn't bad. He also didn't know how she felt about his approach to Megan Hollister, but that was another variable for her to have to contend with and decide whether it mattered or not.

He did feel that he had planted enough seeds in past conversations so that if Megan specifically told Nathalie the words *every…moment*— and he felt she would—then Nathalie would be sure to be ready at the Borelli estate on Saturday. For his challenge of *that moment* to work, he needed her there. He stretched out his legs with a relaxed assurance.

Tomorrow was Friday. His memory would not let that simple connection alone. That date, long ago, had been a big day. A life-changing day.

He had felt the aircraft shudder before he heard the *thunk* sound. He knew it wasn't simple turbulence when Salvatore, the co-pilot, dashed from the cockpit and descended into the fuselage from the galley. In a few moments he could hear Salvatore as he raced below through the fuselage belly to the rear of the jet.

His little brother, Charlie, sat preoccupied with his Etch A Sketch.

His mother relaxed absorbed in reading a paperback book whose cover she hid and didn't look up as she turned the page.

He knew why she hid the cover from sight but didn't really know anything about the book though he wondered what it was about. There was an image of a woman lying on her back with a bare breast exposed. That was the glimpse he had gotten when they had boarded. The book had a strange title, *The Tropic of Cancer,* which he worried was about the disease or hopefully maybe like *Age of Aquarius* or some new age crap. It was by Henry Miller.

Years later, he would read it wanting to know what was so riveting that she didn't look up at the sound of the *thunk*. It was notorious for its adventurous sexuality—even banned in some places—set in Paris and France in the 1920s and 1930s.

He would think of this and on how his mother thought of his father for years to come. His parents loved each other. That he knew. But he wanted to know what they thought of each other *in that way*. It remained an emotional curiosity never resolved.

He heard Salvatore race back from the tail to emerge quickly up into the galley.

He called out to the open cockpit: "The hydraulics—a forced break!"

He could hear his father respond. "Forced?!"

"A timed charge!" Salvatore jammed himself back into the co-pilot's seat and buckled in!

"That bastard! It's your airplane," he could hear his father, Roland, say to Salvatore.

"My airplane," replied Salvatore and took command but the control wheel froze up due to falling fluid pressure in the hydraulic system. He wrestled with it to keep the plane level!

His father quickly unbuckled and came back into the main cabin.

His mother had closed her book. Something was very wrong. That was clear.

His father looked at his mother and simply said, "It's Renzinger."

He would always remember the look of fear and resignation that flooded his mother's face. Whatever it meant was not new to her.

His father looked at them. Even Charlie looked up from his Etch A Sketch.

"I love you all. Buckle up," his father simply stated.

Eli grabbed for his seat belt as his mother buckled in Charlie then quickly retook her seat.

"We'll get there," his father said to all of them. He then turned to his oldest son. "You're going to the Louvre. Count on it."

Charlie wondered, "And Mama's ring?"

"Yes, that too," his father replied turning to Charlie.

For a fleeting moment, his father placed his hand on his mother's shoulder. Was it reassurance or farewell? His father's face filled with an acceptance of some truth, but what he didn't know at that moment. His mother pressed her hand on top of his father's. The pressure of his parent's touch on each other was firm; he could almost feel it himself. His parents looked into each other's eyes for a split second. His father pulled his hand away from his mother's shoulder to dash back to the cockpit. He remembered it as *ripping away*. In dreams for years he would hear a *whoosh* as their hands separated. It was his father's back he last saw as he flung himself back into the pilot's chair when the Bombardier 600 lurched sideways.

"Mom?!" He could still feel the urgency and plea for assurance in his young voice.

His mother forcibly shut down her own fear—an image he had never forgotten—to push a smile onto her lips. "Your father's going to get us home."

&

"I've got something." Ian hunched over his computer screen reading.

Nathalie and Megan watched him on the Zoom connection.

"There was a crash in the Mediterranean off the coast of France in 1984. Let me share the screen."

The article he shared was from The New York Times archives. It popped up on their devices—Nathalie's computer and Megan's phone.

"It was a Bombardier 600 business jet whose flight originated in Rome and went down about two miles southwest of Saint-Tropez.

"Saint-Tropez!" Goosebumps raced up Nathalie's spine.

"There were no survivors."

"Are you sure?" Nathalie pressed him, unwilling to accept that conclusion.

"That's what it says. The plane was a corporate jet for CRM, a New York technology company that manufactured high-speed miniature chips. Apparently the CEO was the pilot."

"That's it?!" Nathalie needed more.

"I'm reading, give me a sec."

Nathalie watched the article on her screen scroll ahead as Ian read further.

Megan ensconced in scrutinizing another website she had pulled up suddenly blurted out:

"Oh my God, look what I found!"

"Let Ian read," begged Nathalie!

"No, no, listen. I looked up CRM. It was a company back in the eighties. Headquarters in Manhattan with manufacturing in Jersey City."

"So what," blurted Nathalie, pissed that Megan interfered with Ian reading.

"Well," Megan said indignantly. "CRM stood for Crositer Renzinger Miniatures."

"Crositer," cried out Nathalie! "This is the crash Katharine Otley spoke about. This is it!"

"Yeah, holy shit, here it is," piped in Ian, finally zeroing in on the last page of the article. "The passenger manifest included the co-pilot and the CEO's family: Roland Crositer, the CEO, his wife, Audrey, and their two sons, Elliot and Charles. Only the bodies of the wife and youngest son were found. The others were presumed dead, lost at sea."

"Presumed…" Nathalie pondered.

"This is wild," exclaimed Megan. "Eli might actually be Elliot!"

"I think it's safe to say this is now not coincidence with his name," added Ian.

"Eli Cross is Elliot Crositer," said Nathalie softly as if she was meeting him for the first time. This landed as a vital piece of information that her father had not discovered.

"Wow, good work, Nattie." Ian was definitely impressed with his sister.

Nathalie didn't acknowledge his heartfelt praise for she had already moved on in her drive to connect the dots. "Vadoma said they found Eli. How? Where? Wandering around on land, washed up on shore? What does found mean?" Nathalie stood up and paced.

"Does it matter?" Ian wondered. "They found him."

"Yeah, but right away or sometime later?" Nathalie paced over to the window and gazed across at The Lucerne.

"What's your point?"

Even Megan wanted to know. "Yeah, what difference does it make?"

Nathalie didn't look at either of them. She remained focused on The Lucerne across the street. "Ian, you were told by Jean-Pierre that Vadoma said that they grew up together."

"Yeah, that's right," Ian said. "Kinda like brother and sister." He wondered what his sister was driving at; what dots in this mystery scenario she connected.

"Well, after they found him, why didn't he go home, back to New York?" she asked.

Nathalie turned around and saw Ian on the Zoom screen. His face told her that he had connected the dots. He knew the significant import of this and let out a long exhale of breath.

"Go home?" Megan wasn't as quick and tried to follow her thought.

"Yeah, why did Elliot Crositer stay in Europe and become Eli Cross?"

Nathalie pressed her hand against the cold, dark glass of her window. The lights were off in the tenth floor deluxe king suite at The Lucerne. She knew he was there, sitting in the dark.

CHAPTER SEVENTEEN

*I'll come to thee by moonlight, though hell should bar
the way."*

"The Highwayman" by Alfred Noyes

"You are not that boy anymore," said Vano simply.

"I don't understand," stammered Elliot, still somewhat groggy.

"You are dead is what they say."

Vano's wife, Lavinia, placed a comforting hand on the young boy's shoulder.

"You have been sick with us a long time," continued Vano. "Much has happened."

"But clearly I'm not dead," protested young Elliot. He looked over at Vadoma, their young daughter who was almost his age—two years younger—searching her face for a supportive glance. She turned away not able to conceal her tears.

This was his first day in many of being relatively clear-headed but none of this made sense to him. These were the people who had nursed him back to health—saved his life even—the one's he had trusted for everything while he recuperated. They had dragged his sand-caked face off the beach as the tide rolled in and before the frigid water could overwhelm his unconscious body and drown him. Why would they make up a lie now?

"Much has happened," Vano repeated. "The ways of the world."

Elliot couldn't clearly focus on anything or anyone for too long, his vision still erratic. The head trauma sustained in the crash from the impact of the water tearing apart the fuselage still affected his vision. A doctor had told them it might clear up. Might. Sometimes the body finds a way to reorganize, to reclaim homeostasis. Sometimes. Elliot had impatiently waited—as much as a teenager could—for *sometimes* to arrive.

He closed his eyes to help him corral his thoughts.

What did Vano mean by *the ways of the world*?

He wanted his parents to tell him what happened. Intellectually he knew they were dead, but emotionally he hadn't been able to fully accept that yet. He'd been found. Why not his parents and little brother—even Salvatore?! The papers had said that no one survived the plane crash. They were wrong about that. They could be wrong about his family.

He wanted to tell someone other than Vano, Lavinia and Vadoma who already knew.

Even with his eyes squeezed shut, the flashes of the jet's impact into the ocean battered his memory. The water ripped a jagged hole in the fuselage bursting at him with explosive force—his mother's arms stretched out for him from her seat—his little brother's Etch A Sketch hurtled by his head—the impact violently wrenched him out of his seat—propelled back into the aft section of the jet!

The jagged metal of the fuselage ripped in half like a torn page of paper. The front section with the cockpit and his father and Salvatore plummeted into the depths. The middle section with his mother and brother shredded and dispersed in pieces like they were shot from a cannon. He got jammed against the fuselage wall of the tail section as it spun vertically like a cartwheel underwater.

All these images flashed by him as he spun with the fuselage until he catapulted upward into the air when the open end breached the surface like a whale. He tumbled back down into the water and his back slapped the surface with a sharp splat! His mouth gulped in searing hot air! *Why was it so hot?!* He blinked from pain and saw the oil-streaked water engulfed in flames.

Sputtering out water and sucking in air, he clawed his way along the surface, pushing aside debris with terrified swipes of his arm. When the flames were behind him, instinct took hold and he swam with intent. He had been on his school's swim team. He hadn't been all that good, but he had been determined, stubbornly determined.

He swam forward, each stroke stronger, each stroke a hope that he would catch up to his parents and brother. Surely they were just out of sight. *Stroke*... He would find them. *Stroke*... They would be okay. *Stroke*. They would get—*stroke*—to the Louvre—*stroke*—for his birthday—*stroke*—just like his father—*stroke*—had promised. The planned trip—*stroke*—the previous year—*stroke*—had been cancelled—*stroke*—because of business. His father had promised—

stroke—that nothing would get—*stroke*—in the way—*stroke*—this year. His father never—*stroke*—broke his promises. They would even—*stroke*—get his mother's—*stroke*—ring.

The stroking rhythm increased until the loss of blood leaking from his fractured skull caused him to slow down and eventually black out.

His next remembered image—his face scraping against sand—his body dragged up from the water's edge in a beach cove outside Saint-Tropez.

He opened his eyes. "I want to go home."

"The news…it says…" Lavinia hesitated.

"It says there is no home," stated Vano definitively. He shot his wife a look that stifled her objection. "We tell the boy the truth. We can't control it, but we can say what it is. He deserves at least that."

Vano placed his arm firmly on the boy's shoulder and spoke with assuredness. "To rise from the ashes you must acknowledge what has burnt and know what has then perished so you waste no time searching for it, for it is gone. Then and only then can you sift through the ashes and see what is still there, what would never burn. With that discovery you rise."

℃

That conversation was long ago. The exact words and more importantly the clarity of the emotions and their visceral impact were immediately recalled by Eli at the slightest provocation; a smell remembered or even a sound brought it all back as if it were yesterday. Eli knew he couldn't evade these feelings; they were part of him now. They fueled his *saudade,* drove him ever onward.

He stripped off his tux as if discarding the weight of the past. He strode naked into the bathroom. He let the shower water get hot—steamy hot—before he stepped inside.

The cleansing he sought lay soul deep.

How to explain the deep, dark ways of the world to a boy who just turned fifteen, whose family had been violently torn from him? As the hot water pounded his shoulders turning them red from the heat, Eli knew the answer. *Tell the boy the truth. The unadulterated truth. Face it. Deal with it. The truth would not change by softening it or ignoring it.*

Vano taught him resilience when things do not change and how to act to change things. This Romani gypsy had set him up to survive. It would take a while but Eli would discover his reservoir of gratitude for this man and his family. Lavinia also spoke of the harsh truth of the world without diluting it but she had an almost mystical manner of easing into it. Perhaps it was her husky voice that gave her words a tantalizing allure as opposed to the sharper clipped speech of her husband. Lavinia's throaty voice reminded Eli of his father's favorite actress, the talented, dark-haired beauty Suzanne Pleshette, and that always reminded him of home.

But where was home after the crash. It would become Europe. Elliot Crositer lived in Manhattan and in the Hamptons. Eli Cross would live in Europe.

Eli stood under the hot water with the pulsating spray pummeling him with memories. He remembered the confusion and his struggle to understand. How did he become erased? How did his home vanish? And his family's money, what the hell happened?! Young Elliot couldn't grasp it—the manipulated system—none of it made sense. Thus his new education began.

Vano had seen it too many times before. Clever men with uber-wealth manipulating the system to make even more, to control more and shield themselves from any accountability. The leverage of *the green* got some to look the other way and others to confirm the lie as truth. This was how young Elliot learned about Renzinger, the sale of his father's company, CRM, and the dispersion of his family's money mostly to charity as there were no living relatives.

The executor of their estate—supposedly an old family friend—was heavily compensated by Renzinger and *adjusted* the execution of the wills and trust in subtle but effective ways. There was no one to scrutinize it or to protest so *all was well.* It had all appeared above board.

Money greased the wheels and the entire process got fast-tracked in mere months, the amount of time that young Elliot needed to recover.

The company became Renzinger's to sell and he and his wife garnered possession of hundreds of millions of dollars with enough payouts to get a good many people to *look the other way* when it became necessary. For Renzinger it had been far simpler than one might imagine. Once the fuse of human behavior got ignited with anticipation of wealthy rewards, the complications of financial manipulation effortlessly minimalized with greed the driving force.

Vano was a clever man too and had learned how to dance around ingrained rules and those with power. It was how he had tricked the hospitals into helping the young injured Elliot before they then disappeared and moved on to avoid paying. It was trickery on a smaller scale but took advantage of the same human behavior. This was scamming as survival not greed's soulless grasping. It was also a very clear acknowledgement that morals were pushed aside to live, not simply chase greed. Morality had ranked relativity in navigating the deep, dark ways of the world. In Vano's way with the world, morals could be bent but not broken.

Becoming Eli and letting go of Elliot was no easy feat but once the decision was made there was no turning back. He became an autodidact and learned by reading and by listening and observing, then absorbing. He learned how to create an entire background of both mystery and veracity. He also learned that the web of deceit and conspiracy against his father was woven by many wealthy participants each wanting pieces of the pie. When he learned how to steal from and disrupt the rich, he was on his way.

His Gypsy *family* knew he wasn't *theirs* and knew he must leave for a bigger destiny. Vano and Lavinia had lost a son, Nikko, from an accident when he was eight and he would've been Elliot's age. Somewhat selfishly they wanted him to stay. Vano understood what Eli set out to do and though he knew the futility of it, he still offered some wisdom from experience—*"It is an endless road to set things right"*—knowing full well the words would not be heeded until lived. That sorrow, Vano kept to himself.

Even after leaving to carve out his own path, Eli gave himself access to the greatest minds by reading. Einstein had captured his imagination long ago. In his wisdom were insightful perception and a warning: *"Time and space are not conditions in which we live, but modes by which we think. Time does not exist – we invented it. Time is what the clock says. The distinction between the past, present and future is only a stubbornly persistent illusion."*

Eli became haunted by time. He wanted to control it, to command what happened with it with a precision that obeyed his design. It was impossible of course. He knew that also.

Yet he became very good at achieving this control in his capers, his *projects.* Why he planned everything with precision with numerous contingencies leaving little to chance and happenstance. Plans so well laid out they seemed natural, real, raising no doubts or suspicions.

The return of the stolen Renoir to the Louvre was an operation smooth as silk; its threads woven with the warp and weft of greed and fear. The greed of the thief—the Baron—*to get as much as possible* and the fear of the thief *to not get caught*—after stealing the Renoir when it was outside the Louvre being *cleaned* at a secret facility. The manipulation of those two aspects of human behavior proved to be simple and could be trusted to hold fast until the desired end.

The **Veritas** International Insurance Agency listed on the business card which Cross had handed to Baron von Hellerstadt had been set up by Cross. The agency was fake but had the façade of reality behind it. First off, its allure was its extreme discretion and iron-clad privacy. Nothing could be traced back to the client; a most desired service since the client desired to secretly *insure* stolen property. There was no internet presence available to the public.

One learned of the agency only through word of mouth from a trusted source who had used its services—meaning from a fence or thief—names and temporary identities given to people hired to play a part. When the perspective client—in this sole case, Baron von Hellerstadt—was surreptitiously contacted he was made to feel special, to be considered a valued member of the highly secretive society that was the lucrative and dark world of stolen fine art.

The fictitious name which Cross used on the business card— Helmut Hauer, from the agency's *Fine Art Retrieval Division*—did have an actual office in the agency's Zurich headquarters. This classy facility consisted of an entire floor of offices tastefully decorated and fully staffed. People were hired without ever seeing Helmut Hauer who hired them. They received a packet of instructions for clerical activities and computer data input duties. Helmut Hauer never came into the office. Photos on his desk were computer generated—a digital pixel family. Verification of agency funds, should a client demand proof, was discreetly provided by the Swiss bank handling the agency's business transactions through a private numbered account.

The morning of the Renoir's return, all evidence of the *Veritas* Agency's existence faded quickly into memory. Furniture and art work donated anonymously to charities as well as wiped-clean computers left nothing which could be traced back to a source. People were paid very handsome bonuses on top of generous severance packages while told only that the agency had been sold and its assets liquidated for profit by the new, unnamed owner.

The last act of Eli Cross leaving The Louvre before dawn was ceremoniously dropping *Helmut Hauer's* last business card in a trash can.

The Louvre got a bill for *Art Restoration and Cleaning* which was how they officially accounted for the painting's absence. The substantial bill was gratefully paid by The Louvre and the government of France thus avoiding the scandal of theft. All told, Eli Cross pocketed €1,500,000 for the *Art Restoration* which included expenses for establishing the *Veritas* International Insurance Agency, another €2,000,000 worth of Siglinde's jewels and another €500,000 for the initial *insurance premium payment* from Baron von Hellerstadt.

Eli had thoroughly enjoyed creating *the sucker's web* that lured and trapped the target. It had required an artist's flair to envision and enact such a lair of deceit and distraction; a true magician's legerdemain was the light touch of the Master Thief.

There were those who sought art for themselves by whatever means for profit and pleasure and those who profited from art for all to see. There was also profit to be made by stepping into those crossroads of desire. A few legitimate entrepreneurs at those crossroads were known. One, however, remained tantalizingly unknowable.

The *unknowable quality* allowed him to take the Renzinger's money, the money that had belonged to his family. Recovering it had become an obsession once Elliot understood what had transpired after his parents' death.

Elliot knew his father had trusted his business partner, Renzinger, from conversations he had overheard his parents having. Then later there were the disquieting more secretive whisperings between his mother and father when the doubts crept in, when trust dangled by thin threads connected only by hope. When Vano had interpreted the newspaper accounts of the plane crash and the company's subsequent sale as well as the dissolution of his family's estate with an insight of what lay between the lines of the straight news, Elliot knew his father had been fooled.

Up to that point, Elliot had maintained an original innocence, his parents desiring to expose and educate him slowly to *the ways of the world* for they felt the core of *innocence* if held onto made for a more soulful life. Renzinger's sabotage was a dagger to the heart of that sacred innocence because Elliot understood that Renzinger's plan—long in the works—was to leave his family with nothing, not even their lives. So precise had been those plans that no one and nothing were left to expose Renzinger's chicanery.

That was the moment that Eli Cross was born…with an infusion of Gypsy blood.

Edmund and Isabelle Renzinger proved to be easier targets than anticipated. Their deceitfully-gained money provided all the high-tech security systems and personnel to keep them safe from the intrusions of the outside world. It did not protect them from themselves.

Eli had taken his time to not only discover the best angle of attack but to immerse himself in the skills needed to implement a plan and to escape detection. The simplicity hidden in the strangeness of human behavior proved to be his key.

Eli discovered that the Renzinger marriage was based on a love of money, not each other. Gadgets were not needed for him to penetrate their high tech security. In their fertile ground of deceit, doubt was a potent seed.

Hatred was a good complement to greed and fear. Its embers could be stoked into scorching flames and that white heat ignited human behavior that could then be melted and molded in whatever direction or shape that was desired. In the Renzinger's marriage, suspicion had become doubt which then generated fear that quickly metastasized into hate which was the kindling needed to feed a fire. Lacking was trust and without that, love was an easy victim.

Eli's knowledge of the Swiss banking system and its shield of privacy, enticing fake personas, a well-positioned shell company and the talents of Vano, Lavinia and Vadoma were a slow simmering stew of subterfuge. Edmund and Isabelle Renzinger breathed in the vapors wafting from that stew and each perceived a way to deceive their spouse and secure most if not all of the money for themselves pending the inevitable divorce.

The one they each trusted to set up the secret transition of assets was Eli Cross; known to Edmund as *Harris Sinclair* and to Isabelle as *Garrett Egan.*

As Sinclair, Eli presented himself as a slick and sophisticated player in the Swiss banking system with elite pedigree via Cambridge and Lloyds of London; always impeccably attired by Saville Row to appease Edmund's snobbery. Their first meeting was on the slopes of Chamonix accompanied by Sinclair's seductively curvy assistant, *Raffaella*, a very game Vadoma in a skin-tight Givenchy ski outfit.

For Isabelle, the persona of Egan was a Montana rancher cowboy turned Wharton School of Business Wall Street whiz to appeal to her desire for a more rugged and rough man. Their first meeting was at his behest at the Claremont Riding Academy on 89th street followed by a ride through Central Park astride two pure-bred Arabians.

Eli gave them both what they wanted to see and hear. He used their greed and mistrust of each other to *let them do it to themselves.* A snowball rolled down a mountain quickly becomes an avalanche.

It was the largest *take* Eli ever made from a score and all he had to do was suggest and they bought into believing. The money was not theirs to have the way he saw it. The desire for it, the addiction to it, had taken his family from him. Eli felt in his soul they needed to lose it all.

When Edmund and Isabelle shot each other to death in a tabloid-perfect culmination of hatred, the wheels of their estate dissolution were naturally turned by *Sinclair* and *Egan* following the greedy dictates of the Renzinger's own authorized deceit. The ownership of their acquired art masterpieces had previously been transferred—with each of their separate and secret approvals—to The **Veritas** Fine Arts Storage Facility in Geneva, Switzerland to avoid taxes after the *death* of their spouse. The true owner of this facility was not either of the Renzingers, as they thought, but Eli Cross.

To create the atmosphere of propriety and legality—and to cover the deceptive transfer of wealth—much of the Renzinger's millions went to good charities like Doctors without Borders, Clean Water initiatives, Habitat for Humanity, Planned Parenthood, Reputable Animal Welfare charities and No-kill animal shelters. In death, despite the grisly greed and *la mort de l'amour,* which spawned the bestselling book and movie, *A Murder So Fine And Fair*, the Renzingers drew a chorus of hosannas for their generous philanthropy.

In the end, the estate's three hundred and thirty-five million was dispersed, though not all went to charity. Eli—in the form of *Sinclair* and *Egan*—left their estate enough for burial.

A good forensic accountant could eventually recognize the trail and ferret out the deception, but why look? Most of the money went to wonderful charities as if the Renzingers wanted it that way. The magician's trick—or the Master Thief—was to get you to look elsewhere or not look at all. The best financial sleuth, if sent on the trail, would ultimately reach a dead end, knowing only that there had been deception. The money by then had wafted through the international financial system like vapor, dispersed into the unknown.

Once the distribution of estate funds to the philanthropic list of recipients was completed, and the Renzingers cremated then tossed at sea, the remnants of the financial holdings went to the purchase of a villa…in the South of France…outside of St. Tropez. The very same villa Eli's family had rented for a summer long ago but had never set foot in because they were killed and the surviving son deprived of his identity. After the dissolution of the Renzinger estate, a Crositer took up residence in the *Maquis sur mer* villa under the name of Cross.

The remaining scraps set up an operation fund and purchased some of the tools for his endeavors, such as the fifty million dollar Bombardier Global 6000. There was also the acquisition of a small vineyard and winery between Arles and Aix-en-Provence to be run by a Frenchman and his Gypsy bride. Vano and Lavinia Lakatos were seen shortly thereafter sculpting and painting in the extended gardens of a lakefront property on Lake Como outside of Bellagio, Italy where they entertained an odd assortment of itinerant travelers who were known to drop by throughout the years. Not surprisingly, plush Turkish towels went missing each time from a few of the bathrooms, and were always replaced without regret or rancor from a large but secret stash for just those occasions.

Every *moment* that had needed to fit, fit precisely. No *moment* had eluded his perfectly arrayed plan. Eli had accomplished that. The self-inflicted murder of the Renzingers by their own hands was an unanticipated—though hoped for—but nonetheless welcome *exit stage left* that accelerated his well laid plans. But revenge and its sweet spoils were *not enough*. There was something missing. Saudade persisted. He was driven ever onward to dispel the yearning.

At last, Eli stepped out of the shower, his skin bright red from the hot pounding water. As he toweled off, his memories would not leave him in peace. Why did he still feel empty from that victory? There was no *moment* that had not fit. It had been pulled off without a hitch. That time.

He also knew that *time* asserting its dominance was only a *moment* away. Dodging that *moment* forever was not given to mere mortals. Einstein understood that. *"A happy man is too satisfied with the present to dwell too much on the future."* Eli couldn't remember when he was last happy. Satisfied with a result from an effort, yes, but happy…not for a long, long time.

Intuitively he knew he was hoping for the future to heal the past. Einstein might have thought *good luck with that.* For the first time, Eli felt tired.

That road to set things right that Vano had spoken of was indeed endless. It had not escaped his attention that he was still fervently driven to set things right, but it exhausted him that the emptiness would not abate.

His next step he knew would be risky. He would be working without a net.

ℰℭ

Nathalie sat alone in her living room. Megan had gone home. Ian had signed off Zoom. It was late. The pages from her father's files on Eli Cross lay in clumps around her and pinned to her bulletin boards like a phalanx of support troops. It was very quiet.

She let the darkness engulf her, much like the soft stuffed cushioning of the chair she sank into which folded up against her legs. A light remained on across the street in the tenth floor king suite of The Lucerne. She was clearly thinking of him. Was he thinking of her? If so, why?

He needed her to do something, that much seemed true. Was it for her benefit, or both of them, or merely him? Was she a pawn or a queen and should she be in attack or on defense? At this late stage there were still missing dots from her father's notes, definitive answers still in short supply. She asked herself questions over and over—even the same ones again and again—for she knew this was more a mental challenge than physical and that sometimes emotion was the devil hiding in it.

Before Megan left and Ian had signed off the Zoom call, more facts—two hauntingly eerie revelations—had tumbled together into the scintillating new pile about Elliot Crositer/Eli Cross—more dots to connect—which had to add up to something. But what? Her skin still tingled from the revelations.

Eerie revelation number one surfaced because Megan—despite at times her scabrous comments on men and sex—was a dyed-in-the-wool romantic. Her most closely guarded secret was that she watched the Hallmark Channel. Even Nathalie did not know this dark fact for only under pain of death would Megan have ever confessed.

Megan's favorite actor, whose character wore the same damn knitted sweater whether it was a Thanksgiving movie or a Christmas movie and always reunited with someone he'd lost touch with from high school, had played a cop in the very non-Hallmark film *A Murder So Fine and Fair* about the Renzingers killing each other. She had seen it three times in the theater even though he had only two scenes. His dialogue—which she knew by heart—had many mentions of the name *Renzinger*.

Seeing that name—*Renzinger*—again when she had read about the company *CRM* in researching plane crashes triggered her memory. While Nathalie and Ian Googled and dug into other avenues of research, Megan brought up old news footage and photos on her phone about the murders. Even though those murders were many years after the plane crash near St. Tropez, Megan was excited that she had connected the name of Roland Crositer's partner with these murders. She had no information pointing to Eli Cross having anything to do with those murders but she had felt a detective's glee in finding at least something that was fascinating.

When she had showed Nathalie a photo of the Renzinger estate where the murders had taken place, Nathalie gasped. For a moment, Nathalie had said nothing.

"What's wrong?" Megan had said, but Nathalie had simply continued to stare at the photo.

"It's just where the Renzingers killed each other. Ya know Eli's—Elliot's—father's partner. Doesn't mean anything, 'cause it was many years later, but it's just…ya know, weird." But those words from Megan had not been consoling.

Nathalie had known differently. Her words then were barely a whisper: "It's not the Renzinger's anymore; it's the Borelli's and it's where the Cartier bash is this Saturday."

"Holy shit," those words had come from Ian on the Zoom call, but not about that eerie revelation for he had one of his own. Nathalie and Megan both looked at his image on Nathalie's computer screen.

"Little tidbit, I found," were the words he had led with and let dangle for a moment too long.

"For fuck's sake, what?!" Megan's irritated response had been more about her thunder being too quickly pushed aside than impatience to learn what Ian had discovered.

"Found out Elliot Crositer's exact age, if he had lived, if he's Eli Cross." Again Ian had let those words hang in the air for a moment. He knew what it meant. His own goosebumps had given him pause. "The plane crash was thirty-five years ago this August, tomorrow, Friday."

Nathalie's goosebumps had shot up like mountain peaks. She knew in her gut then what he was going to tell them. Her woman's intuition burst into fire at that moment.

"Elliot Crositer would be fifty this year." Ian paused again and drew in a long breath. "He'll be fifty…on Saturday."

"Holy shit!" Megan's goosebumps had poked out as words.

Sitting in the dark, thinking back on that moment, Nathalie realized that Lieutenant Donelli had been right. Cross was hell-bent on pulling off his score right under their noses. How could he not? The Renzinger connection to where the Cartier jewels will be and the amazing coincidence of his birthday on that day were as if the universe lined up the perfect test of his *moment* that did not fit and whether he was up to the challenge to overcome it. This was how she knew—and felt—that he was definitely committed to this plan of action.

The light was still on in his suite at The Lucerne and she realized that the newly uncovered information shed more light on her prey. It was the first clear hint of vulnerability, something emotional that could give her the upper hand if she knew how to exploit it.

The CRM company had been sold very quickly and the Renzingers became very rich very quickly and the Crositers were very quickly gone. Except one Crositer wasn't. What did that feel like, she wondered? Did it have a lasting impact or had he learned to put it behind him?

If it still ate at him, even drove him, then it could be a glimpse of a man who was not perfect and unstoppable but in fact broken, leaving a vestige of something that was vulnerable that he didn't fully control.

It excited her that this would allow her to know him more truthfully. This could be something he can't cover up and therefore something she could trust. This private crisis inside his psyche was also sexy to her, drawing her to him to defeat him or perhaps—from a strange rush of sudden feelings— help or save him and in the process to finally know him.

Her resolve waffled.

Think, don't feel, solve this, connect the dots she implored herself. What was he doing? Find the flaw. It was there she reminded herself. It was somewhere in his plan, the plan at the Borelli estate, once the Renzinger's. The confluence of circumstances was too perfect for him not to be there. The *moment* was there. Be waiting for him at that *moment*.

She needed to piece together the nature of his potential vulnerability, of his being human and not just a precision instrument who never made a misstep. Her confidence of her ability to beat him at his own game rose exponentially. It might cost her, the steps needed to be taken to gain the upper hand, but she felt it would be worth the price. She would be completing her father's quest and possibly avenging her mother's indiscretion.

What she didn't anticipate were the feelings that his vulnerability generated. It surprised her because part of her wanted to help him. She remembered that despite all, her father found something in him— almost inexplicably—to like.

Her hesitation to pounce bothered her. Was it a woman thing this hesitation to act strongly, decisively, and instead feel compassion? Would the men she competed with hesitate?

Her jaw set tightly. She would not be weak. She shoved down those rising feelings.

This was no time to get soft! She was *on the case*!

The light snapped off in the king suite across the street.

She knew it was in the dark that he operated. The theatre of the thief held hidden secrets. She remembered one other piece of information they had uncovered: *Maquis sur-mer*. It was the name of his villa in Saint Tropez. Ian had said *maquis* meant thicket or craggy scrubs which abounded in that region. But Nathalie knew it had another meaning, one of honor in France. It also meant *armed resistance fighter*. Maquis was the name given to the French Resistance in World War II. Like the thicket it was tough, hard to kill, and everywhere. It was also relentless.

She needed a shower. That would clear her head, set her resolve.

In the shower, the hot, pulsating streams of water loosened up her muscles but also released a torrent of feelings she didn't expect. Suddenly off balance, she had to brace her right arm against the wall for stability.

It shocked her all the little things which gushed up from memory that she felt were sexy about him. His stunning good looks were one thing, potent yes, but not as emotionally resonant as the *little things*. Those touched her…deeply…and came as a destabilizing surprise.

The way he sometimes flicked his fingers against his hair, not once, but always twice, and in the same spot. Nothing was out of place; it was just something he did. The way he had spoken about a favorite movie with unrestrained childlike appreciation. The way he would hold his gaze on her eyes waiting for a response. The patience in his silence. None of these things had anything to do with sex but they all shot shivers up her spine. The warmth between her legs was not from the hot water.

Quickly she shut off the shower and slammed the door against the flow of feelings.

Toweling off, the brisk rubbing of her skin dry locked in her resolve. She was her father's daughter and would do what it took to connect the dots.

Her nightgown had no sooner drifted past her shoulders and cascaded down her body like slippery silk when she felt the chill. A window was open. The breeze crept toward her.

She had not left a window open, not in this weather. A distant police siren rose like an omen heard too easily from the street through the open window.

Her hand silently slid her Sig Sauer off her nightstand.

She waited. Listened. Silence, except for the lace curtain lightly slapping the window sill when fluttered by the breeze. Everything else was still. There were no moving shadows.

She took a slow breath to steady herself…and then she knew. She smelled the faint, but distinct blend of a very unique, musky cologne. His cologne.

Eli Cross was in her apartment.

CHAPTER EIGHTEEN

Love is a journey, not a destination

Roy Croft, poet

It was her fantasy come true; a male intruder, presumably using the roof of the building next door had swept in through the open window. But she was not a sexually repressed sixteen year old Catholic school girl. This still unknowable man was here. But for what purpose?

She hid the gun behind her back, clicked off the safety, and stepped into the darkness of her living room. A figure dressed all in black sat in a chair. His fingers flicked his hair twice.

A little thing.

She dared not move in the darkness. She didn't trust herself. Not yet.

Her antique chair creaked as he shifted his weight on it in the dark.

Nathalie instinctively stiffened, bracing herself to respond.

A long moment of intense silence filled the space between them.

He seemed content to not move, and then—

"I have a similar antique chair in France," he said.

The casual tone of his announcement unnerved her.

"They told me it was from the court of Charlemagne," he added. "This one feels better."

Cross stood up from the antique chair and into a shaft of moonlight. Dressed head to toe in clothes of black stealth, the image did nothing to ease Nathalie's tension.

"I wanted to see you," he said without moving closer.

"You could've called."

"Where's the fun in that?"

"Or the intrigue..."

"Also the romance," he offered.

Casually tossed off as playful banter, the words felt more like little daggers flying out of the darkness at each other, probing the defenses. Who would lose their cool first?

The look in his eyes when he had said romance disturbed her. She had expected a challenging edge to it—like the others—but instead it floated toward her with a hint of innocence, tossed out with a sense of hope—maybe not hope, more like a plea—like wanting someone to toss a life preserver. Only a fleeting moment of feeling from him, but she had felt it.

"Then there's that small matter of trust," stated Nathalie.

"Yes," replied Cross. "What are we going to do about that?"

He held her gaze in the lingering silence. Another *little thing*. Once again.

Nathalie swore under her breath as she felt her limbs tingle with anticipation. Feelings! They could be so unfair. She held his gaze with a solid stare to get back in the game. Her heart beat faster. To slow it down she needed to be cold and calculating. Trusting Cross seemed out of the question which stymied her at this crossroads, unable to move forward with confidence.

The moonlight bathed their faces once again in a cool glow. Both faces guarded their intent, so much held back. The desire to break through the other's emotional wall intensified. Something had to give. Eli cast his eyes at her front door to break the stalemate.

"You changed your locks," he said.

"Yes, thanks to you; cost me a small fortune." She glanced at the open window. "The window entrance was only something romantic I'd dreamt about…until now."

"The reality's much more difficult, trust me," said Eli brushing some building dirt off his black pants.

The room plunged back into shifting darkness as the moon drifted behind another bank of clouds. A sharp gust of breeze slapped the lace curtain against the window sill. The *slap* hung in the air like a warning shot.

"Trust. There's that word again," said Nathalie with a challenging smile.

Eli did not respond or move. He remained dead still.

To Nathalie it felt like the stone-like stillness of the crouched lion just prior to attack. She needed to set him off balance if even for a moment.

"I trusted you to bring me a glass of wine—not a difficult endeavor—and yet you left the party instead." She watched his eyes for the glint of vulnerability of his *Elliot Crositer* identity possibly exposed. Had Nathalie heard his exchange with Katharine Otley? Had she connected the dots? The vulnerability was fleeting, but she caught it before it vanished.

"You said surprise me," he calmly explained, any vulnerability now smoothly covered up. He looked at the window. "I thought this was a better surprise."

"Yes…but where's the wine?"

He lit up with a genuine smile, without a planned agenda. He smiled because he liked her style. He couldn't help it.

To Nathalie it was a small sign that she momentarily had the upper hand. She decided to press that advantage.

"I'll let you off the hook for the wine; just return the jewels from the Waldorf Astoria gala."

"Well, if I had them…"

"But you know where they are," stated Nathalie.

He did not immediately respond. The words tossed back and forth in the darkness had been flares checking the battlefield, hopefully illuminating an advantage. Neither one had edged closer to the other…yet. The darkness between them remained untested space.

His presence at her home held clear intent.

The lack of movement from Eli jacked up the tension in Nathalie's muscles. Her grip tightened on her gun. The hard metal still remained hidden in the soft, flowing, silky folds of her nightgown.

"Perhaps that's one of many myths about me," he finally said.

"You told me not to discount the power of myth."

"When there is no clarity, people require myth," he stated.

"Yeah…and I think you enjoy the mythical allure that hangs around you because the trail of that story is easily manipulated." With her eyes she called him out.

"Much clarity will be revealed at the Cartier bash," Eli replied directly.

"And yet you're still insisting on not being there where stealing anything that night would be the ultimate challenge."

"I've fully explained that," he said simply.

"You made a point of reading to me from that Old French manuscript. I remember the words. *The goddess is but for a moment, and yet, for all eternity. Chasing her is elusive for she is ever-present, though seems unattainable. Acquiring her is sweet surrender."*

Eli smiled appreciatively at her remembrance. "That it is."

Nathalie felt the solemn truth of his tone behind the words.

"But Eli…" She let the familiar use of his name linger in the air as a lure, an enticement. "You need to test your *moment,* the one that does not fit, and you can't do that if you are not there, which is why I don't believe you. That challenge is too hard to resist. That's your Goddess."

This woman, so like her father, made the field of play thrilling. The slightest misstep on his part and he would fall to her sword. Something about her made him unsteady, not unlike her mother. He felt most alive facing someone worthy of all his skills.

His next words flowed with respect. "How do you know that it's not you?"

"Me? The Goddess?" This Nathalie did not expect.

"If you saw yourself through my eyes."

Those eyes had always bothered her, the vibrant blue, the lively flecks of green, and now the sincerity pulled her in like a rip tide. She longed to swim in their dangerous current.

"It's just the nightgown," she flippantly responded to steady herself.

His eyes never left her. That look—the gaze of a man enthralled with a woman—a tossed fishing net that slowly floated down over her head, clinging to her body and—

"Call it my Goddess shroud," she tossed off to fully regain her composure.

"You wear it well."

"Maybe…"

She remembered her plan. To take charge! Thoughts raced through her head. She couldn't possibly be the Goddess he chased—as enticing as that might seem—for she had never met him before that night at the Rainbow Room. If she was his Goddess—a fleeting thought if there ever was one—the Goddess would be in charge! That was all she needed to feel.

"But I don't surrender," she stated simply as fact. "So you'd best stick with another Goddess, your perfect crime where everything— every *moment*—fits."

He moved toward her slowly, his words chosen with precision. "Yes, sweet surrender, to make the Goddess yours, to own that *moment* when everyone is trying to stop you."

The dark space between them lessened with his every step.

"The coup de grace," he stated pointedly.

A sudden small shaft of moonlight slashed across the dark space between them as the moon emerged from a swirling river of clouds. He stopped as if facing a barrier from that light.

On either side of the thin shaft of light stood milky darkness and uncertainty.

Nathalie awaited his next move, but Cross just stared at her.

"This is exactly why the impostor will be there," he said. "But if you are not there…then the security is not complete and the challenge not enticing enough."

This was clearly a gauntlet thrown. Should it be picked up? Nathalie searched his eyes for any hint of a lie, but his gaze was rock steady. Trust was still elusive.

"Donelli says there is no other thief. It's you."

"The guessing will be over soon," was his only response.

"I want to know."

"What do you feel?"

"That you can't always trust your feelings."

That was the truth this moment to Nathalie. Perhaps that was what locked in her plan, a mentally calculated risk to turn the tide in her favor. She knew the cost. The worst part was that she didn't know if her father would approve of her method. She had to thrust feelings aside and commit to her plan of action—the door she intended to open to trap Eli—knowing there'd be no turning back. Would her father have clear-eyed pride for her taking charge or would he be disgusted with her choice of action. This was the only time she was glad her father was dead.

Cross moved next to her…his breath on her face.

Nathalie looked into his eyes...unwavering.

"You don't fall in love too easily," he whispered.

"Well, if I was wrong about you, maybe you're wrong about me."

The sexual edge in the air cut through the pretense. Their skin felt electrically charged.

"You think we know each other?"

Cross said those words with a tone of hope, not sarcasm. The humanity of his inquiry did not deter Nathalie from her plan.

"We each know how to break the rules," she said with assuredness.

"With rules there must be a game."

"And what game are we playing?"

Now her eyes were the lure. Nathalie could feel the electricity crackle between them.

Cross gently caressed her hair... her face.

"How do you know I won't take you out of the game?"

His hand slid around her throat. A distinctive *click* signaled her gun cocked into his ribs.

"A girl learns early on to be responsible for protection."

Nathalie slid his hand away from her throat. Cross eased her gun away from his ribs.

Her breath quickened. His hands remained unmoving and deathly still on her body. A touch so light a breath could pass between his fingertips and her skin. Her anticipation deepened, primed for the next move. But his fingertips remained still like a breath held. Intent melted, and she felt the battlefield bathed in a gentle wave of warm acceptance, not of giving in, only of the connection of mutual sweet surrender; yet it came with a warning: *who's in charge here?*

Their lips met in a tingling kiss, soft lips exploring, his arm circling her waist pulling her closer; bodies then pressed together, the kiss deeper and deeper until their breathing blended with the rustling of the sheer lace curtains in the whispering night air.

The bedroom, shrouded in darkness, mere footsteps away.

Nathalie gently broke the kiss, separated their lips as her hand pressed against the small of his back and turned him toward the bedroom, taking the lead in this passion dance. She guided him into the darkness. The Goddess was in charge.

What unfolded in the darkness was not at all what she planned. The moon was aloof; it's reflected light swallowed by mountainous clouds. Clothes fell away in a slow graceful dance, no tearing asunder, but fabric gently sliding against skin; the movement unseen in the darkness, but felt. The softness of the touch, brushing ever so lightly against her skin, sent cold shivers coursing through her body breaking the dam of guarded emotions and releasing rivers of increasing warmth. She felt her grip on committed plans slipping.

Softness like water can penetrate the hardest wall. She hadn't prepared for softness.

The heat of passion, the kind that burned hot only to flame out did not erupt. She had been prepared for that and ready to not be carried away by it but to use it to get him to drop his defenses and reveal his emotional Achilles heel.

Instead, waves of gentle exploration—not hot passion—generated enveloping warmth. What she felt would be explosive was more deeply dramatic in its quiet expression. He didn't *take her* in a move of masculine conquest which she had expected; no he gave himself to her. She was in charge…but slowly, losing control. When her power to control ceased to be power, then only the rhythm between them had control, and they were both carried along by it.

And those eyes…his eyes…never left hers. She never wanted to look away and she didn't. She could see his every feeling in his eyes before it expressed itself in touch. She experienced connection with this man in ways that before had only resonated in her daydreams about men. But this was real. She was most assuredly awake. Nothing had ever felt like this.

Feelings continued to roll in inexorably like the tide, unstoppable, until they were both awash in them. It was delicious and deep and soulful, so much more than merely physical.

How could this be, Nathalie wondered? She had intended to utilize all the allure of being a woman and pull him deep inside a web of emotional and physical manipulation, to use sex as a weapon. Then, with his defenses softened, his vulnerability would be apparent and she could then do what her father had not been able to do; he would be *Muldooned,* and by a Seeger.

Instead, swept up by the swirling sensations, her body and spirit felt freed from gravity and soared with the wind in playful flight. When he was deep inside her, they moved in shared motion, nothing forced, nothing rushed.

Her eyes urged his movement and his eyes urged her response.

A blended rhythm of harmony entwined their bodies in a dance of feeling connected by their eyes more than skin. Their orgasms were not consciously sought but rather arrived as a natural crescendo of delight to this man-woman symphony, but it was not the key moment for her; it was not that *moment* of deeply revealing truth.

No, that had occurred earlier and it had taken Nathalie by surprise.

Her sharp inhale of breath at the sudden impact had marked its arrival.

It happened in a pause, like the silent space in music, in a moment of cessation of touch. She caught his eyes and a glimmer of something deep inside. The visceral impact hit like a lightning bolt. In nature, the lightning flash vaporized water and heated the air around it to 54,000 degrees Fahrenheit, five times hotter than the surface of the sun, forever transforming the environment. In the heart, the flash of insight seared an indelible image on her spirit.

She couldn't put any words to it—then or later on—for it was simply an inner presence she detected within him, an insight that there was so much more to this man. It so touched her it pushed aside all mental calculation and manipulation. All in a fleeting lightning bolt moment. She would always remember her thought at the time: *what the hell just happened?!*

The love-making continued after the lightning bolt moment and was definitely real, and that legitimacy surprised her. But the lightning bolt moment floored her. That special moment of insight—a knowing beyond words—exploded all her plans. She had to rethink everything.

Her shattered plans were not from the euphoria of sex. She felt a deep sense of connection from this experience in the dark more than the lingering glow from the actual sex. Connection disrupted her plans. She had to understand, really understand, what it came from and could it be trusted.

How different this all was from the intense physical explosion of sexual passion from the past experience with Graydon Hutchings, and then possibly the threesome with his wife, Eshana, in The Lucerne. That had set her straight on what she wanted and didn't want in a man or a relationship.

She wanted connection.

So what the hell was this feeling of connection with this man, this international master thief and God knows what else?! Why had she never encountered this feeling with anyone before?! This timing sucked! It was so brutally unfair!

All these thoughts raced through her mind while their bodies remained entwined in a gentle embrace. The lingering pressure of his leg against hers, his arm cradling her shoulder, and her head resting on his chest only added to her quandary. She now understood her father's confusion concerning Eli and for the first time saw her mother's indiscretion in a new light.

The lightning bolt insight moment revealed to her something deeply worthy, a quality of character about this man. She certainly hadn't seen it fully expressed yet. The thought exploded in her head: *so how the hell do you trust that?!*

This shock collided with the cold realization that this feeling, this heartfelt connection in a relationship, had been missing her whole life. No man she had ever been with got to her like this man. What she felt, she felt soul deep; it's veracity undeniable and because of that she felt damned, for this connection with this still unknowable man came with her worst fear. Could she trust it?

In a pitched battle with an adversary where her career and possibly her life were on the line, being a dewy-eyed romantic didn't play to her strength. Clearly, she abhorred the idea of being one of those women who were whipped every which way by their emotions. She saw those women getting manipulated. Not her. No sir. No way.

She would use this insight for…then again…maybe she wouldn't use it all. Emotions could be tricksters. She knew—with feelings kept in check—that she was an intelligent, practical woman with a pragmatic lock on life. She trusted that.

Lightning bolt moments were a mystery and possibly only…myth.

A ribbon of moonlight escaped the grasp of the clouds and rippled through the fluttering curtains and rolled in waves across the floor to the edge of the bed where naked feet entwined with each other in gentle caress. Hidden in the shadows once again lay the suspicions. Nathalie, her head on his chest as her fingers rhythmically brushed across his skin, wondered about her next move and what he was thinking. Suspicion's claws reached out from the darkness and clutched at her nakedness.

She was suddenly unsure.

What had his experience been, manipulation or connection? His long, slow, deep breath warned her to stay quiet, to let his response, hopefully his words, be her guide. She waited…

"There is a touch you have," he softly began, "when you forget yourself that is...sweet surrender."

Nathalie said nothing. Those words and especially his tone informed her that this was the most emotionally open expression she had felt from this unknowable man. It was a doorway that she knew might only be open for a short, unguarded moment. She desperately needed to slip inside.

She hesitated to expose her knowledge of *Elliott Crositer* to him as her entrance card. That was the secret ace up her sleeve to be played only when necessary…and yet she realized that time may be now even though it risked him exiting the game before he could be caught red-handed with the goods. Once again, he would then slip through the net of a Seeger. Daughter, like father, would lose her perp.

Her fingers brushed across a scar along the side of his chest. The texture told her it had not been placed there by nature. She cast her eyes down to the raised and roughly crinkled patch of skin. Immediately she knew this was her way in. She recognized the scar. It was a bullet hole.

"Does this hurt?"

"Only the memory of it," he said.

Nathalie heard the ripple in his voice, a crack in his armor. This was her chance. This was Cross being real. She sensed the struggle in him to face this, to deal with it, to admit that he wasn't the perfect machine of precision he had invented. This was connected to the yearning she had sensed in him.

He turned his head toward her, but said nothing.

Nathalie felt his eyes begged for help. Was this the young boy shouting out from the past hoping the man would listen and respond and…and what? Save him, she wondered? Stop him or set him straight? And if the man—his older self—wouldn't respond, then maybe this woman? She wasn't sure but she knew this was part of what drove him.

"Tell me... please," Nathalie said softly.

For a moment, he said nothing, as if weighing his options and the safety of each choice.

"It was a gift…from Monte Carlo," he finally said.

Nathalie remembered the challenging words of Jake Kracauer in the Regency hotel when he said Cross used to be the best but lost his nerve: *Ask him about Monte Carlo.*

"Monte Carlo…?" Nathalie gently probed.

"I don't really talk about it."

Nathalie took a chance. "If you trust me..."

Cross took an uneasy breath...all pretenses or posturing vanished.

"I had marked several patrons of the Casino," he began, "and was ready to unburden them of their jewelry. Almost six months to the day that your father died. Had he not gotten sick, he may well have caught me before that night. Something I will never know."

He was silent for a moment, simply remembering.

"Your father was relentless in his pursuit, but appreciated the artist's work. What I did lacked its spark when he was gone. And when you are not pushed hard, you relax, you get sloppy...and I took a bullet in my side."

Uncomfortable and unable to remain connected to her, Cross slipped out of bed into The Regency bathrobe Nathalie had bought at the hotel.

It seemed to her that his newly expressed vulnerability needed the protection of space between them. He crossed to the window and gazed down to the street below...

"That's the first moment that didn't fit for you, wasn't it?" Nathalie had him where she wanted him.

"It comes to us all," he shrugged.

"But it came before you were ready to accept it."

His painful look back at her revealed a piece of his heart. Nathalie wondered if the challenge of the Cartier International bash on Saturday was all about answering Monte Carlo.

"It is what you make it." Nathalie hoped her words might encourage him to let go of his driving need to chase the Goddess, his *moment* that did not fit.

Cross stared at this woman he had just made delicious love with and knew things were unfolding as he had hoped and intended. He sensed she had felt a connection that surprised her and had her second guessing everything. He trusted that sense because he had felt a connection also. This was emotionally where he needed her to be. This heartfelt concern would eat at her until she would be at the Borelli estate to stop him, or save him, which is just what he needed.

He returned his gaze out the window to the street below. Something caught his eye; a curl of cigarette smoke rose out of the shadow behind a streetlamp. Parked next to the streetlamp was Marty

Lefkowitz's Blackhawk motorcycle. Cross stepped back from the window's edge into the protective shadow of the room but continued to watch the street.

"The doctors in Monaco said that I died on the operating table, but somehow came back. As I recovered, I began to feel as though this was my second life, and it should be different."

He turned from the window to face her…as if a new man.

"So I changed. And I went straight."

Nathalie searched his eyes for the slightest flicker of truth, waited for her intuition to kick in and confirm it, and hoped for another lightning bolt moment of deep insight. That *still small voice* within her—that divine whisper—was awfully damn quiet. The only thought which emerged: *he was too damn good at keeping things hidden, at being unknowable.*

He offered a knowing smile. "Perhaps your father caught me after all."

Nathalie thought *if only that were true.* She still felt it was up to her. Deep down that was not unknowable to her.

Tomorrow was Friday. Only one day left. The Cartier international bash was Saturday.

CHAPTER NINETEEN

Women, like men, should try to do the impossible. And when they fail, their failure should be a challenge to others.

Amelia Earhart

A museum curator placed the sturdy fine-art-protection cabinet near *The Cellini Lovers.* It served as its vessel for the journey to its owner's home. A steel protective rim ten inches in height encased the bottom of this high-tech packing crate and framed a solid weighted base. The statue would fit inside the upper cabinet and rest on top of this thick heavy base.

The interior walls of the crate were lined with layers of plush material which would mold to the sculpture's shape like memory foam and hold it tightly in place cushioning any side-to-side or up and down movement without so much as a hint of a blemish on its marble surface.

The outer walls protecting the inner cabinet were thick fiberglass which had been heated and fusion bonded with an impregnable polymer resin coating. State-of-the-art for fine art.

Once loaded, the masterpiece sculpture would be safe and secure for travel.

The Baronfeld was currently closed to the public. Preparation for packing ensued. There was much work to be done. Several exhibits were being dismantled, including the room with *The Cellini Lovers,* and the precious art work sent back to the various patrons and museums who had loaned them to The Baronfeld. These exhibits must be cleared out by Saturday night for the first thing Sunday morning the new shipments arrived; some of those masterpieces also owned by members of the Baronfeld family.

Cross handed Benny, the security guard, a clipboard as Nathalie watched the exhibit dismantled by art restoration experts.

"This is your schedule," Cross said." Every step is to be followed—precisely."

"Yes, sir," replied Benny.

Benny clung to the clipboard as he watched the sculptures and paintings moved carefully by the experts from their exhibit positions. The newly discovered Cellini masterpiece of the entwined lovers still rested on its original perch. Cross stared at the small statue with admiration.

Nathalie folded her arms around him. "Thinking of the passion of the artist?" Nathalie teased as she nuzzled his neck. She unfurled her finger toward the eternally entwined couple. "That position was more challenging than I thought."

"Yes...we did suffer for our art," Cross gamely replied.

"Nobly..."

Gilbert, the other guard, watched as two art restoration experts lifted the Cellini sculpture from its pedestal and placed it gently in its awaiting cabinet.

Cross took Nathalie by the hand and led her out of the exhibit.

"Will you ship them?"

"Carry by hand, every one that I'm responsible for."

"Anxious owners," Nathalie said squeezing his arm in jest.

"Especially with me guarding them." Cross felt perfectly at ease with her ribbing.

As they passed through the main lobby, Nathalie recalled the last time she traversed this floor with him, a gun at her head and few options to stop a theft and save her life. How things had changed.

Change…perhaps the one thing to trust; there will be change.

One dynamic change occurred that sprung clearly from him. After the night of lovemaking with Eli, the visual images of the other men who had been lovers in her life suddenly became fractured pieces of memory only, never a complete face when she attempted to recall them. Struggle as she might, her mind's eye saw only dissipating fragments of image that soon vanished like mist before a breeze. The face that emerged each time out of a gust of fresh air always became his—his smile—his eyes.

What the hell was this feeling?! She had clearly never felt it before. This was the real deal, whatever it was, and everything before a mere forgery. The elements of his character that remained still unknowable pressed her to keep probing. Something inside though had changed. She was not the same woman he had met in the Rainbow Room.

"Your lesson of being a thief with The Cellini Lovers..." Nathalie suddenly said, letting the words hang without conclusion.

"Yes..." Eli waited for her to make her point. He was in no hurry.

"Your cell phone would've pinpointed you there," said Nathalie, pointing out a flaw in his flawless plans.

"Would it?"

"It can be tracked."

"But to this location...or somewhere else that night?" Eli let that teasing tidbit hang in the air between them. "If you know how to do it, it's rather simple. All part of your preparation."

"And the security cameras? Even if we weren't seen we would've been recorded. We were in clear sight."

"I only needed to be worried about being seen not recorded to teach you the lesson. If I wasn't handling security, and actually stealing it, there was a way to avoid being recorded."

"How?"

"I can't tell you all my secrets. You might be tempted to try them and get in trouble."

No answers for Nathalie in this line of probing, except one; there were still secrets. Perhaps playful probing was more effective. "Didn't last night teach you that I can take care of myself and stay out of trouble?"

"In surprising ways...yes." Eli's answer seemed genuine as he squeezed her hand. "I remember..." he said then suddenly chuckled from a memory that stopped his words. "I remember something your father told me. About you and Ian when you were little."

"What...?" The sudden insertion of something so personal from her past into their conversation unbalanced her. Something else— something personal of her family—that her father shared with this thief that he wanted to put in prison?! It rankled her that he was privy to so much more of her past life than she was of his.

"He said you were very sure of yourself, even at seven, and couldn't be persuaded otherwise. You insisted on doing things that got you in trouble."

"He told you these things?" Nathalie felt that her father sharing such personal memories with him somehow violated the sacred space of her own memory because she had not chosen to share it. It was supposed to have remained hers. She didn't know how to react to this intrusion.

"There was one incident in a grocery store. He said you and Ian wanted a box of cereal on a top shelf. You were told no because you couldn't reach it. He said you turned and stared at it…thinking…then scampered up a pyramid stack of large juice cans and grabbed the box. But when you tossed it down to Ian, you slipped and the whole stack came crashing down. You hit your head on one of those cans but you wouldn't let yourself cry."

"Dad was really pissed," Nathalie said remembering.

"Yeah, but he was also proud. He valued determination."

"I knew I could reach it, but I didn't know how to get down. I still have a little scar from that under my hairline."

"We all have our little scars," Eli said wistfully.

She stared at him, remembering the discovery of his bullet wound scar and its impact on him; yet it was her words *didn't know* which clung to her thought as a warning. She suddenly knew that was her own Achilles heel with him; she didn't know what she didn't know! She didn't want *to slip and fall* again! No more scars.

"How much else did he share?" Now there was a clear edge to her voice.

"He loved talking about your family."

Why did her father share these personal feelings with him? Was it all part of making your adversary your friend—keep your friends close, but your enemies closer? That was wisdom from *The Godfather*. Her father often joked that everything she wanted to know about criminals and his job as a cop—or life for that matter—she could learn from *The Godfather*. She sure as hell had gotten close to Eli…but what had she really learned?

But she wasn't the only one who had gotten close to him. The image which rose up before her out of a swirling witch's brew mist was a haunting one…her mother and Eli Cross intertwined like *The Cellini Lovers*, naked and…and what?! In love?!

Each time she slammed that image out of her thought, it would rush back in like water shoved up an incline with nowhere else to go but back down. The image assaulted her relentlessly again and again. Each time in detail that was raw and cut deep—the nakedness, the touch, the moans of pleasure, the passion.

Her mother was formidable. She'd seen her dig in her heels, stand up to tough situations and not back down. How could she have been so weak with him?! This feeling plunged the whole sense of her parents' marriage into grave doubt. Their love was one thing she trusted to be true! Even though she was a grown woman, this change was shattering, leaving painful shards embedded in her heart!

"And what did my mother share with you?!" Nathalie spit the words out in explosive frustration!

"Nothing I should tell you. It's not my place. I owe her that."

Eli was resolute in his tone. But so was Nathalie.

"I want to know about you and my mother!"

"I expected this last night."

"I thought the bedroom would get a little crowded if I brought my mother into it."

Eli knew that silence would not deter her. The little girl who went after the cereal box would keep coming at him as a woman until there was some satisfaction.

"Your mother doesn't let life slip by. When she makes a choice, she can't be swayed. You're a lot alike."

"Is that what last night was? Completing the affair—mother, now daughter?!"

"Is that what you feel?"

"My father was crazy about her!"

"Because she was a match for him right down the line!"

"And I've been right with you every step of the way!"

"Almost...but not about this," Eli said.

He stated that as a fact which left no room for argument.

Nathalie wondered what she might have missed. Maybe nothing, but she sure as hell knew what she had experienced—and it was painful.

"When they returned from Paris, they separated for a year! Did you know that?! But my father wanted her back." She shook her head in heartbreaking confusion. "She made him court her all over again!" Her eyes held sheer amazement. "And he did." Tears flooded her eyes like a surging tide. "And he died in her arms." The tears fell freely and soaked into her blouse. She didn't care, she wasn't ashamed, she wasn't holding back. The long-held pain flowed out.

"She's a remarkable woman," said Eli, unable to offer any other comfort.

With a heart that was breaking, Nathalie spun around and walked away.

"Is this good-bye?" Eli called out after her.

Nathalie stopped but did not turn around to look at him. She stood in silence for a long, lingering moment, then… "Not if we're having dinner tonight."

"Eight o'clock?" Cross offered.

Without looking back, Nathalie simply nodded, her shoulders sagging.

"I'll have my driver pick you up."

He watched her walk out the front entrance into the sunlight. With each step the sadness and resignation in her body language lifted. He couldn't take his eyes off her. This woman got to him. There was no *give up* in her. She was as formidable as her mother. He had dealt with that once before in Paris. Though he didn't know it at the time, he was aware of it now that his actions then and that decision changed the course of his life. Now the daughter was in his crosshairs, to see if the *moment* was his, to know whether the Goddess would surrender.

He knew it was time to take care of loose ends, set the final stage.

&

In the Seeger's backyard in Jackson Heights a cobblestone path rimmed with trails of flowers led to a vegetable garden where Odile carefully loosened the earth around the strawberries. Plunging her fingers in the soil always felt like therapy. The sensations carried memories. She and Nate had spent his downtime growing vegetables together. Shared time she cherished. Now each scratched area of ground grated against her fingernails and reminded her that he was gone.

She needed to find her therapy—her soothing memories—further back when touching the earth carried the anticipation of discovery. Her fingers sought solace in the earth back to her childhood in France.

Odile Trenet first had cultivated flower boxes on the window sill ledge outside her family's apartment in Paris when she was little. The thrill of seeing a sprig appear never lessened as she got older. One spring she planted flowers which replicated the colors of the French flag in order left to right: blue, white and red. She beamed when many a cry of *merveilleux* rose up from passing pedestrians on the street below.

During the summers in Provence at their place in Arles, she learned of the many qualities in the dirt which made their way into the wines of the region such as rosemary, currant, and her favorite, lavender. They were days of innocence filled with exploration. Escapades of fanciful delight fed by unleashed childhood imagination led her to the banks of the Rhône River and daydream adventures traipsing through olive groves. Here her passion for art, for drawing the images she saw as she lay in the cool grass, burst forth. Always there was the earth which grounded her; her back pressed into the soil soaking in its energy. Many times she came to the family's long outdoor dinner table with her hands caked with dirt.

The long festive table stretched from dappled shade provided by a mixed clump of Mediterranean pines, platanes and one lone fig tree into the soothing warmth of the arms of the late summer sun. The seven sisters, a row of towering Cypress tamed the fierce and fickle mistral winds which roared out of the Rhône Valley and otherwise would've scattered the meal and its dishes to hell and gone. Odile watched them bow before the masculine god of wind and his blustery might but never lose their strength or dignity which was why she bestowed on them their feminine name: the seven sisters. As an only child these sisters were her protectors.

She never felt lonely in those lazy summer days because the evening meal was always populated with her parents' friends. There was much laughter and convivial discussions which most excitedly often turned into boisterous arguments where sometimes food took flight across the table. When pigs flew—mostly the cooked morsels— she quickly covered her wine glass to prevent the splash from unintended intruders. Allowed wine at a young age, as was the French custom, she found her day come full circle with each sip as it brought to her lips the taste of the magic within the earth.

Even now as an adult living in America, every handful of dirt was smelled to discover the aromas within, the hidden magic. In Queens, few of the aromas of France wafted forth, yet each handful always held out hope. Odile was absorbed in her work nursing the strawberries until she sensed something in the air...an aroma from her past...one that carried a clash of memories...an extremely unique, musky cologne. She breathed it in to be sure there was no mistake, that it was real and not rising from her imagination. Without turning she called out...

"Eli?"

"Oui, Odile, c'est moi."

The voice behind her was as smooth and confident as she remembered. She turned to see Eli Cross standing on the cobblestone path. They stared at each other, across time and memories. So much of what had been felt and experienced between them in Paris hung in the weighted silence between them. They both knew there were no words…

"I can't stay long," Eli said simply.

"It's better that way," Odile acknowledged.

"I wish it were different."

Words of hope they both knew could only ever be a wish. She studied his eyes, the ocean of blue and green that held so much for her, and he met her gaze with sincerity. He owed her honesty, the unvarnished even if painful truth.

"I want you to know I've been with your daughter. Nathalie's everything you are...and more. As formidable as her father."

"Does she know now about Paris?"

"It wasn't for me to tell her."

Odile knew then she would soon face the irrefutable moment, the moment when the truth that was so carefully blocked and guarded against has broken through and will not be denied.

"I wanted it to rest with Nate and me…and leave my children their memories untainted."

"She has your strength."

"She loved her father very much, Eli."

Cross stepped forward, knelt down and took her in his arms.

"There's not a day goes by that I don't think of him," said Eli softly.

She clung to him...gaining strength from memories…then broke the embrace and took his hands in hers.

"Nathalie's my daughter, Eli. I love her more than my life." Odile said almost as a warning.

"Then trust her."

"And you? What are you going to do?"

"What I have to," he stated simply.

"This is not Paris," she said, feeling the all-to-true painful truth.

"No…it's not," he admitted.

He lifted her hands to his lips and planted a kiss...then stood up and walked out of the garden without looking back. Odile watched him go, knowing that there was nothing she could do to stop him and that she would probably not see him again.

෫෨

The building housed a private school for children with learning difficulties. That had merit, he supposed. Even better, a portion of the structure was in use as the school's art center. Art, he knew, must be nurtured, and remained as always precious to him. But the memory of what once was here was not only historical but deeply personal.

He wished he had returned sooner, before the change and reconstruction for one last look, a final lesson even, and of course a farewell journey down its ramp and through the fabled oversized doors.

A taxi accelerated and flew by aggressively close behind him. His legs squeezed the flesh beneath him to steady his ride and his hands tightened the leather reins. The horse, a grey Arabian was well-seasoned on urban streets and did not spook easily. Nonetheless, Eli grimaced at the stupidity and careless disregard of New York drivers, a distinct downside to this energized city.

With one last look, he turned the horse from 175 west 89th street and proceeded at an easy walk toward Columbus Avenue and eventually Central Park West. Memories trailed behind him of that building and the genuine moments of happiness he had experienced there.

Twelve years ago in 2007, the doors of Claremont Riding Academy and its stables closed. Until that day, he had had the opportunity only a few times as an adult to re-experience firsthand the smells and sound from his childhood when he and his father performed dressage routines in the small riding arena. Navigating between some of the support pillars as well as staying clear of other riders in the crowded space improved one's horsemanship skills rapidly.

Built in 1892, Claremont was the oldest stables in the city and even housed many of the horse carriages for use in Central Park. Watching the horse-drawn carriages traverse the series of ramps that led down from the upper levels always thrilled him. The horses had such grace and poise in their expression of elegant power.

He thought it would never close. He also thought his father would still be alive.

Both memories only; he rode onward toward an uncertain future and Saturday night.

A parked car door suddenly opened in front of him blocking his path. A cane extended past the door frame, then a leg, and pulling himself out using the door as a brace, Ian Seeger confronted Eli Cross and the Arabian. Undeterred by the size of the horse, he pressed his case.

"I'd like to talk to you," Ian said forthrightly.

"Another Seeger, isn't it? Ian?"

"Yeah, I wanna get somethin' straight here."

"You have your father's brassy side," said Eli, "not unlike your sister."

"Yeah, well, she's our topic today."

"I thought she might be." Eli offered an appreciative smile.

Another car zipped by recklessly close and Ian flipped off the driver with his cane while Cross settled the Arabian with professional command!

"Do you ride?" Eli asked, yet again unfazed by the aggressive driver.

"If it's got a motor."

"You should try flesh," Eli said as he patted the horse. "Much different feel of power. My grandfather used to ride here at Claremont at the turn of the last century and my father and I did dressage and then the bridle paths in Central Park. So it holds a bit of history for me. I even rode through the park once with your father."

"I didn't know he rode." This was a surprising fact about his father. Even more surprising was that he was learning it from Eli Cross.

Ian could imagine his father jousting with Cross, complete with suits of armor, a battle to the death right out of *Ivanhoe*. It might even have been over love for his mother. But just a ride in the park…that was a new one…and more unsettling than fascinating. How he wished his father was still here to ask him what the hell that was all about!

"He didn't really," Eli chuckled fondly. "But he was game." He paused in remembrance and then continued with sincerity. "He was a fine man."

"Yeah, a good cop," Ian wondered what else might be revealed about Cross from this conversation.

"That he was. He said you were a political warrior, no taste for the streets."

"I chase the bad guys with words." Ian shifted uncomfortably with his cane.

"Being a writer's a noble pursuit. Your father admired it. He bet me that you'd win a Pulitzer. Laid money on it."

"You may have to pay up."

"It would be my pleasure."

It was an unexpected gift to Ian to hear about his father's admiration and pride for his chosen work and he did not doubt the truthfulness of Cross's words. His sincerity was real.

Cross was s a tough man to dislike. Ian understood more of his father's notes now.

But that did not solve the dilemma of Nathalie, and Cross sensed it in Ian's eyes.

"You are concerned for Nathalie because you think I am a thief planning on using her."

"Yeah, you could say that. I don't want my sister hurt."

"It is your sister who has the upper hand on me, I'm afraid. I didn't expect to meet someone...special, like Nathalie."

Ian wasn't ready for the look of truth in Cross's eyes or for words that made his sister the woman of a man's desire. What he didn't know fully was if this was a good or a bad thing.

"Yeah...women can do that to you," was all Ian offered.

"I had never let them get that close. This is a new game...and she plays it better than I."

Ian wondered if he was seeing a man in the quandary of love or spinning a web of manipulation. This was one of those moments when he craved knowing what the missing pieces of his father's notes were and how those dots connected.

"Sometimes if you lose, you win," Ian said.

"Yes," Eli smiled warmly. "Sweet surrender. Aptly named."

"Surrender's not in the Seeger dictionary," said Ian directly. "Consider that carefully."

"I have. The Seeger women know their strengths more than you think, more than they will admit, and I know it's the same for the Seeger men."

"Remember that," Ian stated as a warning.

"I'm counting on it."

With a light lift of the reins and gentle pressure from his heel on the Arabian's flank, he eased the horse past Ian and on down toward the park.

As an adversary, Ian felt admiration for Cross, much like he remembered from his father's notes. Cross would take one right to the edge of guesswork with charm and firmness of intent without divulging his true purpose. That unknowability demanded unfailing vigilance to keep the playing field even.

Ian knew that somehow for reasons he could not yet pin down, Nathalie was in Eli's crosshairs. She had become integral to why he was here and what he was planning. Ian also knew he had learned well from his father, and if it was necessary, he was prepared to shoot first to protect his sister.

CHAPTER TWENTY

In this world there is no force equal to the strength of
a woman determined to rise.

W.E.B. Du Bois

Nathalie watched the rehearsal astonished at the spectacle.

This was destined to be a uniquely memorable event in the Hamptons where memorable often became commonplace. Dancers adorned each other with precious Cartier jewels placed on their bodies in rhythm with the music and prompted by specific choreographed movements all ending in a frozen tableau image of French pointillist painter George Seurat's painting *A Sunday Afternoon on the Island of La Grande Jatte.*

This required the perfect timing and placement of people in period costume—even dogs—props such as blankets, scenery in the form of trees and a projection of the Seine River. The performers held this frozen effect in silence for a full minute to not only allow for the expected applause on Saturday night, but for the audience to fully appreciate the effect, and most importantly, to allow for the surprise of the final Cartier denouement.

Laser focused beams of white light added a dazzling homage to the painter's pointillist style during the re-creation of the human-scale painting. Pinpoint rays of light struck the Cartier jewels bestowed on the actors within the painting landscape and minute shards of tiny dots of light burst forth as if applied from an invisible brush stroke. Pointillism by light.

Some of the music came from the Pulitzer Prize-winning musical *Sunday in the Park with George* which was inspired by the painting. The music and lyrics were by Stephen Sondheim with book by James Lapine. Rumors abounded that Sondheim and Lapine and the stars of the original Broadway production, Mandy Patinkin and Bernadette Peters, might be among the VIP invited guests. Those rumors were professionally started to spread the word that this was a *must see and to be seen at event* for if *they* were coming, then *everyone* might be there.

To maintain one's professional status and social standing, attendance was required at an event like this. The rich and famous enjoyed being seen by each other when the celebration involved rubbing elbows with great talent, seeing great talent perform, and on this vaunted evening, having a gander at priceless gems and jewelry.

It was impossible not to be drawn in and entranced by this creative production.

Nathalie watched the performers where in their frozen state not even a muscle twitched, even the dogs. It was eerie. She thought back to the breathtaking moment that led up to the emotional impact of the frozen silence. Pinpoint spotlights timed with the music highlighted the sparkling jewelry on each actor at once which cascaded rainbow-colored shards of light dancing among the space which would be filled with guests thus encasing the audience in the pointillism style. It was splashy, hypnotic, spectacular and distracting.

Distracting was a key element of a thief's plan. There was plenty for the eye and ear to be distracted by from the vibrant, dazzling production and whatever the rich and famous were doing in the crowd on Saturday night. Keep them distracted while the thief absconded with the goods. Nathalie stared at the riveting stillness of the actors within the painting's humanly rendered landscape and wondered how and when and where Eli Cross would meet his *moment*.

The renowned French luxury goods conglomerate, Cartier International, had spared no expense to mount this production. That was first apparent in the rental of the Borelli estate. Now seeing the extravagance and intricacy of the entertainment presentation, she was most impressed. Major Hollywood talent agency heavyweights, Creative Artists Agency and William Morris Endeavor, provided the musical and acting talent along with the director, writer, choreographer, and production technical support. Simply getting CAA and WME to play ball with each other was the coup of the year.

Anyone who was anyone in society and the entertainment business would assuredly be here on Saturday night. The wealth on display would be dazzling on a galactic scale. She had to be ready for Eli Cross. There would be no venue anywhere this year on the globe like this gathering of the uber-elite. This would be his ultimate test, no doubt.

The concept for the Cartier bash, this variety of tableaux of live artistic expression whereby masterpiece paintings were recreated utilizing costumed actors, props, silken backdrops and computer projected images paid homage to The Pageant of the Masters held annually in Laguna Beach, California. This east coast variation added a storyline, musical numbers and dance which highlighted the Cartier jewels and culminated in the frozen image of a masterpiece painting when the music stopped and the actors held their pose exactly as the painter had expressed on canvas.

The Seurat painting was set to be the finale in the grand ballroom of the estate but other famous paintings were to receive the same but smaller more contained treatment in other designated areas such as the tennis courts, grotto pool and art studio.

What a canvas on which the Master Thief could paint his heist as a work of art, a masterpiece for all time, Nathalie thought. A *moment* made for Eli Cross.

She gazed around the glorious potential crime scene. The performers and production crew were unconcerned with what occupied Nathalie and Lieutenant Donelli's every waking moment. Donelli stood off to the side completely uninterested in the stunning performance now still frozen. Instead he poured over blueprints of buildings and their exits and entrances marking key posts for the detectives who accompanied him.

Nathalie shifted her focus back to the stage as the tableau returned to life and movement.

New music brought the entrance of a thief all dressed in black wearing a black bandana mask which tied in the back ala Zorro and carrying a plush black velvet pouch. In a stylized, cleverly choreographed number, he moved with great stealth and grace among the painting's human figures. He deftly lifted the jewels from one woman after another and slid them with ease into the black pouch. Policemen in period uniform from the late 1800's of the Seurat painting entered from all sides and dramatically closed in on him as part of the choreographed dance.

Individual pinpoint spotlights clicked off at the moment the jewels were stolen from each woman; the dazzling shards of light vanished that had been bouncing off the gems. All timed to specific beats of the new pulsating music. This continued until all the jewels had been stolen and the spotlights doused creating the illusion of a rush of darkness and an unsettled emptiness.

Nathalie felt the thrilling effect as it captivated one's attention entirely.

The music darkened and intensified. Just as the crescent-shaped curve of policemen surrounded the thief, he spun forward to be face-to-face with the lead actress whose frozen form blocked his only escape. She suddenly animated once more and reached out at the music's crescendo and ripped the mask off his face! The music stopped and in the crashing hushed silence, she stepped closer toward him and pulled him into a deep, passionate kiss.

Everyone, including the policemen, registered shock. Now exposed—and kissed—the thief pulled a dazzling ring from the black velvet pouch! A spotlight pinpointed the ring and colored light exploded around the ballroom! The thief dropped to one knee and pulled her hand closer, placing the ring on her engagement finger. With her cry of "Yes!" the performance ended.

The director and choreographer consulted with each other on their notes as the cast waited in place. After a moment, the director called out "You're all beautiful my darlings, grab a bite of something or someone delish and we'll see you all tomorrow afternoon for final prep." Everyone scampered off the performance floor, grabbed backpacks, exchanged hugs and kisses and sauntered out into the evening as the sun set over the estate grounds.

Donelli had never looked up once from his blueprints. Nathalie knew Donelli didn't give a shit about the art which had occurred right in front of him. None of it held any allure. He was here to end Cross and his unblemished streak. Dead or alive, didn't matter to him. How could he not, even for a moment, appreciate the art which surrounded him?! What a bitter, empty life.

Nathalie gasped at the thought that suddenly struck her: *The art.* Not Donelli's dismissal of it, but *the art itself.* Why hadn't she seen this before? It was right in front of all of them. Chills ran up her spine. It wasn't the jewels! It was the art! The art masterpieces at the Borelli estate and those on loan from museums for this gala—they were the prize!

Sculptures and paintings from world famous artists worth millions lined the walls and occupied prominent placement in all the venues where the frozen performance paintings would be recreated. Nathalie realized the jewels and their dazzling presentation were the distraction, a focus which captured the eye and the imagination.

Eli's plan and his brilliance were suddenly so clear to her. It was ridiculously simple. Simplicity, he had told her was his ideal. What was simple stood naked and exposed before all but without being seen for it was *so simple* to overlook its presence right in front of you.

She realized as she thought it through that the distraction had been initiated over a week ago. The theft of the Waldorf jewels was a set-up, a distraction of its own, so all the focus would be on the Cartier gems and not the art masterpieces in plain sight! Sure, she thought, the art could've been targeted and stolen long before this, but not under the eyes and noses of such a prominent crowd! Eli Cross was setting his own stage, establishing the gladiatorial arena for the test of his *moment*.

She approached Donelli.

"You're gonna need more men," she stated.

"We got things covered," Donelli said dismissing her as lint.

"I'm sure you do," she said. "Each performance venue."

"We've been over this," said Donelli losing patience. "The tennis courts, grotto pool, art studio, after each one the jewels are gathered by the guards and taken to the ballroom for the finale."

"And the guards leave those areas," said Nathalie calmly.

"Yeah—with the jewels! Pretty fuckin' simple."

"And no one stays behind."

"Yeah, everyone's goin' to the next performance. What the hell's your problem?!"

"You never really cared about art," said Nathalie stringing him along.

"So what."

"The paintings and sculptures staged in those areas are all masterpieces. They're beautiful. They're also worth a small fortune and they'll be unattended. He knows how to disable the security alarms on the artwork if no one is guarding them." She let that sink in for a moment. "Right under our noses, right?"

Donelli paled as he connected the dots.

"The jewels are the set-up, the distraction. The art is the prize. Eli Cross is an art lover," said Nathalie. "He's been telling me all along and I didn't see it."

"Holy shit…" Donelli realized she was right.

"Yeah, it's why you need more men," Nathalie simply said. "He's scoped out the estate, even knew it from years ago, probably caught the rehearsals. He knows the guards leave. So have some guards carry the jewels to the ballroom just as he expects. But now leave a few behind, at least three, more than he can handle or would risk taking on. And tell them not to leave the area no matter what noises or distractions occur. If they don't leave, he won't enter. His plans are simple, always. This will over-complicate things for him."

"So he'll just split and we'll lose him!" Donelli was disgusted with that outcome. He wasn't going away empty-handed this time, his bloodlust was high.

"No, he always has a contingency plan," said Nathalie. "Cover the art, make that impossible, and he'll put his sights on the jewels."

"They're still a helluva temptation," Donelli acknowledged.

"Especially since we're guarding them. He'd love lifting them right under our noses."

"We'll be ready for that."

"Good," said Nathalie and with that she turned and headed for the nearest exit marked on Donelli's blueprint.

"Where you goin'?"

"I've got a dinner date," said Nathalie. "Can't be late. I'm being picked up."

She didn't tell him that it was dinner with Eli Cross. She also didn't tell him that after watching the rehearsal she knew when and most probably how Eli would take the jewels after he was forced to drop his plans for the art masterpieces. That knowledge she kept to herself. She wanted to be one step ahead of the boys…for many reasons.

℘

The breeze down Central Park South grew sharp and crisp. Nathalie stamped her feet on the hard pavement of the sidewalk to get them warm again. Christ, she thought, at least Manolo Blahnik could have the decency to design something warm that was affordable and not ugly! She supposed it would be stretching the boundaries of adversarial combat too far to ask Eli to warm up her feet after he picked her up; this she felt even though they had already made love which definitely confused the hell out of everything, especially because it was heavenly and there was that lightning bolt moment.

It felt like she was on a stakeout but without the cup of coffee and a warm unmarked car to sit in. Stealing precious jewels were one thing, but making her wait in the cold?! That demanded *Muldooning!*

Whew, her mind rambled like a teenager festering about an Instagram insult.

That thought sickened her and she calmed herself back down into being a professional insurance investigator…an investigator who wore a stylish outfit that was not warm. Gotta look good when on the job when it included dinner was her only excuse.

Where was he?! She was in the right spot for sure. Across from the Essex House but before West Dr. She was glad she was not waiting at her apartment building or at The Lucerne. Somehow that felt weird, too personal. But where was her limo or cab or…

"Would you like to climb aboard?"

The driver of the Hansom cab horse carriage had pulled up right behind her. Nathalie had faced away from the flow of traffic to keep her face turned from the increasingly biting, cold breeze and had not even heard the clip clop of the horse's feet. The line-up for the Hansom cabs servicing the public was further down. Why, she thought, was this old guy stopping here?

"Oh, no thank you," Nathalie said. "I'm waiting for someone."

"Indeed you are," said the driver in a mellifluous voice. "Eli would like you to climb aboard so we can rendezvous in time. Melvin doesn't feel like trotting tonight."

Melvin was a ten year old dapple grey Percheron standing sixteen-three hands and a thick muscled seventeen hundred and fifty pounds. He was a towering beauty.

Nathalie looked up at the striking behemoth. "Well we wouldn't want to upset Melvin."

"Melvin's a sweetie, you'll see," the driver said as he hobbled down from the carriage and opened the door for Nathalie. With a smile, he added "I'm the one can get ornery."

Decked out in a light grey, long-tailed morning coat over a Pittsburgh Steelers sweatshirt with wrangler jeans rising out of a pair of black pirate boots and a black top hat creatively staved in at the top and bent into a slight angle that gave it a sexy lean, he doffed his hat with a sweeping gesture to invite her inside.

"Name's Mosey."

Nathalie immediately felt at ease although she knew it was wise to remain wary.

"Make that Nathalie for me."

"The French spelling I understand, mais oui?"

"Oui, c'est vrai."

Nathalie studied her driver as he gathered the reins in his left hand. He had a kind face, a strong face, sitting under thick, tight, salt and pepper hair. He was lean yet sinewy strong. She guessed around seventy. He sported a stubble beard more out of an independent streak than reluctance to use a razor, she felt.

Mosey at a quick glance was a grizzled old con man, but that glance would miss so much. He had the air of a man who had been places and done things. Whatever restrictions came from the bumps and grinds along those adventures he now carried with grace. He knew who he was and how to handle himself. He had to. He was a black man in America.

She liked him right away, couldn't help it. Perhaps she might learn something from him about Eli Cross that would make her case. The strange part of that feeling lay in the dual fork in the road to her case. One path clapped him in irons when caught red-handed with the goods. The other road, the one not yet taken, held the hope that she could talk Eli out of risking everything. This she knew might be her last chance to reach him, to change him. But change a man? When had that ever worked for her? She hoped to learn something from this man who held the reins. Some insight or leverage to change the game to her advantage.

She settled back for the ride.

Mosey lifted the reins and with a slight flick, Melvin moved off at a steady walk and turned on West Dr. into Central Park. The lights of the city in the buildings rimming the park sparkled like stars in the crisp night air. She needed to be picked up like this for dinner more often, she thought.

"A clear night, but with a wee bite. Wrap yourself in the blanket. It's what it's there for," Mosey said as Melvin plodded along. The rhythm of the Percheron's hooves against the pavement provided a lulling sound that invited relaxation.

Who needed winter gear when there was a soft, thick blanket, she thought. She wrapped it around her legs and tucked it in over and under her shoes.

"Melvin don't mind the cold if he's had some hay to heat him up. Named him after a badass dude I'd met. Melvin Van Peebles. You know his work?"

"I know he first got started in France because it was hard for a black filmmaker to get work here in the states then."

Mosey turned around to look at her, quite surprised she would know that.

"My mother is French and she thought he was quite provocative," added Nathalie. "She admired his grit. His first film was shot in France and based on a French language novel he wrote. I got all that from my mother. She actually read the book and saw the film. Said he had something to say."

Mosey was quite impressed. "I think I'd like your mother."

"Then of course *Sweet Sweetback's Baadasssss Song* put him on the map," Nathalie said, then added, "A true independent. I like those kinds of filmmakers."

"A brother carvin' his notch," said Mosey with respect.

Nathalie hesitated and then opened up a new line of questioning hoping for some insight.

"Eli met my mother. Did you know that?"

"Did not know that. She like him?"

After an uncomfortable pause, Nathalie said softly, "You could say that,"

"Most…women…do," Mosey said drawing the words out slowly as if proven fact.

That angle of inquiry yielded nothing but a twist in her gut. Nathalie hoped there had to be another way to get something useful out of him.

"You like Independents, me too. Always like the road you pick yourself," said Mosey. "Like Cassavetes, that John Cassavetes. Now that dude could be black. His film *A Woman Under the Influence* with that actress wife of his, Gena Rowlands, she's a force I'm tellin' ya. Losin' her grip on everything in that story, man I been that crazy before. And Peter Falk tryin' to keep it all together for her. That was some badass shit. Too bad Cassavetes and Melvin never made one together."

"That could've been something," Nathalie mused.

"You and Eli talk about favorite movies? He's got quite a few."

"We sort of did, yeah," Nathalie said recalling her awkward conversation with Eli in his hotel suite. Nathalie realized she had better get him off the movie kick which could go on forever since it sounded like Mosey has seen more than a few.

"He hadn't seen most of mine," Mosey said. "They're kinda offbeat and—though there was one—one we both dug. *Searching for Bobby Fisher.* That's a little gem. A true story. Better look that one up if you haven't seen it."

"I'll do that. So where are we going?" interjected Nathalie.

"My own route. Picked it out myself. Like to mix it up. Especially like the Bandshell, Strawberry Fields, Sheep Meadow, Belvedere Castle and of course the Lake."

"And what about Eli?"

"He'll find us."

As she listened to Mosey talk about his favorite places along their route and even where some scenes of movies were filmed, her thoughts drifted. How do you catch a thief really? You must know how they think. We move at the speed of thought. Be ahead of his next thought and catch him on arrival.

"You two think alike?" Nathalie suddenly asked cutting him off.

"Sometimes we see things the same."

"But you've known him a while, long enough to know his ways," Nathalie pressed him.

"Goin' on twenty years. Smart as a whip. He could steal your next thought."

"He can take your breath too," said Nathalie to keep it light and get him to drop his guard.

Mosey chuckled. "Yeah, seen him do that."

He turned around to Nathalie and let Melvin follow the path on his own.

"You must be somethin' though. Saw it in his eyes. He talked about you...different."

"Probably something he ate," she said.

Mosey liked her. She was all right in his book. He knew Eli Cross was a big boy and knew what he was doing. "You didn't know I was pickin' you up, so I'm thinkin' he didn't talk to you about us—him and me.

"Not a word."

"We pulled a couple jobs."

"You two? Together?"

"Yeah, not tellin' you what though. I know you're tryin' to stop him. But we made out real fine then. Real fine. I wanted more, but I was gettin' a step slower, you know. He saw it, I didn't. So, he paid me to go legit."

"Paid you?"

"Yeah, knew if I pressed it, I'd buy time—hard time. He made it okay to go straight. Must've cost him, 'cause I've never had a need. Ever."

Something new she learned. Something about his character. Maybe she could change him. Maybe he actually wanted to. Was this what her father saw in him?

"Did he get you this job, Mosey?"

"Nah, that was me." He patted his top hat. "Wanted to look sharp."

"And you do!"

The insight she garnered wasn't extensive, but it was significant. It showed her an angle to tap into Eli's vulnerability.

"Mosey, I think maybe we got somethin' in this Eli Cross."

"That we do."

A Blackhawk motorcycle on a parallel path stayed even with their slow pace in the carriage. The rider was watching them. It was Lefkowitz. They did not notice him.

Mosey looked at his watch. "About time. He's never late."

Up ahead, Eli Cross cut across a bridle path on horseback, on the grey Arabian. He did notice Lefkowitz on the Blackhawk motorcycle. He did not divert from his path to the carriage.

Nathalie watched his expert horsemanship with admiration. She had to admit to herself that the man had style. She also felt she knew enough about him now to understand that he didn't arrive on horseback because it was cool, but because he enjoyed it.

Eli pulled alongside them. "Mosey, I hope the wine is chilled."

଼

The Hansom cab rolled past the Sheep Meadow and then Bethesda Terrace and the Loeb Boathouse as Eli spread out hors d'oeuvres and finger sandwiches from a black cooler under their carriage seat. Dinner was light but refined and delicious. Eli's Arabian horse was tethered to the back. Mosey kept a gentle hand on the reins while he whistled to himself.

Under the canopy, Eli and Nathalie cuddled under the blanket as they ate and sipped their wine, a pinot grigio...from Oregon, not Provence this time.

"How can you not like *Tootsie*?! Nathalie couldn't believe he could be so dense.

"Dustin Hoffman in a dress was a turn off. Not attractive." Eli plucked another finger sandwich from the plate into his mouth.

"She was—he was—adorable!" Nathalie jabbed a finger sandwich at him. "Adorable!"

"Made me cringe."

"Oh, you're—and you never laughed?!"

"Never. Nothing funny about it."

"Mosey, how can he…?!"

"He's kidding," Mosey said.

"What?!"

"He's kidding, look at him."

Eli wore a grin from ear to ear. Nathalie punched him in the shoulder.

"You laughed your ass off," insisted Nathalie!

"I did," Eli admitted. "I was completely assless after seeing it."

"Okay." Nathalie was relieved. "It's one of the all-time greats."

"All time, any time," agreed Eli.

"How'd you like not having an ass?"

"It was great. I was just an asshole."

"You got that right," Nathalie said as she gulped the last of her wine.

God it was so hard to hate this man. That would make arresting him difficult if she couldn't talk him out of chasing his *moment.* He had an amazing way, she thought, of pulling you into life and completely forgetting about the task at hand—her case, the missing jewels—where the only thing that mattered was the moment right now and enjoying that moment.

But where was the thief in this moment right now? At times, she knew she couldn't find him because he wasn't there. This was one of those times. She felt like she was chasing a ghost.

The magical almost fairytale nature of her strange connection to this still unknowable man rose to storybook level as the carriage approached Belvedere Castle. Resting upon Vista Rock, nestled behind a forest of trees with its formidable stone walls, the square tower with its arched windows and the hooded turret tower rising up toward the clouds conjured up images of Camelot in her head.

The reflected moonlight off the waters of the lake-size Turtle Pond created an inviting carpet of light up to the castle walls. Would he be Arthur or Lancelot? Or more to the point was he Merlin? A dream flash of being swept into the castle vanished quickly before finding emotional roots because she knew this *building* actually housed the Central Park weather station.

She thought, *keep it real.*

But for a moment…there was the flash of a dream.

In their *relationship,* she knew a storm was brewing, the type of storm that sent ships to a watery grave. Still…the magic of this visual moment was somewhat intoxicating.

Nathalie took this moment to reach across what divided them.

"There's so much more to experience," Nathalie said.

"So much…what?"

"So much of everything. Don't you think we get wiser with more life experience?"

"Yes, we get better at what we do, maybe even be the best."

"Maybe being the best is knowing what really matters," Nathalie replied pressing her point and hoping it resonated with him.

Cross poured two small glasses of the pinot grigio as the serene clip clop of Melvin's feet carried them along past Belvedere Castle. He raised his glass in a toast.

"To your heart and thoughts.

Nathalie clinked her glass with his. "And the one moment that doesn't fit."

"To elude that moment," he said just before sipping.

Eli leaned closer. Nathalie did not lean toward him. She waited…and made him slide over next to her to receive her lips. It was a small gesture but he got the point. She wanted him to leave his *moment* behind if he wanted to linger in her world. Mosey's whistling carried them down the lane...both knowing that nothing was really resolved.

Mosey and Melvin took them all the way to Nathalie's apartment building. Mosey pulled back easily on the reins and Melvin stopped at the curb. Across the street chained to the streetlight was the Blackhawk motorcycle without its rider. Eli offered his hand as Nathalie stepped down from of the carriage and blew Mosey a kiss which he caught and tipped his hat.

"Why don't you drop by later," she said, then kissed him. "I'll leave a window open."

If she could get him into bed one more time she knew she could change him.

Cross looked at her across a long silence. This time it didn't feel sexy to her; it was unsettling.

"What is it?"

"It's all set for the impostor to be trapped. I won't have to be there, as I've told you. I'll be gone before the party's over."

"Your carriage turns into a pumpkin past midnight?" Her heart sank as she offered those playful words. She knew that *play* was over.

"Yes," he said with a genuine smile, then added with clear serious intent, "And Lieutenant Donelli will know where I stand."

It infuriated her that he could lie to her face like that after all they've shared and experienced. She knew he would be there attempting to master the *moment* and create his work of art in the theft of the decade. Her face never registered her irritation. She was in command of her own game at this moment. But her heart ached. "Then I won't see you after tonight."

Neither one has wanted to face this moment.

"Don't be so swift to outline the future," Eli said offering a glimmer of hope. "We have right now. Let's not let it slip away."

He pulled her into a deep kiss. Their arms found each other and clung tight.

Nathalie withdrew her lips from his. "Now is nice."

"What a fine twist of fate, you and I."

"Keep that in mind," Nathalie said as an emotional demand that bordered on pleading. She stepped out of the carriage.

This lady had taken a piece of him and he knew it. He watched her enter the building then tapped Mosey on the shoulder. Mosey flicked the reins and Melvin pulled away from the curb back into the night.

Cross settled against the worn leather of the seat, his thoughts adrift...until his eye caught the Blackhawk motorcycle chained to the light post across the street.

"Mosey, stop. Something's not right."

Cross leapt from the carriage and dashed back to her building and into the lobby just as the elevator doors closed giving him a fleeting glimpse of Nathalie…alone in the elevator.

CHAPTER TWENTY ONE

Life and death are balanced on the edge of a razor

The Iliad, Homer

The little jolt-bump that always started the elevator rising both amused and annoyed Nathalie. Amused her because it was like the comfortable and quirky habit of an old friend. Annoyed her because if she was just slightly off balance, like tonight, it made her instinctively reach for the wall for support. She was never in fear of falling so it annoyed her even more that she couldn't ever stop the automatic reflex to grab the wall. She felt stupid even if no one else was around. Sighing in frustration, she searched her purse for her keys, unaware that above her the emergency roof hatch was open.

Nothing but darkness lurked up above to the eye through the open hatch as the elevator rose up the shaft, but the sound of the cables and fly wheels echoing against the steel and concrete walls rushed in to fill the space in the elevator cabin.

She still couldn't find her damn keys in the cavern that was her purse.

In the lobby, Cross watched the floor numbers light up on the elevator panel – 4 – 5 – 6.

In the elevator Nathalie was oblivious as a green nylon cord, looped as a hangman's noose, lowered out of the darkness right over her head. Nathalie snatched her keys triumphantly from her purse. The noose dropped around her neck—snapped tight—yanked her up—onto the tips of her toes which brushed the floor struggling to make contact!

Keys and purse crashed to the floor! The purse contents spewed across to the closed door. She clutched at the nylon cord to pull it from her throat! The tight fibers chafed her skin and the tension threatened to crush her windpipe each time she slipped off her toes! Her fingers got a grip but the nylon cord was anchored tight from above the hatch! It also held her in the center of the elevator box so she couldn't reach the wall with her arms or legs for support. Only the tips of her toes kept her from suffocating!

A face appeared out of the darkness of the open hatch above her; a face she had never wanted to see again. Marty Lefkowitz. He dropped through the roof hatch and tore her hands away from the cord, pinned them behind her, and trussed them quickly like hog-tying a calf at a rodeo!

Nathalie fought to catch her breath as she slipped off her toe grip and the nylon cord squeezed her neck!

Marty shoved his face against hers—nose to nose—his nose the hammer of hell, she thought!

Marty said, "Don't struggle. The cord won't pull as much; you might be able to breathe."

Nathalie fought to steady her swaying body.

Lefkowitz watched her stretch her toes to the floor establishing contact!

"I'll bet you took ballet as a little girl," said Marty. "Nice little pink dress. Made your parents cry. Am I right?"

Nathalie glanced at the floor indicator lights.

"Oh, we're not stopping on your floor," Marty said." Nice little override trick I learned."

Lefkowitz wore leather gloves and had a 9mm Beretta strapped to his chest on a bandoleer like a ghetto pirate. He moved around her like a forest sprite on speed. This wired intensity along with a speech delivery which slid between languid phrases and staccato bursts made Nathalie think of a mind unhinged. As she fought to sustain her balance, his razor-edged madness unnerved her to her core. There was no way to assess his next word or action.

"Ever see the view from your roof?"

Nathalie gasped at his words and he stuffed a gag in her mouth in that same breath.

"Thanks for helpin' me pick this out" Marty said as he tugged on the green nylon cord. "I really like the green."

The rooftop resembled a dark platform paved with layers of hot tar and felt sealed with a membrane. Remnants of gravel which was the outer layer prior to being replaced by the membrane were still scattered about. More modern renovations and tiled surfaces were in the works with a few sections under construction. The roof held structures of various heights like a wooden water tower and new air conditioning power plants that rose into the darkness of the night sky like looming, giant tombstones and mausoleums, a graveyard in the sky.

The stairwell door burst open and Lefkowitz yanked Nathalie along by the nylon cord tightly secured around her neck. She tripped and fell hard to the rough roof paving, several gravel pieces embedded into her skin releasing a thin trail of blood down her leg. He dragged her behind him by the tight nylon cord to the far edge!

Panicked, she grabbed the rope behind her head and propelled her legs against the roof to shove herself along and get closer to him and take some more of the pressure off her neck as he yanked her across the roof. The sharp points of her Manolo Blahnik heels tore through the membrane into the felt and hardened tar beneath. That gave her enough traction to keep her windpipe from being crushed. For this one night, every penny of the ridiculously expensive shoes was worth it.

Reaching the far edge, he pinned her chest down with his knee and quickly trussed her ankles together just as he had done her hands in the elevator. He stood up suddenly but kept one leg pressing her chest to the roof as he clamped the other end of the nylon cord to a repelling system that had already been anchored into the wall by a series of pitons and carabiners.

Lefkowitz jerked her to her feet by the neck cord. Nathalie coughed and sputtered to breathe from the choking pressure and pain of the cord. He spun her around and shoved her face over the edge, forcing her to look.

Far below, headlights from passing cars sprayed fleeting splashes of light into the alley that then glistened off of discarded plastic trash bags. It was a dirty place to die splattered across the pavement amidst the garbage. Nathalie swayed from a rush of vertigo. Lefkowitz steadied her.

"Not just yet." Marty stepped back and took a camera from the back of his bandoleer. "This is for my buddy, Eli." He snapped several photos of Nathalie while she struggled to maintain her balance standing at the edge of the roof with hands and feet tied. "You should smile. He probably likes your smile."

He snapped off another shot but Nathalie didn't smile. Tightly held terror never looked like a smile, especially with a gag that pulled her lips into a ghastly grimace. Everything was happening too fast. She couldn't get a grip on reasoning while drowning in waves of fear.

"Suit yourself," Marty said. "He won't see these until morning. Even though he's probably comin' back here tonight. At least that's his usual MO. To bestow one last sweet kiss before you become the sacrificial pawn in his plan."

He popped off a final shot.

"But this time he won't see you," Marty continued as he gestured over the edge, "'cause you'll be hangin' around the building."

He reveled in simply staring at her—his captive prey—savoring every fleck of fear that raced across her eyes.

Nathalie tried to take advantage of this long, sickening moment and her eyes darted around the roof, desperately searching for a way to tip the scales. But another wave of panic rushed into her throat and she suddenly felt she couldn't breathe.

Marty checked the cord on her neck. "Sorry if the cord's too tight and tough to breathe. It's gotta be that way to snap your neck. So, you know…sorry."

"Are you…" Nathalie asked barely choking out the syllables because of the gag.

"What?" Marty could barely understand her. "Here," he said as he yanked the gag out of her mouth. "Just say it, no one's gonna hear you up here." He was certainly right about that, not with the noise of the city rising up from the streets.

"Are you working with Eli?" she asked, her breathing coming in short gulps from fear.

Marty's eyes narrowed into two narrow slits and his lips curled from disgust as if he'd just been insulted. "No." Then real pleasure lit up his face. "This is just for me. He had plans for you for his big night tomorrow. This is gonna screw everything up." Lefkowitz nestled his cheek softly against her face. "You're probably askin', what did I do to deserve this?"

He swiftly planted a gentle kiss on her lips.

"You trusted him."

Marty's satisfied chuckle chilled her to the bone. Talking a deranged psycho—who liked his work—out of killing her required deft reasoning yet asphyxiating fear choked off her thoughts!

Lefkowitz placed his hand on her chest and then gripped the clothing between her breasts. Feet and hands trussed and now trapped in his vice-like grip, Nathalie couldn't move. He curled and tightened the bicep of the arm that held her dress pulling her slowly toward his face. Then lips to lips, Marty whispered: "Ain't love a bitch."

Nathalie's eyes widened with fear and her body tensed. She knew the meaning of those words and the final committed look in his eyes. In the next breath she knew he would thrust his curled bicep forward like a shot put and send her off the roof. In desperation, she drew a final breath, and clamped her teeth onto his shirt collar locking the two of them together!

Surprised, Marty had to release the grip on her dress to yank his shirt collar out of her mouth. He tugged at his collar. Her teeth held tight. He slapped her face! She bit down harder! In a rage, he tore his shirt collar from her mouth ripping the cloth!

"Fuck you, you bitch, this won't fuckin' stop me!"

A sudden surge of new ideas shut off the faucet of rage and he took a moment to calm himself. He stared into Nathalie's defiant eyes reevaluating his next move. He grabbed her dress once more, but this time he pulled her back from the edge further onto the roof.

"All right, all right," Marty acknowledged. "That's one for you. So…well done…we'll start again. I do love this." He smiled with sincere enjoyment. "And love's better the second time around, right?" As he reached out to grip her dress once more…

"Marty…" The voice was Eli Cross.

With his back to Cross, Lefkowitz drew the Beretta from his bandoleer and calmly turned around to face him. Cross held his Walther PPK in his left hand ready to shoot. His right hand was cupped loosely by his side, fingers curled. The back of his right hand faced Lefkowitz.

Eli never looked at Nathalie; his gaze riveted on Marty.

"What do we do now?" Eli asked.

On the roof, the two men stood separated by ten yards of darkness. Lefkowitz stepped in front of Nathalie. She was still dangerously close to the edge. One false move on her part and Lefkowitz could shove her over the edge before Eli could do anything about it. Her life depended on whatever Eli Cross did next.

"I was gonna send you pictures,' Marty said. "But now I get to see your face when you realize your plans are all screwed."

"Are we still disturbed about Ingrid?" Cross knew this would keep him thinking…at least for the moment.

"Well...I liked her." Marty gestured toward Nathalie. "And I think you like this one." He gestured again over the edge of the roof. "It would make us even."

"Ingrid set you up, I didn't," stated Cross simply.

"You made her believe you'd split the heist with her!"

"Ingrid believed what she wanted to. So did you."

"It would've worked, you know that! No one ever got into the Louvre that way—but I did—and it all would've worked!" Marty still felt incredulous that Eli had let their plans fall apart, even after all these years.

"It was a brilliant plan you had," said Cross. "Almost perfect...except for that one *moment*."

"She left me hanging from that skylight," Marty spit out bitterly! "I got seven years! French prisons have a certain Je ne sais quoi fucked quality, ya know!"

"You got caught because you were sloppy. You were always sloppy."

"Not tonight," replied Marty. "This is very neat. You're not gonna shoot, 'cause if you hit me, it takes her over the edge."

Eli took a moment, a moment to allow Marty to savor the simplicity of his revenge plan. But Eli knew that the sword of revenge and retribution cut both ways. Everyone got bloody. He was ready. There was always a sacrifice if *the moment* was to be met.

"Marty, you know I don't like to lose. You don't think I had other plans in case she didn't work out?"

A flicker of doubt raced across Lefkowitz's eyes.

Nathalie wondered what the hell Eli was talking about.

"If you had done all your homework," Cross said emphatically, "then you would know that." His stare unflinching, his path committed to; no turning back.

Marty's eyes nervously darted back and forth seeking the truth. He wondered what he might have missed. The last indiscretion with Eli Cross cost him seven years in prison.

"I'm going to trust you, Marty. I'm going to put my gun down so we can both walk away from this."

Cross calmly leaned down and placed his Walther PPK on the surface of the roof then stood up. Nathalie couldn't believe it. Neither could Lefkowitz. It unnerved him, especially how calm and sincere Cross was, and how quickly he committed to this *surrender*.

"Walk away, Marty."

Lefkowitz did the math. Nothing added up to his liking. Why was Cross doing this? He looked down at the Beretta still in his grip. He felt this should be his moment. It was there for the taking.

"Seven years is a long time," Marty said bitterly.

Lefkowitz raised his gun and took deliberate aim at Cross.

Eli whipped his right arm toward Lefkowitz! His fingers uncurled with a snap, releasing an oriental throwing blade that embedded deep into Marty's chest! The Beretta dropped from Lefkowitz's hand!

Cross rushed toward Nathalie as Lefkowitz staggered back over the edge of the roof plummeting downward into the darkness but not before he had grabbed onto Nathalie's nylon cord! The end of the nylon cord was still tightly secured around her neck!

The slack from the pile of coiled rope unspooled rapidly and snapped taught against…Eli's hands as his flying leap grabbed the cord just in time; his strength and his body weight jammed against the low roof wall stopped the impact from reaching Nathalie's neck!

Over the edge, Marty hung on with sheer grit. With a gurgled growl, he propelled his legs off the side of the building like a repelling mountaineer arcing out over the alley!

On the rooftop, the sudden surge of Lefkowitz's weight broke Cross's hold on the nylon cord and jerked Nathalie by the neck toward the edge! She dug her feet against the torn and loose roof membrane and clawed the surface with her hands and fingers to slow her slide over the short wall at the edge.

Cross clutched the nylon cord in front of her head bracing his legs against the short wall as they slid along and into it, taking the tension off her neck just as over the edge Marty crashed back against the wall, the impact driving the knife blade deeper into his chest! Marty's weight and arcing action stretched Eli over the edge of the wall, his knees pressing to keep him from being pulled over.

Staring down into the darkness of his own possible death below, Eli saw the last flash of fire in Lefkowitz's eyes drilled right at him. Marty Lefkowitz lost his grip on the nylon cord and dropped through the darkness to the pavement below extending a final one finger salute!

Nathalie exhausted from effort and fear collapsed onto the torn roof membrane. Cross lifted the cord from her neck and freed her hands and feet. Eli was no longer calm and cool.

"I thought I'd lost you," Eli said, clearly shaken.

Nathalie took in rapid gulps of air as the paralyzing tension and fear released in waves of convulsion. But the thoughts racing through her head were even faster.

She thought she knew this man who saved her! She felt like she didn't know shit!

"Those things you said to him..." Nathalie searched his eyes for the truth, for something to trust, anything that was real and not part of a plan!

"You're alive, aren't you?"

He cradled her in his arms...but it didn't feel comforting. She clung to him, her mind spinning. *He told Marty he had other plans. What other plans?! Did he mean that?! And what the hell happened at The Louvre?! Did he use Marty?! Set him up?! Was she next?!! And who the hell was Ingrid?! A secret accomplice he still used?! Or another sacrificial pawn?!* Just like her father she wondered if she had been taken in by this guy's style and charm?! *Fucking hell!*

Still holding Nathalie with one arm, Eli punched a number on his cell with his other hand.

"Mosey, the alley. You'll know what to do."

He clicked off the call and fully embraced her once more.

His arms felt more like entrapment to her than protection. There had been dinners and dancing, clever and revealing conversation, wine and emotionally enthralling sex, and now death. His words to Mosey were so simple, so swiftly activated as if common place; so, so...normal like there was nothing to it. How easily he handled death, and this had been a brutal, frightening death. How often had he covered this ground? Those eyes of blue and green that she wanted to swim in, were they no more than a drowning pool? Once again her heart broke and her mind shrieked!

This was never simple, and trust was hauntingly tricky, if even possible at all.

"Eli, we have to call the..." Nathalie didn't finish for she knew in her gut what his answer would be.

"No, it's taken care of. You don't want to complicate things. Too much to explain."

Nathalie suddenly realized that if she said *no, that she was going to do the right thing and call the police*, then she might still go off the roof like Marty Lefkowitz. Her death would be easily cleaned up by Mosey—what's one more body—and wouldn't stop Eli's plans for tomorrow night, especially if he had a plan B already locked in.

Being tied up dealing with a complicated police investigation could prevent him from facing his planned *moment* at the Cartier bash at the Borelli estate. That, she reasoned, he wouldn't allow to happen.

"Do you want me to stay with you tonight?" Cross offered with sincerity.

That thought, once exhilarating and enticing, filled her with dread.

She even flashed on Megan rambling on about the movie *The Day of the Jackal* and the Jackal character being in bed with some countess. *He just leaned over and softly kissed her on the mouth with his hand gently on her throat. So quiet, no struggle, just a kiss and she was dead.*

She was still in shock and not reasoning anything real well at this moment. To fall asleep with him, she would have to trust him.

"No," she said quietly but firmly. "I just want to be alone."

CHAPTER TWENTY TWO

The warmth of the sun woke her up. It was a comforting, penetrating heat that made her not want to move. Nathalie knew full well that the trauma of last night had not been a dream. Sometimes though, reality had a way of engulfing you in ways that felt so strange it could only be a dream. Today of all days she had to see things clearly. This was Saturday. Trauma must be shoved aside, dealt with later. Tonight was Cartier. Tonight was Cross. Tonight held the *moment.*

Marty Lefkowitz was a bad man. She had no doubt of that. He had tried to kill her, not for investigating him or getting in his way, but simply because he thought Eli Cross liked her or even more importantly planned on using her in his next heist. When it came to dealing with Cross, unlike her father who had expressed *no regrets* in his file notes, Marty Lefkowitz was driven by revenge, his soul riddled with it.

What had Cross done to him? What had he said on the roof last night? She struggled to remember, to recall it. Something about Ingrid…about a heist at The Louvre. *Ingrid set you up, I didn't*—that's it—that's what he had told Marty. But it wasn't that simple. There were two sides to this coin. She had to acknowledge that as painful and disheartening as that felt. Eli's hands were dirty too. What was it? Something Marty accused him about…oh yeah…*You made her believe you'd split the heist with her!* That's what Marty had nailed him with. But it was Eli's response that felt so familiar to her: *Ingrid believed what she wanted to. So did you.* Those words were familiar to her because they contained the feeling of her father's note from his file: *I knew him too well. Maybe he wanted me to.*

What unnerved her, like a parasite crawling under her skin, were Eli's quiet, simple skill and the casual aplomb with which it was rendered. Cross had come prepared to kill. Not only with his Walther

PPK, but he had an oriental throwing blade and used it with expert precision. Deadly. Noiseless. Unlike a gunshot, it was not intrusive to its environment except for ending a life. How often had he been called upon to use this method? Was it just this once in saving her life? Or was he a skilled, professional killer like Megan had suggested as well as a master thief?

Then there were his words to Mosey. *You'll know what to do.* Simple. Clean. A known shorthand between them. That had to mean they had dealt with body disposal before. Didn't it? How many times before? Was this part of his MO? This added a whole other layer of consideration for Saturday night at the Borelli estate.

She wondered how easy it would be for them to dispose of her body. It was extremely hard for her to *Muldoon* someone if she was dead. Maybe the lightning bolt moment in bed together which revealed a deep part of his soul to her just didn't go deep enough to light up this area of darkness.

Quickly, she checked the TV news channels, her Google news feed and Facebook. Nothing. Not a single mention of Marty's death in the alley. No one even saw any of the scuffle and fight on the roof. It was like it never happened. How could that be? Hadn't anyone seen anything? Some busybody, someone gazing out their window, someone passing by the alley! How fast did Mosey *clean up* the alley?

This was damn freaky. This was also New York. She had to get dressed.

She would fill Ian in; he should know, but not Donelli, not yet. Certainly not her mother.

ℂ

Preparations were in full swing for the evening's festivities in the Hamptons.

All the outdoor performance areas, the tennis courts, basketball court, swimming pool and water lily grotto pond were encased in giant tents for any weather challenges and for the necessary security requirements to protect the art masterpieces.

The mini-performances of frozen artwork created with actors and props happened here. They each contained scripted dialogue and character interplay which created a storyline prior to attaining the climatic frozen image of the smaller great paintings and a cliffhanger ending in the ongoing storyline. Each venue viewed in order set up the conclusion of the story to be unfolded in the banquet hall and culminating in the frozen tableau image of French pointillist painter Georges Seurat's painting *A Sunday Afternoon on the Island of La Grande Jatte.*

A canopied tent went up on the south lawn where caterers set up table displays. Waiters underwent final instructions for the proper presentation of the culinary delights in store for the uber-rich and fabulously famous attendees.

An emergency medical tent had been set up off to the side nestled within a grove of trees to keep a low profile. Also tucked away out of sight and mind stood the Security HQ. Nathalie found Donelli inside as he poured over a blueprint of the estate grounds with Swat Team members.

Donelli pointed up to the rooftop of the main house where several Swat snipers deployed into positions at each extreme end. Nathalie quietly watched everything coming together until Donelli turned to her.

"You wanna add anything to this?"

"I think you got it covered."

"The extra men you suggested will enter the smaller venue tents unobtrusively after each final mini-performance and the removal of those jewels."

"That will definitely make those art masterpieces a no go for him," Nathalie said.

"Forces everything to the banquet room and the finale."

Nathalie nodded. She still had no intention of telling Donelli how Cross would most probably make his play for the jewels when the art masterpieces were suddenly too dangerous to attempt. That was for a Seeger to know and act upon.

Looking around at the enhanced security preparations, she knew Eli Cross was taking on the impossible. A nervous flutter in her gut bubbled up releasing a sudden wave of emotion of deep respect; her skin tingled. If Eli actually pulled this off and triumphed over that *moment that did not fit,* he would deserve all the treasures taken. A sacrilegious thought for sure as her father's daughter, yet she couldn't help the feeling that flushed her cheeks with anticipation. She knew she had suited up for this challenge, a true measure of beating the boys…or not.

Donelli suddenly grabbed her arm and pulled her aside away from the others.

"You think your little event last night means anything to him?"

Nathalie's eyes widened. She stalled her response to not get trapped into blurting out something about her attack from Lefkowitz. He couldn't possibly know anything about…

"Yeah, that's right," Donelli said acknowledging her shocked look which she couldn't fully repress. "Your little rooftop soiree. Not exactly dinner and dancing was it?"

"I don't know what you're—"

"You don't think I've had eyes on him—and you?!"

Stunned, Nathalie simply stared at him, her jaw open in astonishment. "You knew and you squashed any investigation?! What the hell is wrong with you?! I was almost killed!"

"Nothing's gonna get in the way of me nailing this bastard," countered Donelli.

His calm assurance rattled her. He really thought of her as lint. Her life—or death—meant nothing to him. It was always only about Eli Cross. He wanted to catch Cross doing what Cross did best. Al Capone went to prison for tax evasion and fraud not for murder. That justice would've disgusted Donelli. He was out for blood—righteous blood— which made him unpredictably dangerous!

"He saved my life last night."

"Yeah," agreed Donelli. "Because he needs you here tonight. He's planning on using you. Then he's done with you, however it works out, alive or dead, not much of a difference to him."

Nathalie didn't want to believe it… but it worried her deeply. She didn't think of herself as a victim or as someone who couldn't see the forest for the trees. A chill raced up her spine as her father's lesson came back to her. In sixth grade, a boy she had liked and trusted had conned her into letting him take credit for her science project.

She went crying to her father when he came home, still in uniform from his shift as a beat cop. Nate Seeger never said a word; he merely wiped her eyes and made her blow her nose. He then handed her a copy of *The Adventures of Tom Sawyer* and sent her to bed. Many pages later she learned her lesson. *"It is easier to fool the people, than to convince them they have been fooled."*

She wondered if she had learned anything since childhood.

⅋

Nathalie opened the door to her apartment and as soon as she had closed and latched the deadbolt, she heard her mother's voice.

"Nathalie..."

Nathalie dropped her keys and purse off in the foyer and walked into her living room to find her mother waiting on the sofa. The bulletin board labyrinth containing the file papers on Eli Cross still in evidence.

"Mom, what're you doing here? Is everything okay?"

"No it most certainly is not." Odile struggled mightily to contain her emotions; her body trembled. "Ian told me what happened." The tears burst from her eyes no longer held back by her usual French élan. This was a mother terrified. "Ma petite fille..." In convulsive sobs she reached out her arms to Nathalie.

Her daughter rushed to embrace her on the couch. "I'm okay... really."

But she was not really okay. All the turmoil within her emotions and her desire to be the cool professional clashed in an explosion of doubt. Nathalie felt cornered. In an instant regression to being a little girl lost, she looked to her mother for help, dropping her façade of grown-up confidence.

"I don't know what to do now. He saved my life, but for what reason? Because I'm just a pawn he still needs to play? Am I the last move in the game?"

"Do you love him?"

Her mother's words caught her breath up short. Such a strange question for her mother to ask—her own mother—after what Nathalie had just been through on the roof last night and considering her mother's past with Cross. She didn't really know how to answer, mostly because she was afraid of the answer, felt it made her weak. But she knew the feeling that haunted her. The feeling that just wouldn't go away. It had to be a weakness! And she hated herself for it!

"Yes, goddamn it...god-fucking-damn it!"

Her mother held her tightly for a long, lingering moment without saying anything.

Nathalie melted into this mother comfort. She wanted to understand, but her confusion had gotten the better of her. She had just told her mother that she loved the man who her mother had an affair with which almost destroyed her parent's marriage. *Fucking hell! What did she have to do to feel sane again?!* She only had the emotional strength to lay her head against her mother's breast and sigh...

Odile chose her next words carefully. "Nathalie, you have to trust your love and see if it's strong enough to stand up to the truth."

Nathalie lifted her head up from her mother's breast and stared at her. *What the hell was she saying?*

Odile took her daughter's face in her hands. "This is what I came here to do."

Nathalie didn't understand.

"It hasn't been easy knowing when to leave you kids alone...to work things out for yourselves."

Odile couldn't continue and needed a moment to collect her emotions before they spilled out and stifled her words...words she had waited many years to express.

"If you want to know what to do about Eli Cross, ma petite fille, then you have to know about Paris."

Nathalie took a deep breath...bracing for the truth...and whatever pain it brought.

"Nothing of what you've been thinking happened."

Nathalie wasn't prepared for that. She felt she at least had known *the what* and it was only *the why* which so painfully eluded her.

"Eli could've used me to get at your father. I was very vulnerable and willing."

"Why were you...?" Nathalie suddenly wasn't so sure she wanted to know.

"I wanted your father to feel the pain that I had felt from his affair."

This knocked the breath out of Nathalie...shattering old images. This truth had teeth!

"Daddy...when? How could he...?"

"He had gotten swept up in the pursuit of Eli Cross, even felt an allure to his lifestyle. Eli saw that weakness and used it, made it so your father met this woman, Ingrid, from Sweden, who seemed to work with Eli."

Ingrid! The name Eli and Marty had argued about. "Ingrid..." Nathalie repeatedly softly.

"Yes. This Ingrid led your father to believe that he could get to Eli through her, that she could be turned. I forced him to describe her. As you can imagine, she was extraordinarily alluring, a true Scandinavian Goddess, chosen for the role. This was all just before Paris."

Nathalie struggled to take it all in. How weak and so easily fooled could her father have been?! She had always felt with pride that her father was as tough and as noble as they came, imbued with iron discipline. She almost retched from a sudden revulsion as she realized that she—with her perceived insight—had been taken in by Eli too.

"Why didn't Cross take advantage of you in Paris?"

"It surprised me, for I can be very persuasive with men."

Her mother's words sounded like those of a sexual predator. Yet, she herself had felt she could be persuasive with men using the wiles of her womanhood. How different the shoe looked when it was on your own feet.

Odile continued. "I went to see him late one night in his suite at the George Cinq. I wasn't planning on going back to your father at our hotel that night. But Eli didn't respond to my seduction which was formidable."

"Why not?" Nathalie was on pins and needles with her emotions.

"Because he knew..." She fought hard to stifle the tears and wiped at her eyes with her fingers brushing the drops away. "He knew that I was still in love with your father... and always would be."

Nathalie took her mother into her arms. "Oh, Mama," Nathalie choked out through tears, "I'm so sorry, the things I thought about you. I feel so ashamed."

Odile clung to her daughter. "Don't be. We all do strange things for love."

The two women held each other in the warmth of a new truth.

"But Nathalie...I don't want you to think too badly of your father. There are some women—and this Ingrid was one—who can get the best of men to do whatever they want. I know this to be true, because I was once that woman…and I used it to get the love of my life."

Nathalie stared at her mother through grown-up eyes. She wondered what other unknown depths her mother possessed but had kept to herself. Human beings were such wells of mystery.

"So what do I do now, Mama?"

"Remember everything you've felt about him and test its truth in your heart."

Nathalie had to know what truth her mother held onto. "Do you trust him?"

"There is something inside him," Odile said thoughtfully, "that he can't change. I think your father knew what was eating at Eli and driving him, but he didn't share that with me. I feel it runs very deep and he lives by that. And that is what I would trust."

Nathalie knew she had to dig deep into the pit of her fears and face all the doubts squarely and with clarity. But it was there, hidden in her intuition, that she heard the whisper once again out of the lightning bolt moment…*trust this*.

CHAPTER TWENTY THREE

Hope is the last thing ever lost.

Italian proverb

A mirror reflected without judgement. It presented an image of certainty. The result yielded clarity, no deviation allowed. To stare into a mirror provided an unwavering assessment. Many could not maintain eye contact when their own truth emerged to face them.

The dressing area mirror in the Lucerne deluxe king suite on the tenth floor filled with the image of Eli Cross when he stepped in front of it dressed all in black, not a tux, but clothes of stealth for work in the dead of night. He stared confidently at his image before him, his eyes unwavering, until he slipped a thin, gold chain around his neck. It held a small trinket—half a heart—which dangled from the chain.

He unfolded a handwritten paper note that read: *Half yours, the other mine. Nathalie.*

When he looked up from the note and locked onto the reflection of his eyes in the mirror, he recalled her words at The Baronfeld Museum concerning *The Cellini Lovers*. Her lovely voice resonated in his head as clear as on that day. *Each flows into the other and back again...endless. La verite éternelle. Their lips so close, the kiss so imminent, and yet forever kept apart.*

His gaze remained riveted, unblinking. But as he remembered his own words, his eyes saddened. *Only in stone. In feeling, the kiss has already happened. That's its emotional impact. That's the power of the art. The feeling is more accurate than the eye. The yearning for something true to last.* It was the saudade, that yearning which haunted him.

He turned away from his image, no longer able to hold its truth. When he looked back, something was different...in his eyes...the assured look was not there.

℁

Eli's thumb-sized drone cylinder from the lesson at The Baronfeld lay on her dresser. Draped in a stunning evening gown, a Givenchy knock-off, Nathalie picked it up. *Every well-dressed man should have one.* Eli's words settled in her heart as a distant echo.

The phone rang. She dropped the cylinder and ran to her purse, fished her cell out and answered it quickly—expectantly.

"Eli?"

"Sorry, it's just me," Megan responded.

"He was gonna call." Nathalie realized how desperately she had been hanging onto hope.

"He still can," Megan said with forced enthusiasm.

"He's cuttin' it short."

"Maybe he won't show. Maybe he really is legit."

"Yeah."

"Is that what you're thinkin'?"

"I'm thinking he liked hitting home runs in Yankee stadium."

"Yeah…" Megan sighed in resignation, but then offered her ray of hope, "But then he met you."

Both women knew the truth hung by a thread and when that thread was cut, it could fall either way.

"I'm hoping," Nathalie offered, "that the look in his eyes the last time we kissed was for real."

"I'll be here," Megan said, knowing that most times all one could do was to be present for a friend.

"I know... thanks."

Nathalie ended the call and reached for her purse. She checked inside for her Sig-Sauer. It was there.

Her hope hung on tenterhooks stretched taut almost to the breaking point. She really didn't know for sure what Eli Cross was going to do. She remembered a quote from Benjamin Franklin her father had written in his note files about Cross: *It is the height of cleverness to conceal it.* Her father had attributed this quality to Eli's *itinerant Gypsy past* and the lessons learned on the road throughout Europe. Tonight, clever and cunning would clash at Cartier.

There was still time before she had to leave. She thought she might as well clean things up, box the files; it would all be over tonight one way or the other. She proceeded methodically, mostly to keep her nerves steady, but also on the slim chance there was something she might have overlooked. She decided that everything—papers, photos and files—would be taken down off the bulletin boards and put in the box they came out of and in the order her father had them. In this small way she honored the discipline he had taught her.

Even with gaps in the notes, her father knew Eli Cross rather well. *Too well* as one of his key notes had offered. In her own discoveries, she had to make reasoned assumptions because she couldn't connect all the dots. There was still no direct line to the truth which could be fully trusted. There were too many missing dots.

Perhaps her mother was right. She would have to trust what she felt in her heart. Many theories abounded that the heart was the seat of true intelligence. She wondered how well that worked when the moment meant life or death.

Aggravation rose from all that she didn't know: the lessons learned from his Romani Gypsy family, the mindset he was taught, and how the plane crash and his family's death changed him. She clung to the hope that she didn't need to know everything about him to stay one step ahead. Clearly he wanted to keep things simple. That was his desired M.O. and that required hidden cleverness as Benjamin Franklin had suggested.

So…what was the simplest moment of the party tonight?

How to capitalize on that?

If she figured it out, he would applaud her. That thought made her laugh for how silly it was because he also may kill her, for *getting away with it* was his pièce de résistance and she would've ruined that. *Was that really what she wanted to do, ruin it?* That fleeting question she didn't want to answer right away. It confused her that the thought was even there…pestering her.

Focus she told herself.

Nathalie then replayed all the stages of the Cartier event in her mind. She'd seen the rehearsals for every mini-performance in all the other venue areas. She actually liked the one in the lily pond grotto space the most. The Monet painting, *Women in the Garden,* prominently displayed there on loan for this one weekend from the Musée d"Orsay in Paris was one of her favorites. The intuition she had when watching the grand finale rehearsal—the one she didn't reveal to Donelli—still felt true.

She felt she had considered every angle. But she so wanted to beat the boys, to outsmart them, that she went over all of it again. She told herself she would be as thorough and anal about this as she was about replacing the Eli Cross files back in her father's case boxes. *Yes, damn it, she wanted him to applaud her.* Shameless self-justification, probably pinned to some deep insecurity, but nonetheless she wanted Eli to salute her. To applaud!

The thought suddenly struck her. *Applause.* It suddenly seemed so *simple.* The cleverness of it all was hidden—or concealed—in plain sight as Benjamin Franklin opined. One left the stage during the applause, allowing time for the applause to build, then returning to take a bow…or not returning and escaping with the goods while everyone was applauding the performance.

Her confidence soared. She had him—and she knew where—and she would be waiting.

During all this thinking time—this now productive time—she had been packing two of the three file boxes she had in her possession. Her father was precise; anal was another word. The papers and files in each box filled the space to the very brim, nothing wasted.

The file papers meant for the final box she had stacked in two separate piles outside the box. The top page on what would go into the box as the bottom stack held a note that stuck out to her. *Justice with style.*

It stood out to her because it veered from the trajectory of notes her father had made that focused on capturing Cross in the act. This sentiment of how Eli worked struck at the heart of why he did what he did and to whom he did it. This note tilted motivation more to the *personal* than to the *monetary* end. Her gut told her to hang onto that thought.

This prompted her to consider if there was a driven purpose to his quest tonight, something that might give her extra insight, a purpose that was more personal to him. This might outline for her what he might be willing to sacrifice—like the art work or the jewels—for something else. That *something else* could be what was directly connected to his triumphing over the *moment* that he saw as his quest.

If retribution was the driving factor then the use of violence possibly propelled him.

Or was tonight all about him, his quest to accomplish the impossible under everyone's noses? That desire would probably be *clean* without violence, a celebration of *wit* instead.

Then again maybe she was overthinking it. Time was fleeting. She'd keep an open mind but it was time to pack it up and get on with it.

She stacked the last two piles on top of each other next to the file storage box when her tea kettle whistled. She dashed to the stove, shut off the burner and poured the steaming hot water into a Yeti thermos filled with Columbian instant coffee grains. The plastic lid with the slide-lock drink opening would keep the instant coffee hot for hours, an elixir to keep her alert into the wee hours. On her toes to beat the boys…actually one boy.

Nathalie placed her thermos next to her purse and returned to the last pile which sat next to the file box. She reached down to pick it up and place it within the box…and stopped. There must be something missing. As it sat outside the box on the floor, the pile did not reach to the top of the box. All three boxes had been filled to the brim when she had brought them home.

She quickly checked that papers weren't set aside near the bulletin boards on the floor or under a chair or a table which she may have overlooked. No, no extra papers anywhere.

There wasn't much time. She needed to leave soon.

Finding the missing pages would have to wait. She grabbed the pile and placed it in the box. She turned to leave but stopped when she saw that the papers now filled the box to the very top. That wasn't possible, for when the papers sat outside the box the level of the pile was shorter than the top of the box by about an inch.

She needed to leave. An inch was nothing. *Don't be so anal!*

Nathalie grabbed her purse and thermos then strode to her front door. She was going to be late if there was even a hint of traffic and there was always traffic in the city! In frustration she yanked the door open—but intuition shoved her arm forward closing it!

She left her purse and thermos in the foyer and went back to the box. The annoying box!

It didn't make sense. Her Dad was anal and thorough and precise. She inherited that itch to get it right. That inch should not be there! Unless…holy shit!

Unless there was a false bottom. Small and unnoticeable. Like an inch deep.

She plunged her arm into the box and slid it under the last file at the bottom. In one swift movement she lifted the entire pile out of the box and placed it on the floor. Nathalie stared inside the box at the bare cardboard bottom; a wave of hope rose up in her gut.

She prayed it wouldn't turn into a rogue wave and sink her hope.

Her fingers felt around the edge of the cardboard base pressing down and against the sides until she gained a purchase on it. The cardboard was wedged tight but not attached. She gripped its edge and yanked upward ripping out the false bottom!

There sat the missing pages! About an inch worth.

Her cell rang. Her hope soared. It had to be Eli! She grabbed the phone.

Goddamnit! It was Ian. She swiped open the call.

"What?!" she snapped!

"Hey, how about Hello," retorted Ian.

"Yeah—hi."

"I'm just letting you know I'm on my way."

"Where?!"

"To the Hamptons, to the Borelli estate. I'm gonna be there."

"Ian—"

"There's no way I'm letting you face this alone," Ian insisted in a tone that left no room for discussion. "Where are you?"

"I'm at home,' Nathalie said.

"Well you better get your ass in gear; this is no time to be fuckin' around with make-up."

"Ian there's…" Natalie hesitated, unsure whether to continue her thought.

"What?" asked Ian when Nathalie's silence lingered too long.

Nathalie wanted to tell him—desperately wanted to tell him—about the missing pages. This was her brother who she loved and who had been a helpful part of ferreting out the pieces to the Eli Cross puzzle and to connecting all the dots and speculating on the missing dots. Detective Nate Seeger was his father also. But she just couldn't tell him, not now, not until she knew what was in those pages. She didn't want her brother's locked-in male sense of wanting to protect her to get in the way and create some gallant, well-meaning boondoggle.

"Nothing," Nathalie sighed. "I'm half out the door."

She quickly clicked off the call ending any further discussion of intended Ian heroics.

Nathalie lifted the inch of missing pages out of the box. What the hell was in them that her father felt had to be kept but also had to be hidden?! The anticipation swept through her as a wave of nausea. She had only a few minutes to digest it all, connect what dots she could, and have it make sense before she had to leave or she would miss the whole Cartier bash and Eli's *moment that didn't fit.*

CHAPTER TWENTY FOUR

One kiss, my bonny sweetheart, I'm after a prize to-night, But I shall be back with the yellow gold before the morning light;

The Highwayman, Alfred Noyes

The black electric Vespa floated over the Bow Bridge in Central Park from The Ramble side like a whisper through the descending darkness. The black-helmeted rider, face hidden by a dark visor, body covered in sleek black clothing for night work, slipped like a ninja through the faint shards of light that kicked off the lake from a drowning sun. Only death draped in a black hooded shroud and carrying a long scythe generated a more chilling feeling.

Waiting on the Cherry Hill side sat Mosey's Hansom cab carriage and Melvin. The Vespa pulled alongside. Strapped to the rear of the crypt-quiet scooter were two large, thick, black, expandable leather saddlebags—empty of their prize for the moment. The helmet came off. This *ninja* had a definite stylish Continental flair but Eli Cross's eyes were deadly serious, focused on the intended job to be done.

Eli wanted to get on with it, but the emotions he wrestled into place were not always obedient. Their incipient rebellion curdled his blood. To hesitate was to invite death. The yearning that had driven him faced its ultimate test this night. *You prep your whole life for this. To pull it off you risk everything that's gone before. If you meet that moment, a new world awaits; if not, it ends.* He realized it wasn't much of a pep talk.

The past encircled him like a whirl of rampaging ghosts—his parents and little brother being the armature that strengthened his plans—the relentless New York cop, Nate Seeger, the respected adversary whose challenge was deeply missed—and the ghosts of possibilities yet to come from the captivating Odile, and from her daughter who he has set up to play a final part.

His cynicism behind the manipulation he had used to engineer and destabilize human behavior had grown heavy and weary and had eviscerated the joy of facing *the moment*. His soul knew the relentless emptiness had to end. It was self-suffocating. There had to be a sacrifice. Therein lay the danger. What was there left to trust?

Eli snapped into action and hauled himself up on the carriage and sat on the driver bench next to Mosey. He handed him a sealed envelope. Mosey hesitated in taking it; this wasn't planned.

"What's this?"

"A numbered Swiss account," Eli replied. "The Bank of Zurich. Only you have clearance."

Mosey looked at his one-time partner in crime clearly worried for he sensed that the impenetrable confidence of this supremely unknowable man had a slashed gash in it.

"I may not come back this time," Eli continued.

"And you do this for me?"

"You're my friend."

Mosey knew an unsolved situation ate at Eli's insides. He also knew that hesitation killed. Eli had warned him of that and had made it safe for him to go straight.

"And what do you do for her?" Mosey asked, clearly knowing the source of his partner's angst.

Cross was abnormally quiet...thinking his answer through carefully.

"Experience the moment," Eli finally said.

"And then move on..." Mosey added to pin him down.

Cross couldn't look at his friend. Mosey saw clearly the hole in Cross's armor that Nathalie had put there. A hole that could cost him dearly.

"You've put her in a tough spot," Mosey said. "Do you trust that?"

That was still a potentially fatal flaw in Eli's final plan. Failure in that area ended everything. Eli had no answer for Mosey.

"I thought so," Mosey sighed. "There's always one that gets ya."

Cross's vulnerability ripped his insides. Vulnerability had not been viewed as strength by Eli in all the capers he had previously pulled as a master thief. In this he disagreed with author-researcher Brené Brown and her plan for embracing vulnerability and thus whole-hearted living.

"It's not a weakness," Mosey said.

"For me," Eli insisted.

"There is a time to trust." Then Mosey added for hope, "And in that moment..."

"...is everything," Cross said wanting it to be true, but not yet knowing how.

Cross checked his watch...the job awaited.

Nightfall asserted itself. Darkness—the playground of the master thief—unfolded before them laying down cover for intended sins.

On his watch face, the second hand swept inexorably forward. In its movement all sounds of the park whooshed into silence leaving only the tick of the second hand echoing in his head.

Eli prepared to embrace the illusion of time. In action, he knew it would proceed swiftly leaving no room for hesitation, but for those waiting, he knew time lingered painfully and produced a level of dullness, a dullness which the thief could exploit. The relentless *ticking* of time was his partner tonight.

&

The guard's flashlight swept the exhibit room of The Baronfeld Museum, past *The Cellini Lovers* which sat in its packing cabinet, a sculpture by Rodin and a painting by Caravaggio. When the sweeping beam fractured through the protective glass case of the rare Old French manuscript; one slash of light also caught the edge of an ancient Egyptian papyrus under glass and another beam fragment landed on a presentation of the Dead Sea Scrolls. All was well.

&

Chauffeured limousines lined up out front of the Borelli estate in the Hamptons as the rich and fabulously famous disembarked for the Cartier International event. The parade of designer adorned bodies paraded along the stone-tiled entry path like a Paris runway as photographers' flashes illuminated the receptive faces.

Inside the canopied security tent, Donelli, his shoulder holster packed with an old-school Colt 1911 .45 caliber, impatiently tapped his fingers against the estate blueprint plans like the ticking hand of a clock. His eyes flicked from one bejeweled guest to another. He hated waiting.

In the grand banquet room of the mansion, jewelry displays sparkled in the sweeping space graced with art masterworks and thirty-foot ceilings with skylights opened to the dazzling display of stars in the night sky. Ian Seeger watched a tuxedoed cop adjust his shoulder holster.

ᔆᖉ

The lone light splashed across Megan's scratched-out legal pad in her DRN cubicle as darkness shrouded the labyrinthine maze elsewhere. The muse offered no ideas. Megan's thoughts were only of her friend. Had she waited at home for any news, her wine rack would've been empty by now. She had stayed at work because she at least wanted to have a clear head for…whatever.

The cardboard cutout of Donald Trump wobbled behind her from the recent thrust of a pair of scissors jammed from worried frustration into his crotch which now dangled like a useless stubby penis. Megan stared at the silent face of her cell phone as another digital minute passed. There was nothing she could do. She knew that. No, not exactly, in rising frustration there was something she could do. Her fingers curled into a fist, her chair spun around, and she punched Trump in the face launching him backwards. The blow bent his head and Trump dropped like a weak-chinned chump hanging facedown into her trash can.

ᔆᖉ

Beneath the Renoir print of *Dance at Bougival* in her Jackson Heights living room, Odile Trenet Seeger sipped a glass of Chardonnay in the strangling silence of the interminable waiting. The romantically entwined couple embraced in a dance once embodied romance and exuded life-force energy, but seemed to her now like frozen ghosts. No longer warm memories, the past that had clearly come home to roost had brought with it a deathly chill.

ᔆᖉ

Nathalie arrived at the separate security entrance on the south lawn of the Borelli estate. She showed her ID and her gun and entered the grounds next to the canopied security tent. The entire Borelli estate grounds had been encircled by security fencing for this one event, not simply as a means of entrapping Eli Cross but as a protection for the rich and famous from unsavory characters and interloper party crashers. Carefully selected members of the press and entertainment news had been placed on a tight leash where disobedience meant banishment. Nathalie moved past the security HQ and headed toward the main house.

The lush surroundings were spectacular, a playground for contemporary gods and goddesses rivaling the celestial stylings of Mount Olympus. One fully expected to see Homer and Herodotus capturing this singular historical and mythic moment with reed brushes on papyrus or, to fit in with the glitterati, perhaps a quill pen upon fine vellum with blood the medium for words for added emphasis and drama. It all seemed otherworldly to Nathalie. It felt like walking through a multi-colored dream. Famous faces glided by her, but her thoughts were elsewhere. They were reeling from an inch worth of paper. What she discovered in those missing pages had forcibly changed her strategy.

Near the end, even as his illness slowed him down, her father had developed an entirely different set of plans for dealing with Eli Cross. The missing pages—the one inch secret pile—were the dots he didn't want connected until they were felt. And he didn't trust just anyone to have those feelings. These dots or *facts* as he saw them were gained by talking with, listening to and observing a man he had sought to *Muldoon* for years; a man whose set-up had almost derailed his marriage and cost him the love of his life. These *facts* needed to be felt to be trusted.

Nate knew that ambitious cops who picked up the chase after he was gone would do so to go after the legend of Eli Cross. Running this fox to ground would put a feather in their cap. It wouldn't be about finding the truth; it would be all about grabbing the glory for catching the legend. They would rely on the cold, hard facts which created the legend. They would only connect the dots they wanted to connect to believe their truth and justify their actions. They wouldn't believe—or even want to believe—these newly discovered *facts* which Nate arrived at over years of applied instincts. But he knew *the legend* had become these new *facts* which revealed the depth of truth in all its layered human complications.

He understood that these new *facts* of who Eli Cross really was and why he did what he did would not be accepted. He knew it because he felt these *facts* revealed that Eli Cross meant to go straight, to leave the field to others. If the cops were chasing *the legend,* he knew they would be chasing a ghost.

So by leaving these *facts*—the missing dots—out of the main file boxes, he preserved the legend to give Eli the space and time to change. The idea came to him from one of his favorite movies, John Ford's western *The Man Who Shot Liberty Valance.* When Jimmy Stewart's character of Senator Ransom Stoddard told the story to the *Shinbone Star* newspaper editor of who really shot outlaw Liberty Valance—a truth that was different from what everyone thought they knew and loved from established history—the editor made a swift decision: *"This is the West, sir. When the legend becomes fact, print the legend."*

Nathalie had watched that film with her Dad at his insistence. He had used it as an example when he tried to explain to her the ways things really were in being a cop; that sometimes the right thing was accomplished by doing something wrong.

Now she understood its impact. Nate's standard had always been *commit a crime, get Muldooned, go to jail.* The missing dots had shown her that her father didn't really want Eli *caught* once Nate knew why he stole and who he stole from. Eli's family had been taken from him by greed. Those who embraced greed offered Eli the opportunity for retribution.

Being rich was not a crime to Eli Cross, the accumulation of wealth and profit by honorable means was worthy of celebration, but the greedy rich whose wealth—many times improperly or unlawfully obtained—empowered them to be above it all whether they be a person, an enterprise, or a government and they needed to be *adjusted* to restore the rhythms of decency. His plan was simple. He manipulated them by getting their greed to hoist themselves on their own petard. Given the chance, evil will destroy itself. Eli Cross learned how to apply grease to the wheels of that self-destruction.

The missing dots connected the past to a new plan. Nate wanted to help Eli turn the page, move past what drove him, and go straight which was the peace he sought in his yearning. In pursuing his case, Nate considered everything—including the Portuguese name given to Cross's Arabian horse—*Saudade*—and its translation: *"the love that remains" after someone is gone, a yearning, a longing.* Nate Seeger knew this wasn't a name given simply because it sounded good.

In hiding the missing pages, Nate took the risk that not connecting all the dots left the door open to speculation about him and even the possibility that Nate had been pulled into considering a caper with Eli because of the allure of that lifestyle.

Nathalie knew that she and Ian got sucked into that track of thinking and it had shaken the foundation of faith in her Dad.

Nate was willing to take that risk because he understood that the *facts* revealed by connecting these *dots* needed to be connected in the heart, not the head. That was a difficult decision for a tough-as-nails New York City cop to make. Yet he made it because the truth needed to be felt to be known and trusted. Nate didn't want anyone—even Nathalie—to simply be told. Even her mother had acknowledged to her the nature of trust with Eli Cross and the need to understand it.

Nate Seeger loved his family and trusted them to understand the truth as he saw it. He also trusted his daughter and son to be thorough and relentless and if they ever delved into the files of Eli Cross they would keep searching to connect all the dots. He knew they would know that something was missing—and missing intentionally—and not give up till they found it.

Nate understood from his many years of dealing with all the darkness of the underbelly of human behavior which he experienced as a cop, that despite it all, the world was good; but you had to look deep and true to see it clearly. Perhaps, Nathalie thought, that *not realizing* this was the *moment* that didn't fit that Eli had been chasing—maybe this was the Goddess.

Reading the missing pages before she left for the Hamptons had overwhelmed her with a poignancy she didn't know how to handle. All of it was so simple, like Eli's requirement for a perfect heist. She thought back to all her encounters and discussions with Eli and wondered if he understood what drove him. As she had closed the door to her apartment, it all hit her and she had to wipe the sudden rush of tears from her eyes; *at heart, Eli Cross was just a boy who wanted to go home.*

She scanned the grounds of the Borelli estate knowing that it was the last dot—the final assumption her father had made—that scared the hell out of her. Nate felt that Eli still needed to prove one last thing before turning the page and going straight. Jean-Pierre Bonnaire, Vadoma's husband, had told Ian the same thing. Eli was working on something, needed to do it, before things could change.

Nathalie feared that pulling off the ultimate heist one last time under everyone's noses was what Eli needed to do to close out his escapades as a master thief. His obsession could consume him before a chance at redemption. Now she knew it wasn't enough to just catch him; she had to stop him before he got caught.

Her thoughts were a swirl of doubts and fierce commitment. *There's no way he's gonna pull this off—not with me eliminating the art as his prize. He's gonna get himself killed. I know there's a good man inside him. I know it. I've gotta stop him!*

Exactly how to stop him hadn't fallen in place yet.

Worst of all, the part that she couldn't control, involved Lieutenant Donelli. She felt trapped and squeezed between the closing vise-like plates of two men's obsessions. Donelli didn't really want to arrest Cross with the goods. He didn't want to risk a trial and any legal chicanery which might free Cross. No, Donelli wanted to kill Eli in the act, to use the *moment* of getting caught as justification in killing him. Donelli wanted *the legend* to end in blood at the hands of a righteous cop *who was owed!*

Nathalie looked up to the roof of the mansion with nervous anticipation. She would have to get to Eli first. To live, he would have to leave without fully testing *the moment.*

℘

The second hand on the wrist watch of Eli Cross swept up to the top of the hour.

"It's time," Eli said.

An intake of breath pushed back against vulnerability. With a slow, controlled exhale an old memory surfaced and brought a surge of deep desire. Something Vano had told him long ago prior to a Gypsy caper, a tricky scheme in the south of France near Arles designed to allow them to eat that day. To assuage young Eli's fear before initiating the dangerous gamble, Vano had whispered an old Spartan war saying: "O Tolman Nika." *He who dares, wins.*

Eli Cross dropped off the carriage and threw a leg over the black Vespa.

Mosey flicked the reins and Melvin lurched the Hansom cab forward into the billowing mist that floated in off the lake and covered the path. Mosey looked behind him, but the Vespa had disappeared into the darkness like a silent specter, an almost invisible getaway vehicle.

CHAPTER TWENTY FIVE

*Life and death are one thread, the same line viewed
from different sides.*

Lao Tzu

The tip of the cane plunged through the soft grass and got stuck in the webbing of the sod that had been laid recently for the event. *What the fuck!* Ian yanked the cane out of the lawn with a tug—an annoyed tug. There were times—and this was one of them—when the cane infuriated him. Emotionally it felt like a ball and chain appendage, one he desperately wanted to discard but couldn't. He also thought of it at times like a possessed monster that had grafted itself onto his body. He had vowed he would never let it attach itself to his soul.

He swatted the grass with the cane in punishment for its audacity in entrapping him. He stared at the polished, black demon gripped in his hand with barely repressed anger. At least it looked sharp. A crutch had no style. This devil stick had style. When he bought it, he had a calligrapher etch a reminder in its handle in Latin: *Incurvatus surgo.* With every step those words were etched in his soul and embraced in his heart: *Unbowed I rise!*

Ian suddenly chuckled to himself. He couldn't chase down Cross tonight, but he could use the damn cane to trip him up if he ran by. Ian knew if he had a steel blade imbedded in the shaft, or better yet, a single shot rifle barrel with the trigger in the handle grip, he would be more versatile. But alas, that satisfaction existed really just in movies and books for someone like himself.

He would write about this serpentine craziness though, that he knew for sure. He would carve out the words in the stones he had overturned in seeking to know and understand this insistently unknowable international master thief. When it all unfurled, he would tell the story of Eli Cross, his sister and his parents, and the strands of web that locked them all together, and the cool August night when it all ended…if he were still alive at dawn to be that story's scribe. And what of his sister? Would Nathalie's role in this tome be one of triumph or tragedy, or in this ever-twisting tale a heartbroken marriage of both?

It was eerie to contemplate. He didn't even know as he thought about it whether the work would be fiction or nonfiction. Right now, the nonfiction parts still didn't add up and made no sense to him because of the holes in human behavior and action. Most likely he would probably have to find the truth through art in a novel where the truth usually resided in its freest form and was finally understood only in the heart.

Whatever direction it took, he would need a title. *Crossing the Line* seemed a good candidate. It contained innuendo and a titillating sense of dangerous action. *Stolen Kisses* had some merit, dangerous romance being one element, until all Ian could see was a book cover with sparkling jewels, a bare-chested man holding a woman with a ripped bodice, and all under the seductive grin of the Mona Lisa. No, he wasn't writing one of those books…although…they do sell like hotcakes. He decided to put a pin in that title. *The Gypsy Thief* then leaped from his imagination. Damn good, he thought. Felt sensual with a hint of intrigue and aroused curiosity.

He realized though he would probably catch flak in this finger-pointing day of righteous-shaming and uber-criticizing from overly insensitive idiots who insisted that some Romani gypsies took offence to being called *gypsy*. What the fuck! There was always something. To be a writer—an artist—meant that he could no longer be a card-carrying member of polite society and still tell the truth. He settled for the image of those protesters standing outside bookstores and libraries in the pouring rain attempting to burn copies of his bestseller *The Gypsy Thief* with some of those lost-soul protesters accidently setting themselves on fire. Oh well… Given what he knew he would have to face tonight and be ready to do in order to protect his sister, the proper book title settled into his head with heavy gravitas: *What the Fuck.*

Ian had seen Nathalie only once since she had arrived. She said she would catch him later and had hustled off to scope out just how and when to stop Eli without alerting Donelli. He didn't understand why *alerting Donelli* was not a good thing, but he didn't really like the prick so he figured Nathalie would fill him in later in time for him to make his own adjustments. He looked around the grounds. *Later* felt like it should be now because the last of the performances of the mini-venues had just wrapped up.

The smaller performances which started the fictional storyline of the connected paintings took place in the tented areas of the tennis courts, swimming pool and grotto pond and had completed with artistic precision. The jewels used in creating the frozen moments of famous paintings had all been properly collected and transported to the main banquet hall for the climatic finale. The art masterpieces in the other tents and locations were well guarded by extra police officers who had quietly taken up their new positions in each venue after each performance thanks to Nathalie's insight and suggestion.

Cross would now be forced to make his ultimate test in the grand banquet hall since the last minute change of security plans with the additional guards were not present during any of the rehearsals. This was clearly a last minute change to the playing field. Without the proper time to work up a simple approach that took into account the extra police, it would be too risky. Worse, it lacked panache. Nathalie knew Cross insisted on simplicity, but enjoyed adding a dash of panache. The stealing of the jewels sparkling in the spotlights of the final theatrical performance offered the panache element.

Donelli was anxious, ready and poised to strike. He and his men had closely watched all the mini-performances and with no theft attempt, Donelli knew it all came down to the finale.

Nathalie had waited patiently until now. She knew Eli's attempt would happen near the end of the final performance. She wanted Eli to leave—without *the yellow gold*—on his own accord. She wanted to save him. She knew telling Ian what she had discovered in the missing pages would just complicate matters at this late juncture and she couldn't risk Ian trying to protect her when she needed to be free to risk implementing her plan. She had to stop Eli. She would have to move fast. Ian couldn't help her with that. Nathalie left the grotto pond to take up her final position. She at least needed to tell Ian something.

Ian moved as fast as his black devil stick would allow to the grand banquet hall. He took a shortcut past the catering tent. He did not notice the black Vespa parked unobtrusively amidst the black catering golf carts used for quick food delivery to the outer limits of the property.

As the black-tie bash entered its final phase, the banquet hall stage awaited the start of the finale performance that would end with the frozen pose of French pointillist painter Georges Seurat's painting *A Sunday Afternoon on the Island of La Grande Jatte*. The audience would be enthralled and captivated without the slightest hint of impending theft. They would be enveloped with the music from the Sondheim-Lapine musical *Sunday in the Park with George* and not hear the shuffling of armed cops scurrying to better vantage points for capture.

For the audience, a thief would be part of the program—a delight—as in rehearsals an actor portraying a thief would enter the stage—an incursion in the grand frozen pose—and be chased by period-costumed cops as he grabbed sparkling jewels off the frozen people in the painting and set them in a black velvet bag.

The thief would finally be trapped by the cops and be face-to-face with the leading lady in the painting who would dramatically animate once more and unmask the thief, planting a dramatic kiss upon his lips. Stunned, he would swiftly pull a magnificent Cartier diamond ring out of his black bag that would shower the audience in rainbow-colored fragments of light when struck by a laser-focused spotlight. He would drop to his knees, not in surrender, but with an engagement proposal for the leading lady who would cry out *Yes!*

It was the perfect setting for a real thief to insert *panache*.

Detective Donelli, in his rumpled tux, watched the banquet hall stage carefully. Extremely pleased with what he saw, he moved along the windowed wall until he stopped next to Ian Seeger who had just set himself in his desired position to watch the proceedings.

"Anytime now, Donelli said."

"You sure?"

Donelli's confidence and delight in soon bagging his quarry were off the charts as his eyes scanned the room. "Oh he's here."

"Has Cross been spotted?" Up to this point, Ian had seen no sign of Eli's presence.

"Trust me, he's here," Donelli stated with confidence." And however he got in—places we intentionally left unguarded—have now quietly been sealed up tight. He's ours."

Ian hobbled away on his cane, over to Nathalie who watched the lighting on the banquet hall stage dim up and down to signal the imminent start of the final frozen tableau and the evening's storyline's denouement. She was riddled with anxiety for what came next.

"Bottom of the ninth, Sis."

"Little boys and their games," she added with an edge to her voice.

Ian could see that she was hurting, torn by what she had to do, but worse she was in love. He knew she would never admit it and he wouldn't force her to face it at this moment.

"You seen anything, any sign?"

She didn't respond, couldn't even look at him.

"People do change," he said. "Maybe you were a part of it."

"Yeah...but home runs are addicting."

"Cross is a big boy. He knows the rules. One day you push too hard. It happens."

"And it's not my life, I know."

"That's right, it isn't," Ian insisted.

"Yeah, everything's just real fine."

In the packed banquet hall, they were surrounded by beautiful people dripping with fame and money. She wanted to tell Ian about her *one inch* discovery but she first waited for her definitive sign, to see if her assessment of Eli's adjusted simple plan was correct.

"What is this stuff worth anyway?" Nathalie didn't really care. What was *stuff* in exchange for a life?

"I think we're talkin' a cool maybe two hundred mil with the jewels," Ian stated." Then there's the art—all masterpieces—a few somewhat...priceless."

"Chump change."

"Yup..."

They both knew full well how tempting it all was and how departing with it would be the Uber-Score of scores.

They watched together until the actors froze into the image of the painting. The audience erupted in applause, but they knew there was more to come. The audience gasped as the actor portraying the thief dashed onto the stage of frozen players.

She watched the thief character carefully as he entered the painting—his mask was different from rehearsals—it covered his whole face and hair. She knew it was him. The mask in rehearsals looked like Zorro and tied in the back—the actor's hair visible. This was a full hooded balaclava, only the eyes were exposed. This was the sign she was waiting for; this was simple.

She knew the actor who portrayed the thief would be found gagged and restrained probably unconscious in a locked mobile dressing room in one of the Hollywood honeywagons normally used on film sets that had been brought in for the cast and production crew. Eli wouldn't risk killing him because it was unnecessary and even without a death penalty in New York it would mean many more years in prison than those for theft. Besides, it lacked panache.

She had very little time to get into position.

"He's here. I gotta move."

Impatiently, Nathalie took a step to leave. Ian halted her.

"Where you goin'?! Where is he?!"

"Things have changed," she stated urgently." I know where he'll be. I know what's simple, how he'd do it. It's the change he had to make once the art was no longer a valid target. Right under your nose, but simple."

On stage the thief moved with athletic grace among the frozen people in the choreographed number in which he extracted the jewels and placed them in the black velvet bag.

Nathalie knew she only had until the end of the sequence—before the cops chased the thief—to get into place. She knew Eli's pivotal action will be down on stage in the painting tableau but that's not where her best chance to stop him will be. Nathalie looked up to the open skylights and the roof.

"I can't make it up there!" Ian was pissed.

Nathalie reached out to her brother with affection.

"Just be down here for me. Don't tell Donelli. Okay? This is a Seeger operation. Dad didn't like that prick."

That worked for Ian, he didn't like Donelli either. Ian noticed her high heels and evening gown.

"You goin' like that?"

Nathalie pulled canvas fold-up sure-grip slip-ons from her purse.

"I came prepared."

She also showed him her Sig. Ian watched with trepidation as his sister headed toward the rooftop access spiral staircase. There was only one way to reach the roof on foot and it was heavily guarded. Nathalie had clearance for the entire estate grounds and all it took was for her to show the cops her security pass and ID and she was on her way up .

The mansion's roof was a sweeping expanse—multi-layered. At night, it appeared as a world of shifting shapes and shadows. She stepped out of the roof door under the moonless night sky. The snipers on the four corners of the roof took immediate notice of her movement. A woman in a ball gown was not expected on the roof. She gave them the proper security hand signal and they returned their riveted gaze to the estate grounds. From their positions they could virtually cover everything.

Nathalie walked toward a position that was over the proscenium stage of the banquet hall. Three large aluminum-framed AC units arranged in a broken triangle formation sat silently at this location. They would not be needed on this cool August night. Nathalie peered over the edge of one of the units. In the center of the broken triangle space, unseen by the far four corners where the Swat snipers were located, was a lone open skylight right over the stage. All the skylights were perfect targets for the snipers save this one.

Three short strides from the AC units was an open-air expanse beyond the ballroom walls which dropped down to a terraced series of courtyard patios. The ground-level travertine patio opened to the sprawling lawn and the outstretched inviting arms of darkness and a gathering mist which rolled in from the damp, cool air off the Atlantic. Soon the mist would thicken on the ground with wispy strands rising to the stars providing even more cover. Nature was laying down the perfect escape fog. She wondered with amazement if Eli had planned on there being fog. He certainly would've checked the weather and known the possibility was there. Sometimes, she thought, it was better to be lucky than good. He probably planned that too.

Nathalie hunkered down on the dark side of one of the AC units tucking her gown underneath her. She chose a loose and light, free-flowing gown for ease in movement—or wrestling. She thought of it as her ballroom-style judogi and she was going to judo his ass into submission if necessary.

She listened to the unfolding finale below. In her mind's eye she felt she could play out Eli's every move. It was a brilliant plan—a dash of style with an injection of humor—and so simple. She felt at this juncture in their journey of cat and mouse, she grasped how he thought. She waited where she knew that thought would take him.

On the stage, sudden heightened electricity shot through the cast. The costumed cops chased the thief but this time, in this performance, with an almost comical sense of timing as they bumped into each other. Gone was the stylized drama of the rehearsals, but the audience delighted in it as the movements appeared so natural to them.

The laughter of the audience caused Nathalie to peer down over the edge of the skylight. *What was happening?!* The audience saw nothing amiss, thoroughly charmed with the Keystone Cops homage. But to Nathalie the thief's movement was out of order from the carefully choreographed rehearsals and so was the tone. The facial expressions of the frozen actors in the painting tableau registered barely suppressed alarm as the thief darted among them lifting off their precious Cartier jewels. They needed to remain frozen and could do nothing; the costumed cops compensated as well as they could with the different blocking this thief tossed into the choreographed number. Collisions with the frozen painting actors seemed imminent; one so perilously close that one frozen woman with an umbrella squeezed her eyes shut bracing for the impact…which mercifully never happened, but she gasped, her relief decidedly unfrozen.

The audience remained enthralled.

The director and choreographer horrified.

Donelli didn't sense any problem. He had never paid close attention to the rehearsals.

Nathalie knew that Eli Cross had paid very close attention through numerous rehearsals. She had thrown Cross a curve ball with the added cops guarding the art masterpieces. His thorough research allowed for rapid readjustments. She remembered the taunting words he tossed at Marty Lefkowitz on her roof: *You don't think I had other plans in case she didn't work out.* That same hubris on display on this night thrust him onward against shifting odds. She knew that very hubris could also get him killed.

The thief spun away from the period-costumed cops who encircled him and found himself face-to-face with the frozen leading lady in the painting.

This initiated the final moment of the night's performance…if things went as planned.

Donelli prepared to move quickly. He knew the jewels were in the black velvet bag. He felt that when the actor left the stage with them, Cross would make his move, perhaps slipping into the crowd of dancers and actors leaving the stage; it might be something simple like a pickpocket attempt and then slip away again in the crush of moving bodies rushing to get ready for a curtain call. Donelli did not know—rehearsals mattered—that the thief holding the black velvet bag on stage was not an actor.

Just before the leading lady animated in order to unmask the thief and plant a kiss on his lips, the thief changed the intended action yet again and extracted a black, pistol-gripped oblong tube strapped to his leg. The actress animated with shock and reached out to unmask him attempting to follow the script despite this change, but he took a step back and raised his arm dramatically up to the roof—and fired!

A wound steel wire shot upward out of the oblong housing; its titanium arrowhead-style blade on the leading edge of the wire embedded in the base of the rim of the open skylight—Nathalie's skylight! With a flick of his finger, he activated the electric hydraulic pulley which rapidly retracted. He rose up off the stage floor into the air above the astonished actors who stared open-mouthed at this blatant stage exit!

With the black velvet bag of jewels clipped to his belt, he reached the rim of the skylight, grasped the roof's edge, let go of the pistol-grip pulley tube and hauled himself up into the darkness of the foggy night on the roof.

The audience exploded into applause at the dynamic, visually audacious finale!

Donelli sprang into action, finally realizing that roof exit was not part of the planned performance. He sprinted out of the ballroom to the grounds yelling into his handset microphone! "He's on the roof not backstage!"

The snipers whipped their scoped-rifles away from the grounds and to the roof's surface, but couldn't see anyone. To them the roof was clear. The triangulated AC units blocked the two bodies grappling with each other.

Down below, chants of *Bravo* intermixed with the applause that continued unabated and built into a thunderous crescendo! The actors rushed out on stage for a dazed curtain call and the applause exploded again to even greater heights!

The noise below billowed out of the open skylights and masked the scuffling sounds of the other two people on the roof. Nathalie grabbed his shoulder when he emerged from the skylight pulling him back behind the AC unit so the snipers wouldn't see him.

In a desperate whisper she uttered, "Snipers!"

He paid no heed and shoved her backwards scrambling to scoot around the AC units.

She latched onto his ankle and jerked his feet out from under him. They were still unseen.

He jammed his foot into her face propelling her backwards.

Stunned and righteously pissed, her thoughts on fire: *What the hell's wrong with you, I'm trying to save your ass!* Before she could grab him again, he slithered quickly beyond the AC units.

The snipers now scanned the grounds with the roof clear and did not see him dashing across the dark roof to the edge that overlooked the courtyard with the series of terraced patios.

She raced after him gripped with panic and dread from the breaths she gulped in—filled with a unique musky cologne scent—the one that prompted her to dub Eli Cross *The Musked Marauder!* She had to catch him—to stop him—before it was too late! With all the commotion down on the grounds and the place swarming with converging cops, she knew he'd never escape even with the help of the increasing fog!

She had to catch him at the roof's edge, to get him to surrender to her—for her!

The mist swirled up onto the roof from a sudden gust of wind off the Atlantic. She could barely see him in the dark, moonless night. She kept her voice soft to be undetected by snipers.

"Eli..."

He turned to her. She didn't attempt to move any closer. He stood on the edge. The safety of the fog beckoned. She knew he could quickly drop down and elude her—only to then be *shot down like a dog on the highway* by a vengeful Donelli!

"Don't...please...for me."

He didn't move. Her heart and hope were in her throat. And then…he merely blew her a kiss and leapt down into the open courtyard and onto the first terraced patio below!

"Oh God," Nathalie gasped! She hesitated only a second then leapt off the edge—her *judogi* ball gown billowed like a parachute—and landed less successfully than him collapsing into the soft dirt of a planted flower bed!

She picked herself up and saw him standing at the far edge ready to drop down to the next terraced courtyard patio. Nathalie pleaded, her heart sinking. "Eli!"

He paid her no mind—escape was paramount—the need to elude the *moment that didn't fit*—and he leapt down to the next level terrace below!

This time she raced down the terrace stairs next to her to the same level patio terrace. He was poised like a cliff diver at the edge of the final drop. Down below the ground-level travertine-tile patio beckoned as the gateway to the fog-filled lawn beyond.

The wind off the Atlantic shoved a heavy fog bank on shore! A whisper-quiet black Vespa could slice through that dark, mist-swirling landscape and quickly vanish.

The opening would be there—she knew he sensed it—his body tensed to move on instinct, to be there when the opening arrived—but he hesitated…and instead of leaping, he looked back at her one last time, a final gaze, perhaps a farewell!

In that moment of indecision, a blustery gust of wind blew the protecting fog away.

She sensed in her gut she had one last chance. One last plea for sanity…and for his life!

"Please, Eli…don't. The *moment's* passed. Give the goddess her due."

He dropped his head as if acknowledging that the opening had closed—this was now the *moment that didn't fit*—he could no longer avoid it.

He raised his head slowly, not in defeat, but in defiance.

Nathalie gasped knowing what he would do at all costs.

Instead of surrendering to her, he doffed his hand gallantly off his head in a salute to her and then…

Spotlights snapped on catching him in crossing beams!

He whipped out a gun—a Walther—but before he could fire, a thunderous hail of bullets struck him and hurtled him backwards. He plummeted helplessly down to the travertine terrace below striking the ground with a sickening thud that broke the tiles in pieces!

Donelli, gun drawn, raced across the terrace like the triumphant hunter to his awaiting prize. Nathalie stayed up on the second level unable to move. She saw that his body was still.

A wave of anguish rolled over her at the bloody denouement. She still couldn't move. It was her heart and not her body that froze in stillness. She gazed down at his body; the sight crushed her soul. He was sprawled on his back, legs akimbo, on the travertine tile of the terrace patio. Blood pooled from underneath his head and torso discoloring the now broken, earth-tone tiles with dark red.

She knew he was dead. The brutal reality sucked out all her breath. She grasped for something tangible to hang onto, anything to make sense of all this madness! *At heart, Eli Cross was just a boy who wanted to go home.* Was that it?! Was that why he pushed *this moment* so relentlessly to the limit?! My God…all to ease his pain. The heartbreak of *this moment* strangled her hope because it suddenly made sense. If he failed to triumph over *the moment that didn't fit,* it would not be failure, but release; for he knew he would be killed and would at last *go home.*

Elliot Crositer would finally be home in the arms of his family. She gasped at the realization: *it was so simple,* making it the perfect Eli Cross plan.

"Game over," Donelli cried out with devilish delight! He had brought down *the legend.* No more frustration at being played the fool while the thief walked away scot-free. Eli Cross was dead! Case closed! The champagne waited on ice. He would be the toast of the department. At last they would all have to admit just how damn good he really was—always was! Even the great Nate Seeger—best clearance record in the department's history—couldn't nab this thief. But now…Lieutenant Victor J. Donelli stood alone at the top having nailed the Perp of perps! From this moment on he relished the birth of his own *legend* as the watchword for a righteous collar would now and forever be *Donellied* and no longer *Muldooned!* It didn't get better than that.

"Stay back from the body," Donelli ordered!

Lieutenant Victor J. Donelli didn't want anyone intruding on his glory! He hustled over and shoved tuxedoed cops aside, clearing the area around the corpse. Cross was indeed a corpse; just how Donelli always had envisioned this moment of triumph—no trials to legally maneuver out of on a technicality—just stone cold dead.

He looked forward to framing one of the crime scene forensic photographs of Cross's bloody and broken body.

Donelli actually smiled when he saw the blood that had pooled from under Cross's hooded head from striking and breaking the multi-colored travertine tiles of the patio that had been imported from Tivoli, Italy at great expense. The rich, bastard thief who loved his art now lay dead on an artistic design. How appropriately ironic, he thought, a masterpiece of death.

But the largest river of blood had flowed out of the bullet-ridden torso and Donelli was most pleased that death had actually come up above on the terraced roof instantly—after Cross's salute to Nathalie—from the impact of three sharpshooter rounds center mass and at least one slug from his own 1911 Colt .45.

The lieutenant had emptied his mag at the thief he hated and he knew for sure that at least one bullet, maybe more, had found their target. All the many hours over many years at the gun range had finally paid off big time!

Ian shoved the blockade of tuxedoed cops aside with his devil stick and disregarding Donelli's orders scuttled quickly over to the body and stood behind the lieutenant. His heart ached for his sister as he saw Nathalie immobile at the rim of the terrace courtyard patio above…a frozen pose in a painting of horror.

Donelli relished having an audience for his victorious reveal and reached down with rising delight to the dead body and slowly, savoring the moment of triumph, removed the mask.

His face in death had not been distorted by bullets or impacting travertine tile. His striking face was fully intact. Easy to identify. It was not Eli Cross!

"That's Jake Kracauer," Ian exclaimed!

Donelli's dismay actually buckled his knees. He was dumbstruck, sick to his core.

Nathalie's heart leapt with sheer joy! A muscle spasm from released tension rolled through her stomach and doubled her over.

Tears no longer held back burst from her eyes. In stunned relief she realized that he really truly hadn't been there tonight. Just as he had told her.

But where was Eli Cross?!

CHAPTER TWENTY SIX

*There are two ways to be fooled. One is to believe what
isn't true; the other is to refuse to accept what is true.*

Soran Kierkegaard

About the time that Jake Kracauer drew his last breath, the Bombardier Global 6000, tail number F-EVLC, soared into the night sky wheels up at Teterboro Airport. The flight plan was Zurich, but over the mid-Atlantic, it would be rerouted to the Venice Marco Polo Airport. The luxurious private jet streaked across the sky toward the breaking dawn in the distance over the stormed-tossed Atlantic.

Seated alone in the main passenger cabin, Eli Cross hoped to catch the first glimpse of the new dawn in his life that ushered in a treasure-trove of possibilities. On the dark, mahogany table in front of him sat the special state of the art steel and fiberglass cabinet from The Baronfeld Museum. The door of the cabinet stood open.

Inside the pristine protective cushioning rested the small sculpture of the entwined man and woman, *The Cellini Lovers.*

Eli Cross had been responsible for its security and safe return to the eldest Baronfeld daughter, Lyudmila, at her private alpine chalet outside Vaduz, Liechtenstein per her specific instructions. Secluded and fortified, access available only by gondola lift, snowmobile or skis. Cross planned on honoring those specifications—gondola lift in with the statue, ski out with his fee having been deposited in his numbered Swiss bank account.

First though, he had personal business in Venice, Italy on the little island of San Giorgio. He would commandeer a different style of gondola there to reach his destination. On that journey he would carry a newly obtained prize. It was not *yellow gold*...it was better.

From out of the hidden steel-rimmed false bottom in the base of *The Cellini Lovers* cabinet he withdrew one of the black Vespa leather saddlebags bulging with its specially wrapped treasure.

Carefully, with the delicate precision of an artist's brushstroke, he unsealed the airtight wrapping which released a *whoosh* of a colorless, protectant gas that had been injected before closure. He peeled back the opaque material especially designed to keep out any harsh light. Resting in his arms lay the rare manuscript written in Old French whose parchment pages expressed the sentiment of *chasing the goddess* which he had shared with Nathalie.

He had no contract protecting this ancient masterwork of art.

But his victory at obtaining it left a bittersweet taste on his palate. Though loose ends had been cleared up, Kracauer and Lefkowitz, so their hatred didn't follow him going forward, and Donelli's spirit had been crushed so he would abandon the chase, Eli did not feel free.

His thoughts were elsewhere. A few fleeting memories fluttered across his mind from some of the escapades with his itinerant Gypsy family, what he thought of as *Lakatos Lessons*. They saved his life. They taught him independent survival. They provided him a bag of tricks created and developed with style and panache which he turned into a road map for his personal path of retribution. The love of art, instilled in him by his parents, Roland and Audrey, never left him. When he discovered that the art world was the wild west of money with billionaires twisting like pretzels to avoid taxes by keeping their precious prizes technically *always in transit,* many times simply between storage facilities in Geneva, he decided that some of these masterpieces needed to be freed from their dark abodes to be seen and appreciated again, an elixir for the heart and soul. His new prize had been freed from its billionaire possessor, but his thoughts fell upon a small trinket.

Into his hand, he dropped the gold chain holding the delicate half-heart from Nathalie.

She had done what he had needed her to do, what he had set her up to do. He had needed her at the Borelli estate doing her best to do the right thing. From the connection he made with her, he knew she would press on in that regard—even though she liked him—to the very end. It fulfilled his *moment.* Now what to do about the emotional detritus left over from that *moment* left the bittersweet taste.

Part of him had doubted—couldn't fully trust—that she would follow through as he hoped. But she had. His dealings with Nate and Odile had left the same bittersweet feelings unresolved. The loss of his family haunted him. The actions of the Seeger family haunted him.

Perhaps he was an itinerant gypsy now, always on the move, always left with a *yearning* in the embrace of *saudade.*

§

Nathalie staggered into her kitchen finally dressed for the day in jeans and T-shirt and heated up the tea pot for a much needed cup of coffee—as fast as possible—two spoonfuls of Columbian instant—to be human again. It had been a long, sleepless night, her thoughts churning over and over about Eli Cross and whether she may actually have meant something real to him or was she simply a useful idiot.

She barely got two long swallows downed into her system when her cell rang. She answered. It was Lisette Granger.

"Are you okay, girl?" Lisette inquired with sincere concern.

"I'm only on my first cup of coffee," Nathalie said trying to make light of things.

"No, no girlfriend, don't shove this aside," Lisette cautioned. "You saw someone shot right in front of you; that's no small thing."

"No…no, it wasn't."

"Did you know that thief?"

"No, not really, ran into him at The Regency once…part of my Waldorf heist research…he was a bit of an asshole…but he liked my hair…still…seeing someone get…"

"Yeah, it's a nasty thing," concluded Lisette worried about Nathalie's disjointed speech. She needed to bring Nathalie's focus back to the present. "Did he have the Waldorf jewels?"

"No, my reputation's still on the hook for them."

"Well that fucking sucks," Lisette offered.

"Were you there last night?"

"No, I was at Fenway, my man was hammering the Yankees, kicked their pussy butts too. He dropped by my Boston hotel after, brought his bat and balls, and scored several more times."

"So, you had a better night," Nathalie said adding some levity to the somber moment,

"You could say," Lisette agreed.

"Yeah, we both got fucked in different ways," added Nathalie.

"Oh girl, we gotta have lunch, something decadent to free your head."

"I'm game."

"Maybe Friday, Tavern on the Green?"

"Maybe, yes," Nathalie said with a slight hesitation.

"No, no—hell yes—c'mon!"

"Okay…hell yes."

"By the way," Lisette interjected, "a little something to lift your spirits so you know all the shit's not droppin' on your head. Someone absconded with a rare Old French parchment manuscript from The Baronfeld Museum last night."

"What?!" Nathalie couldn't believe it. *Fucking hell, that bastard!*

"Yeah, slick as can be, just vanished. Some masterpieces were being returned as part of the normal rotation and they're all accounted for, but that manuscript…it's in the wind."

Of course it was *in the wind,* Nathalie thought, probably literally, on board a Bombardier private jet going…wherever!

"The thief had a touch of style and a sense of humor though," added Lisette.

Nathalie wondered what *panache* Eli had added to his evening's escapade.

"In place of the manuscript," Lisette suddenly laughed. "You gotta love this. The thief left a copy of *Don Quixote* by Miguel de Cervantes in the display case. A copy," she chuckled again from the sheer pleasure of the humorous hubris, "purchased from Barnes & Noble," and splayed open to a highlighted page, but with a touch of class though because they chose the resplendent Edith Grossman translation. I sent you a link with the page."

There was a knock at Nathalie's front door, a short pause, and then the sound of a key turning in the lock followed by Megan with two cups of steaming coffee lattes.

"Shit comin' down is right," Natalie sighed. "Friday then."

"High noon," Lisette said as she clicked off the call.

Megan handed Nathalie her latte so she could be a two-fisted coffee imbiber if she wanted.

"You know a rare manuscript is missing from The Baronfeld Museum. Worth a small fortune," Megan proudly stated as if she'd scored a journalistic scoop.

"Yeah, that was Lisette filling me in," said Nathalie.

Chapter Twenty Six

"Oh…" Megan said disappointed that she wasn't first with the news.

"Grabbed a burger with Lisette and our mutual friend Denise Yamura—the one from Lincoln Center—the other day. That MoMA friend of yours is a soul-sister sass-sorceress. We gotta jam with her more often. She makes me laugh—hard. She was on a wild, sassy rant about her ballplayer boyfriend pouring the meat to her gash garden then answered the phone and shifted into elegant, erudite sophistication in the same breath, ended the call, picked up the rant rhythm without missing a beat."

"Gash garden…"

"Exactly—Vagina—how good is that?!" Megan said excitedly. "You gotta laugh; it's like right out of a warped edition of *Good Housekeeping*. Fell off her tongue just like an irreverent song. I'd never come up with that but I'm white so what the hell do I know," she said laughing!

"Pouring the meat…" Nathalie slowly repeated.

"Yeah, I'm gonna use that one if I ever find a meat-pourer worth keeping."

"Hopefully your meat-pourer can do the dishes, some laundry and a little vacuuming."

"Goes without saying," Megan quipped.

Nathalie resisted but then succumbed to an emerging smile and Megan hoped she had been able to turn the tide and lift Nathalie's spirits on this somber morning.

"Maybe you can join us at high noon Friday at Tavern on the Green," Nathalie offered.

"High noon. Count me in," she said, then added a lilting refrain, *"do not forsake me oh my darlin'."*

"What?" Nathalie wondered confused, not getting the lyric reference."

"High Noon," Megan said as if it were obvious, then getting a blank stare from Nathalie, quickly added "Gary Cooper, Grace Kelly, great old movie!"

Nathalie still didn't get it that the words were from the title song.

"Never mind," Megan quipped giving up. "Does Lisette know about you and Eli Cross?"

"No—and don't say a word—nothing—or I'll—"

"Okay, okay," Megan said, hands up in surrender.

Pain etched itself on Nathalie's face, unmistakable emotional pain.

Megan realized that no amount of ribald humor or switching subjects again would lift the pressing weight of defeat and despair off of Nathalie's heart.

"Last night when I thought he was dead…" Nathalie couldn't continue because her breaths suddenly only came in short staccato bursts as she struggled to repress full-on sobbing.

For a moment, Megan panicked and didn't know what to do.

Yes she did, she told herself, she wanted to tell her best friend that all this really, really sucked, that she was the best friend she'd ever had and didn't deserve any of this shit, and that fuck she really had to stop shaking 'cause it was freaking her out, and that none of this shit would've happened if she had just met a guy and not some international master thief, and she felt really bad now that she hadn't slept with Eli because then they could commiserate together like they did about Vinnie, and that maybe fuck it, they should just ditch men altogether because they were…they were men and too much assembly was required and they fell apart like all that Ikea crap, but that would only leave women and she'd never told her about the lesbian affair she had for four weeks which was actually great for three weeks because the softness was so nice and she didn't have to explain her body to her lover because she had the same body but then the craziness started because women are like jigsaw puzzles and some of the boxes get shipped with pieces missing so it didn't make sense cause there were weird holes, and fuck, guys were jigsaw puzzles too but they didn't even come with a picture of how they should look, so, the two of them should just get a dog, rescue a dog and they'd rescue us right back, that's what she wanted to tell her, that, and that sometimes you just wanted someone to pour the meat to your gash garden and then leave so you could sleep. She wanted to tell her best friend all this and how much she loved her and needed her to be well all in the four seconds that all these thoughts and feelings raced through her.

But she didn't.

Instead, Megan stepped forward and hugged her.

The hug felt good. No words. Just the hug.

The hug stopped the shaking.

Nathalie liked the hug, melted into the hug and needed the hug to know she wasn't alone.

Megan had said all she needed to say with the hug.

Once again, Nathalie breathed normally.

"You really think Eli took that manuscript?" Megan asked bringing things back on track.

Nathalie thought of what Eli told her was his most effective device: *Usually a smile.*

In spite of the heartbreak, she nodded to herself, for she had to admit that smile of his was dazzling, and in its truest form it was lit from within by something utterly captivating. Nathalie finally looked at Megan but didn't respond, instead led Megan over to a box on the coffee table.

"This came by special Express Mail postal courier this morning," Nathalie said. "Sender unknown."

Megan opened the lid of the box and freaked! The contents were all jewels—dazzling jewels—layers of staggeringly expensive baubles that only the ridiculously rich would own.

"Wow... are these the stolen jewels from the Waldorf?"

"That's them," Nathalie said.

Megan picked up a necklace. "This would be fabulous with my black evening dress."

"I've had similar thoughts all morning."

"So this is how it feels."

"This is it," Nathalie stated.

Both women stared at the glistening fortune in gems...fantasizing about another life.

"Not without a certain..."

"...rush," Nathalie said concluding the thought they both felt.

"Yeah..." Megan agreed wistfully.

The jewels were a reality slap in the face for Nathalie.

"He stole these to draw attention to himself while he was in town with The Baronfeld Museum exhibit. He knew Kracauer was planning on hitting the Cartier party and that was the diversion he needed. Everyone would be expecting Eli Cross to rise to the ultimate challenge."

"But someone was imitating his style," Megan said. "He didn't lie to you about that. Jake Kracauer was the impostor."

"Yeah, he didn't lie about that," Nathalie said with a sigh that contained no consolation. "And he didn't steal the masterpieces he was guarding at the museum." She tossed Megan a knowing smile, including her in the collusion. "But then, he wasn't guarding everything."

"And the manuscript was fair game," stated Megan confidently following that rabbit down the hole.

"And so was I."

That was the harsh fact. No getting around it.

"He returned the jewels," Megan reminded her as a form of solace. "You get to score points for recovering them. You're not in trouble anymore...unless we want to improve the accessorizing of our wardrobes."

Nathalie wasn't embracing Megan's humor and Megan still so wanted to cheer her friend up to help kick start what she knew would be a long, emotional healing process.

"So you don't get to live in the south of France, so what?"

Nathalie took a sip of the latte which Megan had brought.

"This is a good latte, thanks."

The two friends shared the moment in silence. The mystery of dealing with men enveloped them both as it always had and most probably always would.

"As usual, there's nothing to prove that Eli stole the manuscript. It's simply missing, with one added touch. Left in its place in the display, a copy of *Don Quixote* by Miguel de Cervantes purchased from Barnes & Noble—but the Edith Grossman translation no less—"

"Oh—well the man does have good taste—horses, jets, books...art."

"Yeah, the book was splayed open to a highlighted page. Lisette sent me this link with the page."

Nathalie brought up the link on her cell phone, looked at it, and immediately knew it well for it was a famous passage from one of the greatest stories and most beloved novels ever written. Its selection was perfect, she thought, chosen with a poignant understanding of its relevance to this *moment*.

She also knew in her heart that it hadn't been left for the police, no, the sentiment was entirely for her.

She handed the phone to Megan, the highlighted section of the page visible on the screen. Megan read the selection in silence.

Nathalie did not need to hear the words. She almost knew them by heart, not from reading the link earlier but because she had memorized them from childhood. It was one of her father's favorite passages, the encounter with windmills, from what he considered the greatest novel ever written. He had shared it with her when she was a little girl and she had memorized it out of love for her dad.

She realized that Eli Cross probably knew all this because her father may have shared that precious memory with him, just like an exchange of beloved movies. Had they also discussed Tolstoy, Dostoevsky, Dickens, Goethe, Hemingway, Fitzgerald, and Steinbeck? Probably. But Miguel de Cervantes would have been the first author's name past her father's lips.

Nathalie knew Eli had gotten so deep into her head it seemed like he owned property there, an entrenched address. And what had she given him of her heart?

She watched Megan's eyes well with tears as she neared the end of the passage.

Nathalie felt the Knight's quest with his friend, Sancho Panza, mirrored some of her journey with Cross, weaving in and out of reality and illusion, truth and fable, and there lying quietly at the end of the path the letters *what do you trust?*

Like Don Quixote, she—and probably her father—were boldly ready to engage in righteous combat with giants, a *Muldooning* of evil if there ever was one. The Knight's faithful servant tried telling his grace that his intended combatants were merely windmills, not giants with long, swinging arms. Windmills…did not hold the promise and assurance of *adventures* so the command was uttered to step aside and pray while he, Don Quixote of La Mancha, entered the realm of glorious combat with giants.

Oh…what signals had she missed?

Megan finished reading and paused to wipe her eyes. "Not without a touch of…" Megan said searching for the right word.

"…panache," Nathalie added to finish the feeling.

Nathalie tossed a letter to Megan, already opened and sticking out of its envelope.

"This came by separate delivery. It's a note that my father had sent to Cross some years ago."

Megan took the letter and began reading out loud, but it was her father's voice that Nathalie heard as Megan read on.

Dear Eli, I admire the gusto and style with which you embrace your life, even though we are adversaries.

ॐ

The Bombardier Global 6000 rose into the clouds as the canals of Venice faded into the distance with Eli's mission accomplished. The half-heart from Nathalie lay across the palm of his hand. He imagined Nathalie reading her father's letter. He remembered every word. He hoped it might assuage some of her distress from his actions. He still heard the assured voice of his former adversary, and hoped he could say *friend,* as the words resonated within his memory.

Knowing you gave me second thoughts as to the road not taken. I found your life addicting and exhilarating. There's something to be said for living life at the edge.

ॐ

Megan continued reading out loud, her voice cracking from emotion as she understood the depth of connection between the celebrated detective and the elusive master thief.

We are very similar, you and I, but our difference is now clear to me. To have chosen your path would have meant not having Nathalie and Ian and Odile in my life.

Nathalie gazed out her window visualizing her father writing those words in his study surrounded by his medals and citations for a lifetime career of being a heralded cop.

Megan paused wondering how all this must resonate with Nathalie…then she read on.

And having them gives answers where before there were only questions.

Shafts of light suddenly broke through the front windows. The eerie timing made Nathalie almost feel that her father had reached out to connect, to tell her that she had done well, a good job, that it was okay, that he understood. Tears fell freely from her eyes as she stared at the Lucerne and the deluxe king suite from where Eli had watched her hatching her plan to trap him and *Muldoon* him.

"He told me not to trust him. He didn't say anything about loving him." Nathalie understood and finally embraced and owned what she knew to be true. "I believed what I wanted to. And he knew I would."

Nathalie picked up one of her father's files and within it his note that she had seen on Eli Cross. She had searched for it and picked it out of one of the boxes last night when she couldn't fall asleep. Nathalie read it out loud to Megan. It felt especially poignant and apropos to her after Megan's reading of her father's letter because she and her father had arrived at the same point.

"I knew him too well. Maybe he wanted me to. No regrets."

It was a bittersweet surrender.

Nathalie gazed out her window as the morning sun glinted off the panes. Her heart felt a ghost image of Eli Cross's jet streaking toward the horizon line...and his new life…without her.

CHAPTER TWENTY SEVEN

*Sometimes we stare so long at a door that is closing
that we see too late the one that is open.*

Alexander Graham Bell

The still waters of the Turtle Pond next to Belvedere Castle in Central Park mirrored the shape-shifting clouds that floated across the water's surface like ghostly galleons. When their Hansom cab carriage had passed by the castle on their last night together, Nathalie had entertained visions of a dashing champion knight and his amorous queen. It was a fleeting fantasy of childhood revisited which that magical night rekindled. Then of course, later, Marty Lefkowitz had tried to kill her. Her knight saved her, but the glow of Camelot had been badly tarnished. She had no longer been sure whether the man who saved her was Arthur, Lancelot, or Mordred. Myth did not seem to hold up well twenty years into the twenty-first century.

Soon, she would have to fully embrace the reality of New York City and get her stalled and imperiled career back on track. But for this last lingering moment, she stood at the water's edge; her half-heart charm dangled from her neck as she stared at the water and the flotilla of clouds which sailed on by and carried with them the echo of memory…from her lesson at The Baronfeld Museum.

So, how would you do this?

I don't know... maybe redirect the beams.

With mirrors?

Yeah, maybe mirrors. And, then…maybe…not.

Keep it simple. That's key. Always. Simple. Less chance of getting caught.

She dropped a pebble into the pond which broke the surface of the water and the resulting ripples carried away her memories. Nathalie checked her watch. It would soon be high noon and she was due at Tavern on the Green for what she hoped would be an uplifting lunch filled with good, rousing, deliciously dirty, raucous humor with Lisette and Megan.

Behind her, she heard the clip-clop of horse hooves on pavement. She turned and was stunned to see Mosey guiding Melvin and his Hansom cab over to her. The carriage was empty.

"How did you know I'd be here?"

"Wasn't hard to figure, bein' a romantic old cuss," Mosey said. "I caught you starin' wistfully at that castle that night."

Nathalie found it strangely unsettling that he used the word *romantic,* like she had been caught being real that night, and somehow less professional.

"He's not coming, is he? You feel sorry for me?"

"Not at all," said Mosey, smiling. "You're a big girl."

"That I am."

"He knows that too and he would be askin' a question of you."

Nathalie didn't get it until Mosey handed her a black velvet ring box. Inside rested a glittering rose-cut diamond engagement ring.

"It's not stolen?" Nathalie asked being properly skeptical.

"It was his mother's. He's never offered it to anyone. And he'd like to know your answer."

"He couldn't bring it himself?"

"Well…thought it might be a bit awkward…and he knew you liked me."

Nathalie laughed at the audaciousness of it all. "I do, Mosey, I do like you." She fingered her half-heart charm that hung from her neck. In that moment, she wrestled through a myriad array of legitimate concerns that prompted serious contemplation. The mystery of it all intrigued her, no doubt, and yet…

"He's asking a lot of this heart," she said simply at last.

"Yes, I think he is, and you'll just have to…"

"Trust him?"

Nathalie gazed out over the pond to the Belvedere Castle walls. What dangers, she wondered, hid within the lure of hope? An enigmatic smile slid across her face; perhaps, as Eli had cautioned her, she shouldn't discount the power of myth just yet.

ൡ

Lunch was a hoot and a half. She laughed so hard her sides ached and she almost peed her pants. But the ache was welcome. Lisette really was a sass-sorceress spewing out words in rhythms like a magical incantation which evoked involuntary guffaws of laughter—loud enough that turned heads at other tables! It was so refreshing to be with someone who had no filter and just let it fly, but always with a heaping dollop of Southern humor! That unleashed inhibition revved up Nathalie's grit and determination to *get on with life!*

One reason Nathalie had so much fun was that she had decided before she got to Tavern on the Green that she would not mention her encounter with Mosey and the offer from Eli which sounded almost ludicrous when she thought of how she'd phrase it in telling the girls.

Now that she was back in her apartment, she was so grateful she never opened that Pandora's box. She'd had enough of all hell breaking loose for a while. Let sleeping dogs lie felt like better marching orders.

In fact, on the cab ride back to her apartment, she had made a commitment to herself that she would turn Eli down, let the past stay in the past, and get on with being normal for a change. Normal sounded good. Normal felt nice. Normal was simple.

Carefully and with the utmost respect, she readied the box of stolen jewels from the Waldorf Astoria heist for its return to Vorhees International Insurance.

Lying separate but next to the stolen jewels, the black velvet box with the engagement ring delivered by Mosey and Melvin oozed vibrations of temptation even though she knew her commitment to walk away was strong. Eli's mother's ring was a work of art and could now be hers...if she dared take that step. She knew her commitment would not waver though.

There were so many thoughts screaming at her that felt reasonable as to why she should not even consider this madness that it was frankly difficult to be impressed with just one. However...*No way in fucking hell should you do this*...did stand out from the rest!

She had to stay on task. Edward Vorhees was not a patient man. *He was also an arrogant prick.* That thought which prompted her not to dance to his tune and feel rushed, also opened the door that let in the demon. The devilish mesmerizing whisper she heard that wafted in through a tiny little fissure in her commitment roused her curiosity which got the better of her...and she removed the ring from the black velvet box...and shoved it on...just for fun.

It was breathtakingly gorgeous, shaped like a blossoming rose, and caught the light with an array of colors shining forth. Clearly it was also exquisitely expensive…and now…as she knew she had to leave…the damn thing was stuck on her finger!

No amount of tugging and twisting removed it from her finger! The application of first soap and then olive oil over her kitchen sink accomplished nothing. It wouldn't budge; it simply dug in as if possessed by some…demon was all she could think of as the sweat of panic appeared on her forehead. The skin of her finger, now cut and rubbed raw, annoyed her but not as much as the stupid inclination to try on the ring just for fun!

The ring was not coming off. Okay…face the music, she thought, just deal with it; it was what it was. So what?! She checked her watch. She had no more time left. She grabbed the box of jewels from the Waldorf Astoria heist and left determined to be done with all this crap.

Ⅎ

Once again, feeling like a child summoned to the principal's office, they ushered her over to the slippery, leather chair as Vorhees and Simmons then checked off the pieces of jewelry one by one against individual photographs stacked in a neat pile next to the jewelry box.

A much subdued and deeply embarrassed Lieutenant Victor J. Donelli glared at her.

Nathalie wanted to keep things professional. She knew a wounded tiger could still be very dangerous. She wanted to be done with trouble.

"You know this is Eli Cross," taunted Donelli.

"They were delivered by special U. S. Postal courier, and they're here, that's what I know," said Nathalie to Edward Vorhees, not even looking at Donelli.

"Victor, that is enough for us," Vorhees told Donelli to satisfy his friend's concern.

Donelli simply chewed on his frustration as Simmons handed Nathalie her check.

"Provided all the missing items are accounted for, this is yours," stated Simmons.

Nathalie took the check with an accepting nod of her head. "Thank you. I think you'll find..."

She then noticed the top photo on the pile.

"...that they're all here," she said with a rising lilt of trepidation in her voice.

The jewels were indeed all there.

But to her horror, she saw the next photo was of the ring that was stuck on her finger!

She quickly covered her left hand with her right hand and aggressively twisted and tugged on the ring!

Simmons picked up the ring photo from the pile of photos, and he and Vorhees then began the search in the box for... "The ring of Countess Yvette De la Grange," Simmons stated. "A ten-carat, rose-cut diamond valued at one point two million."

Nathalie repressed her rising panic! *Holy shit, 10-carats, $1.2 million!* There could be no possible sweet explanation for her having this, so with a final, brutal tug—"Ahh!"—she grunted in pain as the ring ripped from her finger tearing more skin off! She clutched the ring in her right hand, squeezed tight, and grimaced from the pain! She abruptly stood up from the slippery leather chair as all eyes were on her from her grunt which had sounded like an explosive burp!

She extended her right hand, fingers closed, and palm down over the box. "I'll leave you boys to your toys." She uncurled her fingers and released the ring down onto the remaining jewels in the box. "All the little baubles," she said as she patted her hand up and down as if her motion was an act of blessing their proceedings.

She hid the ring finger of her left hand, which was now bleeding, took her check...and gracefully walked toward the door.

"Ms. Seeger, I underestimated you," said Vorhees, stopping Nathalie in her tracks.

She turned back to face him, praying that she hadn't been found out.

"Thank you, sir, not a problem anymore." She then turned to Donelli. "And you Lieutenant?"

Donelli was as stone-faced and irritable as ever. Nothing had changed.

"When it comes to Eli Cross...you Seegers never learn."

The blood from the ripped skin on her ring finger was dripping on the plush carpet.

"Mr. Vorhees, when you need a job completed, you have my number," said Nathalie.

Dignity intact, Nathalie walked out the door, blood droplets trailing behind her.

In the lobby of the international insurance firm, by the elevator, she felt a surge of pride. A river of confidence coursed through her consciousness. The job was done.

She had closed the case. The jewels were recovered as she had promised: *And this Seeger is definitely in the game—for the whole ride.* Another drop of blood hit the floor as the elevator door opened. She had held her own with the best of the boys. The blood loss had been minimal.

EPILOGUE

*Does the imagination dwell the most Upon a woman
won or a woman lost?*

The Tower, **William Butler Yeats**

A new café had opened in Nathalie's neighborhood, a French-style café and patisserie named *Le Bon Chance*. It was even within sight of The Lucerne adding to the European flair.

Nathalie sat by herself at a small round table for two and nursed a café au lait that was divine. The aroma seemed straight from Les Deux Magots or Café Flore in Paris and the mouth-watering croissant could go straight to her hips. She didn't care. She'd wear it with joy. She also knew she would invite her mother. There was much still to talk about, to process…to try and understand.

Work was good. She had just wrapped a complex case of fraud for a major insurance company and had received a healthy bonus. Her reputation was on fire—in a good way. She was fielding offers on the same playing field as the guys—and she was out-scoring them. She smiled to herself as she sipped her café au lait. Her life was settling into a certain *je ne sais quoi* satisfaction.

Her brother Ian had happily plunged into writing his next novel: *The Gypsy Thief.* In it he intended to fictionalize *the legend* of Eli Cross using the new name of Sam Simone for the character of the Master Thief. He toyed with the idea of Sam actually being short for *Samantha.*

Even Megan had carved out a new path. She was locked in rock 'n' roll mode. Megan had been put in charge of her own ad campaign at Delacorte, Redfield & Nanning, not just the graphic design. She was crazed with pressure, doubting every decision, but loving it. She had drawn prison bars on top of her cardboard Donald Trump whose head was still bent.

Megan was also actually speaking to the breathtakingly stunning receptionist creature and had discovered she was a decent human being and not a privileged, self-centered, entitled bitch. Simone—that was the creature's actual name—had even introduced Megan to her brother, Theo. Nathalie had wondered if he was a U-Penn Wharton School or Yale graduate, but Megan had set her quickly straight. No, he was a Bowdoin grad with a degree in English. Nathalie thought she had then said he was a professional conversationalist, but she said no—a conservationist, who had three dogs and liked hiking in National Parks. He also apparently looked like movie star Bradley Cooper with a light, rugged two-day stubble that was…Nathalie knew what it was even though Megan had simply stared off at nothing and had never finished the sentence.

Nathalie hesitated for a moment to think it; not wanting to jinx anything, but she knew that Megan was actually…happy. She hadn't seen her in weeks. And that was okay. Her best friend was in a good place.

Nathalie was enjoying being single. There was much to be said for the single life. When one was confident and responsible only for oneself, the world took on a certain glow of possibilities. She was actually contemplating taking a vacation, by herself.

Europe beckoned. How could it not with The Lucerne across the street and *Le Bon Chance* tucked nearby. She felt drawn to the South of France…St. Tropez…then thought better of it. Perhaps a Viking Riverboat Cruise along the Rhine. Did German princes still live in castles? Maybe not a good idea. Italy—rent a villa in Tuscany—that felt safe. Lying under the Tuscan sun or under a Tuscan artist or vintner or even an olive farmer, his hands slippery with olive oil as he massaged her back, her thighs, her—

No, it had to be Lake Como. Set against the picturesque scenery of the Alps in Northern Italy's Lombardy region. Yes, that had to be it. Pasta in paradise serenely sequestered and pampered at the five-star Villa d'Este Lago di Como. She might even meet movie star George Clooney. He had a villa somewhere on the lake if he hadn't sold it yet. But then he was married to Amal, a gorgeous and brilliant international law attorney working on human rights causes, and they had children they adored. Well…maybe the three of them could…no, she had ruled that out years ago.

No, just explore the beauty, and experience the serenity by herself. She was worth it. She deserved that. Maybe her ring finger might actually heal in the Italian alpine air.

She finished her croissant and looked at that finger where she had yanked off the diamond ring of Countess Yvette De la Grange. The skin was still scabbed over. What the hell was going on under there?! Why was it taking so long to heal?!

"You had it on," said Eli Cross, his voice shocking Nathalie out of her European travel plans and scab-healing befuddlement.

Had she actually heard his voice? She had. Cross was standing over her shoulder gazing down at her ring finger. She was at a loss for words until she realized the truth might carry some weight.

"It got stuck."

"I wasn't sure of your size," said Cross.

"Your *mother* had smaller fingers."

"Apparently."

"Your mother!!" Nathalie was full-on indignant. "It was part of Countess Yvette De la Grange's stolen collection!"

"Yes, she stole it from my mother," insisted Cross.

He paused only momentarily to gauge Nathalie's thoroughly incredulous glare.

"In Paris," he continued. "Thirty-five years ago. Took me a long time to track it down."

She stared at him…not yet taken in by this tall tale.

"Even longer to take it back," he said annoyed. "And now you've returned it to her."

Nathalie was nonplussed. Unconvinced.

"But what's more important," Cross said as he met her stare, "is why did you put it on?"

Nathalie was momentarily taken aback. There was a different light in his eyes. Something natural. Something…real? The hopeful, playful boy inside the man? Could it be? What was he doing here anyway?

Once again, he'd not been caught *with the goods,* not caught with anything that was missing. He'd gotten away with everything he was after—*everything*—there wasn't anything he didn't have. He couldn't possibly be here for…

"Well," said Nathalie offering a simple response, "it had been given to me."

"Yes," said Eli. "Along with a question…which needed an answer."

"You used me to steal—from the Baronfelds! You may have returned their *Cellini Lovers,* which they paid you to look after, but then you stole their Old French manuscript!"

Cross pulled out a chair and sat down at her table as he signaled the waiter.

"Espresso, s'il vous plaît."

"You're gonna need a lot more than a little espresso to explain this to me," she said not being swayed by his casual *savior faire.*

"An espresso is to be savored...an enjoyment of time," he calmly explained.

He was not at all put off by her annoyance, in fact he expected it, and knew he had it coming so he accepted it with grace and settled in to tell his story.

"It has always amused me," he said, "that so much of the art in the Museé du Louvre feels French when so much of it is not from France. Leonardo Da Vinci's Mona Lisa is Italian because he's Italian; the Venus de Milo is Greek. They are not alone, there are many other examples."

Eli luxuriated in a small sip of espresso when the waiter placed it before him.

"But to be in France," he continued, "unlike other cultures, is to be...French. Much of this has to do with the Louvre itself. It bestows on its resident art works a certain transcendence which they would not obtain elsewhere to the same degree. Would they still be great works of art, of course, without hesitation, but the Louvre enshrines them with an eminence that is...well...French."

"And this is your half-assed excuse for stealing the Old French manuscript because it should be back in the Louvre?! Was it ever in the Louvre?!"

Nathalie grabbed the waiter as he passed by. "I'm gonna need another café au lait—a really big one—I might be here a while."

"Are you familiar with the masterpiece painting *The Wedding at Cana* by Paolo Veronese, the Italian Renaissance painter who was based in Venice?"

"No," said Nathalie and grabbed the waiter again as he turned to leave. "Add another croissant to that café au lait would ya?"

"It's a giant canvas, twenty-two feet by thirty-three feet of wonderfully rich colors. It depicts Jesus changing the water into wine, a miracle the Italians took to heart no doubt."

He savored another sip of espresso. Nathalie marveled how he could stretch out that experience. There probably were only about four small sips in that tiny little espresso cup.

"It was painted for the monastery of San Giorgio Maggiore in Venice in 1563."

"That's really nice," Nathalie said facetiously. "So a lot of monks got to stare at it while they got drunk."

"Until Napoleon ordered it taken to France as part of one of his imposed peace treaty requirements. He looted the art of many conquered cultures. After his defeat at Waterloo much of the art was eventually returned. But not this painting."

Nathalie, despite her annoyance at him for…well, for everything, couldn't help but notice that this story held a poignancy for him. Perhaps there was a real point to be made from its telling. Nathalie gulped the last of her first café au lait and bit off a sumptuous piece of the newly arrived croissant.

"This painting," he continued telling her, "had been badly damaged during the ten months it took the French forces to cart it back to the Louvre. When it should've been returned, the curators of the Louvre convinced the Italians that it would be irreparably damaged in the journey back to the monastery in Venice and should remain in the Louvre for the benefit of posterity. The Louvre sent, instead, some minor painting that's been mostly forgotten."

Eli indulged the last sip of espresso. He sat quietly for a moment. Nathalie watched him with anticipation for what came next. He tapped the waiter as he passed by again and pointed to his espresso cup.

"Un autre s'il vous plait," Eli said.

"So," Nathalie wondered after Eli didn't continue, taking note though that his French accent was perfect, like a native. "Are you planning on stealing it back for the Italians this time?"

"No, of course not, it belongs in the Louvre. But it is thought of as being French now."

"Okay…is there more you're planning on telling me?"

Eli pointed at her croissant. "Can I have a bite of that?"

"Sure," Nathalie replied, "If you don't mind missing a finger."

Nathalie pointedly rubbed the scab on her ring finger. Eli got her message.

"So, you were wondering, the manuscript," Eli said getting on with his tale.

"Yeah." She held her croissant up in front of him and indulged another mouth-watering bite, wiped her lips, and smiled a becoming smile.

"Art had always been taken with a clear sense of entitlement by those who could take it. The Nazis did it on a scale and with more violence than Napoleon ever did. The possessors of great art have imagined themselves endowed with a sense of cultural élan by simply having it."

Eli paused. Nathalie felt his clear sense of disgust with the unjust ways of the world.

"The balance should be restored," he simply said. "But even now, they make that a crime, for who wants to part with something of great value that they obtained."

Nathalie recalled her father's note: *Justice with style.*

"The manuscript…" Eli said and then stopped.

"The French manuscript," added Nathalie feeling a river of goosebumps flow up her arm.

"Yes. It was actually written by a French monk for the monastery of San Giorgio Maggiore in Venice while he lived there. He was escaping persecution in France and they took him in and provided him sanctuary and sustenance."

Nathalie tilted her head down, eyes on her croissant, so that the tears welling up in her eyes would not be so blatantly obvious.

"Napoleon's armies removed the manuscript from the monastery when they saw that it was written in Old French and learned that the author was French. The Baronfelds obtained it from France with the power of their money, never acknowledging its provenance. Simply put, it has now been returned to the Church of San Giorgio Maggiore in Venice. It has returned home."

Nathalie couldn't look up because tears were now flowing freely down her face. She slid the remainder of her croissant over to him without looking.

"Here, you finish it," she said sniffling.

Eli took a bite of the croissant and thought it was actually as good as those he had in Paris recently. He savored another sip of the second espresso brought to their table.

Nathalie finally sucked it up and got a grip on her emotions. So many dots from her father's notes were making more sense now. This man seated with her had more facets than the 68 carat Elizabeth Taylor diamond given to her by Richard Burton. There were also so many questions that had no answers yet and bugged the hell out of her.

"You pulled me in to all this," Nathalie said. She downed a gulp of her second café au lait for courage. "Did you set me up on purpose or was I just convenient because of my father?"

"Would it disturb you to know that your recommendation to Edward Vorhees at Vorhees International Insurance and thus your job covering the Waldorf Astoria event came from the *Veritas* International Insurance Agency who gave you their highest rating?"

"Who is *Veritas*?"

"A company founded by Helmut Hauer in Zurich."

"And Herr Helmet Hauer is…" Nathalie paused for the truth was dawning on her.

'No one," Eli stated simply. He imbibed another sip of espresso.

Nathalie realized that *no one* liked espresso. All the points he had scored for returning the manuscript just vanished. She downed another gulp of latte.

"And the Waldorf display cases—the tricked out ones?" she asked with disdain.

"Probably switched out on delivery would be the simplest," he shrugged.

"*Veritas* trucking?!"

"Something like that," Eli said, rather pleased with himself.

"You set me up to fail, to humiliate me!"

"Did you? Were you?"

"No, I kicked ass!"

"You returned all the jewels."

"Yes, of course."

"And how did you get them?"

Flustered, Nathalie shot back, "The U.S. Postal service always delivers."

She knew he was trying to make a point, but what exactly she didn't know yet.

"There's a lot I don't know about you," she said in frustration.

"And I you," he stated as a simple truth.

For the first time in a while she decided to trust the goosebumps which tingled her arm.

"Before you came to New York for the Waldorf," Nathalie said moving on to another tactical approach. "Your jet was at Orly in Paris at the same time that a Renoir which had been rumored to be missing—thought stolen actually—suddenly appeared in the Louvre in time for their special one-time exhibition on the Impressionists. Its untimely absence was attributed to restoration and cleaning. Did you have anything to do with its *return*—sorry—restoration?"

"Well, I was fortunate to be one of the first to see it again," he said as a sly grin slid across his face, "before the long lines started. Have you always been interested in aviation?"

"Not till I met you," she stated with a satisfying grin.

"You are good."

"Good, I'm the best…Elliot."

He stared right at her, pleased to hear his real name from her, knowing that she had to be clever and dogged to discover it. He offered her a genuine, appreciative smile, the kind she recognized as lit from within; this time from the release of a secret long repressed.

"When our plane crashed off of Saint Tropez we were on our way to Paris, a business trip for my father, but mostly to take Charlie and me to The Louvre for the first time and to get my mother's ring back."

She could see in his eyes that the past was still so painfully close.

"Your parents changed me. The way your father, this righteous cop, respected my ways, and actually wanted to give me the chance to turn the page. The nature of their love, the connection they had, and especially your mother's forgiveness of your father and her refusal of me. Their love made me see what I had lost with my cynicism, made me recognize the emptiness of retribution, the futility of it, and the joy that it robs from you."

Nathalie realized this was not a hardened, unknowable thief before her but a man struggling to find himself, to rise above the hurt and hatred and be the man he imagined when just a boy before the family that he loved was stolen from him.

"How did all this become about me? Was it just to steal the manuscript?"

"I wanted to know if those qualities had rubbed off on the daughter."

"Well hell, yes! That's why I went after you. I was gonna *Muldoon* your ass!"

"I wanted you to try to Muldoon me and throw my ass in the hoosegow! How could I respect you if you didn't?"

"This was all some crazy type of test?!"

"I had to see if you'd do the right thing—and you did."

"But why? You didn't really need me to steal the manuscript.

"You were never about the manuscript," he said.

"Then why me?!"

"I saw you give the eulogy at your father's funeral. No one knew I was there."

"Oh my God…"

All the intersections of their lives and her parents that she had learned about in building the case against this man and now this…at this very personal and intimate moment of her past. She suddenly felt extremely vulnerable as if he knew too many of her inner most secrets.

"I had never seen you or Ian before, even though your father had spoken about both of you fondly. I left before you or Ian or Odile could see me, but I heard everything you said."

Even now, he could recall her words—every one of them—and see her proud and poised presence at the lectern next to her father's coffin, her strength shining through though her heart was clearly breaking. Even watching from the shadows in the back of the church, her eyes were radiant to him. She was a vision that lit up his heart like a lightning bolt moment.

"Do you remember what you said?"

She nodded, tears pooling in her eyes, for each word was forever etched in her heart.

"I yearn to talk to him again. I'm tempted to believe this ending has stolen his words, his love. But the way he lived and loved my mother and my brother Ian and I are the words he left us. When love looks at you like that, it can't be taken from you like a thief in the night because it is you. You see yourself in them, you are love. That is what my parent's marriage showed me. For all his kick-ass toughness,

that's what my father gave to me. Love that never leaves. And that's what will wipe these tears away."

He stood before her feeling she was as radiant a vision as when she spoke then.

"I felt so much had been taken from me," he said. "I wondered if it was still there, hidden under all the pain. The Portuguese have a beautifully haunted word for it—*saudade*—for it means *the love that remains after someone is gone, a yearning, a longing.* I had to know whether what you said and felt was real. I had to know that woman— to know you—to see if that's who you really were, and if I could trust that."

Nathalie was astonished, now more vulnerable than even moments ago, because she had never had a man wanting her for the right reasons, the shared life values. She suddenly saw herself in him, their journeys so similar and entwined like the limbs of *The Cellini Lovers* and the feeling she knew they shared on seeing the sculpture when she proclaimed that *Each flows into the other and back again...endless. La vérité éternelle.*

This vulnerability required deep trust.

The vulnerability that Eli felt from expressing his long-held emotions was both frightening and empowering. He felt he had come full circle. His *moment that didn't fit* had nothing to do with the perfect heist. His way of looking at the world through the lens of his past pain was the real *moment that didn't fit* and must now be eluded with every breath. Its usefulness had been served; it had propelled him forward in search of healing.

Through all the chaos and pain, a trust emerged, against all odds and rising rivers of cynicism that threatened to obliterate all hope. It came in a whisper from the heart so soft it defied belief and offered a new reality if brave enough to grasp it and step forward without fear.

It was time to be fully present.

Saudade was now simply a beloved Arabian horse, not his sorrow.

Eli reached over and took a drink from her café au lait. She made no move to stop him. "Nathalie, do you know that a hundred thousand pieces of art stolen by the Nazis have never been returned?"

"That could keep someone very busy," she replied.

He nodded and simply smiled.

Nathalie shook her head…that smile…what an incredible device…captivating…and so simple.

"You were going to ask me a question about the ring," she said hopefully. "I'm not afraid of windmills." Now she smiled. "Maybe you should ask your question again."

"I can't," he said.

He got up from the table and waited as the disappointment spread across her face.

He was going to walk away, she thought! Nathalie felt the goosebumps receding, seeking a safe hiding place, never to venture forth again. Wasn't that always the way it goes. Put yourself out there—trusting—then *smack*!

"I need the ring…to ask the question," he said.

Oh…"

A few goosebumps returned…cautiously.

"I'd have to steal it back."

Ohh…"

A few more goosebumps climbed on board the emotional roller coaster and strapped in.

"Might need some help this time."

"Losing your touch?"

"Just keeping it simple."

"Ohhh…"

Her hope teetered on the edge and she dared not breathe.

He looked into her eyes with a penetrating gaze.

"Do *you* want to steal the ring back?"

She looked into his eyes, plunging into that ocean of blue and green.

"I do," she said.

He took her left hand and gently caressed her ring finger. His touch made it feel better.

"Do *you* want to steal the ring back?" Nathalie held her breath from asking.

"I do," he said.

Their eyes were riveted on each other.

"Are we really doing this?" she wondered.

She stood up from the table and faced him as he took both her hands in his.

"I think we just said our vows."
She searched his eyes...for that *moment...of trust.*

℘

The Bombardier Global 6000 dropped through the clouds and descended on Paris at night, the most sparkling of jewels in the world and an art masterpiece of the heart's desire.

The sweeping beam of light from the spire of the Eiffel Tower invited them with its glow of *joie de vivre,* and the *Goddess, la confiance de l'amour,* guided them, always one step ahead, yet leaving a bright and beautiful trail to follow.

Nathalie gazed out the window with tingling anticipation. Eli thoroughly enjoyed seeing the radiant light in her eyes that had captured his heart years ago.

It all spread out before them in the city of light...and lovers.

Nathalie suddenly gasped recognizing a large structure below bathed by the glow of the moon and laced with sparkling lights as the jet passed over. Excited, she pointed: "That's the Louvre."

"Yes, it is," said Eli. "Do you remember what I told you about the masterpiece painting *The Wedding at Cana* by Paolo Veronese?"

"The one stolen from the Italians, now hanging in the Louvre?" She wondered where this inquiry was going and exactly what the glint in his eye was from.

"Yes..."

"You said it was very large," Nathalie added.

"Yes. It needs space. It rests in the Salles des États, the largest room in the Louvre."

Nathalie, now nervous, added quickly, "You told me it's much too big to carry out without damaging it...so it really needed to...stay in the Louvre."

"Exactly," said Eli.

"Right, good," said Nathalie exhaling a sigh of relief.

"In that same room, right across the hall is another Italian painting," said Eli.

"Oh..." Nathalie's nervous goosebumps returned.

"It's much smaller and rather easy to carry," stated Eli simply.

"Oh, really..." Nathalie's lips felt bone dry.

"It was never shown to the family who commissioned it," added Eli.

"Really?" Nathalie's throat dried up now.

"Yes," stated Eli, "They paid for it and never saw it."

"Well, they're probably dead now, right? So taking it back wouldn't…" Nathalie thought, what the hell was he planning?! Was he pulling me into this?!

"The lady never saw her own portrait and yet she's still smiling," said Eli.

Nathalie stared right at him. "Oh my God…The Mona Lisa…Eli, that should really stay in the—"

"Her smile beckons," said Eli.

"Not to be taken back to Florence!"

"You'll see," said Eli calmly. "We'll go pay a little visit to Lisa Gherardini del Giocondo. Her eyes look right into yours. You can almost hear her asking: Who am I? Who are you? What is real? The eternal mystery behind her smile whispers that *life is a state of mind.* So choose. Perhaps this is the purpose of art and what draws us to it."

So much to this man she desired to unravel; so much more depth to explore which she realized meant more goosebumps to encounter…a lot more.

"And your mother's ring? I mean that's really why we're—"

"Oh, we're definitely stealing that back," stated Eli.

Nathalie knew the journey of *trust* was tricky but clearly never boring. What was that Yeats quote she loved so much and found so intriguing? Woman won, woman lost…oh yeah, she remembered: *"Does the imagination dwell the most upon a woman won or a woman lost?"*

Much the same for a man she thought—and for trust—there was no real pat answer.

It was the time spent getting there.

Nathalie looked into the eyes of this mysterious yet most promising man. What she felt gazing back at her gave her the desire to completely be her own self. Was that an invitation she wondered? The mystery and the wonder merged into a feeling which pressed her lips into an enigmatic yet entrancing hint of a smile.

Eli recognized the challenge.

Nathalie Seeger of Manhattan matched Lisa Gherardini del Giocondo of Florence with a smile which might take a lifetime to understand.

"But really, your mother's ring, right?" A lump sat precariously in Nathalie's throat with that question uttered as a plea.

"Of course, the ring…"

At first his words brought relief from the nerve-wracking and unknown *what if*; yet there was again, a drift in his voice, his tone, which instead of a definite period at the end of that sentence intimated an ellipsis—three dots—a hint of something else. An ellipsis opened a door into a silent space; it dangled an invitation to the imagination. An ellipsis didn't offer simply a binary choice, either *this* or *that*. No, it was something else, something from the great sages of ancient times hidden in sacred texts. Classical Latin historically called it *tertium quid*, a third something. All the mysteries of the infinite universe overflowed with *third somethings.* All romance—or holy terror— contained *third somethings.*

Nathalie couldn't breathe with her breath suspended in the swirling rush of infinite *third somethings.* His words *"Of course the ring…"* echoed in her head and vibrated her heart right up into her throat. Was *Of course the ring* a complete sentence with a safe and happy ending or…or…?

She waited until Eli took a breath and yes, damn it, there it was— the ellipsis!

"…but then…" and Eli's tone drifted off.

Off into what?! *But then* what?! Nathalie's mind raced. *But then…!* Another twist in the tortured trail of trust perhaps?! Getting lassoed and hogtied back in?! *But then*—words that could thrust open Pandora's box for sure, and…and Oh, God…this man. What in the holy hell was he thinking…?

But then she took a slow, deep breath and let it ease out.

She had come to know there was grace and even power in embracing uncertainty.

Eli Cross watched with delight as the enigmatic smile returned to her face.

Nathalie Seeger knew a true dance of equals awaited.

After all, this was Paris, and *but then…*held such promise.

AU REVOIR

DEAR READER

The author and publisher would be grateful if you could take a moment to share your review online. Search for 'Chasing the Goddess' at your preferred bookseller or/and on Goodreads.

Thank you!

ACKNOWLEDGMENTS

A book does not write itself and the author is aided by many kind people. I would like to personally thank friends and colleagues for their cherished assistance in bringing this novel to my equally cherished readers. The following talented and accomplished dear friends gave of their time and lent their insight in reading an early draft and providing excellent feedback: Ginny Partridge, Chris Dickie, Esther Bloch, Neil Tardiff and my beloved sister, Marcy Froehlich. Wayne Alexander's sharp acumen as my attorney is matched by his integrity, honesty and kindness. Tatiana Fernandez was instrumental in helping to create a stellar cover design with her layout expertise and artistic vision. A very special thanks is due Brian Schwartz for his expertise, insight, knowledge and friendship as the guiding guru behind the Indie Publishing that has packaged this book. He is a proven expert in the field of Indie Publishing through his Wise Media label and has helped countless authors find success through the years. He makes the process fun! Brian Schwartz can be reached at www.selfpublish.org. And with deep affection and gratitude for my wife, Katrina Sanders, for her love and support, and for reading several drafts of the novel despite her own busy schedule.

ABOUT THE AUTHOR

I'm a Pittsburgh kid who grew up dreaming of telling stories that might make people's lives a little better, which led me from Ithaca College, where I met my first mentor, the great Rod Serling, and then on to Hollywood and forty exciting years as a writer-director-producer in film and TV—on series like *MacGyver*, *Scarecrow & Mrs. King*, *Hart to Hart*, and *The Outer Limits*–and working with icons from Paul Newman, Katharine Hepburn, Burt Lancaster, Suzanne Pleshette, Mary Tyler Moore, Robert Wagner to George Clooney, Sir Anthony Hopkins, Ryan Reynolds, Francis McDormand, Richard Dean Anderson, Kurt Russell, Henry Winkler and Ron Howard, earning membership in the DGA, WGA, SAG-AFTRA, and ATAS along the way. Now living on a California ranch with my wife, and a variety of animals, including four horses—happy rascals all—I've channeled my passion for storytelling into my first solo novel, believing that something sacred emerges from every story we share as authors and readers; so I invite you into the soul journey of CHASING THE GODDESS. Find out more about me at www.BillFroehlich.com.